A PAST UNEARTHED

Return of the
Condor Heroes I

ALSO BY JIN YONG

JIN YONG

Return of the Condor Heroes I

A PAST UNEARTHED

Translated from the Chinese by
Gigi Chang

MACLEHOSE PRESS
QUERCUS · LONDON

First published in the Chinese language as
Shendiao Xialü (1) in 1961; revised in 1976, 2003

First published in Great Britain in 2023 by MacLehose Press

This paperback edition published in 2024 by

MacLehose Press
An imprint of Quercus Editions Ltd
Carmelite House
50 Victoria Embankment
London EC4Y 0DZ

An Hachette UK company

A CIP catalogue record for this book is available from the British Library.

ISBN (MMP) 978 1 52941 753 1
ISBN (Ebook) 978 1 52941 751 7

1 3 5 7 9 10 8 6 4 2

Designed and typeset in Columbus MT by Patty Rennie
Printed and bound in Great Britain by Clays Ltd, Elcograf S.p.A.

CONTENTS

CHAPTER ONE

THE WIND HARD-HEARTED, THE MOON CRUEL

I

"Leaning over the autumnal water, the Yue maiden picks a lotus flower,
From the tapered sleeves of light silk,
A pair of golden bangles peek.
She catches her reflection, glorious like the blossoms she gathers,
She plucks a sprig, strands from the stem linger and stir like her heartstrings.

Ripples lapping the bank in the evening breeze,
The thickening fog, the drifting haze,
She cannot see the companions she has set out with.
The murmur of song fades as the scull makes for land,
The sorrow of parting draws towards the Southern shores."

MELODIOUS SINGING FLOATED ACROSS THE MISTY WATER. A group of girls tittered and chattered on a small boat as they hummed Ouyang Xiu's famous lyrics to the tune of "Butterflies Adore Flowers". They too had been collecting lotus blooms and their seedpods and were now making their way home in the retreating sun.

With the approach of Moon Festival, the air no longer burned with the fire of summer. Its cooler touch was beginning to dress the South Lake of Jiaxing in the cloak of autumn, filling out the lotus's fruits and curling the broad lotus leaves layered over the water surface.

The frolicking reached the ears of a Taoist nun standing amid a row of weeping willows lining the lakeside. She had been there for some time, gazing at the watery expanse. The gentle wind of eventide tugged at the hem of her apricot-yellow habit and caressed the long hair of the horsetail whisk tucked into the back of her collar. The horsehair fluttered along with her heart, mirroring the words sung:

Strands from the stem linger and stir like her heartstrings.

Snatches of song continued to ride on the breeze, seeking out the ears of those on land.

"*The wind hard-hearted, the moon cruel,*
People, in the gloom, have changed.
Revisiting places of old, all is but a dream,
And, for naught, the wrenching in the gut remains . . ."

The forlorn words were chased away by giggles.

"What's there to laugh about?" the Taoist muttered to herself. "Little girls can't possibly comprehend the bitter sorrow captured by Ouyang Xiu."

Holding up her left hand, she was mesmerised by the blood glistening on her palm. A sigh poured out of her chest.

She was not the only one watching. A dozen *zhang* away, a bearded man lurked among the vegetation not far from the waterside. His hushed presence was betrayed by a gasp stirred up by the second song.

A ROWBOAT, carrying five young women, emerged from the rippling lotus leaves and glided across a lake as smooth as a sheet of glass. The older girls, around fifteen and sixteen, sang as they propelled their vessel forward, while the two younger passengers, both aged nine, chatted between themselves.

"Cousin, look." Cheng Ying pointed towards the rows of willows by the shore.

"The old crank's still sitting in the same spot!" Lu Wushuang was amazed.

"The uncle will be upset if he hears—"

"I'm right, though!" Lu Wushuang cut her maternal cousin short. "Who wears a bib like a baby at his grand age? I'd love to see him so provoked that his beard bristles!" She then picked up a lotus pod from the deck and hurled it at the man.

"Cousin, no!"

Their skiff was still a good few *zhang* from the bank, but Lu Wushuang's aim and strength were admirable for her age. The seed head flew straight at the man's face. He tilted his chin up, opened his mouth wide and caught the fist-sized capsule between his teeth. Then, he started to chew and swallowed the fruit whole – including the inedible cup and shell that protected the seeds.

The girls exchanged a look of shocked amusement and burst into giggles. They steered the boat over, hopped ashore and approached the strange man together.

This was the first time they set eyes on him up close. His glossy black hair and beard, wild and unkempt, stuck out like porcupine quills. His features were divided by deep grooves and wrinkles, giving him the appearance of an ancient in his seventies or eighties. A plain robe, indigo in hue, flowed down to his ankles, obscuring his build, and around his neck was fastened a piece of silk that would have been worn by an infant to keep their clothes clean at mealtimes. The tattered fabric was embroidered with the pattern of a cat chasing after butterflies, an auspicious motif symbolising longevity.

Cheng Ying went up to the seated man and tugged at his robe

3

to get his attention. She took a lotus pod from her bag and broke the capsule into two. After that, she picked out a dozen seeds or so, peeled the green casing and pulled out the bitter germ in the core before offering the little ivory-coloured balls to the man.

"Uncle, it tastes better this way."

He grabbed a handful of seeds and tossed them into his mouth. A subtle, fragrant sweetness spread on his tongue, neutralising the harsh acridity left by his indiscriminate gobbling moments ago. He gave the kind-hearted girl a nod and a grin, snatched what remained and chomped them down with relish.

When he was sated, he sprang up, roared into the sky – "Follow me!" – and sprinted into a clump of mulberry trees.

"Let's go after him!" Lu Wushuang seized Cheng Ying's hand and pulled the reluctant girl along.

"Your mother will scold you for this!" one of their older friends warned.

Lu Wushuang pulled a face, flung away her cousin's hand and took off on her own.

Cheng Ying hurried after her little cousin. Being six months older and less impetuous in nature, she could not leave Lu Wushuang chasing a stranger while she headed home by herself.

The three teenagers, disturbed by the man's peculiar behaviour, called on their young playfellows to turn back, but they did not give pursuit, for it was deemed inappropriate for maidens of their age to be found in the company of grown men who were not their closest kin.

Lu Wushuang and Cheng Ying ran after the old man, but how could their short legs catch up with the wide strides of an adult male? The man stopped several times to wait for his young acquaintances, but he soon grew impatient. He scooped up a girl in each arm, tucked them under his armpits and sped away.

Now the air whooshed by and the undergrowth whipped past. Panic seized Lu Wushuang and she shrieked, "Let me down! Let me down!"

The man responded by racing faster. Lu Wushuang twisted round and bit him on the arm, but his muscles were so tough they made her teeth ache. She returned to screaming and shouting once more.

Suddenly, the man came to a halt and set the girls down.

Cheng Ying took one look at the surroundings and the blood drained from her cheeks. Burial mounds, all around. She had braved the journey without making a sound, but the quaver in her voice right now revealed her nerves. "Uncle, it's time for us to go home."

The man scrutinised her, saying nothing.

Cheng Ying thought she could recognise sadness, self-pity and hurt in his gaze. Feeling sorry for him, she suggested timidly, "If you're lonely, come to the lakeside tomorrow. We'll peel more lotus seeds for you."

The man looked away and sighed wearily. "Ten years! It's been ten years!"

A heartbeat later, his focus returned, and he pinned the girl with a feral glare. "Where is He Yuanjun? Where is she?"

"I – I don't know who—"

The man grabbed Cheng Ying by the arms and shook her, barking the same question over and over.

Tears pooled in the girl's eyes, but she tried to blink them back, along with her fear.

"Go on! Cry! Let those tears fall!" he hissed through closed teeth. "You were exactly like this ten years ago . . .

"I won't let you marry him. I refuse. You say you don't want to part from me. You say you're grateful for everything I've done for you. You say you'll be heartbroken to leave me. But you must go with him.

"Pah! Lies, hogwash, each and every word! If you really are that heartbroken, why don't these tears fall?"

Ashy pale, Cheng Ying bit her lip to stop herself from flinching, while a voice inside urged: *Don't! Don't cry! Don't let those tears fall.*

"You won't spare a drop for me!" he yelled, still jolting the girl back and forth. "Not a single tear! What's the point in going on living?"

Abruptly, he let go, bent from the waist and rammed head first into the closest tombstone. *Thump!* He crumpled to the ground. Blood cascaded down his face.

"Run!" Lu Wushuang grabbed her cousin's hand and bolted, but the older girl dug her heels in after a few steps.

"We should check on him." Cheng Ying's conscience would not allow her to leave the stranger to bleed out in the wild.

"If he's dead, will he turn into a ghost?"

Lu Wushuang's words sent a chill through Cheng Ying. She would rather not encounter the uncanny, and had no wish to be manhandled and subjected to crazed jabberings again.

"I'm not scared. He's not a ghost. He won't hurt me." Cheng Ying mumbled under her breath as she trod tentatively back. At the sight of the man's bloodstained face, she overcame her fears. "Uncle . . ."

He answered with a groan.

Feeling bolder, Cheng Ying crouched down and pressed her handkerchief over his bloody wound. The fabric was soaked through presently, but she stilled her trembling hand and maintained force over the gash until the bleeding stopped.

"Why do you help me?" The man forced his heavy eyelids apart. "Why won't you let me die?"

"Does it hurt?" Cheng Ying asked softly, relieved that the man had regained consciousness.

Sighing, he said, "Not in the head, but in the heart."

That was not a response a nine-year-old could comprehend.

How can such a nasty cut not hurt? Cheng Ying wondered as she untied the cloth belt around her waist and used it to bandage his head.

"Never to meet again. Is that what you've decided?" The man exhaled. "You've made up your mind, haven't you? So, this is how we're going to part. You really won't shed a tear for me?"

Blood had stained the wrinkles on the man's face, but his despondent tone and pleading eyes made him less terrifying.

A dull ache swelled in Cheng Ying's heart and two streams of tears glistened on her cheeks.

The man's features lit up with joy when he saw the girl weeping, but the next instant, his expression was darkened by anguish, and – *wah!* – he broke into sobs.

Teardrops were now rolling rapidly down Cheng Ying's face, like pearls slipping off a broken string. She threw her arms around his neck.

Lu Wushuang was baffled by this emotional display. An irresistible urge to laugh rose from her belly and she hooted in merriment.

"Why are you in such good cheer?" The man dried his eyes and addressed the heavens. "'I'll never leave you.' Those words were on your lips all the time. Then you grew up and you forgot everything you'd said. The only thing on your mind is your new friend, that pasty-faced popinjay." He turned back to Cheng Ying, studying her features. "Yes! Yes! You are Ah Yuan! My little Ah Yuan! You can't leave me – I won't allow it. I won't let you go off with that white-faced swine!"

The agitated man clasped Cheng Ying in his arms, as though afraid she would abandon him there and then.

Lu Wushuang quietened down. The last thing she wanted was to draw further attention to herself.

"Ah Yuan, I've finally found you!" the man went on. "Let's go home. You'll stay with Papa always, won't you?"

"Uncle, my papa died a long time ago," Cheng Ying said in a low voice.

"I know. I'm your adopted father. Don't you remember?"

Cheng Ying shook her head. "Uncle, I've never—"

The man howled and shoved the girl roughly. "Ah Yuan, why do you deny our bond?"

"I'm not Ah Yuan, Uncle. My name is Cheng Ying."

"You're not . . . Ah Yuan was your age . . . twenty years ago. She's all grown up now. She doesn't want her papa anymore. There's only room in her heart for one person – that scoundrel Lu Zhanyuan!"

Lu Wushuang gasped audibly.

"You know him, don't you?" The man loomed over her with a scowl.

Lu Wushuang smiled, trying hard to appear undaunted. "He's my uncle. Papa's big brother."

"Where is the bastard?" The man seized her by the arm. "Take me to him! Now!"

"He's not far from here." Lu Wushuang forced out a laugh but could not mask the tremor in her voice.

He let go and spoke in a friendlier tone: "Take me to him, little girl!" Then he mumbled to himself, "I've looked everywhere. Three whole days. All over Jiaxing. At last, I've found you, Lu Zhanyuan. I've come to settle our account!"

Disturbed by his words, Lu Wushuang rubbed her sore arms and answered back defiantly. "You hurt me! And I . . . I can't remember where my uncle is."

Rage distorted the man's face, but he recalled in the heat of the moment that she was a mere child and arranged his features into an unsightly smile.

"Grandpa was bad and he apologises to you," he cooed as he reached into the inside pocket of his robe. "Grandpa has a sweetie for you."

And yet the hand stayed within the folds of his clothes.

"You lie! You haven't got any sweets!"

The man's countenance turned savage again.

"He's over there." Lu Wushuang pointed out two towering scholar trees some distance away. The next thing she knew, she had been scooped up again and tucked under the man's arm, with her cousin secured under the other.

The man ran straight for the trees, barging through shrubs and leaping over any streams that stood in his way.

TWO BURIAL mounds lay side by side under the verdant canopy. Knee-high vegetation hinted at the age of the memorials.

The man set the girls down, his eyes fixed on one of the headstones.

Here lies Master Lu Zhanyuan

"When did he die?" he demanded.

"Three years ago," Lu Wushuang replied.

"Wonderful!" The man broke into a cruel smile. "Too bad I wasn't there to slay the cur myself." He threw his head back and let out a mirthless cackle. His laughter, steeped in anguish and woe, travelled far into the last light of the day, through the thin mist that had begun to shroud the brushwood.

Lu Wushuang tugged her cousin's sleeve and whispered, "Let's run home."

"The pasty-face is dead. What is Ah Yuan still doing out here?" the man asked himself out loud. "I'll take her back to Dali. Yes, that's what I'll do. Little girl, take me to the wife of your dead uncle."

"Can't you read?" Lu Wushuang gestured at the other tombstone.

Here lies Madam He of the Lu Clan

"There's my auntie," she added.

"What? No! You're lying!"

"Papa said Auntie died not long after Uncle's death. I – that's all I know."

"No, no, no, no, no!" The man wailed and roared and beat his chest. "You can't be dead. You can't be. I told you I'd come for you in ten years. You can't die before we meet again. Why – why didn't you wait for me?"

He howled and stomped like a tiger provoked, swiping his foot into the closest scholar tree. The trunk creaked and groaned; the leaves shook and rustled.

The girls retreated as far away as possible, squeezing each other's hand for comfort. They watched with shock as the man clamped his arms around the tree trunk, yelling and shouting, trying to pluck it from the ground.

"You promised! Have you forgotten? You said we'd see each other once more. Why did you break your word?"

The man's voice cracked and grew more hoarse with each word he bellowed. He squatted lower and summoned his inner strength. Vapour rose from the crown of his head like a steamer on the boil. The muscles in his arms bulged from strain. He tucked in his chest and tensed his back.

"Up!"

The tree snapped in half with a mighty crack, but the roots remained tangled deep underground.

"She's gone . . ." he muttered, still clutching the broken tree trunk.

"Gone!" He tossed the load away.

The leafy crown, like an unfurled umbrella, sailed through the air.

The man's attention was drawn to the monuments once more. He read out the characters chiselled on the stone. "Here lies Madam He of the Lu Clan . . . That's Ah Yuan . . ."

He squeezed his eyes shut and opened them again.

"Ah Yuan!"

He hailed his smiling, bright-eyed daughter, who was standing where her headstone had been. Then he noticed the strapping, handsome youth next to her, so close that his shoulder was touching hers.

"I'll kill you! You seduced my daughter!"

He lunged at the young man with his forefinger extended. A lethal jab aimed at a vital point in his chest.

Bone-crushing pain shot down his hand. The blow had landed on the tombstone.

"You can't run!" he shrieked, following up with two consecutive palm thrusts.

Thump, thump! Twice in a row, he struck the stone slab, but in his maddened rage he was undeterred. Each missed attempt fanned the flames of his wrath higher, riling him into channelling more and more of his *neigong* power.

A dozen strokes later, the memorial was covered with blood.

"Stop, Uncle!" Cheng Ying cried. "You're hurting yourself!"

"I'm fine! Let me kill the rat first!" He cackled wildly. "Die, Lu Zhanyuan!"

He grew hushed all of a sudden, staring blankly ahead.

"I've come all the way to see you. Let me see you. I have to see you!"

As these words poured from the man's lips, he plunged his fingers into the earthen mound under which Madam He lay in eternal rest. Like two shovels, his hands dug into the soil again and again, scooping out clump after clump.

2

LU WUSHUANG AND CHENG YING BOLTED AS FAST AS THEIR legs would carry them, but they lost their way in the deepening gloom and had to ask for directions home. It was pitch-black by the time they entered the Lu family manor.

"Pa! Ma! A madman is digging up Uncle and Auntie!" Lu Wushuang shouted as she sprinted into the main hall.

But her father, Lu Liding, did not seem to have heard her. He sat with his back to the doors, his attention held by something on the far wall.

The girls followed his gaze.

Nine handprints on the whitewashed surface, arranged in three neat rows. Two at the top, two directly below and five on the bottom. Blood red in colour.

Lu Liding turned to his daughter, sounding distracted. "What did you say?"

"A madman is digging Uncle and Auntie's grave!"

"What? No!" He shot to his feet.

"Uncle, it's true." Cheng Ying confirmed her cousin's words.

Lu Liding looked between his daughter and his niece. He would not put it past his impish child to come up with such a tasteless prank, but the orphan of his wife's sister would never have agreed to play along. Something within urged him to take the children at their word.

"Tell me everything," he said.

Lu Wushuang, giddy and giggly, recounted their adventure, but her father grabbed his sabre and rushed out long before she had reached the end. Lu Liding hotfooted it all the way to his brother and sister-in-law's burial site. Though he was primed for the worst, the sight of the desecrated and defiled memorials left him shaken to the core.

Both coffins had been pulled out of the ground, their lids prised open. Lu Liding braced himself to look inside. The remains were gone. Clumps of lime, torn scraps of paper, cotton paddings and other materials used to dress and embalm the bodies had been tossed everywhere. He forced his racing spirits to slow down and examined the caskets. The timber bore many scars, rough and deep.

Shock, rage and grief rushed to his head. Who could hold such grievances against his brother and sister-in-law? What kind of animus had fuelled this unspeakable act? There was nothing more abhorrent under the heavens than to have one's final resting place violated.

Lu Liding regretted not asking his daughter more about the culprit. He drew his sabre from its scabbard, eager to bring the offender to justice, but he had no idea how to study the surroundings for clues as to his whereabouts. He had been trained in the martial arts by his late elder brother, but he had never put his skills into practice. He was well provided for by his affluent family and comfortable with his lot – as such, he had never had any desire to venture in the *jianghu* to find fame or fortune. With nothing to guide his search, he circled the area but did not come across anything or anyone out of the ordinary. Before long, he was standing at the burial site again, unsure what he should do next.

Eventually Lu Liding found himself back at home, sitting in the same chair in the main hall. Once more, he was transfixed by the nine gory handprints. His brother's final biddings came to mind.

Big Brother said he had an enemy, Lu Liding reminded himself. A Taoist nun called Blithe Li the Red Serpent Celestial – savage, ruthless and a supreme master of the martial arts. Brother believed this woman would seek retribution from him and Sister in the tenth year of their union.

If he closed his eyes, Lu Liding could hear his brother's voice again.

"I'm not going to get better. Promise me, you will make sure your sister-in-law takes herself far, far away from here, three years from now."

He remembered his tearful pledge and the shocking news that followed: his sister-in-law had committed suicide the night her husband succumbed to his illness, so she could keep him company in the netherworld.

And this is the year the Taoist nun had been expected to come for her revenge. Lu Liding began to make connections between the day's events. But when Brother and Sister departed this world, any such grievances should have died with them. What does the woman hope to gain by coming here?

He eyed the blood-red marks on the wall, and another memory surged to the forefront of his flustered mind.

Brother said the Taoist nun likes to leave bloody handprints on the wall or door of the houses of her victims as a sign of the carnage to come. Each print stands for one life that will be taken.

She made nine marks here, but there are only seven of us, and that includes the servants. Maybe she didn't know about the passing of my brother and sister when she first got here? That must be why she sent someone to steal their remains . . . Such a black-hearted she-demon!

Wait, when did she leave the marks? I was in the house all day – until just now! How could she have come and gone without anyone noticing?

Lu Liding shuddered at the possible answers. In that moment, the shuffle of footsteps sounded from behind. Two hands, small and soft, shielded his eyes.

"Guess who, Papa?"

Lu Wushuang was three years old when she first played this game with her parents. They responded with such effusive laughter that, afterwards, whenever she sensed that they were in low spirits, she would cheer them up this way, without fail.

But, today, her father brushed her away. "Papa's busy. Go play in the rear courtyard."

Lu Wushuang pursed her lips. Rarely had she been dismissed so offhandedly by her doting parents. She readied herself to bid for her father's attention.

A manservant entered before she could work her charms. "Master, we have visitors."

"I'm not at home."

"They are travellers seeking shelter for the night. She did not ask for an audience."

"She, did you say?"

"Yes, a mother with two boys."

"Not a Taoist nun?"

"No. They appear to be from an honourable household. Their clothes are clean and well presented."

"Very well. Take her to the guest quarters and bring them supper."

"Yes, Master."

After the servant left to carry out his orders, Lu Wushuang jumped to her feet and raced into the courtyard. "Papa, I'll go greet them!"

Lu Liding was left on his own again. He knew he ought to speak to his wife about the imminent threat . . . When at last he hauled himself out of his seat, Mistress Lu had already entered the main hall. He led her to the wall with the handprints and told her what he knew.

Mistress Lu listened with a frown, then asked her husband, "Where should we send the children?"

"I don't know." He sighed, gesturing at the wall. "The girls are marked too. It won't be easy finding refuge."

15

"There are only seven of us in this house. Why nine . . . ?" Mistress Lu felt her strength deserting her as tears welled up in her eyes.

Lu Liding put his arm around her shoulders. "I think those two at the top are for Brother and Sister-in-law. Those below, I assume, are for us. The five prints at the bottom must be for Wushuang and Ying – and the servants. Who can say what terrible things happened that she should wish to demean Brother's remains and spill the blood of every one of us? Brother never told me."

"You think she sent the madman?"

"Yes. Who else?"

Noticing the sweat and grime on her husband's face, Mistress Lu said, "Go and change out of these dirty clothes. We will brave what comes next together."

"It is unlikely that we will escape unscathed tonight," Lu Liding said as they walked back to their rooms. "But we will live and die preserving Brother and Sister's good name."

Mistress Lu mumbled in agreement, though her heart ached at the thought of their doomed fate. She had practised kung fu with her husband for many years, but they had never been a part of the wider martial world. Still, she was aware of the honour and esteem her brother- and sister-in-law, Lu Zhanyuan and He Yuanjun, had commanded in the *jianghu* and the glory they had brought to Lu Manor. She understood that it fell now to herself and her husband to live up to their deeds and preserve the family's reputation.

LU LIDING and Mistress Lu had just stepped into the rear courtyard when they heard a tile crack overhead. Lu pulled his wife behind him and looked up to see a boy sitting atop the courtyard wall. He was stretching his arms out, trying to reach a tendril of trumpet-vine blossoms that extended from the perimeter fortifications.

"Careful!" "Watch out!" A chorus of warnings sounded from below.

Lu Liding now noticed his daughter Lu Wushuang and his niece Cheng Ying crouching with another boy in the greenery.

Were they the traveller's sons? He was not impressed by their antics.

"Give it to me! I want it!" Lu Wushuang shouted when the boy at last managed to pluck the stems he was reaching for.

The lad flashed a smile then threw it to Cheng Ying. The girl caught the sprig and offered it to her cousin, but Lu Wushuang was not pleased. She snatched the flowers, tossed them to the ground and stamped the orange-red petals into a darkened mess.

Lu Liding and his wife stopped for a while to watch the children – carefree and oblivious of the bloodshed to come – before going into their rooms with a sigh.

"Cousin . . ." Cheng Ying eyed the trampled branch.

Lu Wushuang scrunched up her nose. "I don't want his flowers. I'll get some for myself!"

With a tap of one foot, she hopped up and grabbed a robust vine of wisteria hanging from a trellis above, which allowed her to pull herself an extra few *chi* higher to seize a nearby osmanthus bough with both hands.

The boy on the wall clapped and cheered at her athletic display.

"Jump over here!" he beckoned.

Cocky and competitive, Lu Wushuang could not ignore the fact that he had snubbed her and given the flowers to her cousin. She was determined to show him that she was capable of plucking a sprig of her choice. She flexed her core, swinging back and forth to build up momentum, then let go of the branch and launched herself into the air, flying towards the top of the wall.

"Grab my hand!" The boy flung his arm out.

"Out of my way!"

She twisted sideways, imitating the manner in which she had seen her father change direction mid-air. But this lightness *qinggong* move was too advanced even for her mother – what chance did a nine-year-old novice to the martial arts have?

"*Aiyooo!*"

If Lu Wushuang had stayed on her original course, she would have gained a fingerhold on the tiles at the very top of the wall, but her airborne manoeuvre had robbed her of momentum and there was nothing she could seize onto now to break her fall.

She plunged. From a height of more than one *zhang*.

The boy in the undergrowth threw himself forward and caught the falling girl. But her left leg still hit the ground and the bone snapped with a sickening crunch. The mighty force of her descent knocked the boy off his feet. He smacked his head on a rock and blood poured down his face. Pressing a hand to the wound, he pushed himself up woozily.

Cheng Ying, meanwhile, had shifted her cousin, who had fainted from the traumatic fall, into a more comfortable position and called for help.

Lu Liding and Mistress Lu rushed out when they heard the commotion. At the same time, a middle-aged woman hurried from a chamber on the western side of the courtyard, and it was she who reached the children first. Without asking any questions, she lifted Lu Wushuang from Cheng Ying's arms and carried the injured girl to the main hall. She set her down and tapped two acupoints on her broken leg to dull the pain – White Ocean on the inside thigh and Bend Middle on the back of the knee. Then she felt around the fracture and began to reset the bone.

Lu Liding watched her assured pressure-point locking technique with alarm, noting also the sword attached to her belt. He had been told she was a mother travelling with her sons. How come she was so proficient in the martial arts? Not to mentioned armed.

"Who are you? Why did you come to my house?" he asked testily.

The woman was too consumed by the task at hand to offer a verbal answer and merely made a noise in her throat to indicate that she had heard his questions.

Though Mistress Lu was worried about her daughter, she could tell the woman knew what she was doing, so she turned her attention

to settling the other children and bandaging the boy's head wound
with her handkerchief.

THE WOMAN had just lined up the broken bones in Lu Wushuang's
leg when a peal of laughter wafted in from outside. The sudden
sound made her jump and her hands jolted. The girl yelped in pain
and lost consciousness again.

"I am here to take the seven lives of the Lu clan. Anyone else –
leave this house!"

On the eaves extending from the main hall's pitched roof perched
a Taoist novice. She carried a sword on her back. The red tassel
attached to the hilt whipped audibly in the wind, and her face was
illumined by the newly risen moon. She looked to be no more than
fifteen or sixteen.

"I am Lu Liding. May I ask if you are a follower of Celestial Li?"

"I am glad you know who I am. Now, kill your wife, your daughters, your servants, then yourself. Save me the trouble of doing the
dirty work."

"You – you . . ." Lu Liding spluttered in rage. He wanted to fight,
but it would be unmannerly to take up arms against one so much
younger and of the opposite sex. While he deliberated, the mother of
the two boys rushed past him and hopped onto the roof, her sword
already drawn.

The woman was dressed in a grey robe, the novice in an apricot-
yellow vestment. Under the glimmer of the moon, a blur of silver
leapt and danced around a swirl of gold. From time to time, gleaming
white flashes were accompanied by a ringing of steel.

Although Lu Liding had never been involved in a physical fight,
his eyes were keen from his martial training, and he was able to follow every thrust of the duelling blades.

The young Taoist opened with measured, defensive moves then
launched unexpectedly into a ferocious offensive. The woman parried

with caution, heedful of the gaps in the novice's counterstrokes, and timed her attack accordingly. *Claaang!* The swords clashed and the teenager was disarmed, her blade arcing high into the sky.

"Who are you, busybody?" she barked as she jumped backwards in haste, her cheeks flushed crimson. "My *shifu* sent me here to dispatch the kin of Lu Zhanyuan." She made a flourish with her hand and sent forth three silver needles.

The woman swishèd her sword and knocked the two projectiles flying at her off course. The third was aimed at Lu Liding. He grumbled under his breath at the underhand attack as he caught the clandestine weapon between his index and middle fingers.

With a sneer, the novice descended from the roof in a somersault and hurried away, leaving the quiet shuffle of her footsteps to the night.

3

"THROW DOWN THE NEEDLE!" THE WOMAN SHOUTED THE instant she landed in the courtyard.

Lu Liding did as he was told. "Is it poisonous?" The tremor in his voice betrayed his fear.

"Extremely."

The woman cut off a length of her belt and tied it tightly around Lu Liding's wrist, then gave him a pill. But even so, in this brief interval, he had lost all sensation in the fingers that had come into contact with the needle, and they were swelling up before his eyes.

The woman pricked the disfigured fingertips with the point of her sword. Blackened blood oozed out.

Lu Liding stared at his hand, shocked by the potency of the poison.

I only touched the needle, he said to himself. If it had broken the skin, I'd be dead already.

He bowed to the woman in gratitude. "I had not realised a Master had deigned to grace this house. I have been remiss in my manners. Might I ask Madam's name?"

"My husband's surname is Wu, and his given name Santong." The woman responded according to the convention of the time.

"Madam Wu." Lu Liding made another obeisance. "I have heard that Master Wu is a disciple of Reverend Sole Light of Dali, is it not so?"

"Yes, you are right. Please forgive me for drawing my sword before a Master such as yourself – I was taught some basic kung fu by my husband."

Lu Liding replied to her courteous remarks with effusive words of thanks and accompanied her back to the main hall. His brother had once told him that, of all the martial Masters he had encountered, the students of Reverend Sole Light were the most accomplished. Once the King of Dali, the Reverend had abdicated to devote his life to Buddhism, settling in hermitic reclusion with his four disciples – the fisher, the logger, the farmer and the scholar.

In Lu Liding's recollection, his brother had mentioned a quarrel with the farmer, whose name was Wu Santong, but the cause of the disagreement was never discussed. He found it surprising that, given the supposed bad blood between the two households, Madam Wu had chosen to stand up and fight on the Lu family's behalf against a protégé of the Red Serpent Celestial.

MISTRESS LU had stayed inside the main hall with the children when her husband and Madam Wu rushed into the courtyard to answer the Taoist novice's challenge. When they returned, Madam Wu checked on her sons, while Lu Liding went up to his daughter. He was relieved to see that she had come to, but her bloodless cheeks and the effort it cost her to hold back her tears made his heart ache.

"The she-demon will soon be here," Madam Wu said to her hosts. "I have every respect for your martial abilities, but Blithe Li the Red

Serpent Celestial is more than a match for the three of us and we have no hope of outrunning her. All we can do is wait here and let the heavens decide our fate."

"What is she like? Do you know why she holds such a grudge against our family?" Mistress Lu asked Madam Wu. "We don't know much . . ." she added when she noticed the woman's questioning gaze. "All we are certain of is that it involves our big brother and sister and that the matter may have its roots in an affair of the heart."

Madam Wu sighed. "I shall tell you what I know, but please believe me, I have no wish to make idle talk about your late brother and sister-in-law. A dozen or so years ago, your brother Lu Zhanyuan came to Dali. At that time, the Red Serpent Celestial was neither this feared monster of the *wulin* nor a Taoist nun. She met your brother and feelings were kindled, but things unexpected came to pass . . . Your brother ended up marrying He Yuanjun . . ."

The woman trailed off, unsure whether to continue. In time, she drew in a breath and said, ". . . and He Yuanjun was our adopted daughter."

Lu Liding and Mistress Lu exchanged glances.

"Ah Yuan was orphaned at a very young age," Madam Wu said, her eyes fixed on the flame of a candle, her hand patting her injured son's shoulder absentmindedly. "My husband and I raised her and loved her as our own. She got to know your brother and they fell for each other, but my husband was dead set against their union. He didn't want her to move to a faraway place. He also took a disliking to your brother, for he believed those from the South, especially the Jiangnan region, to be cunning and slippery . . . But Ah Yuan ran away with him nonetheless.

"On their wedding day, Blithe Li and my husband both turned up to protest their union, but they were thwarted by one of the guests, a Buddhist monk from Celestial Dragon Temple in Dali. He made them promise to leave the newlyweds in peace for ten years. My husband was so provoked by that day that he has not been in his right mind since. Neither myself nor his *shifu* and martial brothers managed to talk sense into him. He has been counting down the days . . . Who would have thought . . . your brother and Ah Yuan were not able to enjoy even ten years of happiness?" Madam Wu bowed her head in sorrow.

"So it was your husband who disturbed my brother and sister-in-law's remains . . ." It was a struggle for Lu Liding to voice this conclusion.

The mortified woman mumbled an affirmation under her breath.

"Then his behaviour was most disgraceful!" Lu Liding knew he ought to address Madam Wu with deference, since the relation through marriage made her his senior by a generation, but he could not hold his tongue in check. "Surely it was not an insurmountable dispute, and if there were deep grievances, my brother's passing should have cancelled them out. Why did your husband disrespect their remains? These are not the actions of a just man!"

"My husband deserves your chastisement. He is not sound of mind, and his words and deeds are often inexplicable. I came here today with our sons in the hope of stopping him from committing further outrages. I am the only person in this world that can temper his behaviour somewhat." Madam Wu paused and turned to the boys. "Bow on your knees to Master and Mistress Lu and beg for forgiveness on your papa's behalf."

Mistress Lu helped the kowtowing boys to their feet and asked them their names. The one with the injured forehead answered. He was called Earnest and was twelve months older than his little brother Erudite, who turned eleven this year.

Madam Wu added that she had been quite advanced in age when she had conceived the boys. By that time, she and her husband had seen the dark underbelly of the *wulin* and decided to give their sons literary names with the hope that they would take the path of letters. However, the boys were only interested in martial matters.

She finished her reminiscences with a sigh, her mind drifting back to around the time the boys came into the world, when He Yuanjun was turning eighteen. It was then she began to notice her husband harbouring an affection for their adopted daughter that went beyond parental concern. As an esteemed member of the martial world, his behaviour had to be impeccable, so he suppressed his feelings. She remembered the explosion of these pent-up emotions when he learned that He Yuanjun had fallen in love with a youth from the South – he would not stop raving about how devious and sly the people of the Jiangnan region were.

Wu Santong's distorted view did not stem solely from his animosity towards the man who had stolen his little girl's heart. It was also informed by the indignation he suffered at Lotus Huang's hands when she tried to gain entry to his *shifu* Sole Light's temple, trapping him under a rock with her guile.

Madam Wu collected herself and said, "I did not anticipate that the Red Serpent Celestial would be here before my husband—"

A gruff bellow sounded from the rooftop, cutting her off.

"Earnest, Erudite, come out!"

Lu Liding and Mistress Lu were shocked that, once again, they had not caught the sound of someone scaling the roof. From his call, they knew it must be Madam Wu's husband, Wu Santong.

Cheng Ying and Lu Wushuang also recognised the voice. The strange man by the lake!

Wu Santong leapt down in a swirl of shadows and, in the blink of an eye, he was back on the ridge of the roof, his sons in his arms.

"Come down! This is Master and Mistress Lu!" Madam Wu called to her husband. "What did you do with the remains? Bring them back!"

The man ignored her as he bounded from roof to roof, carrying the boys aloft.

WU SANTONG had set forth without a specific direction in mind, and soon found himself in a forest. He placed his younger son Erudite among the undergrowth.

"Wait here. I'll be back," he said, and took off with his firstborn Earnest still tucked under his arm.

"Papa! Papa!" Erudite called.

But Wu Santong was already dozens of *zhang* away.

It was by no means Erudite's first experience of his father's mercurial ways. Being left on his own in desolate woodland on a dark night was frightening, but he believed his papa would eventually come back. Erudite settled against a tree while he waited. His eyelids soon grew heavy and he started to doze.

BACK IN Lu Manor, Wu Santong's sudden and fleeting appearance had baffled Lu Liding and his wife, but Madam Wu was relieved to see him take off with their sons.

"My husband may not be in his right mind, but he is acting sensibly tonight." She smiled at her confused hosts. "We shall find out if my assumption is correct very soon."

Lu Wushuang had fallen asleep in her father's arms and Cheng Ying was struggling to keep her eyes open. Mistress Lu wanted to take the girls back to their room to rest, but Madam Wu stopped her.

"Wait a little while."

A short time later, Wu Santong's voice sounded from above.

"Toss them up."

His lightness kung fu was so effective that Lu Liding and Mistress Lu had failed to detect his arrival yet again.

Madam Wu carried Cheng Ying out of the main hall and threw her up into Wu Santong's waiting arms. So shocked were the Lus, that, by the time they had registered what was happening, Madam Wu had also passed Lu Wushuang up to her husband.

"What do you think you're doing?" Lu Liding demanded. He leapt onto the roof to give chase. Blackness, all around. No sign of Wu Santong or the girls.

"Master Lu, come back!" Madam Wu called. "My husband means well!"

"Explain yourself!" He jumped back into the courtyard.

Mistress Lu said to her husband, "I believe Master Wu has taken the girls away so they will come to no harm at the she-demon's hands."

"Right . . ." But that did little to dispel Lu Liding's anxiety, for he had not forgotten Wu Santong was the madman who had desecrated his brother and sister-in-law's grave.

Madam Wu heaved a sigh and tried to put Lu Liding at ease. "After Ah Yuan married your brother, whenever my husband caught sight of young women, he would fly into a fury, but he seems to be quite taken by your daughters. He cast a glance of concern towards them when he came for Earnest and Erudite – that's why I thought he would come back. I truly hope the fog in his head will clear after this . . ."

Lu Liding and Mistress Lu had been at a loss about how they should face their enemy, as they doubted they could protect their daughter and their niece, but now that the girls had been carried to safety, they could focus wholeheartedly on preparing for battle. They strapped on their blades, filled their pockets with secret weapons, and sat in waiting in the main hall, their eyes closed to preserve energy.

Over their decade-long marriage, the husband and wife had had their share of disagreements when it came to running the household, and yet, at this moment, knowing that they were about to face a ruthless monster and were unlikely to survive the encounter, they sought solace in each other's company and found courage in holding each other's hands.

A HINT of a song, sung by a gentle female voice, drifted in from a distance with the dawn colours.

"I ask the world, what is love?
Why does it inspire vows beyond life and unto death?"

The singer's enunciation was crisp, and with each word uttered, it was clear she was getting closer. By the end of the second line, she was outside Lu Manor.

Lu Liding, Mistress Lu and Madam Wu exchanged a look of shock. How could anyone move so fast?

Craaack! The robust timber bolt securing the main gate snapped and the heavy wooden double doors flew open.

A beautiful Taoist nun strolled in with a smile. Dressed in an apricot-yellow robe, she was not quite thirty years of age.

"Who are you?" The manservant rushed to block the intruder.

"Stay back!" But Lu Liding's warning came too late.

Blithe Li the Red Serpent Celestial flourished her horsetail whisk and lashed the serving man over the head with the unconventional weapon. His skull was crushed instantly and he was dead before he could make another sound.

Lu Liding charged with his sabre drawn. Blithe Li turned slightly, gliding past him, and flicked her whisk again. This single swipe snatched the lives of the two maidservants.

"May I ask where the girls are?" the Taoist enquired with an upward curl of her lips.

Catching each other's eye, Lu Liding and his wife lunged side by side as one, their blades flashing. Now they had seen the woman kill their household staff in a flash without hesitation, they knew they had no hope of surviving the encounter, but nonetheless, they threw themselves into their attack.

Blithe Li twirled the whisk's steel handle, preparing a counterstrike, but before she could send the weapon's lethal scourge in the direction of the Lus, she noticed Madam Wu poised to enter the fray, her sword raised high.

"Since we have company, I shall not shed more blood inside this house." The Taoist spoke in a mild, melodious tone. If one ignored her deeds, it could be said that she was the embodiment of feminine charm – sparkling eyes, perfect teeth, fair and flawless skin, graceful comportment.

True to her word, Blithe Li then sailed up to the ridge of the roof, her movements so lightsome it seemed she did not even need to lift her feet.

Lu Liding, Mistress Lu and Madam Wu scaled the heights in pursuit of the Taoist, but their coordinated attack was waved away by a casual swish of her horsetail whisk.

"Master Lu, were your brother still alive, I'd have spared you and yours –" the vengeful woman paused for emphasis – "if he grovelled to me and cast that strumpet He Yuanjun aside. Alas, you are out of luck. Your brother died too young."

When Blithe Li had arrived in Jiaxing, she had sent her disciple Ripple Hong to seek out Lu Zhanyuan and his family, only to discover that the man she had come to hunt had been dead for three years, along with his wife. Infuriated that he had slipped through her clutches, Blithe Li decided she would take her revenge on his kin, and left nine bloody handprints in his family seat to herald her arrival. Seven for his younger brother Lu Liding and his family, including their servants, and two for Lu Zhanyuan and He Yuanjun. Her intention was clear: she would claim vengeance from the dead.

Outraged by the Taoist's gleeful contempt, Lu Liding swung his sabre, screaming defiance. "Who wants your mercy?"

Mistress Lu and Madam Wu joined the assault, attacking from two sides, but Blithe Li paid them no heed. She had eyes only for Lu Liding. The man's kung fu was average at best, but his stance as he held his blade reminded her of her faithless beloved, Lu Zhanyuan.

A sharp pang of loss seized the Red Serpent Celestial's heart. Realising she would never see the Lu Family Sabre repertoire in action again once she had dispatched this man, she reined in her offensive to keep the three fighters buzzing around her, so she could tease out more of Lu Liding's martial knowledge. A futile attempt to cling onto a shadow of her erstwhile suitor.

4

SQUAWK! A LOUD AND PIERCING CAW TORE INTO ERUDITE'S sleep. He parted his eyelids to see that a new day had dawned. Two enormous white birds were wheeling in the sky, their wingspans reaching at least one *zhang*.

Amazed, he cried out, "Brother, look at the hawks!" He had forgotten that his father had left him on his own in this woodland the night before, disappearing with his elder brother Earnest.

Before long, a couple of low-pitched calls sounded not far behind. A girl emerged from the trees, waving her arms at the gliding raptors.

The birds of prey began to descend at a leisurely pace. They tucked in their pinions and landed next to the girl. She glanced at Erudite before patting them on the back.

"Good condors," she said approvingly.

Erudite looked on with awe. The magnificent creatures were taller than the girl!

"Are they yours?" He ventured a few steps closer. "So these birds aren't hawks? They're called condors?"

The girl pursed her lips and eyed the approaching boy with disdain. "I don't play with children I don't know."

Erudite ignored the terse reply and reached out to stroke one of the birds.

The girl whistled and the condor flicked his wing, flipping the boy over.

"Wow, they obey your commands! I'll get Papa to find me a pair of these birds too," Erudite said as he climbed to his feet, not at all offended.

"Ha!" She rolled her eyes.

Snubbed for the third time, Erudite at last felt a little awkward,

29

staring down at his feet, but a short while later, he heard the girl ask: "What's your name? Why are you playing here by yourself?"

He looked up to find her studying him, her hand lost in a mass of white feathers. She wore a silk dress, pale green in colour, and a long string of pearls around her neck. A pair of slender eyebrows framed her animated eyes, and her skin looked as soft and smooth as cream. He had never seen a prettier girl and he desperately wanted to be friends with her.

"I – I am Erudite Wu," he answered haltingly, afraid that she would rebuff him again. "I'm waiting – for my papa . . . What about you? What's your name?"

"I don't play with strays and wastrels." The girl crinkled her nose and hurried away.

It took a moment for Erudite to comprehend her remark. "I'm not a wastrel!" he yelled, running after her. He was confident he could catch up easily using lightness *qinggong*. After all, she looked two or three years younger than him and he was much taller, with longer legs.

The girl stopped when she was several *zhang* ahead and turned round to taunt him. "You think you can catch me?"

"Of course!" Erudite gathered his *qi* and increased his speed.

The girl took cover behind a pine tree and waited. She slid her foot out the instant he ran past and hooked his ankle. He stumbled and tried to steady himself by rooting his feet with a Cycad Pillar move, but she followed up with a boot to his backside.

Erudite fell face first to the ground. He felt his nose. Not too sore, but it was unnerving how red and slimy his hand had become. Blood was dripping from his nostrils and the front of his robe was already stained with crimson streaks.

In the meantime, panicking at the sight of blood, the girl had taken flight, but she froze when a gravelly voice barked: "Hibiscus! You're being a bully again!"

Erudite turned around. A gaunt old man had appeared next to the girl. He seemed to be lame in one leg, resting most of his weight on an iron staff. His hair was frosty white at the temples and the pupils of his eyes were milky and opaque.

"No!" The girl shot back. "It's got nothing to do with me! He tripped. Don't you make a thing of it before Pa."

"I may not have the use of my eyes, but I can hear very well," the old man retorted.

The girl linked arms with him and pleaded, "Grandpapa, you won't tell Papa and you'll help the boy. I'm right, aren't I?"

The blind man hobbled up to the boy, grabbed him above the elbow and tapped the Welcome Fragrance acupoint on the side of his nose.

Erudite was amazed that this mere touch was enough to stop the bleeding, but his mind now turned to the tight grip around his arm. The long steely fingers were locked to him like an iron clamp. He tried to wriggle free but without success. Growing apprehensive, he recalled a Miniature Grappling move his mother had taught him, and drew in his forearm to trace a half-circle with his hand while rotating his palm upwards and out.

It surprised the old man that the child was able to extricate himself with such intricate kung fu. Nonetheless, he quickly recovered and seized the boy by the wrist.

Erudite summoned his strength to resist, but this time his struggles were in vain.

"Child, be not afraid," the man said, releasing his grip. "Tell us your family name."

"I am of the Wu clan."

"You don't sound local. Where's your home? Why aren't you with your parents?"

Erudite was not sure how he should answer. A whole night had passed since he had last seen his mother and father.

Noticing the tears pooling in the boy's eyes, the girl drew her finger across her cheek in a gesture to shame him and launched into song:

31

> *"Shame, shame, shame,*
> *Dirty little puppy,*
> *Eyes red and teary,*
> *Whine, whine, whine!"*

"I'm not crying!" Erudite yelled defiantly. He then gave a flustered and jumbled description of what had happened since his arrival at Lu Manor the night before.

When the old man had patched together a general outline of events, he asked the boy about his family and his kung fu lineage, and was amazed to hear that the signature move of their martial branch was the Yang in Ascendance pressure-point locking technique and the lad's father was Wu Santong of the Kingdom of Dali.

"Your father is a student of Reverend Sole Light?" he asked, seeking confirmation.

"You know our liege? Have you met him? I haven't had the honour." Erudite was thrilled that this grandpa had heard of the former ruler of Dali.

Wu Santong had served as Captain of the Imperial Guard during the reign of King Gongji, which was Sole Light's formal title before he renounced his throne and his birth name, Duan Zhixing, to take Buddhist vows. Whenever Wu Santong talked to his sons about his past, he always referred to his *shifu* as "our liege" and naturally Erudite had picked up this form of address.

"I have never had the privilege of meeting the King of the South, but I have long admired his reputation. The Reverend performed a great act of kindness for Hibiscus's parents, so, in a way, we are connected. You mentioned your mother came to Lu Manor to confront her enemy. Do you happen to know who they might be?"

"Mm . . . I think Ma said something about Red Snake Li to Master Lu . . ."

"Red Snake Li?" The old man repeated the name under his breath then struck the butt of his staff against the ground. "Blithe Li the Red Serpent Celestial!"

"That's it!"

A grave expression darkened the man's face. "Stay here. Don't leave the woods. I'll take a look."

"Grandpa, I'll come with you," the girl pleaded.

"Me too!" The boy cried a heartbeat later.

"No, no, no, it's too dangerous. I'm no match for this bloodthirsty she-demon, but I must help our friends in their moment of need. Be good. Listen to Grandpa. Wait here until I return." The old man limped off at great speed, supported by his staff.

"He moves so fast!" Erudite was thunderstruck to see such agility from a blind and lame old man.

"Why are you so surprised? You know what's truly awe-inspiring? My papa and mama's lightness *qinggong!*"

THE PASTORAL sounds of farmers labouring in the fields and conversing in song accompanied the sightless, grizzled man into Jiaxing. He had grown up in the city and was familiar with its roads and trails, but he had never been to Lu Manor and did not know its precise location. Though he ranked alongside the late Lu Zhanyuan as one of the city's most renowned martial artists, they had never crossed paths, for his family was of the marketplace while Lu hailed from a clan of statesmen.

The man asked for directions along the way. As he approached Lu Manor, he picked out the ringing of steel in the distance. He was well aware that he was not as skilled as the Red Serpent Celestial and would likely meet his end if they fought, but he could not possibly stand by and leave a student of Reverend Sole Light to face such a terrible opponent alone – not when the Reverend had done so much to help those he held most dear.

He paused at the manor's main gate and listened. A fierce tussle was taking place high up . . . on a roof. From the different voices shouting and the tap of footsteps on the tiles, he deduced that three fighters were working together to take on one common enemy – and they were hard pressed despite their numerical advantage.

WITHOUT WARNING, Blithe Li let out a whistle and stole away from her three opponents. She leapt down from the roof, launching a ferocious mid-air attack with her horsetail whisk, aimed at the neck of the aged martial artist leaning on a staff by the manor's main gate. She was confident that the new arrival would only be able to adopt a defensive stance, and was not at all concerned about leaving her core unguarded or being airborne while the whisk struck home.

The old man twisted his staff sideways and thrust it at his assailant's right wrist. Usually, this type of heavy weapon was clubbed downwards or swung horizontally, its great weight put to good use as it was smashed into or slammed against opponents. However, he was brandishing it like a sword, driving its point home with nimble agility.

The Taoist nun responded with a deft twitch of her wrist, sending the horsetail whisk coiling around the head of the staff.

"Yield!" she commanded.

The supple horsehair threads reversed the force of the man's counter-manoeuvre, sending a jolt down his arm and causing his grip to loosen momentarily. He planted his feet and skewed his body aslant to better resist the woman's leveraged strength.

Blithe Li was shocked to see the iron staff still in the man's grasp. This martial technique had never failed her before.

Known as Grand Duke Fishing, it had been inspired by a nugget of ancient wisdom. According to legend, an old man called Jiang Ziya had taken to angling with a straightened, unbaited fish hook, which he dangled above the surface of the water. When challenged about this unusual set-up, Jiang explained, "Those willing will be caught." His sage words won him a place at the court and he became a renowned advisor to the king.

Blithe Li's move allowed her to flip the force of an incoming blow and use it to disarm her opponent. Now, seeing it fall short for the first time, she swivelled a touch to the side as a precaution and suddenly noticed that there was nothing but white in the old man's eyes.

"You are Ke Zhen'e!"

In that she was correct. The blind old man was indeed Ke Zhen'e the Flying Bat, the eldest of the Seven Freaks of the South.

AFTER THE second Contest of Mount Hua and the death of Genghis Khan, Lotus Huang and Guo Jing were married in a ceremony officiated by her father, Apothecary Huang. The newlyweds had decided to settle with him on Peach Blossom Island, away from the bustle of the mainland. However, in a matter of months, the Martial Great was finding the additional company disruptive and infuriating, and sailed away on his own, leaving a letter saying that he had embarked on a journey to find a secluded spot to live out his days in tranquillity.

Knowing her father's preference for solitude, Lotus let him be, assuming he would get in touch within a few months, and yet, two years passed without a word from him. She returned to the mainland with Guo Jing on a double quest to find her father and their *shifu* Count Seven Hong – from whom they had also received no news – but their wanderings were cut short after a few months, when Lotus discovered that she was with child.

Spirited and mischievous, the young woman had never been one to sit still for long, and now that she was expecting, she had to change many of her habits, leaving her in a particularly foul mood. Of course, she laid all the blame on Guo Jing and grew so short-tempered with him that a quarrel would arise from the most trivial matter. Guo Jing bore her cantankerousness with a patient smile and soothed her ill humour with gentle words until a grin returned to her face.

When Lotus reached full term, she gave birth to a daughter and

35

named her Hibiscus. The new mother had resented the child's presence when she was carrying her, but she changed her mind the instant she held the babe in her arms. Lotus doted on the newborn and Hibiscus was insufferably spoiled by the time she was twelve months old. There were times when Guo Jing was unable to turn a blind eye and tried to discipline her, but Lotus would stand, resolutely overprotective, by their daughter's side. As a result, the little girl grew even more petulant.

When Hibiscus turned five, Lotus initiated her into the world of the martial arts, and from then on, no living creature on Peach Blossom Island was able to enjoy a moment's peace. Birds had their plumage plucked and smaller animals had their fur trimmed. The hermitic retreat was now ruled over by chaos.

On the rare occasions when Guo Jing was tempted to raise a hand to discipline his unruly daughter, Hibiscus would loop her arms around his neck, pull funny faces and plead softly. He always ended up heaving a sigh and lowering his palm.

Neither Apothecary Huang nor Count Seven Hong sent word back to Peace Blossom Island over the years. Although the couple were well aware that no harm could befall the Martial Greats, they wanted to know how the two men were faring.

Guo Jing had tried to persuade his First *Shifu* Ke Zhen'e to move to the island, but the older man preferred carousing and gambling in the boisterous company of common folk from the marketplace of his hometown of Jiaxing. For the eldest Freak, life on Peach Blossom Island would be too quiet, too isolated. He declined every invitation, until one day, he presented himself unannounced. He had had a bout of bad luck with his wagers and racked up a sizeable debt – his disciple's remote residence was the perfect place to hide from his creditors.

The couple were overjoyed to see him, welcoming him into life on the island and refusing to let him go back to the mainland. Little by little, Lotus teased out the real reason behind his visit and sent men to pay off his gambling debts discreetly. Oblivious to this, Ke stayed on the island and became young Hibiscus's companion.

The seasons flew by. Hibiscus had turned nine, and Lotus had still heard nothing from her father. She decided to return to the mainland with Guo Jing to look for him. Ke Zhen'e insisted on accompanying them and, of course, Hibiscus refused to be left behind. When they set sail, Ke said, "I don't care where we go – as long as it's not Jiaxing."

Laughing, Lotus replied, "First *Shifu*, I've dealt with your creditors. You don't owe anyone money."

That settled it. Their first port of call was Jiaxing. Once they had found an inn, Ke Zhen'e caught up with his old friends and learned that an elderly man in a blue-green robe had been seen a few days ago, drinking on his own at the Tower of Mist and Rain. Lotus was thrilled by this possible sighting of her father and commenced a search of Jiaxing and its surrounding villages, while Ke Zhen'e showed Hibiscus around the city of his birth.

WHEN KE Zhen'e arrived at Lu Manor, he was astonished by how quickly Blithe Li had detected his presence and extricated herself from her three opponents to deal him a wicked blow. He was aware of her formidable reputation and never imagined that he would be her martial match, but he had not expected her to be as fearsome and accomplished as his mortal enemy, the late Iron Corpse Cyclone Mei. To guard his core, he launched into the Exorcist's Staff, a sequence he had devised to counter Mei's kung fu, fending off a dozen of the Red Serpent Celestial's quick-fire attacks.

The Taoist nun was impressed: Blind, lame and well past your prime, yet you're still on your feet! The false-hearted Lu Zhanyuan was not lying when he had said the Seven Freaks of the South were the martial elders of Jiaxing.

These reflections were interrupted by a roar and a rush of energy closing in from behind – Lu Liding was leading his wife and Madam Wu in a charge. Blithe Li knew she needed to take decisive action.

If I injure this old man, his protégé Guo Jing will come after me
. . . I'd rather not get on the wrong side of a hero of that stature.

Thus resolved, she flicked her wrist. The silvery horsehairs
straightened themselves out and hurtled spear-like at a major vital
point on the Freak's chest.

Ke Zhen'e could feel the change in the air as the whisk's soft hair
stiffened, thanks to an ingenious manipulation of internal strength. It
was not an attack he could withstand head on. He thumped his staff
on the ground and propelled himself out of range.

Blithe Li strode after the blind man, as though poised to launch
another offensive, but, in the next moment, she snapped her body
backwards, bringing her within two feet of Madam Wu.

Startled, the mother of two swiped her palm down at the Taoist's
forehead.

With a subtle sway of her waist, Blithe Li avoided the blow, her
lithe movement resembling a narcissus in the breeze. Then she shot
her hand out and – *pak!* – struck Mistress Lu in the lower belly, sending her sprawling to the ground.

Lu Liding hurled his sabre at the Red Serpent Celestial and lunged
after it, his arms thrown wide to lock her in a stranglehold. He was
ready to die in order to bring down his wife's assailant.

The Taoist nun had abhorred all contact with the opposite sex
since she had been spurned by Lu Zhanyuan, and she interpreted
Lu Liding's attack as an attempt to sully her chaste body. She swung
the whisk around, knocking the airborne sabre to the ground. Then,
with a swift twirl – *swash!* – she dealt him a crushing blow to the
crown of his head.

With Lu Liding and his wife laid low in the blink of an eye, Blithe
Li disappeared into the rear wing of the manor in a blur of orange
before Ke Zhen'e or Madam Wu could react. She searched every
room for Lu Wushuang and Cheng Ying, but found no sign of the
girls and set alight the firewood store by the kitchen in frustration.
She then returned to face the two fighters still standing, offering
them what she imagined was a winning smile. "This impoverished

nun has no quarrel with Peach Blossom Island or the Venerable Reverend Sole Light," she announced in a courteous tone, making a polite gesture to show that they could leave in peace.

Needless to say, neither Ke Zhen'e nor Madam Wu had any intention of abandoning the injured Master and Mistress Lu, or letting the vicious serpent get away with her wanton brutality. Spurred on by blinding fury, they charged, weapons held aloft.

Blithe Li twisted away from Ke Zhen'e's iron staff and swiped her whisk sideways at Madam Wu's sword. Once the horsehairs had curled around the steel, she unleashed her *neigong* power.

Madam Wu felt two opposing forces grip the metal blade – one pushing out, one drawing in. *Kaaak!* The sword snapped in two, its point hurtling straight at her face. Yelping, she ducked. The shard whizzed over her head, chilling her scalp and sending locks of her own hair fluttering down.

The hilt flew Ke Zhen'e's way. Sensing the air parting, the sightless man swung his staff and batted the stump to the ground. Then, hearing Madam Wu's cry, he spun his weapon and whipped up a whirlwind to drive their opponent back. This gave him a chance to slip a hand into his pocket and grip three poisoned devilnuts between his fingers. He was about to launch his secret weapons when he recalled the woman was notorious for her silver Soul of Ice throwing needles. What if these projectiles were as stealthy and underhand as rumoured and he was unable to detect them by ear?

Blithe Li's patience was wearing thin: It's time to show you my true powers, or you won't know I've been holding back, you blind fool!

With a graceful sway of her hips, she sent the whisk's silver strands twining round the head of Ke Zhen'e's iron staff.

Ke's arms jerked as the whisk was pulled taut. He tightened his grasp, applying his inner strength. Just as his energy was coursing through the metal pole, the force that had been tugging at his weapon vanished. His arms and legs and bones and joints were now pushing against nothing.

Blithe Li waved her left hand, sweeping the Exorcist's Staff to one side, and rested her palm on the blind man's chest. "Master Ke, this kung fu is called the Red Serpent Palm."

"Go on, harlot. Do your worst!" he shot back.

It was clear there was nothing the eldest Freak could do to defend himself. Madam Wu dived at Blithe Li in the faint hope that she could force their foe back. To her surprise, the Taoist did withdraw, jumping up and tapping her foot on Ke's staff to vault sideways.

"It takes courage to see off my disciple," Blithe Li said to Madam Wu as she hung in the air. She then let out a titter and stroked the woman on the left side of her face.

Madam Wu was stupefied. The hand was soft and smooth. The touch gentle and soothing. She stood dazed, watching as Blithe Li landed lightly on her feet then disappeared among the willows with a few effortless leaps. Then, exhaustion overwhelmed her. Although she had survived by the skin of her teeth, the attacks she had launched had depleted her reserves of martial power. She slumped to the ground, unable to move.

Ke Zhen'e was in an equally battered state. It was as if he were being crushed and suffocated by a huge rock on his chest. He gasped and heaved a few times before he could recover sufficiently to calm his breathing with inner *neigong* technique.

The air was now growing hot and murky with black smoke. The fire started by Blithe Li had already claimed a sizeable portion of Lu Manor. Madam Wu pushed herself to her feet and, with Ke Zhen'e's help, shifted Lu Liding and Mistress Lu into more comfortable positions. It was clear the couple were living out their last moments, for the simple act of breathing was almost too much for them.

What should we do? Madam Wu asked herself. They're too injured to be moved, but I can't leave them to the fire . . . As she deliberated, she heard a familiar voice bellow from the distance: "How fare you, woman?"

Her husband was back.

CHAPTER TWO

THE SON OF AN OLD FRIEND

I

"HOW FARE YOU, WOMAN?" WU SANTONG CALLED AGAIN AS HE
hurtled towards Lu Manor.

"I'm over here," Madam Wu answered. Although part of her was
annoyed that he had not been with them to face the Red Serpent
Celestial, she was relieved he had not abandoned her, and moved by
his concern for her well-being: it was the first expression of such care
in a decade.

Wu Santong was more dishevelled than before, his robe stained
and ripped, but the bib around his neck – used by his adopted daughter He Yuanjun when she was a babe – was undamaged. He scooped
Lu Liding up in one arm and Mistress Lu in the other.

"Follow me. Quick!"

He shot to his feet and plunged into the forest, leading them on
a circuitous route for several *li*, twisting east and meandering west.
Eventually, he stopped before a sizeable deserted kiln that had once
been used for firing winemaking vats.

Madam Wu was thrilled to find her sons unharmed inside, sitting
on the floor next to a small bed and playing a game of pebbles with
Cheng Ying and Lu Wushuang.

The girls broke into screams when they saw Master and Mistress Lu covered in blood.

Picking up their wails of "Mama" and "Papa", Ke Zhen'e gasped. "Oh no, we've led the monster here!"

"What do you mean?" Madam Wu looked at him with wild eyes.

"She wants to kill the children, but she doesn't know where—"

"That's why she didn't hurt us."

Hearing his wife's words, Wu Santong strode outside, and planted himself before the kiln's low entrance. "I'll deal with the Red Serpent!"

"Ying . . ." Lu Liding's chest heaved with the effort of speech. "Handkerchief . . . in my shirt."

Cheng Ying wiped her tears and reached into the inside pouch of her uncle's shirt to retrieve it. The neatly folded silk was embroidered with scarlet flowers in four corners, each blossom paired with an emerald green leaf. The once-white fabric had yellowed with age, but the coloured threads still retained their vibrant hues. So skilled was the artist that the decoration looked most lifelike.

"Tie . . . around your neck . . . don't take it off."

Nodding, Cheng Ying obeyed her uncle.

Mistress Lu was barely conscious, but at her husband's voice, she forced her eyes to open. "No! Our daughter . . . give it to Wushuang."

"We promised . . . Ying's parents," Lu Liding croaked.

"And leave your own . . . to die?"

"Wushuang goes with us . . ."

An agonising spasm seized Mistress Lu's body. Her eyes rolled back and she passed out.

THE HANDKERCHIEF was the love token Blithe Li had given Lu Zhanyuan. The scarlet thornapple, Dali's most famous flower, represented the young woman and the green leaf symbolised her beloved, a pun on the pronunciation of his family name *Lu* and the colour green, as they sounded the same. It expressed her belief that theirs was a perfect match, and they would always be together, leaning close and complementing each other.

Lu Zhanyuan had expected Blithe Li and Wu Santong to wreak havoc in the tenth year of his marriage and planned accordingly. However, he had not foreseen that he would be struck down by a sudden terminal illness ahead of time, leaving his brother and his kin with no-one to defend them.

Wu Santong did not worry Lu Zhanyuan, for he knew the man was not out for blood, so he merely advised his brother to avoid the superior martial Master, but Blithe Li's fearsome reputation had reached his ears in the intervening years, as she terrorised the *jianghu* with her vicious and hard-hearted ways. Hoping that the handkerchief would remind her of happy moments in their shared past and dissuade her from bloodshed, he bade his brother to tie it around his neck if the situation turned desperate.

Lu Liding had not produced the keepsake earlier because he would not lower himself to pleading with the she-demon, but there was a chance it could help Cheng Ying. The daughter of his wife's elder sister, she had been entrusted to his care when her parents passed away. Now that he had no hope of fulfilling his promise, the best he could do was to bestow the memento on her in the faint hope it might save her life.

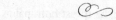

CATCHING MISTRESS Lu's reaction, Cheng Ying offered the handkerchief to Lu Wushuang. "Auntie says it's for you."

"It's for cousin Ying to wear," Lu Liding wheezed weakly.

"Why don't we tear it into two?" Madam Wu suggested. She could tell that the piece of fabric carried great significance for the family.

Lu Liding parted his lips to speak, but could not draw any air into his lungs, so he nodded to give his consent. Madam Wu ripped the fabric down the middle and handed the two halves to the girls.

Wu Santong had been drawn back inside the kiln by their discussion, and he noticed, for the first time, a black mark on the left side of his wife's face.

"What – what is that?" he asked with a quaver in his voice.

Madam Wu raised her hand to her cheek. Numb. She could feel nothing. Not even the touch of her own fingertips. She remembered Blithe Li's strangely gentle caress. Could she have smeared poison on her palm?

But before she could ask her husband to describe the visible symptoms, a peal of laughter rang in the wilderness.

"Toss the girls out, dead or alive. Or I'll fire up the kiln!" The threat was delivered by a female voice, crisp and tuneful like silver bells.

Wu Santong rushed out, coming face to face with Blithe Li. They had last seen each other a decade ago at Lu Zhanyuan and He Yuanjun's wedding. The young woman was not quite twenty then and she still looked just as youthful today. The only change was the way she dressed: she now wore the habit of a Taoist nun. Judging from her appearance, one would assume she was a well-born lady pledged to be a lay renunciant. There was nothing to hint at the seasoned, cold-blooded killer within.

The sight of Blithe Li languidly swirling her horsetail whisk convinced Wu Santong that he would stand a better chance if he were armed. He sized up a chestnut tree growing beside the kiln, its trunk as wide as a standard rice bowl. Deciding it could stand in for his usual weapon, a metal rake, he thrust both palms with a *ha!* and snapped it in two.

"Impressive!" Blithe Li said with a smile.

Wu Santong hefted his makeshift weapon. "It has been ten years since we last met, Miss Li."

It was a term of address the Red Serpent Celestial had not heard since the day she had renounced the trappings of the temporal world. Those two simple words flooded her heart with the sweetness of youth and the first taste of love, but it quickly curdled into bitter rancour, when the image of He Yuanjun clouded her reminiscence.

It was He Yuanjun who had snatched her future – a lifetime with her beloved. It was He Yuanjun who had condemned her to a cold, solitary existence.

Being in the jilted woman's presence again stirred something in Wu Santong's shattered heart. He had accepted that his love for He Yuanjun would always remain unrequited, but he could not help feeling cast aside when she married Lu Zhanyuan.

The memory of what had happened after he and Blithe Li tried to disrupt the wedding banquet came back to him now. He had watched her massacre the entire household of a respected kung fu Master – more than twenty lives, male and female, young and old. He had not intervened, for he had not known that the bloodlust was merely fuelled by bile. He had not realised she was unacquainted with those she had slain and that there had been no feud to speak of: their sole offence was sharing a name with his adopted daughter – He, a common family name – though they were tied by neither blood nor marriage. When he eventually learned of the truth behind the carnage, he regarded Blithe Li with terror and disdain, despite his own internal turmoil.

And now, noting how her face flitted from tenderness to cruelty, he truly feared for the girls.

"Master Wu, step aside please," Blithe Li said. "I have left nine handprints in Lu Manor. I *will* kill the girls."

"Lu Zhanyuan and his wife are dead. You have mortally wounded his younger brother and sister-in-law. Why can't you spare the little ones?"

The Taoist shook her head with a wry smile. "Step aside, Master Wu."

Wu Santong tightened his grip on the tree trunk. "Miss Li, you are too stony-hearted. Ah Yuan—"

Blithe Li's face darkened at the mention of her rival and she cut him off. "I have made a solemn oath to kill whosoever mentions the strumpet's name in my presence. I trust you have heard that I once destroyed sixty-three warehouses and ferry wharfs on the *Yuan* River because their names contained that abhorrent character. Master Wu, you said that word yourself, do not blame me for my response."

Blithe Li knew she could not afford to underestimate her opponent's kung fu. Wu Santong might be of unsound mind, but he had been trained by Reverend Sole Light himself. The most prudent course of action would be to strike him dead before he could retaliate. She raised the horsetail whisk and lashed it down at Wu Santong's head. The delicate weapon fell with ferocious might, whipping up a gust that sent the man's ungroomed hair into a wild dance.

Wu Santong countered with a blistering swipe of the tree trunk, sweeping its branches and leaves into the woman's path.

Recognising the blow was too powerful to tackle head on, Blithe Li glided out of range. She then darted forward before he could pull back his strength, unfurling the whisk's flowing silver horsehairs at his face.

This was the moment Wu Santong had been waiting for. Blithe Li was now within his reach. With a flourish of his right hand, he speared his extended index finger at a vital point on her forehead. This move from the Yang in Ascendance repertoire might appear sluggish to the uninitiated, but its unpredictable and ever-changing course made it nigh on impossible to evade.

Blithe Li shot backwards in an Inverted Strike of the Bell and landed one *zhang* away.

Awed by the effortless way she flitted back and forth at will, Wu Santong channelled more strength into each swipe of the trunk. He managed to keep the Taoist at bay, ten paces from the kiln, but with such an unwieldy weapon, there would always be gaps in his offensive.

At the first sign of a pause between one move and the next, Blithe Li would steal in with a counter-attack, swift as a bolt of lightning. In those moments, it was the might of Yang in Ascendance that sent her scuttling back. If it were not for this supreme pressure-point locking kung fu, Wu Santong would have been at her mercy.

As the tussle progressed, he began to show signs of strain under the weight of his makeshift weapon. The Taoist seized the opportunity to creep closer, watching out for her chance.

Up she flew in a swirl of reddish gold, alighting at the very tip of the tree trunk to thrash the horsetail whisk downwards from her elevated position.

Startled, Wu Santong lowered his weapon, ramming the leafy branches against the ground to throw Blithe Li off balance. The woman let out a girlish chuckle at his futile attempt and darted up the length of the trunk.

Wu Santong twisted to the side and extended his arm in an acupoint jab without relinquishing his grip on the trunk. With a sway of her hips, Blithe Li drew back to the crown of the tree. He tried shaking her off, swinging his weapon from side to side, but none of these efforts succeeded in dislodging her. It was as if she was an extension of the branches, moving with their every quiver.

Blithe Li bided her time. She was now in a position of absolute dominance. As long as she remained perched on the hefty weapon, it was rendered redundant, and her weight was adding to the strain placed on her opponent. She could attack to her heart's content, and delight in towering advantageously over her foe.

Feeling increasingly beleaguered, Wu Santong knew the slightest slip would cost him not just his life but those of everyone inside the kiln – his wife, his sons, the two girls, the injured Master and Mistress Lu, and Ke Zhen'e. He could not allow that to happen. He mustered his *neigong* strength and swung the tree trunk hard and fast in sudden swerves to shake the Taoist off.

2

"HIBISCUS! SUMMON THE CONDORS!" KE ZHEN'E YELLED FROM inside the kiln. He had caught the sound of the girl's footsteps as she hovered on the fringes of the fight. "Get them to attack this wicked woman!"

Whistles and commands answered his call. As Hibiscus emerged from her hiding place, where she had been watching the scuffle unfold, the large white birds swooped down on Blithe Li from two sides.

The Taoist leapt off the tree trunk in a flying somersault. But, instead of landing on the ground, she hooked her left foot around a bough and took shelter among the branches.

Missing their target, the condors flapped their wings and soared into the sky. A moment later, they dived once more at the girl's urging. Their steel-like talons plunged into the leaves, raking and tearing.

Their synchronised attack reminded Blithe Li of a *jianghu* rumour that Guo Jing and Lotus Huang had trained two exceptional birds of prey. Though she was confident that the feathered creatures could not hurt her, their association with Ke Zhen'e, Guo Jing's *shifu*, was troubling. If the birds were indeed those fabled raptors, then their master and mistress were likely to be nearby. The arrival of two such exalted martial Masters would certainly put victory in doubt. She veered away from the condors' claws and flicked the horsetail whisk, catching one of the birds on the wing. A screech of agony rang out as a shower of silvery feathers rained down.

"Don't be scared! We can handle this nasty woman!"

The galvanising call attracted Blithe Li's attention and her eyes lighted on Hibiscus Guo for the first time. She could find no fault in the girl's features – her skin was like the finest jade or the purest snow, her eyes and brows were as perfect as those traced in famous paintings of beautiful women.

Is Lotus Huang her mother? she wondered. The daughter of Apothecary Huang is known to be a great beauty. How do her looks compare to mine?

The Taoist's mind had strayed from the fight and she was sending forth her horsetail scourges a touch slower.

Wu Santong had been growing anxious at his inability to overpower the Red Serpent Celestial even with the help of the

49

condors. Noting her distraction, he gathered every last drop of *neigong* power into his arms and hurled the tree trunk upwards into the air.

The surprise move caught the woman out. She lost her foothold and was sent several *zhang* skywards. The condors beat their wings and drew level, pecking at her with their sharp beaks.

If Blithe Li were on the ground, they would have posed little threat to her, but mid-air, she had no leverage to repel them in their natural environment. She swirled the horsetail whisk, whipping the long hairs into a circle of protection over her head and her face, then flicked out a flowing sleeve.

Three Soul of Ice needles took flight. One shooting towards Wu Santong. The other two whizzing at the condors.

Catching a flash of silver, Wu Santong threw himself to the ground and rolled to the side, but the needle still grazed his left calf. As he tried to haul himself back to his feet, he lost control of the limb and foundered, falling to his knees. He forced out a burst of inner strength to straighten his leg, but numbness had now spread to his hip and he sprawled face down. He pressed his hands against the ground to heave himself up. It was no use at all – he could no longer move any part of his body.

"Santong!" Madam Wu rushed to her husband's side. "Where are you hurt?"

He grunted in acknowledgement and tried to tense his back to hoist himself up. Not a single muscle would respond. The poison in Blithe Li's clandestine weapon had paralysed him.

Up above, the condors arced their wings and soared, but the needles were fleet too, parting the air with a buzz. One tore past the top of the male's foot, slicing open the thick layer of scute.

"Come back!" Hibiscus called, yet the birds would not heed her this time.

Blithe Li beamed at the girl. "Little sister, your last name is Guo, isn't it?"

Hibiscus studied the stranger. The lady can't be wicked – she's too beautiful and charming! Feeling reassured, she replied, "Yes, my name is Guo. What's yours?"

The Taoist strolled over and offered to take her by the hand. "Come, I'll show you somewhere fun."

With a thump of his iron staff, Ke Zhen'e propelled himself out of the kiln and stood protectively before Hibiscus.

"Go inside!" he ordered the girl.

"What're you afraid of? I don't eat children," Blithe Li said merrily.

Before Ke Zhen'e could retort, the sound of someone humming a popular ditty echoed among the trees, followed by the crunch of fallen leaves and twigs underfoot.

A boy in tattered clothes, twelve or thirteen years of age, came bounding up. He clutched a live cockerel in one hand.

"Oi, what are you lot doing standing outside my front door?" His defiant eyes flitted between Blithe Li and Hibiscus Guo. Tilting his head to one side, he made a sucking noise with his tongue, flashed a flippant grin, then he said, sleek as oil, "A great beauty and a little beauty! Have you young ladies come to call on me? I've never known such pretty faces."

"Why on earth would we visit a guttersnipe like you?" Hibiscus shot back, her lips pulled tight.

"Then why are you outside my house?" The boy's grin broadened as he pointed at the kiln.

"You live in this filthy hovel?" The girl regarded the dilapidated structure with disgust and turned away, scanning the sky for her condors and whistling commands to draw them back.

Blithe Li, meanwhile, was striding towards the kiln, giddy at the prospect of completing her revenge. She would rather not dally further and test the veracity of the old adage, a long night is fraught with dreams, in case Guo Jing and Lotus Huang turned up looking for their daughter.

Madam Wu leapt to her feet and planted herself before the kiln's entrance, her sword aimed at the approaching Taoist nun. "Don't you dare!"

"This is our young friend's residence. It is not for you to bar me."
Blithe Li thrust her open palm straight at Madam Wu's sword. Just
before she impaled herself, her wrist turned a touch and her fingers
slid along the flat of the blade. The simple action pushed the sword
upwards and back. The whetted edge grazed Madam Wu's forehead,
leaving behind a streak of blood.

"I beg your pardon." Smiling, Blithe Li glided past the mother
and hunched a little to step through the entryway. Once inside, she
tucked the whisk's handle into the back of her collar, and snatched
up Cheng Ying and Lu Wushuang. Then she tapped her foot without
turning round and flew outside with her prey. As she whipped past
Ke Zhen'e, she kicked his staff from his grasp.

The boy was appalled, his innate sense of justice awakened by
the girls' screams. "Great beauty, shouldn't you have asked *me* – the
master of the house – before barging into *my* home and taking *my*
people?" he asked in an arch tone, launching himself at the Taoist
nun and grabbing her in a bodylock. "Unhand them, now!"

Blithe Li's heart skipped a beat. She had never imagined that
she would be caught off guard by an untrained boy in this intimate manner. She had always maintained a chaste distance from the
opposite sex in accordance with the customs of the time. Even during her courtship with Lu Zhanyuan, she had acted with impeccable
decorum. But now, the boy had his arms around her waist, violating
all codes of propriety.

An unfamiliar sensation took over her body. Her strength seemed
to be draining away. She rallied what little internal energy she could
control and flicked her wrists, sending the girls to a spot several *chi*
to one side. After that, she reached behind with her right hand and
seized the boy by the back of his shirt, poised to unleash the power
mustered in her palm to scramble his heart and lungs.

The Red Serpent Celestial had dispatched more men than she
cared to enumerate with her eponymous palm kung fu over the past
decade, simply because they revealed the faintest lecherous intent.
And yet, now, she hesitated, even as the boy's jaunty "great beauty"

rang in her head. She could not explain why she had not found such words from his lips repulsive, like the jeers of the *jianghu* men who lusted after her. In fact, she was rather flattered. His compliment seemed heartfelt despite his glib tone, and because of that, she was unable to harden her heart and strike him dead.

Urgent caws cut her musings short. The condors were swooping at terrifying speed. She made a flourish with her left arm, unfurling her sleeve and hurling two Soul of Ice needles at her airborne attackers. The birds beat their wings, shrieking in panic, but the lightweight projectiles were flying faster than they could gain height.

Yet Blithe Li's grim satisfaction was punctured by a low swooshing noise whizzing in her direction. The next thing she knew, her needles were falling from the sky. She flung the boy away and leapt over to where her secret weapons had clinked to the ground.

All she found amiss were two tiny specks of the most ordinary grit.

I can't send mere pebbles flying with such velocity or precision, she noted with alarm. I'd better dispatch the girls quickly and get away before it's too late.

Thus resolved, Blithe Li spun round and aimed a palm thrust at Cheng Ying's back. Just before the strike made contact, she noticed the girl's neckerchief. The aged white silk was embroidered with scarlet flowers and green leaves. The love token she had made for Lu Zhanyuan.

She halted, hauling back the deadly force in her palm.

I was still in his heart?

The realisation dredged up tender feelings from bygone days as she tried to fathom why he had held onto the relic.

Is he begging me to spare the girl?

Unable to settle on an answer, Blithe Li decided to kill the other girl first. She drew the horsetail whisk from her collar and lashed its silver strands down onto Lu Wushuang's back.

But again, something gave her pause. Around the girl's neck, an identical handkerchief gleamed in the sun.

There can't be two of them. One must be fake!

A voice snarled in her head, and with a flick of her wrist, the deathblow was whipped into a less ferocious whirling scourge. The horsehair curled around Lu Wushuang's neck, wrenching her around.

Blithe Li was determined to find out why there were two handkerchiefs, but a faint swoosh hummed in the air, drawing her full attention. A tiny piece of rock was zooming towards her back with unnerving speed. She twirled her weapon around. In one fluent movement, she freed the girl and swung the whisk's steel handle at the flying gravel. The force of the clash tore painfully at the muscles between her thumb and forefinger. Her palm seared with unnatural heat and her body shuddered. Her weapon strained against her grip, threatening to fly out of her hand.

The shock of being nearly disarmed reminded Blithe Li of her earlier resolve to get away. She grabbed Lu Wushuang and vanished in a gale of lightness *qinggong*.

"COUSIN! COUSIN!" Cheng Ying scampered after the Taoist, but how could a nine-year-old hope to keep up?

Rivers and canals criss-crossed the fertile plains of the South. Cheng Ying's way was soon blocked by a stream. She ran along the bank, calling Lu Wushuang's name. Suddenly, she caught a glimpse of a swirl of amber sweeping across an arched bridge to her left, and in a flash, she found the Taoist nun standing before her.

Alone.

"Where's my cousin?" Cheng Ying demanded, choking down her fear.

Blithe Li's eyes lighted on the girl's face, lingering over her fair, unblemished skin and delicate features.

"Your looks will break hearts, perhaps even your own," she observed in a glacial tone. "I shall grant you death to spare the world the tribulation."

The Red Serpent Celestial raised the horsetail whisk, flicking the long strands over her shoulder. Poised to thrash it down, to crush the girl's skull and crack open her ribs, she flexed her arm, whipping the horsehair into the air, and yet, all she managed was to pull them taut. Shaken, she twisted round, but before she could fully turn to face whoever was thwarting her, the force trapping her weapon flipped upwards, plucking her feet off the ground. Blithe Li went along with it, springing one *zhang* high and spinning a half circle. The descent gave her time to draw her left palm over her chest in defence, while with her right she injected a blast of inner strength into the whisk and thrust it forward the instant she landed. The soft strands stiffened into a spear-like point.

But there was no-one there.

A phantom? The question flashed through the Taoist's mind. Whoever it was, their speed was beyond the limits of the corporeal world. She had never encountered such an adversary over the hundreds of battles she had fought. Drawing back the horsetail whisk to deploy her Primal Sky and Earth technique, she wove a circular web of protection five *chi* in diameter and wheeled about to catch a glimpse of her elusive opponent.

Just a few exchanges of breath had passed since Blithe Li had raised her whisk to kill Cheng Ying. The girl was still standing in the same spot, but a tall wiry man in a pale teal robe was now towering beside her. His face was as if carved from wood, betraying no expression – it was impossible to tell if he was alive or a stiff corpse. One hurried look was enough to fill the beholder with repugnance.

Blithe Li scuttled back two steps, sickened by his unsightly features and unsettled by her failure to detect his approach. She could not recall any *wulin* Master known to sport such a terrifying visage, but as she parted her lips to ask his name, she heard him say: "Go on, little lass, give this nasty woman a beating."

The girl glanced at the man, who had bent low to be at eye-level with her, and mumbled, "I'm scared."

"Be bold and strike."

Cheng Ying was too intimidated to even lift a hand.

The man, running out of patience, grabbed the girl by the back of her robe and flung her at the Taoist.

Blithe Li reached out with her left hand to catch the girl. Her palm was inches from Cheng Ying's waist, when – *swoosh!* – deadening soreness spread from the crook of her elbow, and her arm flopped to her side. She had been hit by another minuscule projectile.

A moment later, Cheng Ying flew head first into her torso. The impact sent the girl's arms flailing upwards.

Pak! A loud, crisp slap caught Blithe Li across the face.

Never so insulted, the Red Serpent Celestial threw caution to the wind and flipped the horsetail whisk around, clubbing its metal handle down at Cheng Ying's head.

Swoosh! A tremendous force knocked the weapon askew, shaking her grip.

Another flying pebble.

Blithe Li was now certain they were the work of this spectral man. A swift retreat was the only course open to her. She secured her grip on the whisk and took one last look at Cheng Ying.

The girl was now standing out of reach.

The Taoist turned and took to her heels. Several steps later, she unfurled both sleeves, leaving a shimmering trail in her wake. A dozen Soul of Ice needles hurtled towards the man. She had launched the clandestine weapons without twisting around, looking back or slowing down. And yet, every single needle was aimed at a specific vital point.

The man sprang up and shot backwards, surprised by this sophisticated and underhand kung fu. The needles flew at great speed, but he was faster. The silver shower fell to the ground in a patter of soft tinkles.

Blithe Li raced ahead, her senses attuned to any movement in the air. The instant she felt the shift caused by the stranger's evasive manoeuvre, she knew her diversion had worked. She launched a single Soul of Ice with a swish of her sleeve.

At Cheng Ying this time.

In no doubt that her secret weapon would find its target, she picked up her pace in case the man went after her. She crossed the arched bridge again and vanished behind a cluster of mulberry trees.

The man lifted Cheng Ying into his arms and hissed at the sight of the silver needle sticking out of her shoulder. With concern darkening his countenance, he took off in the opposite direction with the injured girl.

3

WHEN BLITHE LI HAD TAKEN FLIGHT, WITH CHENG YING IN pursuit, the boy had volunteered to go after the young girl, following her cries to a stream. Here the vista was more open, giving him a good view of the surrounding countryside, but he could neither see the girl nor hear her voice. He was walking along the stream, looking for traces of her whereabouts, when his eyes were drawn to something catching the light near the foot of an arched bridge. He squatted down to take a better look.

Silver needles, lying on the ground. At least a dozen of them.

He picked one up. Its slender shaft was engraved with an intricate pattern. He had never seen such finely crafted needles. Intrigued, he collected them with care, placing them on his left palm.

A large centipede scuttled over to where the boy had found the needles and rolled onto its back. He poked the immobile insect. Dead. He spotted a number of ants in the loose earth around it. Most of them were dead too. He prodded those still scurrying around with the point of one of the needles. They circled on the spot then shrivelled up on their backs. He toyed with a few other insects within reach. They all met their end after coming into contact with the needle.

The boy was thrilled by his find. They would be very handy in repelling mosquitoes and flies. However, his excitement was soon dampened by a lack of sensation in his left hand. He flexed his fingers to see what was wrong and was shocked to find that he could barely control his muscles.

They're poisoned! he thought as he flung the needles away and examined his hands. A black tint had stained his skin. The centre of his left palm, where he had gathered the needles, was the colour of ink. He rubbed his hands frantically on his trousers, hoping get rid of the blotch, but the numbness spread even quicker, creeping up towards the crook of his elbow.

The boy had experienced a similar tingle once before, when he was bitten by a viper. He nearly died from its venom and this was how the wound had felt. *Waaah!* The memory sent tears pouring down his face.

"You are feeling the poison's power," a grating, metallic voice rumbled from behind.

The boy twisted round in alarm. A grizzly man, holding himself upside down, standing on his palms instead of his feet. His hands were resting on wooden blocks, while his arms were held straight, his legs squeezed tight, and his feet pointed to the sky.

"Who . . . who are you?" The boy shrank back, startled.

The man flexed his arms, shot three *chi* into the air and landed right in front of the boy, mumbling, "Who am I? I . . . I want to know too . . ."

Terrified, the boy bolted, but a rhythmic clacking pursued him. *Tak, tak, tak.* He stole a peek and the sight sent his spirits scattering in fright.

The man was scrabbling forward on his palms. With each stride, he smacked the wooden blocks against the ground, beating out the sound of his approach. His gait, though topsy-turvy, was incredibly swift. He was lagging a mere few hand-widths behind.

The boy galloped as fast as his legs would carry him. A sudden gust of air ruffled his hair.

The man had dropped down from above and planted himself in his way.

"Mamaaaa!" Shrieking, the boy spun round and took off in the direction he had just come from, but his two legs could not outrun the eccentric stranger marching on his hands.

However many times the boy turned and fled, the man always managed to catch up and plonk himself down in his path, landing a little closer with each leap.

The boy wanted to shove him away, but the poison had taken hold of his arms – he could barely move or feel them. His legs wobbled and he slumped to the ground, soaked in a sweat of panic and terror.

The man fixed his eyes on the boy and said, "Running around has hastened the toxin's hold on your body."

"Grandpa!" The boy straightened into a kneeling position to demonstrate his deference. "Help me! Please!"

The man shook his head, but the boy was undeterred. "You're so skilled and powerful! I know you can!"

His flattering words elicited a smile.

Noting that the stranger's stern demeanour had yielded somewhat, the boy gushed, "You run so fast on your hands! No-one under the heavens can measure up to you!"

Evidently pleased, the man let out a booming cackle, shaking the branches of the nearby trees. "Turn over. I'll take a look."

The boy flipped into a headstand, supporting most of his weight with his right arm, which he could just about manipulate. The upturned position allowed him to get a better look at the man. High nose bridge, deep-set eyes. Greying bristles – silver among black iron – stuck out from his chin.

The man scrutinised the boy with a deepening frown. From time to time, he squeaked and squawked to himself in the jangling sounds of a strange tongue.

"Good Grandpa, kind Grandpa, you will help me, won't you?" the boy entreated.

Charmed by this good-looking, sweet-talking youngling, the man said, "I can help you, but you have to promise me something."

"Grandpa, I'll obey your every command."

"You've read my mind." The man grinned.

The boy was already having second thoughts. What if he tells me to go down on all fours and shove my face in dung, like a dog?

Sensing hesitation, the man snarled, "Fine! Die, if that's what you want!" He bent his arms then straightened them, propelling his body into the air, and touched down several *chi* to one side.

The boy tipped himself the right way up and ran after the man. "Grandpa! I give you my word! I'll do whatever you say!"

"Swear!"

"If Grandpa purges this poison from my body . . ." the boy began solemnly, for the deadening sensation in his left arm had now reached his shoulder. "I shall obey your every word. If I break my promise, then let the poison return."

The boy darted a look at the man, who was nodding in approval, and felt rather smug that his hollow vow had fooled him. After all, as long as he avoided those needles, how would he ever fall prey to the same venom again?

The man flipped onto his feet, seized the boy's left arm and massaged the muscles. The effect was immediate. The boy could feel his senses being restored.

"Please don't stop, Grandpa."

Scrunching up his brow, the man shouted, "Call me Papa!"

"Papa died a long, long time ago."

"How dare you disobey me, son!"

The boy now realised what the man had wanted from him – but, even though his father had died before his arrival in this world, leaving him forever envious of those who grew up enjoying paternal love, he was not so desperate for affection that he would tie himself to a lunatic and promise to be his son.

"Do as you please!" The man strode away, on his feet this time, mumbling a string of curious, incomprehensible words that bore the quality of an invocation.

"Papa!" The boy hastened after him. "Where are you going, Papa?"

A wild guffaw answered. "Come over here, son. I'll show you

how to force the toxins from your body." He recited a mnemonic and explained his method for reversing the flow of *qi*.

The boy must first assume the headstand position, then invert the direction of his blood and breath. Only then could he force the venom out from where it had entered the body. As a novice to the martial arts, he would only be able to maintain the upturned posture and altered circulation for a brief period, pushing out tiny amounts of poison. To fully cleanse his body, he would need to perform this exercise every day for at least a month.

A fast learner, the boy managed to apply the technique straight away, driving some of the numbness from his arms. After successfully channelling his *qi* for a short while, a few droplets of black liquid oozed from his fingertips.

"Excellent!" The man was impressed. "That's enough for today. I'll teach you something new tomorrow. Now come along."

"Where are we going?" The boy had not expected this.

"You go where Papa goes . . ." The man trailed off, distracted by a series of harsh cries from above. He looked up to see two white raptors gliding through the sky. As his eyes followed the winged creatures, the furrow on his brow grew deeper and he started to smack himself on the forehead.

A futile attempt to jolt his memory.

All of a sudden, he stopped. His eyes flashed in recollection and a dark cloud descended over his features.

Yelling unintelligibly, he flipped into a handstand and took long swinging strides with his arms. Each time he struck his palms on the ground, he sprang further and higher until he disappeared into a dense thicket.

4

"PAPA! PAPA!" THE BOY SCRAMBLED AFTER THE MAN, BUT IT was impossible to keep up with someone so fleet on their hands. As he tried to determine which way the man had gone, a rush of wind stirred the back of his hair. He looked around to see the condors touching down. Presently, a man and a woman emerged from the trees and approached the birds.

The fellow looked around thirty, his chest broad and his back straight. His large eyes were balanced by thick eyebrows, and a thin moustache framed his top lip. The woman, a year or two younger, was elegant and captivating.

Her vivacious eyes tarried over the boy's face, then she turned to her companion. "Doesn't he remind you of someone we once knew, Guo Jing?"

THAT MORNING, Lotus Huang and Guo Jing had set out early to seek news of Apothecary Huang and overheard talk in a bustling teahouse about a blaze at a certain Lu Manor. Lu was a fairly common surname and there were Lu Manors by the dozen in Jiaxing, but when Lotus heard the name Lu Zhanyuan, she knew she had to see for herself.

The fire had burned out when they arrived on the scene, but Lotus concluded that it was arson as soon as she stepped over the main gate and spotted three charred bodies in the smoking debris. She had never met the master of the house, but she knew that he and his wife, He Yuanjun, were lauded for their kung fu. It was implausible that anyone under the care of two capable martial artists would fall victim to an ordinary house fire.

Lotus ventured further into the rubble and called Guo Jing over, pointing to a group of handprints on a half-collapsed wall.

Although blackened by smoke, it was still possible to make out a hint of their original blood-red colour. They were made more ghoulish by the fact that only the lower half of the palm was still visible of the two marks in the top row.

"The Red Serpent Celestial!" Guo Jing gasped.

"Blithe Li is reputed to be as skilled and vicious as the Venom of the West," Lotus said as she picked her way through the wreckage with caution, searching for clues that might reveal what had taken place.

A small ornamental pond not far from the derelict wall grabbed her attention. Dozens of goldfish were floating belly up. She went closer to see what had caused the carnage and noticed two silver needles glinting on the very edge of the pool. The tip of one of them was touching the water.

Lotus shuddered at the grim effect of the notorious Soul of Ice needles. She picked them up with the aid of two broken twigs and lifted them gingerly onto a handkerchief she had placed on the ground. After wrapping the poisonous secret weapons securely with the cloth, layer upon layer, she put the parcel in her bag.

Once they had looked around the rest of the manor, Guo Jing and Lotus began to search its surroundings. Eventually, they came upon the condors and the boy in rags.

A RIPE stench hit Guo Jing's nostrils before he had time to consider whom it was the boy resembled. He sniffed the air, hoping to work out where it was coming from, but straight away, his head began to throb.

It was then that Lotus noticed the male condor's left foot had swollen to twice its usual size. Examining it, she found a shallow cut on the outermost scaly layer. The tissues around it had already started to putrefy, giving off the foul stink they had detected in the air.

Guo Jing came over at Lotus's urging and was horrified by the sight. Turning to her in the hope that she would have an explanation and a remedy, he noticed a black tint on the boy's left hand and blurted out, "You've been poisoned too?"

Lotus grabbed the boy's arm, rolled up his sleeve and pricked a blood vessel on his wrist with her dagger. She massaged around the cut to let the toxins out, but was surprised by the colour of the vital fluid.

Bright red. Not stained dark by venom.

How could that be? She had never seen a case where the skin was black with the poison but the blood was clear. Needless to say, she had no idea that the boy had pushed the contaminated blood towards his fingertips with the reverse flow technique he had learned from the eccentric stranger – the poison would not travel up his arm while this internal kung fu was in effect.

Lotus took three Dew of Nine Flowers pills and offered one to the boy. "Chew before you swallow." Then she fed the remaining remedies to the condors.

Mumbling thanks, the boy accepted the pill with both hands in a way that showed total appreciation and gratitude. A floral fragrance wafted up to his nose. When he crushed it between his teeth, a sweet aroma spread through his mouth and, as it moved down to his stomach, a cooling sensation reached the Elixir Field in his lower belly.

Guo Jing, meanwhile, had been reflecting on what he had seen since stepping foot in the ruins of Lu Manor. He tilted his head back and let out a long whistle. Birds were startled from their perch, taking flight and cawing frantically. The power of this high-pitched sound stirred branches and swayed leaves, reaching far, far into the distance. Just as his call started to dissipate, he followed up with a second cry, building upon what had come before, multiplying, reverberating, as though a thousand mounted soldiers were galloping into battle.

Lotus understood that her husband was issuing a challenge to Blithe Li the Red Serpent Celestial. As he launched his third whistle, she summoned her *qi* to the Elixir Field and let out a trill of her own.

Guo Jing's tone was rich and full of majesty, while Lotus's was crisp and buoyant. Together, they conjured the image of a hawk soaring wing to wing with a warbler, flying higher into the blue yonder, and despite the difference in size, the warbler never lagged behind.

Their song circled the nine heavens, reaching the ears of every person for miles around. Blithe Li was speeding through the woods with Lu Wushuang when she heard the first whistle. She dared not pause in case the man in green was still pursuing her, but she promised herself with a swish of the horsetail whisk that she would determine in person if Guo Jing's fame were justly deserved.

Yet, when the second whistler joined in, a chill struck her core. The two voices were in perfect harmony. The newcomer brought a supple radiance, amplifying the strength of the original call. They were opponents she was unlikely to get the better of. The thought of the two of them, husband and wife, roaming the *jianghu* together, lending each other support just as they blended their voices, turned her world to ash – dead and devoid of colour – for she was all alone, without a companion.

The woman heaved a sigh and set Lu Wushuang down, resolving to let her go. But the instant she set eyes on the torn handkerchief around the girl's neck, stabs of pain transfixed her heart. She grabbed the child and took off again.

AFTER MAKING the arrangements for Master and Mistress Lu, Ke Zhen'e, Wu Santong and Madam Wu waited at the kiln for the boy's return, hoping he would bring good news about Cheng Ying and Lu Wushuang, but as time passed, it began to dawn on Madam Wu that she should take her sons and her injured husband to safety while she still had the strength. Ke Zhen'e decided he ought to do the same once he had sent the Wu family on their way, in case it was Blithe Li herself who returned. The whistling sounded when he was about to set off with Hibiscus for the tavern they were staying at.

"Papa! Mama!"

The girl ran, following the call, and leapt straight into her mother's waiting arms.

"Ma! Grandpapa sent a nasty Taoist nun packing just now. His kung fu is amazing."

Lotus and Guo Jing exchanged a look. They knew if Ke Zhen'e were to encounter Blithe Li, it was unlikely that he would come out on top. Lotus smiled at her daughter's exaggeration, but Guo Jing was not going to let her get away with an outright lie.

"I've raised you to always tell the truth," he said with a stern face.

"Grandpapa's kung fu *is* amazing. Or else, how did he become your *shifu*?" Hibiscus stuck her tongue out and scrabbled off. She was not going to hang around to be scolded. She ran past the boy and beckoned him to come closer. "Hey you! Why don't you pick some flowers and make me a coronet?" She looked him up and down, taking in his threadbare rags and blackened palms. "Wait! No, stop. Don't do that. Your hands are dirty. Your clothes are dirty. You'll make the flowers dirty! I don't want to play with you. Shoo!"

"Who wants to play with you?" The boy stormed off in a sulk.

"Young man, wait!" Guo Jing called. "There's still poison in your body."

The boy paid no heed and continued his march, his chest puffed out and his chin held high. He took care to place his feet down firm and resolute, and prayed that his confident stride would hide his insecurity and his injured pride. He could not let it be known how deeply the girl's words had affected him.

But Guo Jing was persistent. "Let us help you. Tell us what happened," he said as he caught up with the youngster.

"Why do you care? I don't know you." The boy cast the man a cutting look as he tried to step around him.

A face flashed up in Guo Jing's mind, its expression mirroring the boy's. "What's your family name, young man?"

The boy shot him a glare and started to run. He had barely managed a couple of paces when he felt a tug on his wrist. He wriggled and wrenched to free himself without success. Frustrated, he swung his fist, hitting his captor in the stomach, but the man bore it with a smile. The boy thought he was being mocked and tensed his biceps, determined to serve up another taste of his knuckles, when he suddenly sensed a strange force sucking his hand towards the man's abdomen. He pulled away until his face flushed red and his arm throbbed painfully, and still he could not free himself.

"Tell me your name and I'll let you go," Guo Jing said, maintaining his good humour.

"My last name is Sai and my given name is Er. Now let go!"

Guo Jing relaxed his stomach muscles in disappointment. It was not the name he had been expecting.

Lotus, however, was too sharp to miss the insult. The boy had claimed to be her husband's sire! And his arch tone and the sly glint that had flared in his eyes were decidedly familiar.

Unable to resist the urge to confirm her theory, Lotus spoke up: "Are you saying you're my father-in-law, young man?" She pressed her palm down on the boy's shoulder. The instant she sensed him mustering his strength to repel her, she withdrew.

Having lost the pressure he had been pushing against, the boy tipped forward and – *thump!* – smacked his forehead on the ground.

Hibiscus hooted and clapped merrily.

Mortified and burning with rage, the boy got to his feet, dusted down his grubby clothes and fell back a few steps. He refused to be mocked, readying himself to curse and cuss with every insult he knew.

"Your family name is Yang," Lotus began slowly, her eyes locked onto his. "Your mother's surname is Mu. And you're called Penance. Am I right?"

The boy gasped, stupefied. How did this stranger know his name? A rush of blood surged to his heart. The poison flowed up his arms. His head started to spin, and he blacked out.

Lotus caught him and Guo Jing rushed up to massage his vital points.

"So he is . . . my sworn brother Yang Kang's son?" His voice trembled with excitement. "How did you—"

"I'll explain later." Lotus cut him off. "He needs tending to."

It did not take long for the youngster to come around. He looked between Lotus and Guo Jing. "You – you know me?"

A trickle of blood ran down the corners of his mouth as he parted his lips to speak. He felt a sting on his tongue – he must have bitten himself as he fainted.

"We are friends of your mother," Guo Jing said. "How is she?"

"She passed on."

5

GUO JING CARRIED PENANCE YANG, WHO HAD DRIFTED OUT of consciousness again, back to the tavern they were staying at. On the way, Lotus told him how she had ascertained the boy's identity. She had noted his resemblance to Yang Kang the instant she set eyes on him, and guessed that, if his mother Mercy Mu had taught him any kung fu, the way he channelled his strength would bear Count Seven Hong's hallmark, since Mercy was once trained by the Chief of the Beggar Clan. The Beggar's students fall forwards instead of backwards when they lose their footing, so she gave him a push to test her theory, and he reacted exactly as she had expected, giving her further proof of his parentage.

When the group arrived at the tavern, Ke Zhen'e settled Hibiscus and the two condors, and left Guo Jing and Lotus to look after Penance. Lotus wrote down a prescription and sent the innkeeper to find the medicinal herbs she needed to counter the poison.

Guo Jing was crestfallen when the man returned with only some of the herbs required. A number of the ingredients were so rare that they could not be found even in a city of trade as well connected and prosperous as Jiaxing.

Lotus knew her husband felt responsible for Yang Kang's untimely death, so it had been an especially emotional day for him, finding his sworn brother's orphan and discovering that the boy had been poisoned.

"Let's go to the woods and forage for herbs," she proposed, as she would not like to leave him behind to fret at the inn.

Guo Jing welcomed the suggestion, but her grave tone weighed on his heart. She would have offered more reassurance, if she were confident about neutralising the poison.

KE ZHEN'E went into Penance's room many times over the course of the day to check up on the boy, but each visit was brief as he was also minding Hibiscus. No stranger to poison himself, the Freak recognised the boy had been afflicted with Blithe Li's Soul of Ice and wished there was more he could do, but the venom on his devilnuts was very different and his antidote would have no effect at all.

Penance felt a hand kneading the pressure points on his chest and emerged from his stupor. He forced his eyes open. In the gloom of dusk, he thought he saw someone climbing out through the window. Alarmed, he pushed himself up, and with the support of the furniture along the way, trundled across the room to investigate.

He leaned out to see a man balancing precariously on his hands towards the eaves of the pitched roof. His legs stretched skywards, his upturned body swaying in the breeze. It looked like he might topple over into the courtyard below.

"You!" Penance could not fail to recognise the eccentric man who wanted to be his father.

"Call me Papa!"

"Papa," the boy said stiffly, though his voice was sweet.

"Come up here."

Penance clambered out and stretched his arms to grab the lowest edge of the roof, but his grip had been weakened by the poison and his fingers started to slip as he was hauling himself up. He braced for a painful fall, and yet, all he felt was his collar tightening. The man had caught him by the back of his shirt. He lifted Penance up beside him before flipping around to stand on his feet.

Creaaaak! Doors opening. West side of the courtyard.

Ke Zhen'e hobbled out, listened, then jumped up onto the roof.

He could make out nothing other than the usual indistinct noises at sundown.

*

THE MAN pulled Penance along and took flight as soon as he heard the squeaky doors, and did not stop until they were in the wilderness beyond the city. He set the boy down and said, "Push out more poison."

Penance did as he was told. A few drops of dark liquid dripped from his fingertips and the stuffiness in his chest eased.

Tears glistening in his eyes, the man patted Penance dotingly on the head. "You're very clever. Smarter than my own lad!"

Penance jumped up and threw his arms around the man's neck, crying "Papa! Papa!" His voice was full of yearning and, for the first time, he was not saying those words perfunctorily or with sarcastic intent. He had always longed for a loving, protective father, as his own had died before he was born. Sometimes in his dreams, a great hero, gentle and kindly, would come to him. He remembered the sense of loss when he woke up to find this paternal figure had vanished. For two years now, since his mother's death, he had scraped by on his own, stealing chickens and sleeping rough. As a homeless orphan, he was shunned and despised and bullied everywhere he went. Though he had not taken to the eccentric stranger at first, he could sense that the man was genuinely fond of him, and his heart was touched by the concern and affection. He could not help beginning to regard the man with filial sentiment – his lifelong wish for a father had at last been fulfilled.

The man was aware that the lad had been unwilling to acknowledge any relationship with him, but now he felt that the emotional outpouring was genuine, that a bond as strong as the ties of flesh and blood had brought them together. They would readily give their lives for one another.

"Good boy!" the man cackled. "Dear son, call me Papa again!"

Penance did so and squeezed him tighter.

"I'll teach you my proudest kung fu, son." Extricating himself from the hug, the man walked over to a crumbling old wall and sat on his haunches. A gurgling noise rose from his throat – *croak, croak, croak* – and he thrust both hands forwards. The structure collapsed in a cloud of dust.

Penance stared at the rubble, his mouth hanging wide open. "What is that kung fu? Will I be able to learn it?"

"It's called Exploding Toad. Work hard and you can do it too."

"Then I'll never be bullied again!"

"Who dares bully my son? I'll flay their skin and tear out their tendons!" The man's eyebrows arched in fury. "Thrust your palms like this. You'll send every nuisance sprawling. However many there are. They won't even crawl back on their feet."

The man was, of course, Viper Ouyang the Venom of the West.

The Martial Great had been driven out of his mind during the second Contest of Mount Hua. Since then, over the course of a dozen long years, he had travelled to the sky's edge and the sea's end, asking himself, "Who am I?" When he passed a place that appeared familiar, he would stay for a while, hoping to stimulate his memory. That was why he stopped at Jiaxing.

Although he had forgotten everything about himself, he had not lost his martial ability and continued to cultivate his internal strength by inverting his energy flow, a method developed from the sham Nine Yin Manual he had forced Guo Jing to set down. As his *neigong* improved, the fog in his head cleared somewhat. He became more conscious that he had been acting, from time to time, in ways uncontrollable and erratic, and had been able to recover certain fragments of his memories. However, the vital clue to his identity remained elusive.

Viper Ouyang began to describe his Exploding Toad kung fu, which was indisputably one of the foremost martial inventions under the heavens. The unique way its users channelled their inner force was inspired by how toads accumulate energy while underground and unleash it when they venture out. The slightest error in the control of this store of strength would see the practitioner coughing up blood and suffering crippling, even fatal, internal injuries, and because of this, the Venom had never passed this technique down to his son Gallant Ouyang. But right now, overwhelmed by paternal feelings, the muddle-headed Master held nothing back, sharing his most advanced secrets with his newly adopted son – a child with the most negligible martial foundations.

Penance was a quick learner and soon memorised the introductory mnemonics. Though he could make little sense of the words, he made up his own brutish interpretation and challenged Viper's explanations. Irate, the Martial Great raised his hand, ready to slap some sense into the boy, but the sight of Penance's face in the moonlight reminded him of his late son Gallant when he was about the same age, and he could not bring himself to strike him.

Sighing, he said, "You must be tired. Go back and sleep. We'll continue on the morrow."

"I don't want to go back. I want to be with Papa." Penance had taken a dislike to the Guo family the moment Hibiscus first shamed him for his appearance.

"I'm not quite right in the head. I'll be a burden to you. Once I am better, we will live together, father and son, and never sunder."

"You will come for me soon, won't you?" Penance's voice was choked by tears. He had not been addressed with such warmth since his mother's death.

"I'll stay close by and keep watch over you. If anyone should cross you, I'll snap their ribs like twigs!" With that promise, he accompanied Penance back to the inn.

HEARING A noise in the courtyard coming from the direction of Penance's chamber, Ke Zhen'e went to check on the youngster. Once inside the room, he was startled to find that he could detect no sounds of breathing. He felt his way to the bed – it was empty. Ke Zhen'e rushed out to search the inn and its surroundings, but the boy seemed to have vanished without a trace. He went back to the room, hoping to find a clue to Penance's whereabouts, and he was fast asleep.

The Freak was about to wake the boy and ask him where he had gone when a gust of wind rattled the roof tiles. It sounded like two martial Masters whizzing past overhead using lightness *qinggong*. He rushed to Hibiscus's room, brought her over to sit with Penance, and stood guard by the window.

Another gust blew over the inn. Ke Zhen'e clutched his iron staff in readiness.

Tap. Tap. The martial artists jumped down from the roof into the courtyard.

A man spoke: "You saw him, didn't you?"

"Can it really be him?" replied a woman.

Ke Zhen'e relaxed at the familiar voices and opened the double doors.

"First *Shifu*!" Lotus Huang greeted the Freak then continued the discussion with Guo Jing. "Maybe we've made a mistake? It's dark."

"I'm quite certain."

"Who?" Ke Zhen'e spoke up.

Lotus tugged at Guo Jing's robe to signal that they should end the conversation, but it was not in his habit to conceal the truth from his mentor, so he answered, "Viper Ouyang."

"He's still alive?" Ke Zhen'e hissed, his face contorted with hate at the mention of his martial siblings' murderer.

"We saw a shadow swerve past the inn on our way back. The man moved very fast and his stance was very odd. We went after him, but he disappeared. He looked a lot like the Venom." Guo Jing lit a wax light and headed further inside the room to check on Penance.

The youngster had been feigning sleep since he returned to his chamber, his ears pricking up at the comings and goings. Although he could not quite follow the exchange, he surmised that this Viper Ouyang was his adopted father and relished the apprehensive tone with which they discussed the man.

"He is much better!" Guo Jing observed with relief.

Lotus went up to take a look and was surprised by the boy's improvement. Colour had returned to his cheeks and he seemed deep in slumber, his breathing smooth and even. She had expected to find Penance's arms more swollen and stained, since the poison had begun sneaking towards his shoulders hours ago when they left, and it made no sense that it had withdrawn by itself. They were still missing some of the ingredients for the remedy, but Lotus decided to crush what they had gathered, which should slow the spread of the toxin. She gave the bulk of the concoction to Penance, then fed a few spoonfuls to the male condor.

IN THE morning, Guo Jing and Lotus were thrilled to see Penance looking further revived, the black stains of the poison having receded some more. They took the chance to ask him about his mother Mercy Mu.

"Ma started coughing one day two years ago – I was around eleven." Penance began to describe the illness that had claimed his mother's life. "She took lots of medicine, but it wouldn't clear up. After a few months, she started hacking up blood. That was when she told me she wouldn't get better and that I should bury her cremated remains in the Iron Spear Temple outside Jiaxing. Because that's where my papa sleeps . . ."

Guo Jing heaved a deep sigh at the mention of Yang Kang.

"Ma died a few days later. I carried her ashes from our home in Changxing. I asked for directions, heading east along the southern shore of Lake Tai until I found the temple. I laid her to rest just outside. Ma also said I should go to Peach Blossom Island to seek Uncle and Auntie Guo—"

"That's me! I'm your Uncle Guo!" Guo Jing interjected, then motioned at Lotus. "And this is your Auntie."

"Uncle Guo, Auntie Guo." Penance hailed his mother's friends, unsure if he was required to show respect by bowing on his knees.

Guo Jing and Lotus acknowledged the youngster and retreated into their thoughts. Peach Blossom Island was not far from where Mercy Mu had settled, but their desire to stay away from the *jianghu* meant that they had never visited or sought news about their old friend over the years. They realised now they had neglected their duty towards her as friends – this was the chance to make amends, by looking after her son, raising him, teaching him and supporting him on his journey to adulthood.

"Why did you not come to us?" Lotus asked.

"Ma bade me to behave with caution on Peach Blossom Island. She said I must be obedient and take care not to offend. Well, since I'm not starving . . ." A burst of bashful laughter. "I haven't made the journey yet."

Penance's reply saddened Guo Jing, but Lotus picked up his undertone – the boy did not wish to beg for charity and live by another's rules.

6

GUO JING AND LOTUS DECIDED TO RETURN TO PEACH Blossom Island as soon as possible, so they could treat Penance's poisoning properly. They headed south-east for the coast, journeying until sundown. That night, they slept at a roadside inn, Penance sharing a room with Ke Zhen'e, and Hibiscus bedding down with her parents.

A creak from the roof tiles woke Guo Jing and Lotus around midnight. Ke Zhen'e's gruff voice sounded from the next room, then they heard the crack of splintered wood and the tapping of footsteps. They jumped out of bed and rushed to the window.

Ke Zhen'e was on the roof, in a bare-knuckle fight against a long-limbed man.

Viper Ouyang!

Guo Jing leapt through the window to come to his *shifu*'s aid. He was about to spring up onto the roof when the blind man howled and tumbled from the eaves. Guo Jing lunged, catching his teacher by the back of his collar and pulling the older man to his feet, inches before he hit the flagstones.

"First *Shifu*, are you hurt?"

"I'm fine. Don't let the Venom get away."

"Yes, *Shifu*." Guo Jing jumped up to the roof.

Lotus was already tussling with Viper Ouyang, her palms flitting in a complicated dance, trading a dozen moves in the blink of an eye. The last time the pair had exchanged blows was more than a decade ago, at the second Contest of Mount Hua. In the intervening years, Lotus had made significant advancement in her mastery of combat techniques and internal strength, and she was able to keep her far more skilled opponent at bay with her intricate, ever-morphing onslaught.

"Master Ouyang," Guo Jing called. "I trust you have been well?"

The Martial Great pulled back, befuddled. "What did you say?" He felt drawn to the sound "Ouyang".

Seeing that Viper had yet to recover his faculties, Lotus thought of a way to tilt the fight to their advantage and cried out in a sing-song voice, "You're called Zhao Qian Sun Li, Zhou Wu Chen Wang."

"Zhao Qian Sun Li . . . Zhou Wu Chen Wang . . ." the Venom echoed, stammering.

"That's right! You're also called Feng Zheng Chu Wei, Jiang Shen Han Yang . . ." Lotus bombarded the confused man with another few dozen names from the *Hundred Family Surnames*.

"Who are you? Who am I?" Viper muttered over and over, his wits thoroughly addled.

"You're the venomous toad who killed five of my siblings!"

The roar blew away some of the haze in the martial Master's

mind, but he was not allowed the time to ruminate. The air behind him parted to give way to something very heavy.

Ke Zhen'e was back on the roof, armed with the Exorcist's Staff, which he had just fetched from his room. He determined Viper Ouyang's location by his voice and swept his weighty weapon down for the kill.

The metal staff was mere inches from the Venom's back when Guo Jing cried, "*Shifu*, take heed!"

Just as his disciple's warning sounded, Ke caught a low whooshing noise hurtling towards him. The next thing he knew, a mighty force had sent his staff spinning from his grasp, toppling him into the courtyard below.

"Hey! Over here!" Guo Jing shouted for Viper's attention. Bending his left leg slightly, he traced an arc with his palm and thrust.

Haughty Dragon Repents, the first of the Eighteen Dragon-Subduing Palms.

Guo Jing had worked on this kung fu every day since he first learned it from Count Seven Hong more than a decade ago. Deceptively simple, it had been fearsome to behold even when he was new to the technique, and now his control was boosted by his mastery of the ultimate repository of martial knowledge, the Nine Yin Manual. If anyone tried to counter the blow head on, they would trigger further waves of energy in addition to the initial surge of internal strength, each burst of *neigong* power stronger than the last. Guo Jing could conjure thirteen such ripples – enough to wear down the toughest of opponents. Even his teacher Count Seven Hong would struggle to match such a feat.

A breeze brushed Viper Ouyang's face, ever so lightly, but it carried with it a pressure that left his breathing ragged. The martial Master squatted down and thrust both hands out, channelling his signature Exploding Toad kung fu.

Straight into Guo Jing's outstretched palm.

The impact unleashed a deluge of inner force from the younger man, crashing wave upon wave over the Venom.

Croaking loudly, Viper swayed under the strain of the onslaught, just about keeping his balance, countering Guo Jing's mounting attack with equal intensity.

As with the Venom and Lotus, the last time the two fighters had crossed paths was the second Contest of Mount Hua. Guo Jing was not Viper Ouyang's match then, but he had made remarkable progress in the intervening years, gaining a rounded and thorough comprehension of the Nine Yin Manual. The Venom had continued to refine his own understanding of the Manual's teachings, but his inverted interpretation had hindered his progression, giving Guo Jing a chance to catch up.

As the fight wore on, Lotus stood in readiness, monitoring the contest, but holding back, for she wanted to allow her husband the opportunity to best the Greatest Martial Master Under the Heavens in single combat.

In this duel of inner strength, potent energy was not only passed between the two men's arms – a considerable portion also travelled down to their legs to secure their footing. And yet the three of them had overlooked the fact that they were standing on a roof, instead of firm ground. The milder climes south of the River Huai meant the rafters and boards on which the roof tiles were laid were not particularly robust, since they did not have to bear the heavy blankets of snow and ice that swaddled the frozen northern winters.

The timber frame creaked and groaned under the strain, and before long, the roof caved in, crashing thunderously into the room below.

Lotus fell through the gaping hole and touched down amid a torrent of tiles.

Guo Jing and Viper Ouyang also descended along with the debris, but they barely registered the chaos they had caused, their palms pushing against each other, their inner forces engaged in a fierce tussle. The section of the roof they were standing on landed on a bed, and the luckless occupant, crushed under their weight, screeched in pain. Guo Jing did what he could to keep his strength from travelling down his legs, but that meant losing purchase underfoot and upsetting the balance between the *neigong* power that was issuing forth from his palm and that which was keeping him upright. The Venom had no such qualms – he could not care less whether the man he was standing on lived or died.

Very soon, Guo Jing began to struggle. He had been repelling Viper's two hands with just his right palm, but if he wanted to bring his left arm into action, he would have to let more energy course to his feet. Unwilling to inflict more harm, he allowed himself to be tilted further and further back.

"Oi! Zhang San, Li Si, muddle turtle!" Lotus yelled, waving frantically. She could see Guo Jing was being overpowered. "Look over here!" Her palm drifted airily towards the Venom's shoulder. It was a move from the Cascading Peach Blossom Palm repertoire. While it might appear to be lacking in strength, the moment it made contact with the body, its power would suffuse the vital organs, and not even a seasoned kung fu artist like Viper Ouyang could escape unscathed.

Distracted by Lotus's nonsensical shout, the Martial Great faltered for the briefest moment. Then he noticed her palm arcing towards him and rallied more power to his own hands, forcing Guo Jing back by half a step. Pivoting to one side, he thrust one hand at Lotus with lightning speed. Five fingers clawing at her shoulder, ready to tear a chunk of her flesh.

Piercing pain ripped through his fingertips. Viper jerked his hand back. He had been savaged by the spikes of the Hedgehog Chainmail, one of the greatest treasures of Peach Blossom Island – no known weapon could cut through it. Sensing another wave of *neigong* power from Guo Jing, the Venom twirled his injured palm around and struck back with all his strength.

Pang! Dust flew, walls toppled, what was left of the roof collapsed. The two fighters careered backwards and came to rest in the courtyard, standing stock-still, their eyes closed, focusing on smoothing their *qi* . . .

Blood spouted from their lips at the same moment.

"Dragon-Subduing Palm!" The Venom of the West let out a wild cackle and vanished into the night.

7

THE INN WAS PLUNGED INTO UTTER CHAOS. GUESTS FLEEING for their lives, their cries echoing in the unlit courtyard.

Shaken by her husband's injury, Lotus took Hibiscus from Ke Zhen'e's arm. "*Shifu*, let's not linger here. Can you please carry Guo Jing?"

The Freak heaved his disciple onto his shoulder and hobbled after the mother and daughter.

They were some distance from the inn when Lotus remembered Penance. She supposed the boy must have run off amid the confusion, but at that moment, she did not have the capacity to concern herself with anyone but her wounded husband.

Although Guo Jing was awake and aware, his *qi* circulation had been disrupted by the power contained in Viper Ouyang's palm thrust, rendering him unable to speak or to move. Without the means to reassure his family, he concentrated on regulating his breathing and channelling his internal strength, hoping to clear the blockages so he could restore his motion.

"First *Shifu*, I can walk now," he said weakly when they had travelled seven or eight *li*.

"How do you feel?" Ke Zhen'e asked, setting him down.

"Better." Guo Jing noticed Hibiscus sleeping on Lotus's shoulder. "Where's Penance?"

"I'll go back for him once we've found a place to rest," she replied.

"I'll come with you."

Guo Jing's words brought a frown to Lotus's brow. "He's very shrewd. He will be fine."

By now, the sky was beginning to brighten, and the trees and houses along the road were becoming more distinct. Lotus caught, from the corner of her eye, a shock of black hair peeking out behind a whitewashed wall, but whoever it was ducked away the instant she looked in their direction. She settled the sleepy Hibiscus in Guo Jing's arms and hurried over to see who had been spying on them.

"Auntie Guo!" Penance greeted her with a simper. "I've been waiting for you here."

"Well, come along then." Lotus eyed the boy, a tangle of questions crowding her mind.

Seeing Penance trotting after her mother, Hibiscus asked brusquely, "Where have you been?"

"Over there. Catching crickets."

"Boring," she sneered.

"No! It was fun! I saw a big cricket beat up an old cricket, then two little ones came along and the three banded together against the big one. But it was unafraid, it hopped high. A kick there, a snap here—" Penance tailed off abruptly.

"And then?"

"Why do you care? You said it's boring."

Hibiscus twisted away in a temper. She had never been so snubbed.

Lotus had no doubt Penance was alluding to the altercation at the inn and mocking them with his little tale. "Pray tell, who won the fight?" she asked innocently, hiding her unease that he seemed to be siding with the Venom.

"I don't know." He gave her a charming smile. "The crickets scattered when you came over."

Like father, like son, she thought with disapproval.

WHEN THEY arrived at the next village, Lotus went to the largest house and asked if they could stay for the night. The householder, hearing that one of the party was injured, immediately invited them in and sent servants to prepare rooms and refreshments.

Lotus was relieved to see Guo Jing eating heartily, gobbling down three large bowls of rice at lunch, but she kept a close watch while he rested on the daybed with his eyes closed to nurse his spirits. Reassured that he was out of danger, she allowed her mind to wander to their interactions with Penance over the past few days. There were peculiarities in the boy's manner that she could not fathom, but she knew she would never get a straight answer and decided to observe him in stealth.

Penance joined Lotus and Guo Jing for dinner, then retired early to the room he shared with Ke Zhen'e. He went straight to bed, but a short time after midnight, he sat up gingerly and listened. Loud snores. The blind man was deep in slumber. He tiptoed out of the room and scuttered furtively across the courtyard, then climbed up an osmanthus tree growing close to the garden wall, leapt from the highest bough to scale the perimeter and climbed down.

The guard dogs picked up the noise and the unfamiliar scent and started to bay, but Penance, who had come prepared, threw them bones he had stashed from lunch and supper, and the hounds quietened down.

Once he had sneaked out of the house undetected, Penance oriented himself by the moon and the stars and walked south-west for seven or eight *li*, until he reached the Iron Spear Temple.

The night before, Penance had followed the injured Viper Ouyang as he withdrew from the mayhem at the inn. At first, he struggled to catch up, but the older man was so incapacitated that soon he could hardly lift his feet. Penance helped him sit down by the roadside and proposed to meet at the Iron Spear Temple the next night, for if he stayed, he would risk jeopardising his adopted father's safety, as he was certain Lotus Huang would come looking for him. He took his leave with reluctance and made his way back to seek the Guo family on the main road leading to the coast.

"PAPA, I'M here!" Penance called as he pushed open the doors of the abandoned shrine.

A grunt sounded from the gloom of the worship hall.

Hearing the familiar voice, Penance felt his way forward and lit a candle stump he found on the altar table.

Viper Ouyang was sitting on a prayer mat before the statue of General Wang Yanzhang the Iron Spear. He looked wizened, his breathing weak. Even though the Martial Great's injury was no more severe than Guo Jing's, he appeared to be in a much worse state. Being a few decades older, he could not recover as speedily as a man in his physical prime.

"You must be starving, Papa." Penance took out half a dozen *mantou*, put them in the man's hands and sat down on a prayer mat.

Viper had not eaten since taking shelter in this dilapidated temple, and he wolfed down several of the steamed buns.

"It'll take at least seven days for the Guo lad to regain his strength," he mumbled under his breath after listening to Penance's description of his day. "His little wife will stay by his side while he recovers, so that leaves the Blind Bat . . . What did I do to him? I think I killed . . . four or five of his brethren? He'll come for me tonight, if not tomorrow, but I'm not in a state to—"

A bout of coughing cut his musings short.

What can I do to help? Penance asked himself, resting his chin in his hands. Dozens of ideas raced through his mind. His eyes lighted on the candleholders on the altar table. I know! The old man can't see. I can set traps.

He pulled off the dusty wax stumps to reveal the pricket spikes and placed the candle stands just inside the entrance. He then closed the double doors, but left a gap wide enough to allow him to balance a metal censer on one of the wooden door panels.

Not yet satisfied, he looked around for other objects he could use against the blind man. The main worship hall was flanked by two enormous iron bells, on the east side and on the west. He went up to take a closer look at one, and estimated that it would take at least three grown-ups, stretching their arms wide, to encircle the mass of metal, and that it must weigh at least a thousand *jin*. He then examined the timber frame and the fixture from which the bell was suspended. Both looked robust, despite the tumbledown state of the temple.

We can hide up here when the blind man comes, Penance said to himself as he continued to explore the rear part of the worship hall to seek what else he could use as a weapon.

Dok, dok, dok. The rhythmic thuds of an iron staff, coming from the path leading to the temple.

Ke Zhen'e!

Penance scuttered back to the altar table. Just as he sucked in a mouthful of air to blow out the candle, he remembered that the old man could not see. He pulled out the wax stump, taking care to keep the flame burning as he set it down. He held the candleholder horizontally and pointed the pricket outwards. Positioning himself in close proximity to Viper Ouyang, he made a silent promise to help his papa repel his sightless foe.

KE ZHEN'E had no illusion about his martial capabilities; his skills were trifling compared to Viper Ouyang's. But when he heard Guo Jing and Lotus Huang say the Martial Great was injured, he knew he had to seize the chance to avenge his sworn siblings. It was unlikely the Venom would risk staying in a local household, and since they were on the outskirts of Jiaxing with limited choice of inns and taverns, it was most likely he would seek shelter in an abandoned building. The Iron Spear Temple was known to the man and not far from the inn they had been staying at. He decided to try his luck there after everyone had gone to sleep.

The First Freak of the South slipped across the courtyard and scaled the perimeter wall in the hush of night. The guard dogs paid him no heed: they were still gnawing the bones Penance had thrown them.

Ke Zhen'e slowed down when he stepped through the main gate of the Iron Spear Temple. He listened, his ear cocked. Breathing, inside the worship hall.

"Old Venom, Ke Zhen'e is here to avenge his brothers and sister." He punctuated his challenge with a thump of his staff.

No answer. Viper Ouyang had been soothing the disruption to his energy flow caused by Guo Jing's blow and could not risk projecting his voice. It would undo his good work, dissipating the *qi* he had pooled in the Elixir Field in his lower abdomen.

Ke Zhen'e called out several more times. Nothing. He threw the double doors open with the aid of his staff and marched into the worship hall. Presently, the air parted overhead. Something heavy was falling on him. He swung his weapon to bat it away. *Dong!* An ear-splitting clang. Metal on metal. A searing pain stabbed at his foot in the same moment. He had stepped onto something sharp, and it had pierced through the sole of his boot. He rolled on the floor to avoid driving the spike deeper. As he landed on his right shoulder, he was impaled by a second one. He plucked out the offending objects, pushed himself up and shuffled forwards, guided by the breathing, taking care not to lift his feet. He halted three *chi* from his target and raised his staff.

"Old Venom, say your last words."

Viper Ouyang had been mustering what *neigong* power was left in his body into his right arm. He had strength enough to launch one thrust – when the staff fell – and drag the blind man down to the netherworld with him.

Ke Zhen'e, meanwhile, was waiting for the Venom to make the first move. He was worried that even in his injured state the Martial Great would still outclass him, and wanted to know what he was facing before he dealt the death blow.

A stand-off. Both poised to strike, but neither willing to take the initiative.

As he waited, Ke Zhen'e thought he could hear his siblings' voices above the Venom's laboured breathing. Zhu Cong, Ryder Han,

Woodcutter Nan, Gilden Quan and Jade Han, urging him to strike, to avenge their deaths. He let out a howl and swung his weapon in a Stones Flogged for the Qin Emperor.

Viper Ouyang drew in a breath, raised his palm, determined to put up a fight. But the air got caught in his chest and his arm dropped, hanging slack. Were he not hurt, a casual wave of his hand would have been enough to send the weapon flying from the Freak's grip; at worst, he could have leapt away from the blow with ease. However, with his body sore and limp, he could not conjure a scrap of inner strength. His only hope was to flop down and try to roll out of harm's way.

Paaaang! The head of the staff struck the floor, cracking the tiles in a burst of sparks. A sideways swipe followed, aimed at Viper's abdomen.

Ke Zhen'e lashed out using his Exorcist's Staff kung fu, each thwack of the metal pole swifter than the last, whereas the Venom's attempts to dodge it were getting slower and slower. Eventually he was caught on the shoulder by a move known as Quell the Yaksha Spirits.

Penance's heart tightened at the heavy thud. He wanted to help, to stop the blind man, but what could he achieve with his paltry martial skills? He would merely be killed – and for nothing.

The staff arced down again. One blow after another. Three times it struck Viper Ouyang. His skin split and his flesh rent. But the Venom was not known as one of the Martial Greats for nothing. His injury had rendered him incapable of evading the onslaught or launching a riposte, but decades of *neigong* training had equipped him with the skill to make minute adjustments to his muscles and energy flow, so, even as he was being bludgeoned bloody and blue, he was able to prevent the bulk of the force causing genuine damage to his bones and organs.

Ke Zhen'e had also sensed that his blows were gliding off the Venom's body and that only one tenth of his attacks' power was being channelled into its target. Resolving to club the man in the head – surely it was not possible to protect the skull in the same way – he raised the Exorcist's Staff, whipping up a menacing squall with the heavy weapon.

Viper Ouyang ducked and swerved, but he could not slip out of the staff's field of influence. It would only be a matter of time before he was hit, and if his skull were smashed . . . He had to make a final gamble.

Seizing the moment when the blind man raised his arm to strike, the Martial Great lunged, grabbing his attacker by the front of his shirt. They were now in such close proximity that it was impossible for the Freak to unleash the full might of the metal staff.

Startled, Ke Zhen'e grasped the back of the Venom's robe and pulled, but the Martial Great held firm. In their tussle, the blind man, being lame in one leg, lost his balance and toppled down on the Venom. As they scuffled on the floor, Viper reached around for a weak point on Ke's flank and found what felt like a hilt tucked into the blind man's waistline. He pulled free a blade with an edge so keen it could cut through metal and slice through jade.

The weapon was Butcher's Knife, and it had once belonged to Zhang Asheng, Fifth Brother of the Seven Freaks of the South. Zhang died at the hands of Copper Corpse Hurricane Chen in the Mongolian desert some twenty years ago, and Ke Zhen'e, the eldest of the group, had since carried it on his person as a token of remembrance. Despite its name, it had never been used to slaughter livestock.

Viper twirled the blade and sliced down at Ke Zhen'e's abdomen. The blind man aimed a punch at his attacker's face. *Thump!* Viper was sent crashing back. Starbursts clouded his vision, his head foggy and spinning, but that did not stop him from hurling the knife at the Freak in one last attempt to be rid of him.

Ke Zhen'e sensed the air parting for the flying weapon and veered out of its path. *Boooong!* The knife clattered against the bell on the eastern side and bounced off. Its point lodged into the timber support, the blade quivering under the force of the impact.

Penance had retreated to that very same bell as the fight heated up. The knife flew past his face, almost cutting his cheek. He scrambled up the wooden frame, his heart hammering in fright.

Since Ke Zhen'e could not see, he relied on his hearing to determine his opponent's next move, but with the bell ringing loudly, it was impossible to distinguish any other sounds. He stood in the middle of the shrine, his hair wild, his head cocked, his knuckles white around his staff. He listened, hoping to catch the scuffles of footsteps, the quiet exchange of breath . . . Nothing, just the unending metallic echoes.

He did not realise Viper Ouyang had already climbed to his feet and slipped across the worship hall. He was now taking shelter behind the bell's iron bulk.

Penance watched the scene unfold in the dim candlelight from his elevated vantage point and grasped its significance. He climbed down, plucked out the Butcher's Knife and struck the hilt on the bell.

Bong! It masked all other sounds in the temple.

Ke Zhen'e lunged, guided by its peals, swinging his staff horizontally.

Boooong! The Exorcist's Staff hit the bell.

The deafening clangour gave the blind man an idea. He batted his weapon into the bell again.

Boooooooooong!

Again. Again. Again.

Clang upon clang, booming louder and louder.

Viper feared the tocsin would draw Lotus Huang to the temple. He could not put up a defence against the woman in his current state. He padded across to the hall, trusting the tolling of the bell would obscure any noise he was making. Little did he know that the sightless man had grown accustomed to the din and could now discern the smallest deviations in its pattern.

Ke Zhen'e continued to strike the bell, pretending that he could not pick out his opponent's faint footsteps. He waited until the Venom had reached the middle of the empty worship hall and prepared to pounce, ready to bring the Exorcist's Staff arrowing down at the man's head.

Viper Ouyang might have lost the use of his inner strength, but a Master of his age and experience was not easily deceived by such tricks and feints. The instant Ke Zhen'e began to tense his right flank and shoulder to strike, the Venom knew his foe was about to launch a blow and shot backwards, propelled by a burst of energy he did not realise he could summon in his injured and depleted state. He was behind the bell again before the Freak had even lifted his weapon.

"If I can't kill you with my staff, I'll run you into the ground!" Roaring, Ke Zhen'e lunged after Viper, pursuing him around the bell.

Watching from atop the wooden frame, Penance judged that his adopted father had not the stamina to outrun the blind man – he must think of a way to intervene. He waved and gesticulated, hoping to catch his papa's attention, but the man was too preoccupied to notice him.

However, after some time, Viper spotted Penance's overactive shadow on the floor, imploring him to head away from the bell. Although he could not understand the rationale, he trusted the youngster to have his best interests at heart. He took a risk and sprinted towards the front doors.

Ke Zhen'e halted, his ears pricked up, trying to determine Viper Ouyang's position.

Pak! Pak!

He was certain the Venom was heading for the entrance. So what was making the noise behind him?

It was Penance's shoes. The boy had hurled them in the opposite direction to cover his adopted father's retreat. Now he hacked the Butcher's Knife down on the robust beam from which the bell was hung. The blade, although exceptionally sharp, was not forged for chopping wood, and Penance, being a child, could muster up little force. However, his desperate attempt did manage to damage the timber, compromising the structure, and the weight of the bell soon told. The support snapped with a mighty crack.

Ke Zhen'e had paid no heed to the racket made by Penance because he had been focused on his martial siblings' murderer, so, by the time he turned his attention to the noise overhead, the bell was crashing down on him. Too late to dodge it, he thrust his staff upwards and – *clooooong!* – struck the lip of the bell, diverting its descent and buying himself time to swerve out from under its weight.

The bell smashed onto the floor with an earth-shattering thump. Then it started to roll, with an echoing roar, into Ke Zhen'e. The collision knocked the blind man off his feet, flipping him round and round, until he came to earth face down, some distance from the temple, bloodied and bruised.

Fearing that Viper Ouyang had a skilled accomplice with him, and unwilling to trust his ears to verifying it, Ke Zhen'e clambered to his feet and limped away.

"Pity!" Viper murmured as he watched the retreating figure, then he turned to Penance. "Well done, son!" The slight quiver in his voice revealed both his appreciation of the boy's quick wit and his awe at the power of the bell.

"That blind man won't be back any time soon," Penance said when he climbed down from the bell frame.

The Martial Great shook his head gravely. "Our blood feud runs as deep as the sea. He will be back as long as he has air left in his lungs."

"Then we must go!"

"I'm too injured to go far." Viper felt as though his limbs would fall off and his bones would scatter across the floor. He could not shift his feet to take one step.

"What should we do then?"

The man thought for a moment, then pointed across the main hall. "Put me under that bell."

"How will you get out?"

"I can lift it once I've restored my elemental *neigong*. As long as the lass doesn't turn up in the next seven days, I have nothing to fear. The Blind Bat hasn't got the wit or the kung fu to get to me."

"But you haven't got any food!"

"Just bring me water. I still have some of your *mantou* buns. I'll survive."

Penance found a large clay basin in the kitchen and filled it from the well in the temple grounds. He set the bowl down under the bell, then helped his adopted father into position.

"Go with the Guo lad. I'll come for you soon, son."

Promising to do as asked, Penance climbed onto the timber support and swung the Butcher's Knife.

Viper Ouyang was trapped under the bell.

"Papa?"

No answer.

Penance called a few more times and came to the conclusion that no sound could penetrate the thick metal. He bade a silent goodbye and hurried away, as he had been out of bed for a long time already. But just as he stepped through the temple's main gate, an idea came to him and he ran back inside. He filled another bowl with water, submerged his left palm and flipped into a handstand. He began to purge the poison in his blood with the method Viper Ouyang had taught him.

It was very taxing to invert one's meridian flow, and beads of sweat were soon lining Penance's forehead. He managed to squeeze out a dozen droplets of venom from his body. Once he had recovered from his exertions, he climbed onto the altar table and pulled long strips off some of the ritual banners hanging from the beams above. He then wound the fabric around a bamboo container for fortune sticks and dipped this makeshift brush into the toxic water.

This will poison the blind old man if he tries to lift the bell, Penance thought as he daubed the bell's metal surface. It then occurred to him that there was danger of his Papa suffocating and he began to dig a ventilation hole with the Butcher's Knife. He hacked and hewed to crack the blue brick floor tile, then used the weapon as a spade to remove the earth underneath. Before long the blade snagged on a rock and snapped. Penance continued to gouge out soil with the jagged stump until he had made a cavity the size of a fist. When he was done, he tossed the broken knife aside without another thought – he had no concept of how prized the sharp thin blade was – after all, it was not his to begin with.

He flattened himself on the ground and shouted through the gap, "Papa, I'm going. Please come soon. And do be careful when you come out, I've covered the bell with poison."

"No venom can harm me. Go. Take care of yourself, my boy, I'll find you."

Penance hovered for a while before turning reluctantly away. He ran back to the village, fearing his absence had been noticed. When he sneaked into his room, he was surprised to find it empty. Ke Zhen'e, who had left the temple much earlier, had not yet returned.

PANG, PANG, pang! Penance was woken up by someone pounding on the door. He clambered out of bed and found Ke Zhen'e outside their room, his face ashen-grey, his whole weight resting on his staff. The Freak lifted his foot to step across the threshold, but he tripped and tumbled head first.

"Grandpa Ke! Are you alright?" Penance exclaimed, feigning concern. He had noticed as soon as he opened the doors that Ke Zhen'e's hands had been stained black by poison. It could only mean one thing – he had gone back to the temple and tried to lift the bell.

The disturbance drew Guo Jing and Lotus Huang over. Guo Jing could now walk unaided but had yet to recover his strength, so Lotus helped Ke Zhen'e to his feet and guided him to the bed.

"First *Shifu*, what's happened?" she asked.

Ke Zhen'e would not answer. He just shook his head.

Lotus's eyes fell on the dark blotches on his hands. "It's Blithe Li, isn't it? I'll hunt her down."

Ke clenched his jaw and eventually squeezed out the words: "Not that woman."

"Who then?"

Ke Zhen'e pulled his lips tight. His pride would not allow him to admit that he, the eldest Freak of the South, had not only been thwarted by a man so injured that he would struggle to summon the strength to string up a chicken, but he had been wounded in the process.

Lotus knew she would only vex Ke Zhen'e if she pressed him, so she let the matter slip and turned her attention to his hands. Mercifully, the poison appeared to be rather mild and had ravaged only the very surface of his skin. She gave him a Dew of Nine Flowers and his faint-headedness, as well as other symptoms, receded.

Given Blithe Li's sadistic and unpredictable nature, Lotus judged that the wisest course of action would be to stick to their original plan and return to Peach Blossom Island at once, so the injured could be tended to and the children would be safe. She could settle the score with the Red Serpent Celestial at a later date. She let Guo Jing know her decision and went to make arrangements for their passage east to the coast that afternoon.

Penance paid close attention to the grown-ups' conversation and was relieved that his adopted father was not mentioned. He watched Lotus Huang bustling around, treating Ke Zhen'e and preparing for their onward journey, and wondered why his papa was so intimidated by this woman.

She may be smart and capable, but she's also dainty and delicate, he observed. Can she be more of a threat than even the blind old man?

A CANOPIED barge carried the five of them down inland waterways towards the Eastern Sea. When the light began to fade, the boat-master moored on the bank to cook dinner, rinsing rice and washing vegetables in the canal.

Hibiscus Guo leaned on the cabin's window frame and stared out, bored by the monotony of the voyage and annoyed that Penance Yang had barely acknowledged her all afternoon. She was scanning the shore, looking at nothing in particular, when she caught sight of two boys huddled under a weeping willow. The Wu brothers, Earnest and Erudite.

"Hey! What are you doing here?" Hibiscus called, excited to see people she recognised.

"Who are you talking to?" Lotus asked.

"Earnest and Erudite. Uncle and Auntie Wu's sons," Hibiscus explained.

Lotus jumped ashore and approached the boys. She had learned from Ke Zhen'e of his encounter with Reverend Sole Light's disciple Wu Santong and how they had fought Blithe Li together.

Noting the boys' tear-stained faces and their mother's unmoving body, Lotus asked them what had happened and where their father was. She could tell from Madam Wu's skin, blackened by venom, that she had been dead for some time.

"We don't know where Papa's gone," Earnest told Lotus between sobs.

"Mama sucked the poison from Papa's wound. Lots of black blood came out." Fresh tears fell with Erudite's words. "Papa got better, but Mama collapsed. Papa then went into a frenzy and left us behind. He wouldn't come back even when we called for him."

Lotus was awed by the woman's selfless valour. "Join us for dinner," she said, signalling to the boat-master to lead them aboard. She then went into town to purchase a coffin, so Madam Wu would not have to lie in the open overnight. The next morning, she led the brothers to the burial plot she had prepared, and together they laid the woman to rest.

Watching as the boys wailed and prostrated themselves over their mother's grave, Guo Jing said, "They should live with us on Peach Blossom Island."

Lotus nodded in agreement then went up to the brothers with words of comfort, before guiding them back to the barge.

When they reached the coast, they changed into a larger seafaring vessel and continued east for Peach Blossom Island.

For decades, the island was held to be as deadly as a tiger's lair or a dragon's tarn. It was rumoured that any vessel straying near its waters would not come back, its crew falling victim to the Lord of Peach Blossom Island's insatiable bloodlust, but since Guo Jing's arrival and Apothecary Huang's move to the mainland, its reputation had improved and there was no need to trick the ferryman with a false destination to secure a passage to the island.

CHAPTER THREE

THE ZHONGNAN MOUNTAINS

I

GUO JING MADE REMARKABLE RECOVERY DURING THE VOYAGE, thanks to an internal *neigong* method from the Nine Yin Manual. To pass the rest of the time at sea, he chatted with Lotus about their adventures on this brief outing to the mainland, and they were both awed by the Venom's prowess – the man had become stronger in defiance of his advancing years. Presently, the conversation turned to their chance meeting with Penance.

"It is a great fortune that we found him," Guo Jing said. "I can at last fulfil my lifelong wish."

"No, I won't agree to it."

Lotus was refusing outright before Guo Jing had even told her what he was thinking about. She was familiar with the pledge made by his father, Skyfury Guo, and Skyfury's sworn brother – Penance's grandfather – Ironheart Yang. Their wives were with child at the same time, and they promised each other, if their children were of the same sex, they would vow to become siblings, and if they were of the opposite sex, the families would be united in matrimony. That was the story behind the fraternal ties that had connected Guo Jing and Penance's father, Yang Kang.

Because of this bond, Guo Jing had always reproached himself for failing to persuade Yang Kang that it was traitorous to ally himself with the Jurchens: Prince Wanyan Honglie might have raised him as his son and heir, but he was still an oppressor and an invader of their homeland, the Song Empire. It was Yang Kang's inability to throw off this wrongful allegiance that had led him down the path of no return to his premature and gruesome death at the Iron Spear Temple outside Jiaxing.

"Why?" Guo Jing was shocked by her bluntness.

"I won't let you betroth Hibiscus to that boy."

"His father was wanting in his morals and behaviour, but the Guo and the Yang families have been close for generations. Penance is a smart and handsome young man. He will surely be a hero of the *jianghu* when he comes of age."

"I fear he may be too smart."

"Aren't you very, very smart too?"

Lotus chuckled. "Well, I happened to fall for someone very, very silly." It was an attempt to steer the discussion in another direction, but Guo Jing was not ready to relinquish the issue.

"It was Papa's dying wish for his child to marry or pledge ties of kindred with Uncle Ironheart Yang's offspring. Uncle Yang wanted the same. But I did not put my heart into looking after Brother Yang Kang and Sister Mercy Mu. I had wanted to invite Sister Mu and Penance to Peach Blossom Island, so they could live a better life, and yet, I don't want you to have misgivings about my feelings towards her . . ." Guo Jing let out a sigh. "Who would have thought Sister Mu would leave this world so soon?"

"Wait . . . so it's my fault?"

"I – I've never—" Guo Jing spluttered, his face flushed red and his ears burning.

"Never what?" Lotus lifted her chin, feigning outrage. "Blamed me?"

"I'd never do that!" He embraced his wife with a placating smile.

Her arms pinned, Lotus cried, "Help! Help! Murder!"

97

Laughing, Guo Jing pressed a kiss on her cheek and let her go.

"The two of them are still very young," Lotus said solemnly. "If Penance turns out as we hope, then you may do as you like."

Guo Jing drew himself to his full height, put his hands together in a gesture of reverence and bent from his waist. "I am most grateful for your permission."

"I have not given my consent." Lotus's demeanour was equally serious. "As I say, it will depend on whether the boy stays upright and true."

Guo Jing was straightening up from his obeisance and halted at an awkward angle upon hearing her words. He collected himself and said, "Brother Yang Kang was led astray because he grew up in the Jin Prince's palace. Penance will live with us on Peach Blossom Island. Nothing will go wrong. And you named him yourself – given name Penance, courtesy name Amend – to remind him that if he errs, he should bring himself back to the path of righteousness."

"How can we pin our hopes on a name? You're called Guo Jing, but are you as peaceful and serene as implied by the character *Jing*? No! You've hopped around like a little monkey ever since you were small!"

Tongue-tied, Guo Jing could only gawk at his wife, unable to find a retort. She flashed him a smile and resolutely changed the subject.

ONCE THEY were back on Peach Blossom Island, Lotus prepared a fresh remedy for Penance that successfully purged the remaining poison from his body.

Although Hibiscus had not seen eye to eye with the boy or thought much of the Wu brothers at their first meeting, the benefit of being young was that she soon forgot why she had not been keen on them in the first place. She was just thrilled to have friends of her own age.

The children's favourite pastime was staging fights with crickets, and they were always on the hunt for new champions. One of Penance's searches saw him climb over Fillip Pavilion and scale Bygone Peak, and he was about to circle Whistle Gazebo, when he heard laughter from the other side of the small hill and rushed over. He found Hibiscus and the Wu brothers huddled in the undergrowth.

Earnest flipped over a stone and – *whish!* – a sizeable cricket hopped out. He leapt after the creature and trapped it between his fingers. He examined his find's physique – angular head, sturdy legs, wide mandibles, robust abdomen – and whooped with delight.

"Give it to me! Give it to me!" Hibiscus called, thrusting her clay pot forward.

Although the boy carried an empty bamboo tube on his person, he lifted the cover of Hibiscus's bowl and said, "Here's your invincible general." Then he noticed Penance watching to the side. "Big Brother Yang, none of your fighters can beat this new warrior."

Not one to surrender without taking up the challenge, Penance took out several bamboo tubes from inside his jacket, picked the fiercest insect in his army and put it in Hibiscus's container. In just a few moves, the new cricket clamped its mandibles over Penance's contender and flung it out. The victor fanned its wings and sang in triumph.

"I win!" Hibiscus clapped and cheered.

"Not yet! I've got others!" Penance selected another cricket, but it suffered the same fate. He then sent in a third one. This last scrapper met a gruesome end – snapped in half by the invincible general.

Penance stalked away, muttering, "This is no fun."

Chirr, chirr, chirr. A cricket's song, coming from the bushes, but in an unusual pitch.

"Sounds like a tough warrior!" Earnest followed the call, parted the vegetation and jumped back with a yelp. "Snaaake!"

Intrigued, Penance turned around and saw a serpent with an elaborated pattern on its scales. The venomous creature reared its head and tasted the air with its forked tongue. Penance hurled a rock and struck it on the head. It quivered then went still.

Chirr, chirr.

The children tiptoed closer and saw a tiny cricket, pitch-black in colour and hideously formed, jerking its body and flapping its wings by the lifeless reptile.

"You want this inky wraith, Brother Yang?"

"Of course!" Riled by Hibiscus's derisive tone, Penance grabbed the insect.

"What are you going to do with it? Don't say you want this weedy thing to fight my invincible general!"

"Why not!" Penance put his fresh recruit into the girl's clay pot. The three-time winner backed away, intimidated by the newcomer. Astounded, Hibiscus and the Wu brothers urged the invincible general on with cheers, but the insect would not engage at all. Meanwhile, the inky wraith was raring to go, its antenna twitching menacingly.

The invincible general sprang up, not to attack but to escape. The inky wraith also leapt, locking its mandibles onto the thorax of the fleeing cricket, and dragged it back down. The former champion convulsed and flipped belly up.

Dead.

The inky wraith, having lived close to its venomous neighbour, had acquired its scent, and that was why the invincible general had reacted with such fear.

Vexed that Penance had killed her champion, Hibiscus was determined to claim his. "Big Brother Yang, why don't you give me your inky wraith?"

"I would . . . if you hadn't given him such a horrible name."

Pursing her lips, Hibiscus turned her cricket pot upside down, threw the inky wraith on the ground, and stamped on the unsuspecting insect.

A rush of hot blood surged to Penance's head. He smacked her cheek with the back of his hand.

The girl was flabbergasted, on the verge of tears. No-one had ever shown her such contempt.

Erudite burst out, "How dare you!" and swung a fist at Penance, a hard thump to the ribs. Penance raised his arm with a blow of his own, but Erudite skipped out of the way with ease. Penance then pounced, hurling his full weight at the younger boy. Earnest stole forward, coming to his little brother's aid. He hooked his foot around Penance's ankle to send the lad sprawling.

Recovering his balance, Erudite twisted around. Taking to the air, he plunged down unceremoniously on Penance and pummelled the older boy alongside his big brother.

Penance, despite being the eldest, could not hope to fend off four pounding fists. He had only learned rudimentary moves from his mother, whereas the Wu brothers had a sound martial foundation, having been initiated by their parents at a young age.

Penance clenched his jaw and endured the beating. Though out-numbered and pinned to the ground, he would not give his assailants the satisfaction of catching a hint of a groan passing his lips.

"Beg for mercy and we'll let you go," Earnest offered.

"Never!"

Thump, thump. Penance's defiant answer was rewarded by two punches from Erudite.

The brothers made sure their blows fell on the clothed parts of the body. If Guo Jing and Lotus Huang saw any bruising on Pen-ance's face, they would all be scolded.

Hibiscus had stopped sobbing once the Wu brothers had over-powered Penance. At first, she worried that they were being too rough, but when she touched her cheek – still stinging hot – she decided he was getting his just deserts.

"Harder! Harder!" she urged, feeling vindicated.

The brothers' fists rained down with less restraint. Thanks to their martial grounding, their punches were more than an untrained adult could stomach. Penance would have already passed out if he had not been shown some basic *neigong* techniques by Viper Ouyang.

Evil wench! Penance growled inwardly, vowing to wreak ven-geance on Hibiscus Guo one day. Gritting his teeth against the pain radiating from his flanks, his back and his haunches, he clawed and

scratched at the earth to drag himself away from his attackers. His fingertips ran over something cool and slippery amid the rough grit and dry soil. The viper he had killed earlier. He seized the dead thing and twisted around to brandish it at the brothers' faces.

The boys screamed and jumped back. Penance threw a vicious punch at Earnest's face, knocking the elder Wu brother onto his backside. Free at last, he scrambled off as fast as his legs would carry him.

"Don't let him get away!" Hibiscus shouted as she raced after the Wu brothers.

Penance cast a glance back. Earnest was in hot pursuit, glowering savagely, blood smeared all over his face. The sight of him sent fresh impetus to Penance's legs. He knew if he were caught, he would face an even more brutal beating. Soon, he found himself at the foot of Sword Trial Peak and decided to scale the crag, praying the steep terrain would give him an edge.

Earnest was determined to catch Penance. His nose no longer hurt too much, but the bleeding had stoked his fear and his temper. He urged his little brother to keep pace, his feet pounding furiously as he ran uphill, but Hibiscus halted half way, too tired to push on.

Penance hurried on until the path ran out. A ravine stood in his way. If he wanted to continue his ascent to the very top, he would have to jump across it. The pinnacle of this crag was where Apothecary Huang had come to test his martial inventions, chosen for its isolated location and treacherous landscape.

Penance looked down into the abyss. I'd rather fall to my death then endure another punch from those stinkers! Thus resolved, he turned to the Wu brothers: "Not another step. Or I'll jump!"

Earnest wavered, but the younger hothead Erudite pressed on, goading Penance as he approached: "Go on! Jump! Your threats don't scare us. You haven't got the guts!"

Emboldened by an upsurge of blood and *qi*, Penance braced himself to take the plunge. He was about to step into the void when he noticed the big boulder next to him was propped up by smaller rocks. An idea flashed through his mind. He was now so blinded by emotions that he gave no thought to consequences. He bent down and shifted some of the supporting stones, then he circled round and pushed. The boulder teetered on the brink then thundered down the steep hill.

Throwing themselves out of its path, the Wu brothers watched with ashen cheeks as the huge rock rumbled past in a cloud of grit and dust, snapping trees and crushing shrubs until it splashed into the sea.

The petrified Earnest missed his step and slid down the hillside. Erudite threw his arms around his big brother, but the momentum of his fall was so great that it sent them both tumbling for six or seven *zhang* until their way was blocked by a tree.

The tumult drew Lotus Huang from the house. When she arrived at the foot of Sword Trial Peak, billows of dust were still hanging in the air. She found her daughter cowering in the undergrowth, half-way up the hill, too scared to speak. The Wu brothers were further up the slope, bruised and scratched all over.

She lifted Hibiscus into her arms and asked gently, "What happened?"

The girl broke down at the question, her face buried in her mother's bosom. She spoke haltingly between sobs, describing how Penance had slapped her for no reason, and when the Wu brothers stood up for her, he tried to kill them with the boulder. She put the blame squarely on Penance and conveniently omitted that she had stamped the boy's champion cricket to death and that he had run up the crag to flee from the Wu brothers' beating.

Though Lotus doubted that she had been told the whole story, the sight of her daughter's red and swollen cheek dissuaded her from asking any questions. The maternal instinct to console her child outweighed the need to discover the truth.

By now, Guo Jing had arrived on the scene. When he learned what had taken place, he was furious, his mood in no way improved by the Wu brothers' dishevelled appearance, but he was also worried about Penance's safety.

"Penance! Penance!" he called, his voice amplified with inner strength as he searched through the vegetation on the way to the peak. He knew he could be heard several *li* away, covering most parts of the island, but there was no answer. Growing anxious, he rushed down to the shore and hopped on a skiff, rowing around the island calling for the youngster until the sun had set and the skies had grown dark.

When Guo Jing returned home, he could find no appetite for dinner. Lotus sat with him, subdued, and did not touch any food either. The next day, the couple resumed their search at the crack of dawn.

2

THE INSTANT HE SENT THE BOULDER ROLLING TOWARDS THE Wu brothers, Penance knew he was due a scolding. When he saw Lotus Huang rushing over, he squeezed himself into a crevice in the escarpment. Huddled up, he watched as the twilight set in and stole the last gleam of light from the waves. His stomach was now growling, and yet he dared not emerge from his hiding place.

Nocturnal silence began its reign. The stars glittered in the heavens and a chilly draught rose from the sea. Hungry and cold, Penance climbed out of his refuge and looked towards the main house. It stood a short distance from the foot of Sword Trial Peak, glowing in the warm light of a dozen candles. He pictured the Guo family and the Wu brothers sitting around the dining table, enjoying a generous spread of mouth-watering dishes – chicken, duck, fish and other meats – while trading nasty comments about him.

Shrouded in darkness and lashed by brine-soaked wind, Penance cursed the early demise of his parents. It was because he was an orphan that he was fated to be snubbed, slighted and looked down on with scorn and disdain at every turn. The only person that had not treated him in such a way was his adopted father. As he brooded on his misfortune, angst, pique and solitude swelled and swirled in his breast.

AS SOON as it was light, Penance crept down to the nearest creek and caught a few frogs. He had filled his belly many times with these creatures in his vagrant days after his mother's death. He gutted and skinned them with dexterous ease, then gathered some dry leaves and built a fire in a nearby cave to make sure the cooking smoke would not alert anyone of his whereabouts, stamping out the embers once his food was ready. He had just stuffed a frog leg in his mouth when he heard: "Penance! Penance!"

Guo Jing again.

I'm not stupid, the boy shot back in his head as he chewed. I won't come out to catch a beating.

Penance stayed close to the cave for the rest of the day and bedded down inside it when night fell. As he drifted off, his adopted father's voice sounded: "Child, I've come to teach you kung fu. We'll give those whelps a good thrashing."

Viper Ouyang was sitting on his heels in the dimness outside, croaks rumbling in his throat. He nodded at his adopted son, then pushed both palms forward.

Penance joined him and copied the action, repeating it several times. His strikes and kicks now flowed with a fluidity he had never experienced before. All of a sudden, Viper threw a punch. Penance tried to swerve out of the way but was too slow. *Thump!* The fist struck the crown of his head. Yelping in pain, he jumped and – *smack!* – another blow fell on his skull.

Penance touched his scalp gingerly. Sore, throbbing – a bump was on its way. He blinked a few times and realised he had hit his head while dreaming. Heaving a sigh, he went outside and looked up at the sky. A smattering of stars were twinkling over the treetops.

Papa, when will you come and take me away? he asked the night.

It had been more than seven days since his arrival on Peach Blossom Island. Viper Ouyang should have recovered his strength and freed himself from inside the bell.

Will you really teach me kung fu as you said? So no-one will bully me or look down on me again . . . After a while, Penance snapped out of his brooding and tried to recall the move in the dream, but the details eluded him. Croaking, he crouched down and attempted to apply the Exploding Toad mnemonics he had been taught on the kung fu techniques he already knew, but they would not meld. He thrust his palms out again and again, trying to recreate the sense of ease he had achieved in the dream, but he could not detect any change in his body.

Disheartened, he let his eyes wander over the dark sea – boundless, without end – and he, a forlorn, forgotten figure on his craggy hill.

A WHISTLE rose above the murmur of the waves.

"Penance! Penance!"

Guo Jing's call jolted Penance from his wallowing. "I'm here! Over here!" he cried, running downhill to the water brink without a second thought.

The instant Guo Jing spotted Penance sprinting down the beach, he steered the boat to shore. He jumped into the shallows and folded the boy in his arms. "Let's go home and get some food into you." His voice was choked with emotion – he sounded almost tearful.

When they arrived at the house, Lotus threw a quick meal together and they ate in silence. No-one brought up the events from the past couple of days.

THE NEXT morning, Guo Jing gathered everyone in the main hall.

"First *Shifu*, I'd like to seek your permission to take four disciples," he said to Ke Zhen'e.

"Excellent!" The blind man gave his support readily.

Guo Jing then turned to Penance. "You won't remember this, but I promised to be your *shifu* when you were a toddler. Your mother held you in her arms and bowed to me. Today, I formally acknowledge you as my student, but first, you must pay obeisance to your Grandmasters."

After that he addressed the Wu brothers, accepting them as disciples, and instructed the three boys to kowtow to Ke Zhen'e and the spirit tablets of the six Freaks that had departed from the world. They completed the ceremony by prostrating before Guo Jing and Lotus Huang, honouring them as *shifu* and *shimu*.

Hibiscus watched the proceedings with amusement. "Ma, do I have to bow too?"

"Of course, it's your turn now."

The girl lowered on to her knees with a giggle and made her reverence as the boys had done.

Once the children had performed the rites, Guo Jing said solemnly, "From now on, you are martial brothers, and you—"

"Martial brothers and *sister*!" Hibiscus corrected him.

Guo Jing shot her a warning look and went on: "As martial siblings, the four of you must love and support each other, sharing your good fortune as well as your hardships. I will not show lenience if you quarrel and fight again."

Penance sensed Guo Jing's eyes resting on him as he issued the warning. You're clearly siding with your daughter, he grumbled inwardly. I'll make sure I stay out of her way.

Ke Zhen'e then outlined the rules that the children, as the next generation of his martial branch, must abide by: they must never use their kung fu knowledge to inflict harm on the upright and virtuous.

The Seven Freaks of the South hailed from different martial lineages and each of them lived by a code of behaviour unique to their heritage. Ke Zhen'e could not recall the individual details, so he summarised a collective outline since the core values were more or less the same.

After that, it was Guo Jing's turn to speak again. "My foundation in kung fu came under the Seven Heroes of the South, and later on I was trained in the Quanzhen Sect's *neigong* techniques as well as the martial innovations of Peach Blossom Island and the Beggar Clan. And yet, the most important lesson in life is that we must never forget our origins, so I will instruct you first in Grandmaster Ke's unique skills."

Lotus had been observing Penance covertly all morning. His focus appeared to wander when Guo Jing recited the martial formula to certain introductory moves. He kept his eyes cast down and his head dipped low. Something in his countenance unsettled her, putting her in mind of Yang Kang.

I didn't kill the boy's father, but I had an unwitting hand in his death, she told herself as disquiet took root in her heart. I hope we are not raising a tiger in our midst . . .

"Guo Jing," she called out. "It's too much work for you to teach all four of them. I'll look after Penance."

"Marvellous idea!" Ke Zhen'e applauded the suggestion. "You can compete to see who trains a better disciple."

Guo Jing was taken by the proposal too. Lotus was a hundred times smarter than him, so Penance would be in capable hands.

"I want you too, Ma . . ." Hibiscus pleaded, knowing her father would be strict with her.

"You only make trouble around me. It's better for Pa to teach you, so you'll learn something."

Hibiscus stole a glance at her father. Finding his stern eyes on her, she looked down without another word.

Smiling at their interaction, Lotus said, "Here's how we'll proceed. We won't interfere with each other's lessons – I am responsible for Penance, and you for the other three. And, children, you must never share what you've learned with each other, because you'll only hurt yourselves mixing kung fu." Once she had received everyone's assurances, she turned to Penance. "Now, come with me for our first session."

Penance followed Lotus to the study, thrilled that he would not have to spend more time with the loathsome trio.

Lotus took a bound volume from one of the shelves and handed it to Penance. "The Seven Heroes of the South taught your *shifu* Guo Jing, and you already know that Grandpa Ke is the eldest. The second of the group was Zhu Cong the Intelligent, also known as Quick Hands. We will start with Grandmaster Zhu's kung fu."

She turned a leaf and read aloud:

"The Master said, 'How can one not be pleased when learning finds application? How can one not be joyful when friends come from afar?'"

Penance could not fathom why he was being taught how to read and write during his kung fu lesson, but he dared not question Lotus, and did as he was told, repeating Confucius's words out loud. Over the next few days, he learned more passages from the *Analects*, without a single mention of martial arts passing Lotus's lips.

AFTER BEING buried in books for yet another class, Penance went out to roam the hills alone. He wondered where his adopted father Viper Ouyang was at that moment and decided to try out the kung fu he had shared with him. He tipped himself into a handstand and turned in circles in the way Viper had done, inverting the flow of his meridians. In time, his limbs grew used to the upturned stance. He flipped back onto his feet, let out a croak and thrust his palms out. A warm, soothing sensation spread from his core to his extremities, provoking a wave of perspiration. This brief exercise was the essence of the Martial Great's most sophisticated invention. Penance had only been shown piecemeal scraps of the technique, but he was sharp enough to grasp the heart of the method and was fortifying his *neigong* foundation without knowing it.

From that day onwards, when he was not studying the Confucian classics with Lotus, Penance would hide away up one of the many hills on Peach Blossom Island and practise Viper Ouyang's kung fu in secret. Sometimes in the morning, sometimes late at night, he trained whenever he could find a moment on his own without drawing attention. He had no ambition to become a supreme martial Master, he merely enjoyed how relaxed he felt afterwards and was left ill at ease if he missed the exercise for just one day.

LOTUS WENT through the whole of the *Analects* with Penance in just three cycles of the moon. It was tedious and trying, but one thought kept her persevering: The boy's mind is as sharp as mine. If he is anything like his father and lacks a moral compass, he'll cause great harm with only a little martial knowledge. It will do him good – and others too – if he focuses on the letters and the principles of the sages.

And so, Lotus drew on her reserves of patience and continued the lessons with the *Mencius*.

It was not difficult for Penance to learn the ancient philosophers' words by heart, but their wisdom was not sacrosanct to him and he did not hesitate to challenge the interpretations. His attitude reminded Lotus of her father Apothecary Huang and it occurred to her that he would have enjoyed teaching the boy.

The months flew by. Lotus did not broach the subject of studying kung fu and Penance stayed mute on that front too. He stopped playing with Hibiscus and the Wu brothers after the fight over the crickets, and kept his distance as he had no illusions regarding his place on the island. He was Guo Jing's disciple merely in name. No-one planned to teach him a single martial move. The next time he got into a scrap with the other three, they would have acquired plenty of new abilities and he would not have a hope of defending himself. They would, for certain, beat him to death. So, there was only one future for him: he was waiting for the opportunity to steal onto a boat and flee from Peach Blossom Island.

ONE AFTERNOON, after another lesson on the *Mencius*, Penance left the study and strolled to the shore. Entranced by the rolling waves, he wondered when he might break free of his shackled existence. His eyes followed the seagulls as they dipped and soared over the ever-shifting white crests. Envy surged in his heart. He longed to live like these birds, free from restraints, able to come and go as he wished.

A whooshing noise from a nearby peach grove jolted Penance out of his reverie. Intrigued, he tiptoed into the trees and found Guo Jing teaching the Wu brothers in a glade. He was demonstrating a move called Prop Up the Beam to Switch the Pillar. It was a part of the Grappling repertoire for which the Sixth Freak of the South – Gilden Quan the Cloaked Master of the Market – was known. The brothers were trying to emulate the action, but failed at every single attempt. Penance could not comprehend why they were struggling so much, since he had already grasped the key to the technique from a distance. Nonetheless, Guo Jing was not at all frustrated by their slow uptake, for he had once been a very dull-witted student. He repeated his explanation and performed the movement again and again, all the while keeping an even temper.

How stupid, Penance jeered, but his sense of superiority soon vanished and he wished he were being trained in their stead. Dispirited, he trundled back to his room and buried himself in bed, napping until it was time for dinner. After eating, he read for a while, but was beset by a restless boredom and decided to go for a walk. His legs took him back to the beach near the glade where he had seen Guo Jing teaching the Wu brothers, and the kung fu move they were trying out came to his mind. He attempted it a few times and gave up, feeling irate.

Why don't I spy on them? I'll learn much faster – and much better – and then I'll have nothing to fear. However, the sparks of excitement fizzled out as quickly as they had been kindled. Wait . . . why would I want to learn from someone who doesn't want to teach me? Huh! Who cares about your wretched kung fu? I'm not interested, even if you beg me! They can beat me to death, so what?

Penance leaned against a rock, nursing his injured pride and lamenting his blighted fate, and drifted off to the song of the waves. He awoke when the sun came up, but instead of returning to the house for breakfast and his morning lesson, he waded into the shallows to look for oysters.

I won't go hungry even if I never touch the food from your precious table, he thought as he built the fire to grill the shellfish. He gazed at the island's seafaring vessels and rowboats anchored in the bay as he waited for his meal to cook, wondering how he could steal one to get to the mainland. No solution presented itself as the sun rose higher. The large boats were too complex to sail on his own and the small craft would not survive the open sea. He decided to practise Viper Ouyang's kung fu to take his mind off this conundrum.

Finding a sheltered spot behind a boulder on the sandy beach, he flipped into a handstand and turned his focus inwards. Soon, his body relaxed in its inverted position and his blood flowed faster, energising his flesh and bones.

"*Oi!*"

The shout shattered his concentration. Strength poured out of his body. A prickling sensation overtook his limbs, then they grew deadened and he collapsed in a heap.

Penance tried to flex his muscles, to push himself up, but he could scarcely move his fingers.

"What *are* you doing?"

Penance glanced around, cursing his ill luck. Hibiscus was standing over him, flanked by the Wu brothers.

The paths and vegetation on Peach Blossom Island were planned according to the way in which each of the Five Elements – metal, wood, water, fire and earth – depended on another for its existence while also holding the key to another's destruction, and this system informed the island's main defence against trespassers. Since the four children had yet to master the underlying principles of the island's design, they kept to a handful of major routes. Penance had thought he had strayed far enough from the others' usual stomping grounds, but alas he was wrong.

He had no desire to engage with them, so he closed his eyes and tried to smooth the uncomfortable roiling within. He had been startled at a particularly vulnerable moment. Little did he know it, but if his kung fu were more advanced, the sudden disruption to his circulation could have paralysed him for life. When he regained some control of his body, he leaned his weight on the boulder, climbed slowly to his feet, and tottered unsteadily away without sparing the intruders a glance.

"Hey!" Erudite stepped into Penance's way. "Sister Guo asked you a question. Answer her!"

"What's it to do with you?" Penance shot back icily.

"Let's play elsewhere," Earnest said to his brother. "We don't bait rabid dogs."

"That's true! Mad dogs bite anything that moves," Penance answered back archly. "I was minding my own business, then I heard a bark and saw three mangy mutts snapping their jaws."

Earnest lunged, swinging his fist in rage, but Erudite pulled his older brother back and whispered in his ear, then turned to Penance. "Big Brother Yang, you have been learning kung fu with *Shimu* for a few months now. Shall we spar and see who has made better progress?"

Penance had only just managed to dodge Earnest's blow and he was about to confess that his lessons were confined to Confucian classics, when Erudite followed up with another taunting question.

"Are you brave enough to take this challenge?" the younger boy asked, not deterred by Penance's snort and frosty sidelong glare. "Of course, we can't let *Shifu* and *Shimu* know. If we get cuts and bruises from sparring, we'll say we've taken a stumble. If the loser squeals to the grown-ups, then he's a bastard dog, a turtle egg! Big Brother Yang, dare you—"

A punch in the eye cut Erudite off mid-sentence. The boy staggered back in shock, almost tripping over his own feet.

"Shame on you!" Earnest howled, pouncing with a fist attack he had learned from Guo Jing.

Penance staggered to one side, but having never been trained in evasion techniques, he could not move fast enough to avoid the blow and did not know how to manipulate his body to lessen the impact. Earnest's knuckles thumped hard into his side, winding him. Now, the follow-up flying kick was whipping into him before he had caught his breath. The move Guo Jing had demonstrated the day before flashed through his mind. He bent slightly from the right knee, raised his left hand and reached under the striking leg.

And heaved.

Prop Up the Beam to Switch the Pillar.

He hurled Earnest upwards and threw him back, sending the boy crashing to the ground.

Erudite rushed up to avenge his big brother, punching from left to right. Penance dodged without realising the blow was a feint and ended up putting himself squarely in the path of the real attack delivered by the other fist.

Whump! A heavy jab landed on his cheekbone.

Earnest sat dazed on the ground for a while before it struck him that he had been toppled by the move he had learned only yesterday. He remembered repeating the sequence many times before beginning to grasp its flow. How come Penance was so adept at it? He clambered up in a black mood and re-entered the fray.

In no time at all, the Wu brothers had landed half a dozen punches on Penance's face and another seven or eight on his back and his sides. They had been better fighters even before they received training from Guo Jing.

Outnumbered and outmatched, Penance stood no chance at all. "Go on, do your worst! I won't run!" He flung his arms about with pure abandon, teeth snarling, eyes wild and glaring.

The feral punches – flying high, low and sideways – unnerved Erudite. "Admit you've lost and we'll spare you." He tried to sound confident as he backed away.

"Who wants your mercy?" Penance hurled the truce back with a flying fist.

Erudite deflected the blow with his left arm and shot his right hand out, seizing Penance by the front of his shirt. Earnest barrelled in, thumping his fists into Penance's lower back. As he arched over in pain, Erudite let go, giving his older brother room to knock their opponent to the ground.

"Yield!" Earnest held Penance in a headlock.

"Never! Mad dog!"

"Yield!" Earnest pushed Penance's face into the sand. "Or I'll smother you."

Coarse grains invaded eyes, nostrils and mouth, suffocating Penance. He gasped, sucking in more sand. He twisted. He kicked. It was futile. He could not wrench free of the hands pinning him down. He could not throw off the weight sitting on his back. His lungs were burning for air, his body bursting from the pain of asphyxiation. A warm stream of *qi* shot up from the Elixir Field in his lower belly unbeckoned, then a wave of energy surged to his extremities, filling him with power and strength.

Penance vaulted up and thrust his palms out. He could not see, his eyes were encrusted with sand, but he thought he had pushed into one of his attackers . . . hitting him in the . . . tummy?

Aaaahhh . . .

A gasp then a thud. Someone had hit the ground.

For a while, the murmur of the sea was the only sound Penance could pick out, until it was broken by a scrabble of panicked footsteps and a boy's hysterical cries.

"*Shifu!* Brother! *Shifu!* He's . . . he's dead! My little brother!"

Penance coughed and spat and blinked and dabbed his eyes. When he could at last see and breathe, he found Erudite lying stock-still next to him, his eyes rolled back, no visible signs of life. The true meaning of Earnest's shrieks began to sink in. Still, Penance could not understand how he had hurt the boy. He had no idea that his body had reacted to protect itself when he was almost choked to death, rallying the *neigong* strength cultivated in the past few months through Viper Ouyang's inverted method and unconsciously letting rip with Exploding Toad kung fu. His head was screaming at him to run, and yet he could not even move his legs, for he had not a drop of strength left in his calves.

Still smeared with tears and snort, Earnest led Guo Jing and Lotus Huang to where his brother lay comatose. Guo Jing lifted Erudite up to lean against him and massaged the boy's torso using his internal strength. A perplexed expression crept onto his face and he turned to Lotus. "It's him."

Realising who her husband was referring to, Lotus spoke to Penance: "Where's Viper Ouyang?"

He did not seem to have heard her, standing dazed on the spot.

"When did he teach you the Exploding Toad?" she continued.

Penance gazed blankly ahead, his lips pulled tight. He looked as though his souls and spirits had taken leave of his body.

Unsure if he had registered her presence, Lotus seized him by the arms and raised her voice. "Tell me! Where is Viper Ouyang?" She repeated the questions several times, but he remained unresponsive.

By now, Erudite had come to and Ke Zhen'e had arrived on the scene, led by a terrified Hibiscus.

The blind man stood looming over Penance, the Exorcist's Staff held aloft. "Where is the villain Viper Ouyang? Where is he?" From Hibiscus's account, he had concluded that Penance must be the Venom's disciple and he could not help extending the hatred he felt towards the murderer of his martial siblings to the youngster. "Speak, or I'll strike you dead!"

Something Ke Zhen'e said jolted Penance back to the present

and he shouted, "He's not a villain! He's a good man! I won't tell you anything! Kill me! I don't care!"

The old man swung his weapon in a towering rage.

"First *Shifu*, no!" Guo Jing cried.

Whump! The metal staff hit the sand next to Penance. The Freak had remembered at the last moment that it was a mere child standing before him.

"Where is Viper Ouyang?" The blind man's voice was quivering with fury – he could not let the killer slip away again.

Stubborn silence.

"You won't say?"

"No!" Penance burst out. "Bring down your staff! I'm not scared of you, blind buffoon!"

"How dare you!" Guo Jing cuffed the boy on the ear.

Sweeping his eyes over every face before him, Penance said icily, "You all want me dead. I'll save you the trouble," and he ran into the sea.

"Come back, Penance!"

But Guo Jing's call only made the youngster wade more resolutely into the crashing waves.

"Wait," Lotus whispered as she grabbed Guo Jing's arm to stop him from giving chase.

Guo Jing struggled against her grip. "He can't swim! We have to save him!"

"Calm down! He won't die." Lotus was convinced that Penance would turn back when the water rose above his head, and even if he went under, she was confident she could pull him out in time. She watched the boy march ahead until he was submerged, showing no fear of drowning. Realising she had underestimated his dogged pride, she rushed into the water and swam out to where he had disappeared. He was already sinking towards the seabed when she spotted him. Once she had brought him back to shore, she settled him on a rock, positioning him in a way that would help his body bring up the brine he had swallowed, and waited for him to come to.

"What should we do now?" Guo Jing glanced between his *shifu* and his wife.

"Viper Ouyang could not have come to Peach Blossom Island without our knowledge," Lotus said with conviction. "Penance must have learned that kung fu before he came here."

Guo Jing lapsed into a brooding silence.

"How's Erudite?" Lotus asked after a while.

"It'll take him a month or two to recover fully."

"I'll go back to Jiaxing tomorrow," Ke Zhen'e declared suddenly.

Guo Jing and Lotus exchanged looks. Each saw that the other had understood the Freak's meaning: he would not live under the same roof as anyone with links to Viper Ouyang.

"First *Shifu*, this is your home," Lotus said. "You shouldn't have to leave . . ."

3

GUO JING SUMMONED PENANCE THAT EVENING. "I WILL NOT press you to tell me what took place today, but you were rude to your Grandmaster and that cannot be tolerated. From this moment on, you will cease to be my disciple and I will once again be Uncle Guo to you.

"I know I am not a good teacher, and I fear my shortcomings will jeopardise your future. I have decided to take you to Chong-yang Temple in the Zhongnan Mountains and ask Immortal Eternal Spring Qiu Chuji to accept you under his tutelage. The Quanzhen Sect is the orthodox school of martial arts, and it is my hope that you will work hard to prime your heart and nurture your character there, so you may become an upright man of virtue."

"Yes, Uncle Guo." Penance accepted his new fate readily.

THE DAY to set out for the Zhongnan Mountains soon arrived. Guo Jing woke earlier than usual, his mind preoccupied by the journey ahead. After checking he had packed everything he needed and there was enough silver in his purse, he led Penance to their boat and bade farewell to those remaining on the island. When they docked on the coast of Zhejiang, Guo Jing bought two horses to take them north. Penance had never ridden before, but being agile and nimble, he quickly grew confident and started to enjoy himself, often galloping far ahead.

The pair travelled at a gentle pace, always stopping after sundown. After many days in the saddle, they crossed the Yellow River and entered the region of Shaanxi. The lands north of this major waterway had been under Mongol rule for some years now, following their defeat of the Great Jin Empire.

Once they crossed into Mongolian territory, Guo Jing sold the horses to purchase two stick-thin donkeys and changed into patchy old clothes of the style worn by the local peasants. He had spent his first eighteen years living in Mongolia and had once served as a general under Genghis Khan on one of the western campaigns – until, that is, he realised the conqueror planned to annex his native southern lands, and left the army on acrimonious terms. Fearing he might be recognised by Mongol soldiers along the way, he chose to disguise himself to avoid trouble.

Penance donned a rough-spun robe that hung below his knees and wrapped his hair in a blue-green cloth. His ill-tempered donkey plodded on sluggishly, and he amused himself by antagonising the wretched beast.

At last they reached the alluvial plains of Fanchuan at the foot of the Zhongnan Mountains. The area was named after General Fan Kuai, who had been instrumental in the founding of the Han dynasty and was granted these lands as a reward for his service. Guo Jing and Penance meandered between fertile paddy fields and verdant vegetable patches that were bordered by lush conifers on the hillocks.

"Uncle Guo, doesn't this place remind you of our own Peach Blossom Island?"

Penance's words brought a wistful smile to Guo Jing's lips. He had noticed how dispirited the youngster had been, and that he had not made a single mention of his time on the island. Now, hearing him refer to Peach Blossom Island as "our own", Guo Jing was moved to regard their surroundings with new eyes. There were indeed echoes of the South in the luxuriant scenery.

"We aren't far from the Zhongnan Mountains," Guo Jing said, trying to make conversation. "Put in your best efforts with the Quanzhen Sect. I'll be back in a few years, and we'll return to Peach Blossom Island together."

"I will not set foot on that island again as long as I live," Penance said with finality, his eyes fixed on the horizon.

Guo Jing did not know how to respond. He had never imagined the boy would prove so headstrong and resolute.

"Are you still upset with Auntie Guo?" he asked after a while.

"Why do you think that?"

Not gifted with words, Guo Jing stayed silent and focused on the road.

AT MIDDAY, they came upon a Buddhist temple built on the ridge of a small mountain. Above the main gate, colossal characters were engraved:

TEMPLE OF PERVADING LIGHT

Guo Jing tethered the donkeys to one of the pine trees by the entrance and went inside to seek refreshments. It was common for places of worship to provide travellers with a simple meal and a place to rest in exchange for donations. The seven or eight monks gathered in the courtyard eyed Guo Jing's threadbare clothes with dispassion.

One of them went to fetch two bowls of plain noodles and half a dozen steamed *mantou* buns.

Penance was sitting on a stone bench in the shade not far from their mounts. When Guo Jing joined him with their food, his eyes were drawn by a stone stele nearby. Two large characters carved at the very top were visible above the tall grass:

ETERNAL SPRING

He put down the noodles, went up to the slab and brushed the vegetation aside to find a poem he knew, written by Qiu Chuji the Eternal Spring Immortal.

> The grey heavens look down on the earth.
> Why does it not save ten thousand souls in pain?
> Souls, day and night, in suffering and torment,
> That hide their gasps, swallow their voices, depart in silence.
>
> Howling at the heavens, but the heavens answer not,
> A matter too minor, too small, too futile.
> Let not the many thousand worlds return to chaos,
> Let not the divine maker create more spirits.

As Guo Jing traced the chiselled strokes with his forefinger, floods of memories washed over him. He was transported back to Samarkand, where he had led the Mongolian troops to victory more than a dozen years before, despite the impregnable city walls. The night after their triumph, he had heard Qiu Chuji, who had just arrived from the Central Plains, recite these very words to Genghis Khan. It brought Guo Jing's mind back to the devastation he had witnessed – and caused – on the road of conquest and the risk he had taken when he had gone against the army's bloodthirsty traditions and refused to massacre the city's inhabitants.

"Uncle Guo, what does it say?" Penance's voice brought him back to the present.

"This poem was written by your new Grandmaster, Eternal Spring Qiu Chuji. He saw the people's afflictions and grieved for them." After explaining the poem's meaning, line by line, Guo Jing added, "Immortal Qiu's martial skills are supreme, but it is his compassion that is his most admirable quality. Your father Yang Kang was a disciple of Grandmaster Qiu and I trust he will treat you very well. If you put your heart into your learning, you can achieve great things."

Buoyed by the thought of being reunited with the Taoist after so many years, Guo Jing did not notice Penance's mood darken at the mention of his father.

"Uncle Guo, can I ask you a question?" Penance said when he had finished eating.

"Go ahead."

"How did my papa die?"

Colour drained from Guo Jing's face and a shudder rippled through his body. He would rather not repeat what Lotus and Ke Zhen'e had told him about that fateful night at the Iron Spear Temple all those years ago.

Noting the shift in his countenance, Penance pressed on. "Who killed him?"

Still no reply.

Guo Jing's reticence reminded Penance of the evasive silence his mother would retreat into each time he asked about his father's end, and it unnerved him. He knew the man's affection towards him was genuine, but Lotus Huang had made a point of keeping her distance and being on her guard around him. And though Guo Jing claimed he wanted to look after him – the orphan son of his sworn brother – he had said precious little about the past.

Right now, his quietness was leading the youngster to ask some very pointed questions: Why won't Uncle Guo tell me anything? Why's he acting so shifty? Is it because he's got something to do with Papa's death?

Penance blurted out the words the second the horrifying possibility flashed into his head: "You and Auntie Guo killed my papa . . ."

123

"Nonsense!" Guo Jing smacked his hand down on the stone stele, so hard that it now sat askew.

Lowering his head, Penance said in a pacifying tone, "Please don't be angry, Uncle Guo."

A loud gasp of shock interrupted this strained moment. Guo Jing and Penance looked over to see two monks staring at them from just beyond the temple's mountain gate, one tall and thin, the other rotund and stumpy in build.

"It's him, isn't it?" The stick-thin Taoist turned to his companion, who nodded in confirmation. They sped off downhill, glancing back every few steps.

Guo Jing assumed the monks were from Chongyang Temple, the home of the Quanzhen Sect, where he and Penance were headed. From their fleet footwork and their age – both appeared to be around forty – he guessed they were probably trained by one of the seven disciples of the Sect's founder, Wang Chongyang. It would explain why they were so affronted to see him strike a stele engraved with their martial elder's words.

Despite Guo Jing's close relationship with three of the Quanzhen Seven – Ma Yu, Wang Chuyi and Qiu Chuji – he had only met a handful of their students, those who travelled west with Qiu at Genghis Khan's invitation more than a decade ago. Still, he had heard that this third generation had been making a name for themselves in the *wulin* with their upright and altruistic deeds.

Curious as to their identity, Guo Jing sprinted after the men. "Elders!" he called out when he was within a dozen *zhang*. "Please wait for a moment. I should like a word with you."

Guo Jing's voice had surely reached them, but the monks quickened their pace instead of slowing down.

Did they not hear me? Guo Jing flexed his left foot and sprang into the air. A couple of leaps later, he was landing in the Taoists' path. He put his hands together in a gesture of respect and greeted them again.

Shocked by how swiftly their pursuer had drawn level, the monks assumed he was bowing to camouflage a strike and swerved to either side.

"What brings you here?" the gaunt Taoist demanded.

"Are the Elders from Chongyang Temple of the Zhongnan Mountains?"

"What's it to you?"

"I am a friend of Reverend Qiu the Eternal Spring Immortal. I am on my way to visit him. May I trouble the Elders to point me in the right direction?"

The stouter Taoist eyed him with a sneer. "Find your own way!" Without warning, he chopped at Guo Jing's shoulder with his palm.

Guo Jing veered to one side, away from the swift strike. But that put him in the course of the other monk's whistling palm slice. He was trapped by a seamlessly coordinated interwoven move, which he recognised as an advanced Quanzhen kung fu known as Closing the Gate.

Their aggressive pincer attack left Guo Jing perplexed. Why were they out to injure him without asking his name or his business with Qiu Chuji? Not wishing to further inflame the situation, he summoned the inner strength needed to protect himself, but took care to keep this energy in check, so there would be no danger to his assailants when their blows connected with his body.

The Taoists could tell from his physical stance that he would not engage, but they decided to follow through with their assault nonetheless. *Pang, pang!* Their palms slapped noisily onto the stranger's flanks.

At the moment of contact, Guo Jing gained a clear sense of the men's martial ability. He was now certain, from their masterful control, that they were disciples of one of the Quanzhen Immortals, and that meant they were his fellows, for he had once been taught by the most senior of the seven, Ma Yu.

The monks, for their part, were staggered that their onslaught had had no effect whatsoever. They had spent more than a decade perfecting this potent joint offensive, yet it was as though they had struck a tattered old quilt with ripped filling. Their blows simply glanced off their foe.

Groaning with frustration, the Taoists exchanged a look, leapt up in unison and let fly with their feet in a rapid series of darting strikes.

Mandarin Duck Interlinked Kicks.

The monks' pugnacity stunned Guo Jing. He found it unthinkable that the Immortals would train disciples who threw punches at strangers without cause. Still, he endured this second wave of assault with the same restraint and – *whump whump whump* – let their feet fall on his torso.

The duo aimed a total of twelve kicks at their foe, but though they knew they had struck him repeatedly on the ribs, the sensation in their toes felt like prodding a soft bag of sand. The man's face showed not even a grimace. Only the mess of dusty footprints on his shirt testified to what had happened. They edged back and, for the first time, took a good look at their adversary.

Thick eyebrows, large eyes. A frank and open face. A common peasant in rough-spun clothes. Nothing remarkable, except . . . he was more skilled in kung fu than their *shifu* and martial uncles!

Penance had at last caught up with the three grown men and was furious at the treatment Guo Jing had received. "How dare you touch my uncle, you stinking Taoists?"

"Penance!" Guo Jing said sternly. "Come here and bow to the Elders."

The youngster stared back with incomprehension. Why should he bend to these bellicose monks?

The Taoists caught each other's eye and – *sha, sha!* – unsheathed the swords at their belts. The shorter monk aimed for Guo Jing's ankle with a Dive into the Sea to Slay the Dragon, while his fellow hacked at Penance's calf in a move called Gust Sweeps Leaves.

Guo Jing could not believe his eyes. The blow would surely sever Penance's leg. What quarrel did the monks have with him? Why were they being so merciless? He turned a fraction, placed the edge of his palm on the hilt of the sword threatening him and deflected it leftwards in a Push the Boat Away.

The monk was aghast to find his arm being yanked around against his will as the blade twisted in his grip. *Clank!* It struck his brother's sword and sabotaged the attack on the boy.

The Taoists jumped back in alarm. Their wrists were numbed from the clash and lancing pain seized the muscles between thumb and forefinger.

The technique Guo Jing had employed was one had he invented, based on the fundamental martial system Bare Hands Seize Blade. He could subdue up to a dozen fighters by pitching their weapons against each other, parrying axes with sabres and flicking whips away with spears.

The monks could not deny that they admired their foe's skill, but it made them all the more determined to beat him. Glaring balefully at Guo Jing, they advanced with their blades held high.

Guo Jing recognised their combined approach as a permutation of the Heavenly Northern Dipper formation. He sighed inwardly, disappointed in his opponents. *This kung fu takes seven fighters to realise its full potential! And your swordcraft still needs a lot of work . . .*

Though he knew the Taoists' attack could not hurt him personally, Guo Jing could not risk Penance being caught by the wake of energy left in the air by the blades. He swivelled to one side, avoiding the keen edges of the steel, and scooped the youngster up in his arms.

"I am a friend of Immortal Qiu," he called out, trying again to end the skirmish amicably.

The rake-thin monk sneered. "Ha! I suppose you're a friend of Immortal Ma too!"

"Indeed, Immortal Ma taught me for two years."

"Oh really?" The squat monk scoffed. "Next you'll tell us our Grandmaster Chongyang trained you too!" The caustic remark was punctuated with a lunge at Guo Jing's heart.

Guo Jing could not fathom why he was being treated with such hostility, but he remained firm in his resolve to avoid dealing blows directly. Having travelled thousands of *li* in the hope of entrusting Penance's kung fu education to Chongyang Temple, it would do no good to offend the boy's future martial kinsmen. Besides, the connection he shared with the Quanzhen Immortals went beyond that of Master and disciple – they had also been comrades-in-arms in battles of life or death. How could he raise his hands against his brothers? His only option was to keep one step ahead of their attacks.

By now, the Taoists knew they had little hope of catching their superior opponent with their swords, but it was their duty to stop him from ascending the Zhongnan Mountains. They signalled at one another and – s*ha, sha, sha, sha!* – sent their blades whirling in a fresh pattern derived from a different martial repertoire, aiming a series of lethal strikes at Penance's chest and back.

Aghast to see such ruthless moves deployed against a child, Guo Jing set Penance down, shot his right hand forward and pinched the flat of the stouter monk's blade between his index and middle fingers. The monk's death-dealing thrust was stopped in its tracks. Guo Jing then turned his wrist inwards and swung his elbow up at the swordsman's nose.

The Taoist tightened his grip, trying to pull free, but he could not shift his weapon by even a hair's breadth. Unwilling to risk having his face smashed, he let go and jumped back.

With one assailant disarmed, Guo Jing sent more force to his fingers and flipped the hilt upwards, knocking it into the scrawny monk's blade, inches before its point found Penance's neck.

Clang! A jet of searing heat shot up the Taoist's arm, followed by a wave of shudders. He dropped his sword, retreated out of Guo Jing's reach and yelled, "This is not over, lecher!" before fleeing with his martial brother.

Guo Jing stood agape, watching them scramble up the hillside. He was no stranger to insults – blockhead, idiot, scoundrel . . . but never had he been branded a degenerate. He grabbed Penance, deployed his lightness *qinggong* and caught up with the Taoists in an instant.

"What did you just call me?" Guo Jing tapped his right foot

against the ground and vaulted over the monks' heads, landing in their path.

"Lecher!" The shorter monk repeated his fellow's slur, then added a clarification as he edged away. "You're only here because you covet the hand of that Long woman!"

Guo Jing was befuddled. *What are they talking about? I don't know anyone of the surname Long. And I'm happily married.*

As he struggled to wrap his mind around this latest development, the Taoists seized their chance and bolted down the trail.

4

"THEY'RE GONE, UNCLE GUO."

Penance's voice jolted Guo Jing out of his confounded state. "Right . . . Who did they say this woman was?"

"They didn't explain." Penance extricated himself from Guo Jing's arms and hurried back to pick up the abandoned swords. "They must have mistaken you for someone else."

"Probably." Guo Jing studied the blades. The characters carved on each hilt caught his eye.

CHONGYANG TEMPLE

He turned the encounter over in his head once more, but still could not make any sense of it, so after a short silence he said, "Let's keep going."

They hiked for several hours, reaching Golden Lotus Pavilion towards the middle of the afternoon. From this point onwards, the path uphill grew more and more treacherous. They scrambled over loose rocks and inched their way along perilous precipices, winding slowly towards the summit.

The light was already fading as they passed Sun and Moon Crag. By the time they arrived at Child-Cradling Crag, where they paused for a brief rest, the moon was peeping out from behind the clouds. In the deepening gloom, a curiously shaped rock loomed large, its silhouette – resembling a mother hugging her babe – silently justifying the name it had been given.

Not long after they had resumed their journey, they found the track blocked by a boulder. The misshapen mass of rock, bearing the outline of a woman hunched by age, seemed to peer down menacingly at them.

Old Crone Crag.

Shrill whistles ripped through the night air. Four Taoists leapt out, brandishing their swords, defiantly barring the travellers' path.

Guo Jing crossed his arms over his chest in a gesture of respect and introduced himself: "Guo Jing of Peach Blossom Island is here to pay compliments to Immortal Qiu."

A tall monk stepped forward with a snigger. "Hero Guo is no shameless miscreant. He is the son-in-law of Master Apothecary Huang and admired by all under the heavens. Turn back now, imposter!"

"I truly am he," Guo Jing said patiently, ignoring the man's belligerent posture. "Immortal Qiu can vouch for me, if you would be so kind—"

"Since you are set on provoking Chongyang Temple," the monk cut him off, "we will show you the true mettle of the Quanzhen Sect!" Lunging forward in zigzagging steps, his sword flashed in an angled slice towards Guo Jing's flank, a move known as Parting Flowers, Flicking Willows.

The other three Taoists repositioned themselves, encircling Guo Jing and Penance with their blades held high.

Guo Jing pivoted away from the strike, wondering if the rules of the *jianghu* had changed in the decade he had been living on Peach Blossom Island. Why else would the Quanzhen Sect accept such hot-headed followers?

"I *am* Guo Jing." He was growing exasperated by their unwarranted aggression. "What can I do to convince you?"

"Snatch this sword from my hand." The tall monk aimed the point of his steel at Guo Jing's ribs. His disdain for his opponent was obvious from the lazy way he thrust his blade forward, displaying none of the nimble agility or oblique, indirect approach prized in the art of swordplay.

Guo Jing waited until the sword made contact with his jacket, then, in the blink of an eye, he raised his right hand, curled his forefinger under his thumb, and flicked the flat of the blade.

Whang! The weapon shot out of the Taoist's grip and flew straight up in the air.

The same whizz rang thrice more. Each time it sounded, a blade took to the night sky, glistening in the moonlight.

Penance cheered when he heard all four weapons clatter to the ground. "Now do you believe him?"

"Demoncraft! Let's not tarry here," the long-limbed monk cried to his fellows. He dashed behind the boulder, leading the way through the mess of rugged rocks under the cover of darkness.

Guo Jing was dumbstruck. He, a lecher who uses demoncraft? He had merely wished to avoid enraging the Taoists further and chose the least confrontational kung fu he knew – Apothecary Huang's prized martial invention Divine Flick, which he had learned from the Martial Great himself when he first moved to Peach Blossom Island. He had even hoped it would help to confirm his identity.

"Leave the swords here," he said to Penance, still unsure if he should laugh off the absurd encounter or feel offended.

The youngster lined up the four blades on a nearby rock, together with the two seized in the initial skirmish. Enthralled by Guo Jing's martial prowess, he wanted to kneel and beg the man to take him back as his disciple and teach him kung fu. The pleading words were on the tip of his tongue when he remembered what had come to pass on the island, and he bit down hard on his bottom lip and swallowed his entreaties.

GUO JING and Penance continued to make their way up the Zhongnan Mountains. The narrow craggy track widened after several turns and there were now clumps of pine trees lining the way.

Claaaang! The sound of steel on steel cut through the air. Seven Taoist monks emerged from the trees, their swords already unsheathed. They were approaching in the Heavenly Northern Dipper formation. Four monks on the left moved in a staggered line, in the celestial positions of Heavenly Power, Jade Scales, Manifest Sun and Shimmering Rays. Together, they formed the constellation's handle. Three men on the right made up the scoop, in the Heavenly Pivot, Heavenly Jade and Heavenly Pearl positions.

"Hide behind that rock and stay put," Guo Jing whispered. "I need to focus."

Penance gave a surreptitious nod and spoke in a loud voice, tugging the drawstring of his trousers. "Uncle Guo, I need a pee. I'll go there." He trudged over, making a show to suggest he was moving away to answer the call of nature rather than to take refuge.

It pleased Guo Jing to see another demonstration of Penance's wits, which, to his eye, were as sharp as Lotus's, but he also worried about the boy's future. Before the fight was joined, he mouthed a silent invocation, praying that Penance would use his intellect to pursue a path of virtue and righteousness.

Guo Jing waited until Penance had found shelter before turning his attention to the monks. They were backlit by the moon, so he could not make out their faces, but there was enough light to pick out their silhouettes. Six of the Taoists had long flowing beards that heralded their age; the seventh appeared smooth-faced and slighter in build, likely the youngest of the group.

It was clear to Guo Jing that the only way to untangle this mix-up was to get to Chongyang Temple, so Qiu Chuji could affirm his identity. He had not come all this way to wrangle with the great man's underlings and he knew it would be best to put an end to their challenge by the quickest possible means. With that intent, he swerved left – to where the North Star would be in relation to the Northern Dipper constellation.

The monk occupying the commanding position of Heavenly Power let out a low whistle as soon as Guo Jing started to move. His six fellows shifted their feet to shadow their foe, ready to fence him in.

In response, Guo Jing took two steps to the right, maintaining his place at the North Star.

Another instruction from Heavenly Power, but the monk trailed off mid-speech. He had wanted the three brothers in the Dipper's shaft to swoop in from the side, but realised at the last moment that none of their swords could threaten their opponent, and neither could the rest of them – not without breaking ranks – whereas their enemy could reach each and every one of them from his location. If they could not strike in tandem or come to each other's aid, the formation would lose its power. He made the signal to pull back.

The Taoist at Shimmering Rays started to retreat. Guo Jing, in turn, strode forward by two paces. The rest of the monks took up their new positions, only to find they were stuck in the same impasse: their spatial relationship had not changed; they were still unable to attack or defend.

The Heavenly Northern Dipper had been devised by the Quan-zhen Sect's founder, Wang Chongyang, for his seven disciples to deploy should they come head to head with their nemesis Viper Ouyang, as individually his students could not match the Martial Great. When adopted by supreme fighters with thorough knowledge of its permutations, it was nigh on impossible to defeat, but on this occasion Guo Jing could tell that, despite the monks' familiarity with the various dispositions, they had little knowledge of the underlying astronomical theories.

It was inspired by the constellation of the same name, the way its seven stars rotate around the North Star, whose astral position is fixed. By occupying this spot, Guo Jing gained absolute control over the formation: he could lead the monks in a charge against a common foe, or keep them locked in their relative locations, unable to unleash their weapons on him.

In his ignorance, Heavenly Power urged his brothers-in-arms to change their bearings again and again. Each time, Guo Jing regained his position of power with a few breezy steps.

Gradually, the Taoist at Heavenly Pivot began to notice something was amiss. "Shift!" he roared, and his companions scattered. Those on the left dashed to the right and those on the right to the left, flipping the formation's orientation. The most senior and experienced among his fellows, the monk was hoping that the manoeuvre would confuse their adversary and wrest back the initiative.

Moments later, the seven fighters were once more in configuration. The two parts of the Dipper had switched place – the constellation now faced south-east instead of west.

From his spot north of the Dipper's handle, Guo Jing regarded the Taoists with a smile. He raised one palm over the other, his feet planted casually a little way apart.

Heavenly Jade in the scoop and Jade Scales in the stem lunged in tandem, their swords flashing, but halfway through their attack, they twisted away and withdrew their strength. They realised that, if they had followed through, they would have plunged their blades into their brethren at Manifest Sun and Heavenly Pearl.

"Stop! Stand down!" Heavenly Pivot had come to the same conclusion.

Reacting swiftly, Heavenly Power whistled through his fingers and led his fellows into a new variation of the formation.

Several leisurely strides from Guo Jing sent the Taoists running frantically in wild circles. If they did take evasive action, their backs would be exposed to their opponent. To the east, to the west, to the south, to the north, they were pulled after him – at whatever pace he set – without any capacity to retaliate or any means to extricate themselves.

Amused by his dominance over the monks, Guo Jing was struck by a mischievous idea. You call me a lecher and accuse me of using demoncraft – he grumbled in his head – I'll show you true devilry!

Clapping his hands together, he cried, "Pardon me!" and took two steps to the left. "Penance, watch. This is demoncraft!" He hopped onto a large rock that jutted out from the ground.

A few of the Taoists hesitated, unsure if they should pursue their foe. All too aware of the fatal consequences of the formation collapsing, Heavenly Power screeched at his companions to follow him as he sprang onto the boulder. However, Guo Jing did not wait for them to find anchorage on the rock and instead leapt over to a nearby pine tree, landing at its very tip. Though they were not on the same vertical plane, he continued to occupy the position of the North Star in relation to the seven monks, and the elevated vantage point gave him a second distinct advantage.

The monks knew they were being toyed with, but in a desperate bid to maintain cohesion, they scrambled up the branches, while cursing the nameless fiend for their bitter humiliation.

"Down!" Guo Jing bellowed, swooping down from his perch with a laugh. As he descended, he grabbed at the ankle of the monk at Manifest Sun.

The power of the Northern Dipper came from drawing the might of seven into one, as each member was supported by their comrades on either side. But since Manifest Sun was being dragged from the tree, Shimmering Rays and Jade Scales had to follow if they wanted to preserve their spatial relationship, and, moments later, Heavenly Pivot and Heavenly Power were compelled to shift too. In the blink of an eye, all seven monks tumbled from the branches.

Guo Jing's exhilarating martial display set Penance's heart thumping and his spirits soaring. If I could learn from Uncle Guo, I'd take any hardship life throws at me, he thought in awe. Why couldn't I be blessed like that brat Hibiscus Guo or the dunderheads Earnest and Erudite Wu? As he lamented his ill fortune, suspicion began to gnaw at his mind. Uncle Guo knows the stinking Taoists' kung fu is shoddy, and yet he decides to take me here . . . Does he not want me to learn . . . ?

The boy was so aggrieved by the possibility that his eyes pooled with tears. He forced himself to look away in a sulk, but it was hard to resist the spectacle, and when he finally took a peek, he was once more enthralled.

By now, Guo Jing had the Taoists sprinting in circles. However, he knew it would be unseemly to keep up the farce for too long. The last thing he wanted was to appear discourteous to Qiu Chuji. Hoping he had convinced the monks of his identity, he held his ground and cupped his hands reverentially.

"Pardon Guo Jing's impertinence, Elders. Please lead the way."

"Lecher!" the monk at Heavenly Power bellowed – he had made up his mind that the stranger could have only developed such in-depth understanding of the Northern Dipper formation because he had ill designs on their martial branch. Hot-headed to a fault, he continued in a booming voice, "We of the Quanzhen Sect never sit by and do nothing when evil is in sight. We will not let you commit your sordid acts in the Zhongnan Mountains!"

"What are you talking about?" Yet again, Guo Jing was thoroughly confounded.

It was the Taoist occupying Heavenly Pivot who answered, his tone much calmer that his brother's. "Given your kung fu, you do not appear to be one who wishes to debase himself. This humble monk entreats you – with good intent. Turn back now."

"I have come thousands of *li* from the South to seek an audience with Immortal Qiu—"

"Why should we believe you?" Heavenly Power butted in gruffly.

"In my youth, Immortal Ma and Immortal Qiu treated me with great kindness. We have not seen each other for nigh on a decade, which is why I journeyed here to pay my respects. I also come seeking their aid in a matter of great import."

A dark cloud descended over the bellicose monk's features as he listened. The word "kindness" was sometimes used in the place of animus in the *jianghu*, whereas "seeking aid" was a euphemism favoured by bandits when they made their demands.

"Oh, indeed," he replied in a barbed tone, still convinced that Guo Jing was an enemy of the Quanzhen Sect and that his words could not be taken at face value. "Next you'll tell me our *shifu* Immortal Jade Sun has done you a *kindness* too!"

"Yes, you are right!" Guo Jing was transported back to the residence of Prince Wanyan Honglie in the now vanquished Jin Empire's capital of Zhongdu. He had been a kung fu novice, merely eighteen years of age, and the Taoist had taken on half a dozen martial Masters to protect him. "It would be most wonderful to find the Jade Sun Immortal, Wang Chuyi, at the temple too."

Hearing this reply, the impetuous Heavenly Power hissed in rage and signalled his brethren to pounce in unison. Seven swords, gleaming green in the cold moonlight, flew towards the vital points on their enemy's chest.

Guo Jing's frown deepened. Was he not being his most courteous self? What could have angered the Taoists this time? If Lotus were with him, she would have detected with a single glance the cause of the misunderstanding. Instead, he had to deal with the situation in the only way he knew. He took a few steps sidewards and occupied the North Star again.

"What can I do to convince you that I truly am Guo Jing from Jiangnan in the South and that I have come to your hallowed mountain with nothing but good intentions?"

Again, it was the fiery Heavenly Power who responded. "You have disarmed six Quanzhen disciples today. Why don't you try taking these seven swords?"

His comrade at Heavenly Jade added in a voice that rasped like a cracked gong, "Never will you strut before the maiden of the Long family, you lewd dog!"

"I have never met any woman of that name!" Guo Jing protested.

"Of course, you haven't," the same monk scoffed. "No man under the heavens has. Call her a strumpet if you dare!"

Guo Jing was shocked. He would never use such a term, especially on a stranger.

The man, however, interpreted his silence as an admission of impure designs. "So, you *are* here for her."

Guo Jing was struggling to follow their logic, but it was evident that, if he wanted to clear his name, he would have to force his way into Chongyang Temple and seek out Ma Yu, Qiu Chuji or Wang Chuyi.

"Let me pass. Or else . . . do not blame me for being uncivil."

The Taoists answered Guo Jing's frosty warning by taking two steps forward, hefting their blades.

"Fight us without using demoncraft!" Heavenly Jade roared.

"But I want to use my demonic skills," Guo Jing said, smiling. "I'll disarm you without using my hands and without touching your weapons."

The monks looked at each other in disbelief. They had experienced the man's exceptional kung fu, but they refused to believe he could snatch their swords in the way he had described. Even the most sophisticated Bare Hands Seize Blade technique still required the hands to do the work.

"We look forward to admiring your footwork," Heavenly Pivot jeered.

"I won't need to use my feet," Guo Jing declared. "I'll deprive you of your steel without making any contact. If a part of my body so much as brushes your weapons, then I have lost and I will turn round and never trouble the Quanzhen Sect again."

Incensed by the grand claim, Heavenly Power flourished his sword. His brethren surrounded their foe in formation.

Guo Jing charged sideways to retake the North Star, then lunged at the Taoist's left flank. Heavenly Power signalled a shift to the right to avoid leaving their backs exposed.

However, Guo Jing defied expectations and kept moving left instead of circling round. At times he moved at pace, at others he dragged his heels. One moment he was dashing straight ahead, the next he was sidling aslant. Whichever course he took, he always occupied the North Star position in relation to the Northern Dipper configuration, forcing the monks to shadow him.

Next, Guo Jing began to run, faster and faster, like a galloping horse, shooting forth several *zhang* with a single burst of speed.

The Taoists' determination in the face of his trickery was commendable. Though they were scrabbling to keep up, they still maintained the outline of the constellation to preserve the connections between the seven stars that gave the formation its power.

They might be at odds, but Guo Jing was thrilled to see the monks at last living up to the Sect's martial reputation. He took a deep breath and picked up his pace, whizzing forward as though his feet had no need to touch the ground. As the North Star, he was the point around which the Taoists pivoted, so a mere few steps for Guo Jing multiplied into dozens for his reluctant followers.

The monks were keeping up – with difficulty – but it was becoming clear which of them had stronger lightness *qinggong*. Heavenly Power, Heavenly Pivot and Jade Scales were more fleet-footed and had better stamina. The rest began to lag behind. Gaps were opening.

The youngest monk was the weakest among them. His mind was whirling, his breathing ragged. He knew he was on the brink of collapse, but if he succumbed, he would wreck the formation from within. Clenching his jaw, he soldiered on.

The hardier fighters adjusted their speed to cater for their floundering brothers. If they wanted to defend each other, it was vital to preserve their constant spatial relationship. Keeping their swords high in a shielding stance, each man mustered every last drop of his *neigong* to stay in the race.

All of a sudden, Guo Jing shouted, "Let go!" and darted left with explosive speed.

The monks swerved after him, and in the same instant, their swords shot out of their hands. Seven blades writhed through the air, like seven silver snakes, landing in a knot of pine trees a dozen *zhang* away.

Guo Jing halted and turned to the Taoists with a grin. The effort they had put into maintaining formation was evident and he was impressed by their discipline and rapport.

But the monks just thought he was gloating. They glared back, ashen-faced, unable to comprehend the uncanny force that had disarmed them. They had, in fact, recreated the children's game of spinning a rope with a stone tied to one end. Their blades were the rocks, and they themselves were the cords tethered to Guo Jing by the connection between the Northern Dipper constellation and the North Star, while the ever swifter laps they ran around Guo Jing provided the swirling action, until enough momentum had been built to wrench their swords from their grasp.

Despite it all, the monks valiantly – and futilely – held their positions. Accepting defeat, Heavenly Power caught his breath, let out a weak wheezing whistle and led the retreat into the woods.

5

"PENANCE?"

Silence.

"You can come out now."

Nothing.

Guo Jing called again. Still no answer. He went over to the boulder where the boy had been hiding and found a shoe discarded in a nearby shrub.

Someone else was watching the fight and they've taken Penance! Guo Jing realised with horror, but when he reminded himself that defending justice and upholding righteousness were among the Quanzhen Sect's founding principles, he calmed a little. Even if the Taoists had mistaken him for a villain, surely they would not harm a child. He gathered his *qi* and raced uphill.

As Guo Jing sped through the landscape, he replayed the fight in his head and found his mood brightening. In the past decade or so, he had only sparred with his wife Lotus Huang and he missed testing himself in real combat situations. It was satisfying to know the moves he had developed were as effective as he had hoped.

The trail grew craggier the higher Guo Jing climbed. Some parts were so narrow he had to squeeze past sideways. He had been finding his way by the light of the moon, but now a mass of clouds obscured it, throwing a pall of gloom over everything. Suddenly, it occurred to Guo Jing that this would be the perfect place to set up an ambush. It was dark and he was unfamiliar with the treacherous terrain. He slowed down, his ears pricked up, listening out for any incongruous sounds.

The clouds parted. The moon cast its lustrous beams over the whole mountain range. Guo Jing had barely taken in the majestic vista when he caught the murmur of breathing in the otherwise hushed night.

Soft. Controlled. Too many overlapping inhalations and exhalations to count . . . Guo Jing pulled his belt tighter and continued onwards, pretending there was nothing amiss.

Soon, the landscape opened up and a flat, circular meadow stretched out before him. A large pond, shimmering in the silvery moonlight, lay on the far side, framed by towering peaks.

A hundred Taoist monks stood scattered across the field, garbed in the religion's traditional vesture of grey robe and yellow headgear. Their drawn swords glittered and gleamed in the half-light.

Guo Jing surveyed the men. At first sight, they seemed to be arranged haphazardly, but in fact, they were in groups of seven, in the configuration of the Heavenly Northern Dipper. He counted . . . fourteen formations altogether.

As a seasoned general who had marshalled tens of thousands of soldiers on the battlefield, Guo Jing noticed the individual units were positioned also in the pattern of the constellation, forming two composite arrays facing different directions but working in perfect synchronicity – one engaging head-on, the other ready to launch surprise attacks. He could not recall Qiu Chuji mentioning this compounding of the Northern Dipper before – it must have been a development of recent years.

This is much more sophisticated than Grandmaster Double Sun's original invention, Guo Jing thought, somewhat unnerved, as he made his approach.

A shrill whistle cut through the stillness of the night. The ninety-eight Taoists moved in different directions, reordering themselves around Guo Jing. Once in position, they regarded him in silence, their swords pointing to the ground.

Guo Jing wrapped his hand over his fist and turned in a full circle, making this sign of reverential greeting to every man present.

"I am Guo Jing from Jiangnan of the South. I have come with an earnest heart to offer my regards to Immortal Ma, Immortal Qiu and Immortal Wang. I hope the Elders will not stand in my way."

A monk with a flowing beard answered, "Sir, you have superb kung fu. Why abandon yourself to demonic companions?" His deep voice was hushed, but each character was enunciated with clarity, revealing the depths of his *neigong* power.

"Allow this humble monk to offer a word of advice," he continued. "Feminine guile has led many astray since time immemorial. Waste not the hard work of many summers and winters for one moment of pleasure.

"The Quanzhen Sect has no quarrel with you. Why come here to aid profligates in their disgraceful acts? Please turn back, so we may meet again without acrimony."

The monk's message was earnest and he seemed to genuinely hope that he could talk sense into Guo Jing.

Who do they think I am? Guo Jing was both amused and infuriated by the monk's entreaty, and he once again wished that Lotus were with him to clear up the misunderstanding.

"I know not what you are talking about. Everything will come to light if you take me to Immortal Ma and Immortal Qiu."

"If you are bent on challenging the Immortals –" the same monk again – "you must face the Heavenly Northern Dipper formation first."

"I am but one man with meagre kung fu. I would not be so bold as to pit myself against the honourable Sect's most treasured martial invention. Please release the child who has come here with me and grant me an audience with the Immortals."

"Enough of your idle talk! Chongyang Temple will not allow lechers to sully our hallowed ground!" The monk flourished his sword, the keen blade humming in the wind.

At this signal, his fellows raised their weapons. Ninety-eight swords slashed and sliced, whipping up a giant web of flashing steel.

Guo Jing eyed the two composite formations: How do I occupy two different North Star positions at the same time? While he deliberated what to do, the two battle arrays came together, weaving a net of swords so tight that even a fly would struggle to slip past.

"Show us your weapon!" the same bearded monk called. "The Quanzhen Sect does not raise its blades against unarmed men."

Guo Jing gave no reply – he was too wrapped up in figuring out a way through. So far, he was certain about two things: it would be difficult to disrupt the two battle arrays, but it would also be hard for them to hurt him.

The Heavenly Northern Dipper draws its power from aggregating the might of its fighters, Guo Jing reminded himself, revisiting the underlying principle of the formation. There will always be members with weaker kung fu. I'll get them moving and see what flaws they reveal. Thus resolved, he whirled round to face north-west, sprinted over to a unit on the periphery, made up of some of the youngest-looking monks, and pushed his palm out.

Shun the Concealed Dragon from the Eighteen Dragon-Subduing Palms.

The youths switched their swords to their left hands and thrust their right palms in unison, combining their strength. They managed to hold their own, but they were caught out when Guo Jing pulled back.

The simple act of withdrawing his force generated a powerful tug that rocked the monks' footing. All seven of them fell face down. The young men recovered swiftly, hopping upright, but their cheeks were now coloured by dirt and shame.

The bearded monk's heart contracted at the sight of his martial nephews being felled by just one move. A distinctive shrill call issued from his lips, and all fourteen Northern Dippers were roused into action. Overlapping, linking up, joining forces. Surely their opponent could not possibly topple all ninety-eight of them even if his strength waxed tenfold.

This next phase of the conflict reminded Guo Jing of the time he was attacked at the Beggar Clan Assembly on the Jun Hill island in Dongting Lake. The vagrants were tricked into believing that he and Lotus had killed their chief, Count Seven Hong. Hundreds of them linked arms and formed walls of bodies, trapping the pair and trying to push them off a cliff. Individually, the beggars were unremarkable fighters, but when they joined hands, they were impossible to repel. Guo Jing had not wanted to use brute force then, nor did he wish to resort to it now. He had no choice but to flit between formations with his fastest *qinggong* to search for weak points.

Dashing east and leaping west, Guo Jing instigated changes in the array with each step he took. In a matter of moments, he had seen enough to know that he had little hope of besting this enhanced version of the Heavenly Northern Dipper without causing harm. Each group was so tightly interwoven with the next that he could spot no deficiencies at all. If there were any, he was not perceptive or quick-thinking enough to identify them in such a short time.

Steel shimmered under the glistening moon. Shadows surged like waves, here and there, back and forth, without ceasing, without end. The ground between each unit was fast closing up and it was getting harder for Guo Jing to find an opening to sprint through. He reminded himself why he had come: he was on his way to Chongyang Temple to find Penance and seek an audience with the Immortals to clear up this misunderstanding. His eyes lighted on a suite of grand halls surrounded by smaller structures on a slope to the west.

That must be Chongyang Temple, he said to himself, darting eastwards in a burst of blinding speed. Then, without warning, he changed direction and sprinted towards the distant buildings.

The sudden acceleration reduced Guo Jing to a grey blur in the Taoists' peripheral vision, whizzing past like a shooting star or a flash of lightning, a dizzying sight that left their heads spinning.

"Watch out for the lecher's trickery!" the bearded monk cried as the Northern Dipper ground to an uncertain halt.

Guo Jing seethed with rage to hear himself besmirched again. What if the slander took root in the *jianghu*? Then it struck him that this same monk had been addressing him and giving commands . . .

He's the leader! If I take him out, the others will falter. Guo Jing turned on his heels and headed straight for the principal monk, his palms poised to strike. But within half a dozen steps, he sensed the presence of men at his back and the units on the flanks were also coming uncomfortably close. He realised he had run headlong into a trap laid to lure him into the thick of the fray, with the bearded commander as bait. He was now beset from every direction. Swivelling to the right, he found fourteen swords thrusting at him in synchrony, each blade perfectly positioned, their sharp points leaving no room for manoeuvre.

"Why do you strike to kill?" The Taoists' heedless aggression was goading Guo Jing into a fit of temper. "Aren't you monks supposed to hold compassion close to your hearts – whoever you believe me to be? You claim you won't raise your blades against an unarmed man, and then try to take my life?"

Before his words could fade into the air, Guo Jing threw himself to one side in a towering leap, his right foot raised in a flying kick and his left hand poised to strike.

A Taoist flipped over in a somersault, his sword now in Guo Jing's grasp. His companions came to his rescue, thrusting six blades in unison at Guo Jing's right flank. He twirled his steel and sliced once. *Claaaaang!* All six Taoist swords snapped in two, but there was not even a dent on the one in Guo Jing's hand.

The swords were standard issue of the same quality, but Guo Jing had channelled his *neigong* strength into his blade, allowing it to cleave through the metal in its path.

A sickly, earthen hue coloured the men's cheeks.

While they stood stupefied, two neighbouring units closed in, swords at the ready. Each monk put their hand on the shoulder of the brother to their left, the energies of fourteen men physically joined as one.

Guo Jing's competitive spirits were roused. This was a chance to test the depths of his inner strength. He brandished his steel, striking down at the blade closest to him, at one end of the human chain, pinning it to the ground.

The Taoist tried to pull free, but his weapon was stuck, it would not budge even by a hair's breadth, as though it had been welded to a heavy bronze cauldron or a huge iron slab. His brothers-in-arms mustered what internal power they could and passed it on through their physical link.

This was the moment Guo Jing was waiting for, all fourteen working together to counter the force he was exerting on the blade. When he sensed the tugging on his sword hand reach its peak, he roared, "Watch out!" and made a flourish with his right arm.

Claaack . . . Twelve swords snapped and two arced into the sky. The monks jumped back in shock and horror.

Guo Jing let out a sigh, disappointed that he had failed to shatter the furthest two swords, and made a note to focus more on honing his control of his *neigong* when training.

The two formations, nonetheless, were not disrupted. The disarmed men were just as adept with their palms, whipping up an interlocking maelstrom to keep Guo Jing at bay. The battle array was not diminished by the loss of twenty-one swords – if anything, it was more potent than before, as the Taoists were treating their foe with greater caution and weighed each move with more care.

Fearing that he would be trapped if he dallied any longer, Guo Jing decided it was time to take the initiative. "Elders, please let me through – if not, you'll have to excuse my brusqueness."

The bearded monk curled his lips into a sneer. You won't break out even if you snap every single one of our swords! He urged his martial kinsmen to close in on their foe, confident that he had exhausted his kung fu and they would soon have the upper hand.

Hunching low, Guo Jing put his warning into action, striking hard for the north-east. Two units from the south-west were shadowing him and he turned his blade on them with a flick of his wrist.

The sword's point twinkled like a star in the wintry night sky, swift as lightning, intangible as the wind, as precise as a secret throwing needle.

Fourteen consecutive stings of the sword, pricking each Taoist on the Yang Valley pressure point on the outside of their right wrist. The monks' grips slackened at the fleeting numbness and their weapons clattered to the ground. They leapt back in fright to examine their forearms. A tiny red mark on the skin, no blood drawn. They were awed by the man's extraordinary control. He could have easily cut their hands clean off, if he had so desired – instead, he had applied just enough inner strength to trigger the acupoints, making sure the blade did not even pierce their skin.

Thirty-five swords lay broken or discarded. For the bearded monk leading the formation, this was a grave humiliation, especially as their enemy had shown such restraint. It would be a disaster if he managed to force his way into Chongyang Temple.

We'll hem you in and crush you to death, the Taoist vowed silently, signalling for his brethren to draw in closer.

Noting the surge of aggression in the air, Guo Jing gathered himself for another lightning assault. He had grown tired of the monks' needless belligerence and decided to give them the thrashing they deserved.

A fresh unit of seven rushed forward to head him off, and Guo Jing made straight for its North Star position. A second squad hastened over. He darted towards them using lightness kung fu and came to rest at their North Star. Another group swooped in. He shifted again, his feet a blur of motion.

It was impossible to occupy the pivotal position for each of the fourteen formations at once, but his raw speed made up for that lack, as he raced from one to the next, spinning the individual arrays around in the process.

Confusion was mounting. The bearded monk ordered his men to draw back and hold their positions.

Guo Jing was impressed that their commander had seen through his attempt to plunge them into chaos by occupying as many North Stars as he could in the shortest space of time. But now that the formations were spread out and there was more room to manoeuvre, he saw his chance to bolt for Chongyang Temple. As he looked towards the buildings scattered on the hillside, flashes of steel and silver caught his eye. He was too far away to make out much more than vague silhouettes and the faintest sounds of battle, but it was clear they were under attack.

Who would be reckless enough to besiege the Quanzhen Sect in their own mountain stronghold? As Guo Jing was asking himself that question, it struck him that the Taoists must have been anticipating an attack given their state of readiness – the formation he was facing had surely not been mobilised for the sake of one unarmed man. He was desperate to get to the temple to find out what was happening, but the fourteen Northern Dippers were advancing once more, drawing an ever-tightening snare around him.

Anxious to break free, Guo Jing conjured a Dragon in the Field with his left hand and a Haughty Dragon Repents with his right, using the Competing Hands method. But at the last second, he switched them round. Now, a Dragon in the Field was hurtling at the men on his right and a Haughty Dragon Repents was flying at those on his left.

The Taoists could not believe their eyes. They had never come across an opponent who could launch two distinct kung fu moves simultaneously. And to reverse them at the vital moment? Inconceivable!

Each wing had braced itself for the attack it had expected. But now their preparations were confounded, and they could not readjust quickly enough to counter the flow of energy.

This was the result Guo Jing was hoping for. With a sudden burst of speed, he darted through the closing gap between the two halves of the grand formation.

The Taoists were well drilled, but they were by no means equals in kung fu or reaction times. Now the slightest lapse in their cohesion proved telling as they fought to withstand the collective momentum propelling the two wings towards each other.

Paaaaang! Two sides clashed. A third of the monks tumbled in a heap of tangled limbs, their noses swollen, their eyes blackened.

The bearded commander avoided the clash by the skin of his teeth, the close encounter sending a surge of hot blood to his heart. He bellowed orders through short, ragged breaths, screaming at his men to get to their feet and regain formation. To be so rattled by the fight was unbecoming of his rank, not just because he needed to be cool-headed in the heat of battle, but because his state of mind ran counter to the Taoist philosophy – attaining peace through inaction and overcoming the firm with suppleness – that underlined Quanzhen kung fu.

By now, Guo Jing had shot clear of the formation and reached the banks of Jade Purity Pond. He cut himself a robust branch from a willow tree and tossed the sword away. Then he hurled the leafy bough out over the surface of the water and flexed his foot, launching himself into the air. When he passed over the soaring branch, he stretched out his right leg and used it as leverage to vault to the far side of the pond.

The leading monk, meanwhile, had been urging his brethren to give chase. They charged full pelt after Guo Jing, but he was already airborne by the time they reached the pond and they ran out of ground to pull back. *Plop plop plop plop* . . . the first half of the formation plunged into the water and those behind stumbled and tripped over their sodden brothers.

CHAPTER FOUR

THE QUANZHEN SECT

I

GUO JING WAS RACING UP THE PATH TO CHONGYANG TEMPLE using his fastest lightness *qinggong* when an urgent tolling of bells tore through the night air.

Bong bong bong bong bong . . .

Alarums! He summoned his *qi* and wrung more speed out of his legs. Up ahead, flames were climbing high into the sky over the monastery. At his back, the Taoist monks swarmed after him, dripping wet and keening with rage.

Guo Jing at last understood why the Quanzhen disciples were being so hostile – they must have assumed he was part of the attacking force. But the monks pursuing him were not his concern right now. He was honour bound to offer help in Chongyang Temple's time of need.

In mere moments, he had covered dozens of *zhang*, bringing him to the outer reaches of the religious house.

By now, a thick pall of black smoke shrouded the entire complex. The hungry fire licked and spluttered, eager to consume everything in its path. It had already ripped through a dozen or so smaller buildings on the fringes, but the main halls, for the time being, were unaffected.

A clamour rose from the heart of the temple. Bellowing voices, clashing steel – the tumult of battle. Guo Jing scaled a high wall for a better vantage point. In the large courtyard below, hundreds were engaged in a fierce melee. The Quanzhen Taoists in their identical reddish-yellow robes caught his eye at once. He counted seven individual Northern Dipper formations, surrounded by an enemy force almost three times their number.

The invaders, all expert fighters, did not appear to be a unified cohort. Men of wildly differing physiques – tall, short, thin, stout – attacked with a variety of kung fu and weapons, dressed in garments from diverse regions, with some even charging empty-handed.

The monks were overwhelmed, but their close cohesion allowed them to maintain a tight defence, whereas their opponents were fighting as individuals, with no thought for anyone else.

Guo Jing was about to make himself known when he heard a sharp whooshing of air coming from inside the hall on the far side of the courtyard. It was a sound he associated with the most formidable of kung fu strikes. Whoever was duelling in there must be far more skilful than those fighting below. He leapt down from the wall and made his way across the square.

With a swerve to the east and a dart to the west, Guo Jing slipped past three Northern Dippers. The monks eyed him with great alarm, but the battle was so intense they could not tear themselves away from the rest of the invaders to check his progress.

GUO JING stole inside the hall. A dozen giant wax lights were burning within, but their glow was feeble compared to the red-hot flames devouring the surrounding buildings.

Seven monks sat cross-legged on prayer mats. Each had one palm raised against the dozen or so men attacking them, while the other hand was placed on the shoulder of the comrade to their right.

Guo Jing recognised three of the Taoists immediately – the Quanzhen Immortals Ma Yu, Qiu Chuji and Wang Chuyi. The other four were younger, and he could only name Qiu's student, Harmony Yin.

They were seated according to the Heavenly Northern Dipper formation. On the floor before them, a white-haired man, also garbed in the same amber habit, lay face down, unmoving.

From where Guo Jing was standing, he could not tell who this elderly Taoist was or whether he was still alive, but the sight was enough to send his blood roiling in his breast.

"How dare you befoul the Chongyang Temple!" he roared, grabbing the two fighters closest to him by the backs of their robes. He had intended to lift them up and toss them away from the fight, but they were more competent than he had expected, their anchorage so firm it was as if their feet were nailed to the floor. He let go and aimed a sweeping kick at their ankles instead.

The men had responded to the initial attack by grounding their footing with the Thousand *Jin* Load technique, but when the upward pull suddenly disappeared, they lost their balance and the kick sent them flying out of the hall.

"Who are you?" A pair of assailants lunged at Guo Jing, their hostility failing to mask their unease at the newcomer's obvious skill when compared to their own martial capability.

Whoo-oosh! Guo Jing thrust both palms in answer, throwing the men back before they could get near. They slammed into a wall, blood spurting from their lips.

The affray came to a standstill. None of the invaders were willing to take Guo Jing on. Meanwhile, Ma Yu and his martial brethren sighed in relief, thankful to have been delivered from the present danger.

Guo Jing fell to his knees and bowed before the Quanzhen Immortals. "Your student has come to pay his respects."

"Watch out!" Harmony Yin shouted as his martial seniors – Ma Yu,

Qiu Chuji and Wang Chuyi – returned the salutation with a nod and a smile.

Guo Jing was aware of the air stirring at the back of his head, but he had remained in a kneeling position, waiting for the attackers to steal close. He pressed his elbows against the floor and vaulted up into the air. The men shot under him, allowing him to knee them in the back at the Gate of the Soul acupoint as he descended. They sprawled face down, acting as his landing mat.

"Rise, my dear Guo Jing," Ma Yu said to his former student, who was prostrating himself once more. "Your kung fu has improved vastly in the past decade."

"Elder, I beg your guidance on what to do with these men," Guo Jing said as he straightened up.

An eerie laugh rang through the hall, cutting short Ma Yu's reply.

Guo Jing spun round to find two men standing right behind him.

One was a gaunt middle-aged Buddhist monk who wore a gold coronet on his head. He was wrapped in red vestments of the style seen in Mongolia. His companion was younger, around thirty years of age. Dressed in a pale yellow brocade robe, with a folding fan in his hand, he was the picture of a wealthy, educated man of gentle birth. However, the haughty, vicious glint in his eye jarred with his attire and the image he was trying to project. Both men carried themselves with an air of solemnity that set them apart from the rest of their horde.

Guo Jing cupped his hands politely. "May I ask with whom am I speaking? What business has brought you here?"

"Who are you?" The high-born man spoke Chinese with an accent that was not of the Central Plains.

"I am a student of these Masters."

"Is that so? I did not expect to find such a character among the Quanzhen monks."

Riled by the man's condescending tone, Guo Jing decided against explaining that he was not a formal disciple. "May I ask what your quarrel is with the Quanzhen Sect? Why did you raise this force and set fire to the temple?"

"A junior has no place in this parley," the man said dismissively.

Guo Jing fumbled for a response.

Smiling, the man flicked open his fan then snapped it shut. "These men are here at my bidding, it's true." He took a step forward. "If you can withstand thirty of my kung fu moves, I will spare these old cow muzzles. What say you?"

The hall was growing hotter. It would not be long before the blaze claimed this part of the temple too. Guo Jing reached out his right hand and grabbed the folding fan, pulling it towards him.

The man swayed, but he managed to cling onto the fan while maintaining his foothold.

Guo Jing had not anticipated this level of martial sophistication. The man's internal energy flow reminded him of his long-ago duels with Lama Supreme Wisdom from Kokonor.

He's probably trained under the Vajra Buddhist martial tradition too, Guo Jing told himself, but he's more agile than the heavyset lama.

Then it struck him how cold the fan felt in his hand.

The frame is made of steel. It's a weapon!

Guo Jing tightened his grip and sent forth a stronger burst of *neigong* power.

"Let go!"

The man turned puce, but, within a breath, his complexion appeared normal again.

Guo Jing could tell the man had rallied all his inner strength to resist that attack. He weighed his next move. If I put in more force and make his face turn purple three more times, I'll be able to overpower him, but I'll do grievous damage to his organs . . .

Smiling, he loosened his grasp. The fan now lay across his open palm, but it still retained the internal power from the man's attempt to wrench it back. Still smiling, Guo Jing injected an additional spurt of *neigong* pushing in the same direction. The combined strength upset the man's balance, compelling him to take a step backwards. If Guo Jing had exerted a fraction more force, he would have been sent flying.

The man flushed crimson when his opponent let go of the fan, because he understood that a superior martial artist had chosen to spare him the humiliation of a crushing defeat before his followers. He leapt back, his arms hanging by his sides, and said in a courteous tone, "I'd be honoured to learn your name."

"My lowly name is not worth the mention, but Immortal Ma, Immortal Qiu and Immortal Wang are among my teachers."

The man doubted the veracity of these words. He was fairly confident that he could defeat any of the Quanzhen monks – including the Immortals – in single combat, having exchanged blows with many of them over the course of the day. How could a student outshine his mentors so? He ran his eye up and down Guo Jing. An honest, open face, rough-spun clothes, nothing exceptional about his bearing. And yet, this man, who looked just like any common peasant, concealed martial depths that were impossible to fathom.

"This inconsequential one bows to your most astonishing kung fu," the man said to Guo Jing. "I hope, in a decade's time, I will have the chance to learn from you again. Now, allow me to bid you farewell – I have some unfinished business to attend to." He touched his hands together in a sign of respect.

Guo Jing returned the obeisance. "In ten years, then."

The man turned to leave, but stopped before he stepped over the threshold of the hall. "I trust the Quanzhen Sect will honour this promise and live by the saying, 'Sweep the snow outside one's doorway,' staying away from my private affairs." He was referring to an established *jianghu* custom: when one party conceded and a date for a rematch was set, it was considered dishonourable for either side to raise their fists before the appointed time.

"Of course," Guo Jing agreed readily.

But Qiu Chuji bellowed at the same time, "I won't wait ten years!"

The roof tiles rattled at this thunderous demonstration of internal strength and the man's ears rang painfully. Had the old Taoist been holding back? The possibility made his heart skip a beat and he hotfooted it outside without further ado. The red-clad Buddhist shot

Guo Jing a glare as he marched after his companion, and the remaining fighters hurried out too.

The Quanzhen Taoists rushed up to their silver-haired kinsman on the floor. Guo Jing could now see that he was Infinite Peace Hao Datong and understood why Ma Yu had chosen to stage the Northern Dipper formation sitting down – even when threatened by powerful enemies and an encroaching fire – for that was the only way to protect his injured martial brother.

The Taoist's cheeks were waxen and bloodless. His eyes were screwed tight. Guo Jing could barely detect his breathing. Untying the man's robes, he found a dark purple handprint on the pallid skin on his chest, the splayed fingers clearly imprinted.

The horrifying mark confirmed what Guo Jing had already deduced – the perpetrator had been trained in the Vajra Buddhist tradition. He was relieved to see that, unlike Lama Supreme Wisdom's Five Finger Blade kung fu, which had almost killed Immortal Wang Chuyi back in the Jin capital all those years ago, this Great Seal strike contained no poison, though the inner strength behind it was more fearsome than that mustered by the lama.

Guo Jing then took Hao Datong's wrist and was assured to find a robust pulse. Decades of *neigong* cultivation according to the orthodox Quanzhen method had preserved the monk's vitals.

2

THE FIRE WAS GETTING CLOSER AND ITS HEAT WAS GROWING palpable inside the hall.

"We need to get out of here," Qiu Chuji said as he lifted Hao Datong in his arms.

"Where's Penance?" Guo Jing asked.

"Who?"

"The boy who journeyed here with me."

"I'm here, Uncle Guo!" Penance called as he slid down from a pillar.

"Were you on the roof all this time?"

"These stinky mon—"

"Hush!" Guo Jing warned. "Bow to your Grandmasters."

Penance made a face and kowtowed to Ma Yu, Qiu Chuji and Wang Chuyi. But when he came before Harmony Yin, who appeared to be the same age as Guo Jing, he muttered, "I don't think I need to—"

"This is Martial Uncle Yin," Guo Jing cut him off.

With reluctance, Penance touched his forehead on the ground and then stood up, refusing to genuflect to the remaining Taoists.

"Penance!"

"It'll be too late if I bow to everyone."

"What do you mean?"

"There's a monk tied up in a room. The fire will get to him if we don't move now."

"Where is this room?"

"That one, I think." Penance pointed east with a giggle.

Harmony Yin eyed the youngster warily before rushing to the side chamber and kicking its doors down. Empty. He then dashed to the next room he could think of in the same direction, the Chamber of Tranquillity where the fourth-generation disciples practised their internal kung fu. He threw the doors open. Through the dense smoke he could make out the outline of a man in Quanzhen habit tied to a bedpost, gasping noisily for air. He cut the ropes and carried his martial kinsman to safety.

AFTER MA Yu and his martial brothers had carried the injured Hao Datong from the hall, they led Guo Jing and Penance to the closest high ground to assess the situation.

The rear portion of the monastery was aflame. The fire flickered its red-hot tongues defiantly at the observers, turning the sky a fierce crimson. There was but one water source on site, a small spring providing just enough for everyday drinking and cooking needs. It could not quench a conflagration on this scale.

There was little Ma Yu and his brethren could do but watch the temple burn. They watched the hungry flames devour the majestic buildings. They watched the timber beams and pillars crack and crumble in the heat and the roof tiles crash to the ground. They watched everything touched by the fire reduced to char and ash. Ma Yu, being the most phlegmatic among the Quanzhen Immortals, was unperturbed by the devastation before him, whereas the hot-headed Qiu Chuji, who had not mellowed with age, ground his teeth and hissed curses at the raging blaze.

Guo Jing was on the point of asking Ma Yu about the attackers when he saw Harmony Yin approach, half-carrying the man he had just rescued. The monk, rather portly in build, was still suffering from his ordeal, coughing and spluttering on the smoke in his lungs, but the instant his watery eyes lighted on Penance, a burst of energy came to him and he lunged.

Penance dashed behind Guo Jing with a chuckle. The inflamed Taoist, bent on catching the boy, shoved Guo Jing in the chest, but it was as if he had thrown his weight against a wall. The man did not even sway, let alone give way. The monk jabbed his finger at the boy and yelled, "You little bastard!"

"Qingdu!" A stern warning from Wang Chuyi.

Lu Qingdu was so blinded with rage at the sight of Penance that he had not noticed he was in the presence of the most senior Quanzhen Masters.

"Your student deserves to die for his trespasses," the plump monk mumbled apologetically. He collected himself and stood with his head lowered, his arms hanging by his sides. He could feel a cold sweat breaking out, dampening his undershirt.

"What has happened?" Wang Chuyi enquired.

"Grandmaster, your inept student accepts his punishment."

Wang Chuyi regarded Lu Qingdu with a frown and asked again, "What has taken place?"

"Oh, yes . . . your student was on guard duty in the rear quarters, when *Shifu* brought this little basta-b-boy and charged me to watch over him. *Shifu* said he had come to the Zhongnan Mountains with our enemies. I took him to the Chamber of Tranquillity, then the ba-b-boy said he needed to relieve himself. I never imagined a mere child would be able to give us the slip, so I brought him to the latrine and freed his hands. He sat there, pretended to do his business, then, suddenly, he jumped up, grabbed the chamber pot and upended its foul contents over me—"

Penance's raucous giggle interrupted Lu Qingdu.

"Why are you so merry?"

The youngster tilted his head back to admire the reddened sky. "I'm in good humour." He beamed. "Have you got a problem?"

"Quarrel not with the child," Wang Chuyi cut in before Lu Qingdu could offer a rejoinder. "Continue with your account."

"Yes, Grandmaster, yes . . . I jumped out of the way and the boy laughed, saying, 'Oh no, Master Taoist, I've dirtied your clothes.'" The monk squeezed the muscles in his throat to imitate Penance's boyish high-pitched voice.

Wang Chuyi furrowed his brow at the absurd noise coming from Lu Qingdu, aghast that his disciple's student was making such a spectacle of himself, while the others tried to hide their amusement.

Unaware of the effect his role-playing had had on the gathering, Lu Qingdu continued. "I was livid, so I lunged, determined to beat some sense into the boy. He tossed more night soil at me, and I launched into a Retreating Rapids to avoid it.

"The filth made me lose my footing, but I quickly recovered my balance. However, in that moment, the wretched sneak stole my sword and, the next thing I knew, its point was pressed against my chest, and the little bast-b-boy threatened to run me through if I moved. Since no man of virtue would knowingly walk into harm, I did as he said. When we were back in the Chamber of Tranquillity, he tied me to the bedpost, then cut a strip from my robe and stuffed it in my mouth.

"I was left in the room, gagged and bound. The fire was creeping closer. If not for Martial Uncle Yin, I'd have been burned alive – all because of this *boy*!" Lu Qingdu finished his account with a glower at Penance.

The monks and Guo Jing looked between the skinny half-grown child and the burly martial man. Their contrasting physiques and abilities made the tale even more ridiculous, and a ripple of laughter broke out.

Lu Qingdu scratched his ears and rubbed his face, feeling so mortified that he knew not where to put his arms and his legs. He was thoroughly baffled as to why they had found his ordeal funny.

Ma Yu was the first to collect himself, asking Guo Jing with a smile, "He's your son, isn't he? He has rather taken after his mother – sharp-witted and mischievous."

"Penance is the posthumous son of my sworn brother Yang Kang."

Qiu Chuji's heart tightened at the mention of the only disciple he ever took beyond the walls of Chongyang Temple. Even now, he was overwhelmed with remorse each time he thought of Yang Kang, for he believed it was thanks to his failings as a teacher that the young man had turned out to be such an ingrate. When Yang Kang had discovered the man who raised him, the Jin Prince Wanyan Honglie, was not merely his homeland's oppressor but also responsible for his true parents' tragic fate, he had continued to think of the Prince as his father rather than sacrifice riches and rank. That ultimately led him down a path of no return.

The Taoist was pleased to learn that Yang Kang had an heir, but sorrow jostled for dominance over his emotions when he recalled the young man's undoing. He studied Penance's face, noting the resemblance around the eyes and the brows, and asked question after question about the boy's life.

Guo Jing gave a brief account of Penance's early years and explained that they had travelled here in the hope that the boy could learn kung fu from the Quanzhen Sect.

"Why don't you teach him yourself?" The request perplexed Qiu Chuji. "Your martial learning far surpasses ours."

"Before we discuss Penance's education, I would first like to beg the Elders for forgiveness. I am most distressed to have caused offence to many of my Taoist brethren on our way here earlier today." Guo Jing then recounted how the monks had tried to stop him from ascending the Zhongnan Mountains, mistaking him for their enemy.

"You are one of us. Apologies are not needed," Ma Yu said, his tone earnest and warm. "Your timely arrival delivered the Quanzhen Sect from certain doom."

"So that was how they breached our defences with such ease!" Qiu Chuji remarked, his sword-sharp brows knitting close together. "I put Zhijing in charge, and that imbecile couldn't even tell friend from foe, leading the formations against you!" Bristling with rage, he sent an aide hurrying for a report on how they could have made such a mistake.

Two petrified monks soon came before the group. "Brother Feng and Brother Wei were . . . tasked with keeping watch at the Temple of Pervading Light," one of them began haltingly. "They sent word back that this . . . Hero Guo struck the stone stele . . . and that he . . . he must be with our enemies."

Guo Jing found it incredible that this simple action had caused the misunderstanding. "I was moved by the Elder's poem and struck the plaque it was carved on . . . Who were these men anyway? Why did they attack Chongyang Temple?"

"It's a long story," Qiu Chuji sighed. "Follow me and I'll show you." With a nod to Ma Yu and Wang Chuyi, he headed further up the mountain.

"Stay here with your Grandmasters," Guo Jing said to Penance. "I'll be back soon."

3

WALKING WITH QIU CHUJI, GUO JING MARVELLED AT HOW THE passing of time had had such little effect on the Taoist. His gait was as firm, steady and effortless as the last time they had crossed paths, more than a dozen years before.

Qiu Chuji stopped when they had scaled the tallest peak towering over the temple. "There's a poem set on the other side of this rock."

The new day had yet to break and there was not enough light to make out the writing, so Guo Jing put his hand on the granite, tracing the indentations with his finger and piecing the poem together slowly, character by character.

> His heart set on bringing down the Qin,
> Zifang forsook his pride to learn from the old and wise.
> Saving his liege from ambush and helping to found the Han,
> Towering and upright, he, a pillar holding up the heavens.
> The realm secured, he departed with a swirl of his robe,
> With the Red Pine Immortal, he wandered and roamed.
> Men extraordinary and tomes exceptional,
> The maker of things would not bestow them blithely.
>
> When Chongyang established the Quanzhen,
> Wide he strode, setting his sights high.
> Strapping, with the bearing of heroes,
> He grasped the chance to seize and conquer.
> Reflecting on mistakes of an absurd past,
> Reining in the heart in the Tomb of the Living Dead,
> Rumour had it when he first set foot on the Way,
> The two Immortals over here met.
> And now under the Zhongnan Mountains,
> On mist and smoke, towers and halls glide.

When Guo Jing reached the final few words, it struck him that the turn and flow of the strokes were fitting the rounded tip of his finger with uncanny precision, as if a bare hand, rather than a chisel, had made the impressions.

"Was this inscribed with a finger?" he wondered out loud.

"Yes, it was," Qiu Chuji replied. "I'm sure you have discerned the differing calligraphy? This poem was set down by two extraordinary figures of the *wulin*. The remarkable Master who wrote the first eight lines was an expert in both the martial and the literary arts – the sort of astonishing talent who only emerges once in a century."

"Would the Elder be able to make an introduction?"

"I never had the honour of meeting the Master. Come, sit down, I'll tell you how this relates to today's events."

Guo Jing leaned against the rock, his eyes on the fading fire and his mind back at Peach Blossom Island. If only Lotus was here, he mused. She loves a good story.

"Did you understand the poem?" Qiu Chuji asked, as if Guo Jing was still the unworldly eighteen-year-old he first met.

"The opening recounts the story of the statesman Zhang Liang, am I right? Lotus has told me about him before. If I recall correctly, Zifang was his courtesy name, and one of the best-known episodes in his life was his chance encounter with an old man on a bridge.

"This old fellow threw his shoe over the side, ordered Zhang Liang to climb down to fetch it, then made the young man stoop and put the shoe back on for him. When Zhang Liang set his pride aside and complied with the demands, the ancient was so impressed that he gifted him a book on warfare and tactics. Zhang Liang went on to help Gaozu Emperor of Han found his kingdom and unite China. He then left the court and his position of power to live as a recluse and to travel with the Immortal Red Pine.

"I can tell the second part of the poem covered events from Grandmaster Chongyang's life, but I fear I don't quite grasp the meaning."

"What do you know about him?"

Guo Jing paused, wondering why Qiu Chuji would ask such an obvious question. "He is the Elder's *shifu*, founder of the Quanzhen Sect and the Greatest Martial Master Under the Heavens at the original Contest of Mount Hua."

"Yes, but what can you tell me about his youth?"

Guo Jing shook his head.

> "*Strapping, with the bearing of heroes,*
> *He grasped the chance to seize and conquer.*"

Qiu Chuji quoted two lines from the poem to illustrate his point.

"*Shifu* was not born to monastic life. He trained first in scholarly subjects before turning to the martial arts and becoming the hero and great man known to the *jianghu*.

"At the time, the Song Empire was plagued by Jurchen invaders. *Shifu* raised the banner of resistance, to stop the Jin from destroying our fields and killing our people. He also took back some of the territories seized, making admirable progress in the Central Plains, but the Song court sought only to appease, so the emboldened Jin forces marched back and forth unchecked.

"Alas, in time, *Shifu* was dragged down by defeat after defeat, many of his followers and fellow fighters dead or maimed. Disheartened, *Shifu* renounced the world and pledged himself to the ascetic life. He called himself the Living Dead and moved into an ancient tomb in these mountains. It was his way of making his resolve known – though alive, he was dead inside – and he absolutely refused to live under the same blue sky as the plunderers of our lands.

"*Shifu*'s friends and brothers-in-arms did try to persuade him to come out and continue their struggle against the Jin, but he was so disenchanted that he could not face his *jianghu* associates and stayed stubbornly below ground.

"In the eighth year of his self-imposed exile, a rival of *Shifu*'s came to the Tomb and hurled abuse for seven days and seven nights. *Shifu* was provoked into accepting the challenge, but instead of fists, kicks and sharp blades, it was sniggers and a sardonic voice that assailed him: 'Now you've come outside, stay outside.'

"*Shifu* realised his foe had not come to fight, but to goad him into leaving the Tomb, so his martial talent would not go to waste.

Friendship took root and the former competitors roved the rivers and lakes together."

"Who was this Master?" Guo Jing was intrigued. "He wasn't one of the Greats, was he?"

"The Master was more gifted in the martial arts than the Heretic, the Venom, the Beggar and the King . . . but because she was a woman, she was rarely seen in public and very few knew of her existence or her name . . ." Qiu Chuji heaved a sigh. "Their rivalry was the Master's way of maintaining a connection with *Shifu*. She was in fact very fond of him, but neither her pride nor the conventions of the time allowed her to be the first to reveal her feelings.

"*Shifu* in time learned of her heart's plight, but his was already pledged to the country's lost lands. You know the age-old question, 'How can one set up home before the invaders are vanquished?' So, he feigned ignorance, and in the Master's eyes, his response was a slight on her person and she felt increasingly aggrieved. Enmity once again dominated their relationship as her love turned sour, and she proposed a contest in the Zhongnan Mountains.

"It goes without saying that *Shifu* never wished to come to blows with the Master, but his reticence to engage inflamed her. She said to him, 'You hold back because you think little of my skills!' and after that, he had no choice but to raise his fists.

"Thousands of moves were exchanged here, on this summit, but a winner could not be discerned. The Master was furious because *Shifu* did not draw on the true depths of his power. 'What am I to you? Don't I deserve a wholehearted fight?'

"*Shifu* did not know how to answer her questions. He was unwilling to use more force, so he made a suggestion: 'Since we can't decide on a champion in a martial contest, why don't we compete on letters?' To which she replied, 'Fine! If I lose, I'll no more befoul your eyes and ears.' Then *Shifu* asked, 'And if you win?' The Master's cheeks flushed crimson, and after a short pause, she mumbled, 'Let me live in the Tomb of the Living Dead.'

"Her answer troubled *Shifu*, for he knew she meant to live with him in the Tomb, and if he wished to avoid further entanglements, he would have to win outright. So, he asked her to define the contest, but she seemed uncertain and said, 'We are both tired, let's return to this tomorrow evening.'

"At dusk the next day, they came to this crag again and the Master set out the rules. 'If I lose, I shall slit my throat here, before you, and needless to say, it will be the last you see of me. If I win, you will let me live in the Tomb of the Living Dead and heed my every word for life; if you refuse to oblige, then take monastic vows – Buddhist, Taoist, it matters not – but you must also promise to build a temple here, in these mountains, and keep me company for ten years.'

"The Master did not present *Shifu* with an easy choice. Of course, winning was out of the question. *Shifu* could never contemplate being the cause of her death. But, if he lost, he would either have to marry her, or become a monk and never unite with any woman in matrimony, and on top of that, he would also have to remain in these mountains for ten years.

"*Shifu* was touched by the devotion of someone as exceptional as the Master, and he could not explain why he had never felt their destinies would entwine as man and wife. It took *Shifu* some time to reconcile himself to the future that had been mapped out for him, but in the end he agreed to her terms, knowing that he would admit defeat.

"The Master then explained how they would compete. 'We will take turns to carve characters on this rock using just our fingertip.' *Shifu* found the suggestion incredulous and asked, 'How is that possible?' The Master then elaborated, 'It's a simple test of our finger kung fu, to see who can make a deeper impression.' *Shifu* shook his head and said, 'It's beyond what human strength is capable of.' But the Master seemed to believe otherwise. 'What if I can? Will you concede?'

"Now, *Shifu* was certain that flesh and bone could not chisel through stone, and if a winner could not be determined, the contest could be set aside, so he said, 'If you can perform such a feat, I'll happily yield; but if you can't, then we are equals and we won't compete again.'

"The Master pulled a wry smile and said, 'You're destined to be a monk then.' She ran her left hand over the surface of the rock, speaking half to herself. 'What should I set down? Among the heroes who cast off their earthly shackles, Zhang Zifang has to be the foremost. He resisted tyranny but sought not rank or riches. He was a progenitor of people like you.'

"With those words, she placed her right forefinger on the boulder and began to write. Wherever she touched, the rock crumbled. She carved character after character into the hard surface, and that was the first half of the poem.

"*Shifu* vacated the Tomb of the Living Dead that very night and in the morning he took the vows of a Taoist monk. He built a small shrine near the Tomb, and that structure, in time, grew into Chongyang Temple."

Guo Jing ran his hand over the characters, stroke by stroke, feeling how the fingertip had shaped the rock in ways no chisel could.

"Her kung fu is incredible," he muttered in awe.

Guo Jing's reaction made Qiu Chuji guffaw. "Well, she fooled *Shifu* and the two of us, but your wife wouldn't be taken in."

"It's a trick?" The younger man's eyes widened.

"What is the greatest kung fu that employs the finger?"

"It has to be Yang in Ascendance."

"Do you think Reverend Sole Light can carve words on wood with that technique? No, certainly not. Then how did the Master manage it? That was a question that haunted *Shifu*. When your father-in-law Apothecary Huang came to visit him, *Shifu* thought perhaps the sharpest of his contemporaries might have an idea.

"The Lord of Peach Blossom Island retreated into his thoughts for a long while after hearing *Shifu*'s tale, then burst out laughing, and said, 'I have yet to fully master this kung fu, but I will show you when I return in one moon's time.'

"Lord Huang came back a month later as he had promised and *Shifu* brought him here. He put his left hand on the rock and felt its surface for quite some time before he began to write. *Shifu* was astounded to see Lord Huang's finger making a deep impression, especially as he knew the man's kung fu was less developed than his, and as such, he could not possibly summon sufficient power to his hand. His mind ablaze with questions, *Shifu* tapped his finger against the rock, and, to his surprise, he pierced the stony surface with little effort." Qiu Chuji took Guo Jing's hand to show him the mark. "Right here."

Guo Jing was amazed to find his finger slipping into a cavity that fitted as if it were moulded around it. He gathered his inner strength and pushed, thinking the rock might be more porous than it appeared, but all he managed was to give himself a jolt of pain without making the slightest indentation.

"I know you won't be able to figure out the secret." Qiu Chuji chuckled at Guo Jing's futile attempt. "Remember the Master ran her hand over the granite before she wrote? When Lord Huang heard *Shifu's* account, he supposed she had something in her possession that could soften the surface of rocks and stones temporarily. That was what Lord Huang was preparing in the month that he was away."

Now Guo Jing was all the more impressed by this mysterious Master, who seemed as knowledgeable and as full of tricks as his father-in-law. His mind wandered to where Huang might be found. He had not sent word back to Peach Blossom Island since he sailed for the mainland a decade ago.

Qiu Chuji did not pick up on Guo Jing's contemplative mood and went on with his tale. "It was never *Shifu's* intention to become a monk. He was resentful at first, but when he immersed himself in Taoist writings, he gained enlightenment and began to understand that everything in life happened for a reason. He also unravelled the wonders of attaining peace through inaction, and turned his focus to the cultivation of the self and the furthering of the Sect.

"If we think about it, without the Master, the Quanzhen Sect would not have existed, I would have never become who I am, and who knows where you would be today."

Guo Jing nodded in agreement. "Do you know this Master's name? Is she still with us?"

"*Shifu* never mentioned her name." Qiu Chuji let out a sigh. "She did many a good deed in the *jianghu* but she was extremely secretive. She passed away before the first Contest of Mount Hua, otherwise, she would not have missed it."

"Did she take any disciples?"

"Herein lies our misfortune. The Master had no protégé, but she shared her extraordinary kung fu knowledge with her maid-in-waiting over the dozen or so years they lived together in the Tomb. The serving woman never had any dealings in the martial world, and yet, somehow, she took on two followers. You may have heard of her eldest disciple . . . What do they call her in the *jianghu*? The Red Serpent Celestial . . . Blithe Li was her name."

"Ah!" Guo Jing gasped. "That woman is most cruel and savage!"

"You've come across her?"

"A few months ago, in the South. Her martial skill is chilling."

"You exchanged blows?"

"No, we only encountered the bodies felled at her vicious hands. She was more callous and hard-hearted than Iron Corpse Cyclone Mei at her worst."

"Well, I for one am relieved that you did not come across her yourself. Her younger martial sister's surname is Long . . ."

"The Long woman?"

"You know of her?"

"I'd never heard of her until today. When I was trying to make my way here, they said I was a demon and a lecher for hoping to seek her hand . . ."

Guo Jing's confusion drew a cackle from Qiu Chuji, but his mirth soon fizzled out. "It seems Chongyang Temple is fated to endure these trials. If our lookouts had not mistaken your identity, the compounded Heavenly Northern Dipper formation would have held back the invading horde and you would have arrived much sooner. Brother Hao would have avoided his injury."

Seeing that Guo Jing was not following him, the Taoist added, "It is her eighteenth birthday today."

"Huh?" This merely confused the younger man further.

"It is believed that her surname is Long, but no-one knows her given name," Qiu Chuji carried on. "The fiends out there have dubbed her the Dragon Maiden, taking the meaning of her family name. And that is how she is most often referred to these days.

"One night, eighteen years ago, the wail of a babe was heard outside Chongyang Temple. The disciples on night watch found an infant girl, wrapped in swathes of fabric, left on the ground outside the main gate.

"It would not be appropriate for a religious community of brothers to raise a female child, but with compassion as our guide, we could not leave her to the elements. However, that night, Ma Yu and I were both away, and as the junior monks debated what to do, a middle-aged woman descended from the hills behind the temple and said, 'I'll look after this poor child.'

"The disciples let the woman take the baby, relieved that a solution had presented itself. When Brother Ma and I returned, we did not give the matter much thought. From the description we were given of her physical appearance, it seemed clear that the woman was the Master's maid. We had met this resident of the Tomb of the Living Dead several times, though not a single word had ever been exchanged. We might be neighbours on the same mountain, but because of the entanglements between our seniors, our mutual existence brought to mind the old saying: 'The same bark and the same crow ring in our ears, yet unto old age and death our paths never twine.'

"Some years later, we heard that her disciple Blithe Li had ventured into the *jianghu*, wreaking havoc and gaining notoriety with her fierce kung fu and vicious ways. We held meetings in the Sect to discuss what we might do to curb her wanton behaviour, but we did not take action in the end as we were wary of overstepping the mark and undermining our neighbour. We left a courteous letter at the Tomb, and yet, it was as if we had tossed a stone into the sea, for we heard nothing back. Blithe Li continued to carry herself in her unbridled ways and no-one from her martial clan tried to restrain her.

"Another few years drifted by. One day, a white banner was hoisted above the thicket of thorns outside the Tomb. We knew the Master's maid must have passed away. Since no Quanzhen Sect follower is allowed to step across the Tomb's threshold, we bowed at the entrance to pay our respects.

"A girl, around thirteen or fourteen years of age, emerged from the subterranean dwelling to return our obeisance, saying, 'Shifu bade me, in her final moments, to reassure the Reverends that she had ways to rein in her errant disciple.' She disappeared the moment she had delivered the message, giving us no chance to ask for details.

"We thought it must be hard for the girl to remain there on her own, and sent her food and other supplies, but each time they were returned untouched by an elderly serving woman. The girl was as much of a recluse as her forebears, and since she already had someone to look after her, it was not for us to meddle in her affairs. Thereafter, as we spent more time travelling to different regions to attend to the Sect's affairs, we didn't give her much thought, but we did notice that Blithe Li seemed to have vanished from the *jianghu* and we were full of admiration for our late neighbour for making good her promise from beyond the grave.

"Last spring, when Brother Wang and I were staying with a hero in Ganzhou in the north-west, we heard the shocking news that fiends from the four corners of the *wulin* were planning to descend on the Zhongnan Mountains in twelve moons' time. Of course, we assumed they were coming for the Quanzhen Sect and sent scouts to verify the rumour, so we could plan our defence. It turned out they were after the Dragon Maiden of the Tomb of the Living Dead."

"But I thought she'd never set foot in the outside world?"

"It was all thanks to her martial sister."

"Blithe Li?"

"Yes. Her. Blithe Li was told to leave when her *shifu* discovered her vicious nature. By then, she had been training for several years, and her *shifu* insisted that she had learned all she could. However, Blithe Li realised before long that she was never taught the most supreme skills of her martial clan, and when she found out her former teacher had died, she forced her way into the underground dwelling. Although she claimed she had come to pay tribute, she was there to oust her younger martial sister and to search for any secret kung fu manuals that might have been left behind by her *shifu*.

"Unbeknownst to Blithe Li, the Tomb was defended by a sophisticated system of traps and snares. She broke through the first two gateways with difficulty, and at the third, she found a letter from her *shifu*, addressed to her. It was an appeal urging her to change her ways, lest she come to a ruinous end. It also stated that her younger martial sister would assume the leadership of their martial branch on the day she turned eighteen, and as the figurehead, she would exercise her power to put their house in order – if Blithe Li persisted in her brutality.

"Li was enraged. She tried to force her way forward but was caught by the snare her *shifu* had set up in this third gateway. If her martial sister had not tended to her wounds, she would have died there and then. But Blithe Li would not be beaten so easily – she returned again and again, though she was badly hurt at each attempt. The last time, she came face to face with the Dragon Maiden. The younger woman was fifteen or sixteen then, and she trounced her martial sister. She could have taken Blithe Li's life if she—"

"Surely this is just *jianghu* hearsay," Guo Jing interjected.

"Why do you say so?"

"First *Shifu* Ke Zhen'e has come to blows with Blithe Li on two occasions. Her kung fu is so advanced that even Reverend Sole Light's disciple Wu Santong could not overpower her. It's hard to imagine a teenager, however gifted and brilliant she may be, defeating someone of her own martial lineage with an extra decade of training."

"Well, that was what Brother Wang heard from a friend in the Beggar Clan, though we may never learn precisely what took place as no-one else was present. Regardless, this is the version that spread throughout the *jianghu*, and it must gnaw at Blithe Li's bruised pride – she's already experienced first-hand how biased her *shifu* was, judging from the superior kung fu skills her martial sister used against her.

"Out of spite, Blithe Li chose a date and let it be known that the Dragon Maiden of the Tomb of the Living Dead was ready to host a Duel for the Maiden."

Guo Jing inhaled audibly. His mind flew back to that snowy day in the Jin capital Zhongdu in his eighteenth year. Yang Kang had met Mercy Mu at such a duel, leading to heartbreak and bloodshed.

Qiu Chuji was thinking about the same event and became rather subdued, but after a moment, he resumed his tale. "Blithe Li made it known that the hero who bested the Dragon Maiden would win her hand, along with the treasures and martial secrets kept in the Tomb. Now, although no-one has ever met the elusive young woman, Blithe Li's looks are highly praised in the *wulin*, and the Red Serpent Celestial herself let it slip that her little martial sister was even more alluring.

"Half the *jianghu* is already besotted with Blithe Li, so if her prettier martial sister is said to be offering her hand, who wouldn't want to try their luck?"

"So the men who attacked you are all her suitors!" Guo Jing slapped his thigh, having at last got to the crux of the misunderstanding. "That's why my Quanzhen brothers called me a lecher."

"Yes, indeed." Qiu Chuji roared with laughter at Guo Jing's gawking expression. "And it came to our attention that these fiends were ready to take arms against the Quanzhen Sect if we interfered in their pursuit of the Maiden. Of course, we were not prepared to offer them free passage through Chongyang Temple to reach her up at the Tomb, so we let it be known that every Quanzhen disciple was to convene at the temple ten days before this supposed Duel for the Maiden. And here we all are – except for Brother Liu and Sister Sun – they are in Shanxi and could not make it back in time. Over the past few days, we have drilled hard, practising all the variations of the Heavenly Northern Dipper formation. We also sent a letter to warn the Dragon Maiden, but received no response."

"Perhaps she's away?"

"No, she is at the Tomb. We have seen cooking smoke rising from –" Qiu Chuji pointed out a crest to the west – "over there."

All Guo Jing could make out through the gloom was a few dark clumps of vegetation. He was still none the wiser as to where the Tomb might be, and he struggled to imagine how an eighteen-year-old could consent to live her life underground – it would bore Lotus to death, quite literally.

"Five days ago," Qiu Chuji went on, "our scouts returned with the news that the fiends were gathering at the Temple of Pervading Light and that their signal was a slap on the stone plaque down there. Leading the ragtag crowd were two Vajra Buddhist fighters, who have made quite an impression in the Central Plains over the past year.

"You wouldn't have heard of them living in seclusion on Peach Blossom Island, but you have just met them. The one who dresses like a wealthy lord of gentle birth is supposedly a Mongol Prince, related to Genghis Khan. He calls himself Prince Khudu. Did you come across that name in your time living with the Khan and his family in Mongolia?"

Guo Jing repeated it under his breath as he pictured the man's refined features and mannerisms, which were not enough to mask a haughty ferocity as well as a certain slipperiness. He had never observed such qualities in Genghis Khan's sons – neither when growing up with them nor later on the battlefield. The conqueror's eldest, Jochi, was staunch and warlike; his second, Chagatai, fiery but meticulous; his third, Ogedai, who had inherited the empire, was generous and even-tempered; and his youngest, Tolui, was full-blooded and loyal. Khudu looked nothing like any of these Princes.

Noting Guo Jing's muted response, Qiu Chuji added, "He might have fabricated his upbringing, but the lineage of his kung fu is unmistakable – it is of the Vajra Buddhist tradition. He first became known on the Central Plains at the start of this year, when he got the better of the Three Heroes of Henan. Not long after that, he was seen in the Ganliang area, where he killed the Seven Overlords of Lanzhou, all on his own, and half the *wulin* rang with his name.

"The Mongol monk is called Darbai. His muscular power is extraordinary and his kung fu shares the same roots as Khudu's – we think he is the elder martial brother or uncle. He has clearly come to support Khudu's suit, since he has already pledged himself to the monastic life.

"When Khudu turned up with Darbai, most of the lechers knew they could not hope to win the Dragon Maiden's hand and set their sights elsewhere. Blithe Li has extolled the Tomb's wealth of riches, from mountains of valuables to a library of martial tracts that detail some of the most admired kung fu techniques, like the Eighteen Dragon-Subduing Palms and Yang in Ascendance. Although most doubt the truthfulness of her words, they wouldn't want to pass up a chance to lay their hands on some scrap of treasure when the victor enters the Tomb.

"Our strength would have been more than adequate to keep these second-rate chancers at the foot of the Zhongnan Mountains, or at worst, we would have had no problem keeping them out of Chong-yang Temple, if only . . ."

Guo Jing parted his lips several times but failed to put into words the feelings of guilt weighing him down.

"*Laughing, I leave home and am free,*
As in West Lake the clouds are reflected and the Moon hangs high
above me."

Qiu Chuji recited the words in a declamatory voice and waved the heaviness away with a smile. "Chongyang Temple is but mere buildings. Even our corporeal form is superfluous, so why should we despair at the loss of a few halls? As someone who has been cultivating *neigong* for more than a dozen years, surely this is something you have already understood?"

"Of course!" A sheepish grin spread across Guo Jing's face.

"I will not deny that when I saw the blaze swallowing the rear courtyards, I snapped like a clap of thunder, but I am now able to view what has happened with serenity. I know full well that my learning lags far behind Brother Ma's – his heart is unburdened and unfettered, even when facing catastrophe."

"It is natural to feel outrage –" Guo Jing tried to offer some consolation – "especially given how wicked and senseless the invaders have been."

"Because the Northern Dippers were set upon you by mistake, Khudu and Darbai were able to lead their pack of rogues straight up to Chongyang Temple with little resistance and they immediately started torching buildings. Brother Hao challenged Khudu, but alas, he had underestimated the man's kung fu – the Vajra martial philosophy is so very different from what we are familiar with on the Central Plains. He was overhasty and got caught out by a palm strike to the chest.

"We gathered around Brother Hao to protect him, but the disciple taking his place in the formation was a less seasoned fighter and did not enjoy the same rapport with the rest of us, so our power was perilously curtailed. If you had not turned up, we would not have held out for long.

"Now I think of it, even if we had set the compounded Northern Dipper on that horde, they would have struggled to block the progress of Khudu and Darbai. We might not have lost outright, but we could not have beaten them as swiftly and as clear cut as you di—"

Bawhoooo-bawhoooo-bawhoooo! A blaring horn cut Qiu Chuji off mid-sentence.

To Guo Jing's ears, there was a note of desolation to the echoing cry. Its resonating tone sent his heart leaping over mountains and his spirits galloping across the steppe. He was once more standing on the rippling sands and endless plains of Mongolia.

But now the horn's call was growing hostile. It was issuing a challenge.

"O sin, wicked sin!" Qiu Chuji exclaimed, his eyes fixed to the west, where the clamour was coming from. "Do you know why he suggested the ten-year adjournment? The scoundrel thought it would leave him free to blaze through the *wulin* unchecked. Well, I will make it my personal mission to thwart him. Come, let's find the rake!"

"Prince Khudu?"

"Who else?" Qiu Chuji set off downhill as he spoke. "He's challenging the Dragon Maiden to a duel."

The horn now boomed with more urgency, its thunderous summons accented by metallic clangs – Darbai had joined in.

"Disgraceful! Two martial Masters tyrannising one young woman!" Qiu Chuji increased his pace, and in a twinkling, he had led Guo Jing halfway down the mountain.

Congregated in a clearing before a dark dense forest were the hundred or so men who had attacked Chongyang Temple.

Qiu Chuji guided Guo Jing around the rock face to a spot where they could keep watch out of sight. Khudu stood at the forefront of the group, blowing the horn, and next to him, Darbai was striking the gold bracelet around his right wrist with a baton, fashioned from the same precious metal, in his left hand. The clangour elevated the call of the horn, inviting the Dragon Maiden to emerge from her dwelling, but the far side of the woods, where the Tomb of the Living Dead was located, remained resolutely silent.

After a while, Khudu lowered the instrument and projected his voice instead: "Prince Khudu of Mongolia wishes the Dragon Maiden many happy returns of her birthday."

Twang, twang, twang – three plucks of a seven-stringed *qin* sounded from the greenwood.

177

"I heard that Miss Long is staging a contest today in which the victor will win your hand," Khudu pursued, thrilled to have elicited a response. "I have come specially to learn from you, Miss, and I hope you will deign to give me instruction."

The zither rattled angrily. Even those not versed in music could recognise the surge of emotion in the timbre. It was sending a clear message: they should vacate the woods at once.

Khudu let out a laugh and continued, "I am of noble birth and I dare say not unpleasant on the eyes. I trust I will be a good match for you and far from an insulting choice."

A feisty strum from the *qin* berated his presumption.

Khudu changed tack and said, "Miss, if you will not show yourself, then I shall come to you." He caught Darbai's eye and received a nod in return. Then he put away the horn and, with a wave of his right hand, marched into the woods.

The horde of men hurried after the Mongol Prince, bustling with anticipation and bumbling into one another. They all wanted to be among the first to enter the Tomb and lay their hands on the treasures within. And they were confident that the young woman could not possibly stop them on her own – after all, the full might of the Quanzhen Sect had failed to contain them.

"Turn back, trespassers!" Qiu Chuji cried out from his vantage point. "Do not disturb the peace of the Quanzhen Grandmaster's former residence."

A few among the rabble wavered, but the lure of riches outweighed their fear of the Taoist monk.

Qiu Chuji and Guo Jing rushed after the intruders, but when they reached the forest, they found them running the other way, fleeing as fast as their legs would carry them. Even Khudu and Darbai had taken flight, looking far more dishevelled than when they beat their retreat from Chongyang Temple.

The astounding sight stopped the two men in their tracks. How did she manage to drive them all away? Just then, the woodland came alive with a buzzing, humming sound. Louder and louder it grew. Great billows, misty white and hazy grey, rolled down from the branches, swarming over the retreating horde.

"What are they?" Guo Jing asked.

Qiu Chuji shook his head, his eyes trained on one of the fast-moving clouds as it caught the moonlight. It swirled around the hind-most intruders. The men went down shrieking, cradling their heads.

"I think they're bees, but they're white in colour!" Guo Jing gasped.

Even as he spoke, the jade-white swarm claimed another five or six victims. A dozen martial men in total were now rolling on the ground, their screeches reaching a heart-stopping, soul-shaking pitch.

Their extreme reaction mystified Guo Jing. Why were they squealing like pigs at the slaughter? Were these bee stings more venomous than usual? But there was no time to consider these questions – a grey cloud was swarming in his direction. Guo Jing turned and ran, but to his surprise, Qiu Chuji stood his ground, parting his lips and blowing a jet of air from the Elixir Field in his abdomen.

Sensing the change in pressure, the apian attackers slowed their advance. Qiu Chuji sent forth a second air stream. Guo Jing followed suit, letting out a gust that built on the stirring already generated by the Taoist monk. A high wind, fortified by orthodox *neigong* power of the highest order, swept into the bees, compelling them to change their course. They skirted around the two men and took off to pursue other interlopers.

More and more fighters were now thrashing in the dirt. Their yowls – punctuated by pleas of "Mercy!" and "Pardon!" – were gaining a shriller and more desperate note with each passing moment.

Guo Jing was baffled. He had met enough *jianghu* rogues to know that they would not beg for clemency or squeal in pain even if they had an arm or a leg chopped off. How come one sting from a tiny bee was enough to send them shrieking for ma and pa?

The low hum of the *qin* thrummed above the trees. Wisps of white smoke rose into the night sky. A sweet floral scent drew the bees back into the leafy canopy.

Qiu Chuji was not just awed by the Dragon Maiden's skill, he was also astonished that no-one at the Quanzhen Sect had got wind of her training the bees in all the time they had been living alongside her on the same mountain.

"If we had known our neighbour to be so omnipotent, the Quanzhen Sect would not have interfered." Qiu Chuji was speaking to Guo Jing, but the words were sent forth with sufficient *qi* to reach the young woman's ears.

Gentle, peaceful notes flowed from the zither to thank the monk for his compliment.

"Miss, you are too kind," the Taoist replied with a hearty laugh. "This humble monk Qiu Chuji and his disciple Guo Jing send our best wishes."

Twang twang. Two flicks of the *qin* strings acknowledged the goodwill, then a hushed silence resumed on the far side of the woods. But the moaning and groaning from those stung by the bees had grown only louder.

"What should we do to help them?" Guo Jing was unable to shut his ears or steel his heart against their howling.

"I am certain Miss Long will have a plan."

Leaving the injured men behind, Qiu Chuji led Guo Jing back towards Chongyang Temple. On the way, the younger man asked the Taoist again about taking Penance Yang on as a disciple.

"Your Uncle Ironheart Yang was a true hero and patriot, and I am thrilled to hear he has a grandson," Qiu Chuji said wistfully. "It weighs heavy on me that I played a part in Yang Kang's downfall . . . Don't you worry, I shall do everything within my power to instruct this child and raise him to be a man of honour."

Overjoyed, Guo Jing kneeled there and then on the mountain trail and bowed in gratitude.

The two men filled each other in on their news from the decade since they had last met as they made their way back. By the time they reached the temple grounds, a new day had dawned. The monks were out in force, clearing the rubble, putting out the last of the embers and sweeping up broken tiles and cracked stones.

Qiu Chuji introduced Guo Jing to those present and pointed out the bearded monk who had led the Heavenly Northern Dipper formations the night before. "This is Zhao Zhijing, eldest disciple of Brother Wang. Of the third generation, he is the most skilled, with the purest *neigong* strength. Let him be Penance's instructor."

The choice pleased Guo Jing, who had witnessed the monk's martial prowess first hand. He thanked the man sincerely for agreeing to take on Penance's education. He stayed on at the temple for a few days to make sure the youngster was settling in, and was present when Penance paid obeisance to Zhao Zhijing, confirming their relationship as disciple and *shifu*.

4

BEFORE GUO JING LEFT FOR PEACH BLOSSOM ISLAND, HE spoke at length with Penance. He tried to impress upon the young man that the Quanzhen Sect was the orthodox school of the martial arts, and that their founder Wang Chongyang remained the Greatest Martial Master Under the Heavens – a legendary figure that no-one, regardless of their kung fu heritage, had managed to best. Mindful that Penance had seen him overpowering the Quanzhen monks on their way to the temple, Guo Jing took care to explain that this was not due to the flaws inherent in Quanzhen techniques, but that the Taoists they had encountered had yet to realise the full potential of their martial tradition.

However, to Penance's ears, these entreaties were just excuses to gloss over the truth of the matter. He was convinced that Guo Jing was offloading him onto this drove of mediocre monks to relieve himself of the burden of bringing him up. He refused to believe a single word of it. He had seen with his own eyes how the Quanzhen disciples had flailed about, flustered and undignified, when their swords were snapped in two. Nevertheless, he pretended to agree, nodding and muttering promises in response to Guo Jing's biddings.

Several days later, Qiu Chuji summoned Penance. The Taoist had been reflecting on his failings as mentor to the boy's father. Ever since Yang Kang's premature death, Qiu Chuji had been haunted by his negligence. It was he who had allowed him to be raised by the Jin Prince Wanyan Honglie in the luxury of the palace, leading directly to his misguided allegiance to the invaders of his homeland.

With Penance, Qiu Chuji decided he would follow the ancient saying, "From stern teachers come outstanding pupils, from a firm cudgel, filial sons." He must be strict, else Penance might stray onto the same path as his father. He lectured the lad in a forbidding tone, warning him that slothfulness and impudence would not be tolerated – he must always work hard and obey his *shifu*.

The uncalled-for scolding had Penance seething – he had never asked to be brought there in the first place! – but he blinked back his tears and agreed to do his best and behave as he should. He wept into his hands once Qiu Chuji had left the meeting chamber.

"You think the Grandmaster has wronged you."

The icy comment came from behind. The startled youngster swallowed his sobs and spun around. His *shifu* Zhao Zhijing was looming over him.

"No." Penance straightened up and placed his arms meekly by his side.

"Then why are you crying?"

"I miss Uncle Guo."

Zhao Zhijing studied his student. He had overheard Qiu Chuji's admonition from the courtyard outside – the boy was clearly trying to fool him with a hasty excuse.

Half-grown and already so devious! This trait needs to be beaten out of him now, while he's still young. Taking the boy by the arm, the Taoist barked, "Why do you lie to your *shifu*?"

Penance eyed the man as a retort took form in his head: Do you think I want to call you *shifu*? I didn't have a choice! Even when I've

183

learned all your kung fu, I'll be as much use as a fart – no, a festering boil – because that's what you are! He had little respect for any of the Quanzhen followers, having seen them routed by Guo Jing, floundering about like petals fallen in an eddying stream. He had also seen Qiu Chuji and his martial brothers scrambling pitifully against Prince Khudu and his cronies – until Guo Jing came to their rescue.

To his mind, the Quanzhen monks' kung fu could not be more commonplace. But he knew the consequences of speaking his mind and bit down on his lower lip.

Zhao Zhijing was visibly provoked by his sullen silence and yelled, "How dare you ignore your *shifu*!"

"What would you like me to say, *Shifu*?"

The monk had never been addressed so insolently by a junior. *Pak!* He cuffed the boy on the cheek with the back of his hand.

Penance scampered into the courtyard, his face red and swollen.

In a few strides, Zhao Zhijing caught up with the lad and seized him by the arm. "Where do you think you're going?"

"Unhand me! You're not my *shifu*!"

"What did you just say, little bastard?"

"Mangy Taoist cur!"

The bond of *shifu* and disciple carried as much weight in the martial world as that of father and son. If a *shifu* sentenced their disciple to death as a punishment, it would be accepted without complaint or resistance. Penance's brazen insult was unthinkable, unfilial and unconscionable.

Ire turned Zhao Zhijing's complexion sallow. He raised his hand, ready to give the boy another slap, when Penance jumped up, grabbed his arm and sank his teeth into the forefinger. Lancing pain shot through the monk's body, demonstrating the age-old saying, "The fingers to the heart connect."

Addled by the shock of being caught off guard by an untrained child, Zhao Zhijing failed to shake the boy off at the first attempt.

Penance, meanwhile, was swept up in a red mist of his own, gripping the Taoist with a strength he had not known he possessed, cultivated with the aid of the *neigong* technique he had learned from Viper Ouyang. He was determined not to let go, even if the monk threatened to run him through with a sabre or a spear.

Zhao Zhijing tried again to rid himself of the youngling. This time, he threw a punch.

"Begone!"

A crushing force hit Penance's shoulder, making him clench his jaw. His teeth clamped down on something hard and he could hear a sickening crunch.

"*Aaaaahhh!*" Zhao Zhijing howled, slamming his fist into the crown of Penance's head. He wrenched open the boy's mouth and let his unconscious body slide to the ground.

The Taoist examined his bleeding hand. The bone had cracked. He would not be able to exert the same force through the finger as before, even when it had healed. Maddened at the thought of his kung fu being forever curtailed thanks to this injury, he kicked out at Penance's prone body again and again in revenge. He then looked around and popped his head into the meeting chamber to see if anyone was about. If word of his humiliation got out, he could never show his face in the *jianghu* again.

Relieved that they were indeed alone, Zhao Zhijing tore a strip from Penance's sleeve to wrap around his bleeding finger. Then he fetched a basin of cold water from a side room and poured it over the boy.

Penance soon came to. He pushed himself back on his feet and flung his fists at the Taoist in manic retaliation.

The man grabbed him by the front of his robe. "You're asking for death, little beast!"

"You're the beast here, stinky dog! I saw my Uncle Guo pummel you to the ground! I saw you crawling over night soil begging for mercy, you feeble, bearded goat!"

Zhao Zhijing slapped Penance across the face once more. This time he kept a watchful eye on the boy's reaction. He had learned from his painful mistake.

Penance thrashed about with his fists, but before he could get anywhere near the monk, he was sent sprawling by a kick. And yet, he dragged himself to his feet, blundering forth and clawing blindly. He threw himself at the Taoist with no concern for his well-being: the man was so repugnant that he could not bear the thought of sharing the same sky.

Had Zhao Zhijing wished to truly hurt Penance, it would be as simple as lifting his arm, but the monk had not forgotten that he was the boy's *shifu*, and if he were too heavy-handed, how would he answer to his martial elders? Still, his patience was wearing thin. Neither his punches nor his kicks seemed to deter the lad – in fact, pain seemed to fuel his fighting spirit.

Seeing several bruises surfacing on Penance's skin, Zhao Zhijing felt a twinge of remorse and decided to end this once and for all. He jabbed a pressure point at the base of the boy's ribcage and locked his movements.

"Enough!" Zhao Zhijing stepped away wearily. The scuffle had quickened his breath and sent his heart racing. Even though it was not at all strenuous on the body, it was wreaking havoc on his peace of mind – he knew not how to keep this recalcitrant child in line. He pinned his eyes on his supposed disciple, and the boy glared back in defiance, with no intention of backing down.

Bong bong bong . . . The stand-off was broken by an unexpected tolling of bells. The call for all Quanzhen disciples to gather.

"I'll free you, but you must promise to behave." Zhao Zhijing removed the bind on Penance's acupoint, but the moment the boy had regained his movement, he lunged. The man scuttled two steps back. "Stop! What do you want?"

"Don't ever raise your hand to me again."

Zhao Zhijing knew there was no time to argue, for those who tarried would be chastised, but he was not ready to relent without imposing his authority. "Only if you behave."

"Fine, but if you threaten me with your fist once more, I'll never call you *shifu* again."

The monk nodded grudgingly. "Come now, it's the Sect Leader's summons." He straightened the boy's ripped robe, grabbed his hand and dragged him to the assembly point, praying that no-one would ask about his swelling bruises and bedraggled appearance.

OUTSIDE THE main hall of Chongyang Temple, Ma Yu, Qiu Chuji and Wang Chuyi sat facing seven columns of Quanzhen disciples arranged by their martial lineage. When everyone was in place, Ma Yu clapped three times for attention and projected his voice: "Eternal Life Immortal and Sage of Tranquillity have sent news from Shanxi. The situation there with Blithe Li the Red Serpent Celestial is proving rather thorny. Eternal Spring Immortal and Jade Sun Immortal –" he indicated his younger martial brothers on either side – "will lead ten disciples to give our brethren support."

Qiu Chuji then spoke up, calling the names of those chosen. "You leave for Shanxi with Jade Sun Immortal and I at first light on the morrow."

The news caused a stir among the assembled Taoists – and some were visibly outraged – but they only started whispering with their fellows after they were dismissed.

QIU CHUJI went over to Zhao Zhijing once he had made the announcement. "Much as we would like you with us, Penance has only just arrived at the temple and we do not want to delay his education, so we have decided that you should stay behind this time." The senior monk then noticed the youth in question was standing with them, and that his face was tear-stained and discoloured by bruises. "What's happened?"

Panic seized Zhao Zhijing. I'll face serious punishment if Martial Uncle Qiu finds out . . . He began to rue his rashness and shot his student a look to warn him to hold his tongue.

Penance pretended not to have noticed the signal – he was secretly relishing the man's discomfort. He ummed and ahhed, acting as though he was too timorous to give a straight answer.

The boy's hesitation was getting on Qiu Chuji's nerves. "Who did this to you? Tell me!"

Penance noted with glee that Zhao Zhijing was quaking with fear and took his time in speaking up: ". . . I took a fall. Into a ditch."

"You're lying. The bruises on your face couldn't have come from a fall."

"Earlier, after Grandmaster bade me to work hard—"

"Yes, and?"

"I reflected on your words, and I am extremely grateful to Grandmaster for giving me guidance. I shall do all I can to improve myself – I shan't be a disappointment, Grandmaster."

Qiu Chuji's complexion brightened at the obsequious remark and he grunted in approval.

"This is how it happened," Penance continued, preparing to flesh out his story. "A mad dog came out of nowhere and snapped its jaws at me. I kicked, I fought, but the dog got more feral. I ran and fell into a ditch . . . Luckily, *Shifu* came by and pulled me out."

Qiu Chuji turned to Zhao Zhijing, looking to him to confirm the veracity of Penance's account.

The man nodded and said between closed teeth, "I rescued him."

Of course, Zhao Zhijing realised that the little stinker had just called him a dog, but he had to go along with the wretched lie if he wanted to keep Qiu Chuji from learning the truth.

"Teach the child well," the senior monk said. "Your Martial Uncle Ma will review Penance's progress every ten days."

Though his whole being rebelled against the idea, Zhao Zhijing bowed and promised to do his best, for it would be treachery of the worst kind to defy his martial elder.

Penance, in the meantime, had been revelling in the success of his jape and did not pay any heed to the exchange that followed, or even notice that Qiu Chuji had started to walk away. It was only when he noticed the smouldering Zhao Zhijing threatening to slap him again that he realised and cried out, "Grandmaster!"

Qiu Chuji turned around – "Yes?" – and saw his martial nephew's hand hovering awkwardly near Penance's face.

Zhao Zhijing pulled back stiffly and pretended to scratch the back of his neck.

Penance ran up to the senior monk. "Grandmaster, who will look out for me when you're away? The martial uncles here all want to beat me up."

"Nonsense!" Qiu Chuji's face hardened, making him look more severe and stern than usual, though he was in truth warm and kind-hearted. Remembering that Penance had lost his parents, his tone softened. "Zhijing, look after this child well. If anything untoward happens to him, you will be held responsible."

The man nodded. What choice did he have?

THAT EVENING, after supper, Penance trundled up to Zhao Zhijing's chamber for his kung fu lesson.

"*Shifu*," he said in greeting, but his arms did not make the customary gesture of deference, hanging limply by his side.

The monk, sitting cross-legged on the low bed, had been brooding over what he should do, and the sight of the half-smile on his disciple's face as he strolled in set his blood boiling again. The day's events had confirmed that Penance was belligerent and intractable, and convinced him that if the boy were ever to make anything of himself in the martial world, he would be a menace, for who could keep such a character in check? However, he had been ordered by both his martial uncle and his *shifu* to teach Penance, and much as he detested the idea, he could not go against his seniors.

Wait! A sudden idea came to the Taoist. Penance knows nothing about Quanzhen kung fu. I can teach him the martial mnemonics, but leave out the training methods. He'll learn a few hundred lines of verse that he can't put into action, and when *Shifu* and the martial uncles check on his progress, I'll say he refuses to put the work in.

Pleased with his plan, Zhao Zhijing said warmly, "Come here, Penance."

"You won't beat me again, will you?" the youngster asked from the doorway.

"Of course not, I'm going to teach you kung fu."

Eyeing the man cautiously, Penance took his time in crossing the room. He had no doubt that the monk's surprisingly affable tone was a ploy to conceal a cunning plot.

Zhao Zhijing pretended not to notice Penance's guarded approach. "Quanzhen martial training starts from the inside," he began, "unlike most other kung fu styles, which begin with external, physical moves before turning to cultivating the powers within. I will now teach you our heart-approach. Memorise it." He began to recite the Quanzhen mnemonics that laid the foundations for internal strength *neigong* training.

Hearing it once, Penance had already committed the verse to memory, but he was mistrustful of the man's intentions.

The rough-snout goat hates me. He'd never teach me anything useful. He must be trying to fool me with a fake formula.

Feigning forgetfulness, he asked the Taoist to repeat the poem — it was just as he had memorised it.

The next morning, Penance asked Zhao Zhijing again and the words that came forth were exactly the same as on the two previous occasions. He was at last persuaded that the monk had not fabricated the lesson's content.

In the days that followed, Penance was taught more mnemonics, but his teacher refrained from uttering even one word that would help him put them into action and cultivate his inner power.

On the tenth day, Zhao Zhijing brought Penance to an audience with Ma Yu, to demonstrate to his martial uncle and Sect Leader that his student had learned the whole of the introductory heart-approach. Ma Yu was delighted to hear Penance's flawless recital and heaped his praises upon the clever young man. It never occurred to the senior monk – honest and artless by nature and a true man of virtue – that he was being duped, that his martial nephew had not taught the boy anything material.

5

AUTUMN CHILL CHASED AWAY THE SUMMER HEAT, WINTRY frost cloaked everything within reach. Months had passed since Penance's arrival at the Quanzhen Sect. He had memorised a bellyful of verses, but he had not received any instructions on how to use the mnemonics to unlock his *neigong* power, nor had he been taught any physical kung fu moves. He was as ignorant of all things martial as when he first set foot on these mountains.

Penance had, in fact, seen through Zhao Zhijing's ploy within days of the first lesson. He could tell that his so-called *shifu* had no desire to share his knowledge, but he was also aware that there was little he could do about it. If he made a complaint to Ma Yu, the meek and non-confrontational monk might say a few stern words to Zhao Zhijing, but all it would achieve would be to goad the rough-snout goat into devising new methods to torment him in retaliation. The youngster decided to bide his time until Qiu Chuji's return, but the moon had grown full several times, and there was still no sign of the Quanzhen Immortal.

Their kung fu is as much use as a cow's fart! I'm stronger being untainted by it, Penance would often tell himself, not greatly concerned by Qiu Chuji's extended absence. His loathing for Zhao Zhijing increased by the day. He detested the monk for his deception, but he knew he should avoid direct conflict and made a show of deference at all times.

THE LAST month of winter stole up on the Zhongnan Mountains in the twinkling of an eye. It was a tradition set by Wang Chongyang that a contest be staged over the three days before the final sunrise of the year, to test the kung fu of every disciple and to judge their progress. As the tournament approached, everywhere one turned, one would find young men working hard on their martial moves, even during the hours of darkness.

On the day of the full moon a fortnight before the coming of spring, the students of each Quanzhen Immortal would spar with their martial brothers in a series of preliminary trials. Ma Yu's disciples and their pupils could be seen fighting in one group, while the protégés of Qiu Chuji and Wang Chuyi were gathered elsewhere in their separate clusters. Eternal Truth Tan Chuduan might have passed away more than a decade ago, but his followers had been receiving instruction from their martial uncles, and they were as competent as their fellows. This year, because of the attack that had lain waste to Chongyang Temple, the Taoists were putting in extra effort, determined to prove to the *wulin* that they practised the most orthodox and effective kung fu under the heavens.

The disciples of Jade Sun Immortal Wang Chuyi assembled under the afternoon sun in a clearing towards the south-east corner of the monastery. Since the Master himself was still in Shanxi, his eldest disciple Zhao Zhijing was overseeing this opportunity to review the progress of the fourth-generation disciples over the year, with regard to empty-handed combat techniques, the use of sabres, spears or secret weapons, and the control of *neigong* power. He would grade each of them and offer comments on their performance.

Penance was the most recent addition to the fourth generation, and therefore the last in line to be tested. As he watched boys his age – novices and others like him who had not taken the monastic vow – demonstrate different kung fu repertoires, he was filled with bile rather than envy.

Zhao Zhijing noticed the sour expression on Penance's face and decided he would make a fool of the boy.

"Penance Yang!" he called once the trial he had been assessing was over.

The youngster made no answer but grumbled inside: Why do you call me when you've never taught me any kung fu?

"Penance Yang, did you hear me? Step forward!"

The boy plodded over to Zhao Zhijing and inclined his body. "Student Penance Yang bows to *Shifu*." He paid obeisance in the secular way like the handful of other lay disciples in the monastery, rather than in the Taoist tradition as was expected of those who had pledged themselves to the religion.

Zhao Zhijing nodded in acknowledgement and pointed to the young monk who had prevailed in the last contest. "He is a few years older than you, but you can spar with him."

"Your student knows no kung fu. How am I supposed to—"

"How can you say you know nothing?" Zhao Zhijing growled. "Have I not been teaching you? What have you been doing all this time?"

Penance lowered his head and did not respond.

"You're indolent," Zhao Zhijing went on. "How will you learn anything when you won't work hard? Give me the two lines that follow this:

"*What is the practice of cultivating the Way of Truth?*
To quell the heart from fancies, to squash the birth of cravings."

Penance recited automatically:

"*The essence of life force brims in noble integrity,*
The light of vivacity sparkles over the empyrean capital."

"Good! Then, what comes after this?" He delivered another two lines of martial mnemonics.

"*Grasping the origin of the mystical passed on by the teacher,*
Beholden to nothing at the coming, leave nothing behind at the passing."

The answer came swiftly and without hesitation.

"Dust and grime of years bygone wiped and scrubbed away,
Zestful and bright the whole being illumines the Great Hollow."

"Very good! You know every word." Zhao Zhijing smiled. "Now, apply the method you've just cited when sparring with your martial brother."

"I don't know how . . ."

"What do you mean?" The monk contorted his face in rage to mask the elation in his heart. "Don't tell me you've never put your learning into practice. Enough of your excuses. Get into the ring."

These verses were key to the cultivation of *neigong*, outlining a method for reining in the heart and curbing the wandering mind, as well as training the essence and nurturing the *qi*. Each line was exemplified by several martial moves, and taken together they formed the introductory fist-fighting repertoire of the Quanzhen Sect.

The watching monks assumed Penance was suffering from a bout of nerves. Many offered the boy words of encouragement, though a handful sniggered and made snide remarks. The majority of Quanzhen Taoists were generous in disposition, but human nature decreed that some would succumb to baser emotions and hold Penance responsible for the humiliating defeat they had suffered at the hands of Guo Jing, and as such they relished the sight of the youngster in distress.

Provoked by the jeers, Penance squared up to his fate – So be it! I'll fight to the death! – and pounced, swinging his arms up and down.

Feral, chaotic blows rained down on the novice. He was caught off guard because Penance performed none of the courtesies that usually marked the start of a bout. He stumbled back, startled, but the distance it put between them allowed him to see that his opponent's footing was not secure. The young monk twisted to one side and kicked low with a Wind Sweeps Fallen Leaves.

Struck on the ankle, Penance hit the ground nose first, but he regained his feet in an instant. Ignoring the blood streaming from his nostrils and the snickers from the spectators, he charged, head down, at his foe.

A weight attached itself to the novice's left leg. The young man looked down to find Penance's arms locked around him in a way he had never before experienced. He chopped his right palm downwards at an angle. Wipe Away the Dust was a move designed to beat back any attack to the lower half of the body.

Pang! The edge of his palm connected firmly with Penance's shoulder. As with the kick to his ankle, Penance had no prior warning of the blow's likely effect on his body or any idea how to counter it, since no-one had taught him any kung fu, whether on Peach Blossom Island or at Chongyang Temple. Burning pain radiated from his collarbone, but it only made Penance more reckless. With his arms still wound around his opponent, he butted his head into his other leg, tipping the young monk onto his back.

Penance scrambled up to straddle his foe, pinning him to the floor with his body, and started to box him about the ears.

And yet, the novice was not ready to give up. He drove his elbow into Penance's chest, winding him, and seized his chance to spring to his feet. Then, with a backhanded push and a flick of his arm, he sent Penance reeling in a move known as Nothing Beholden, Nothing Left.

Penance fell heavily and painfully to the ground. Assuming he had won, the young monk bowed with one hand raised to signal the end of the bout. "Brother Yang, thank you for your forbearance."

The gesture meant nothing to Penance. He charged again, like a possessed tiger, taking another two or three blows on the chin before being knocked down once more. But this only made him bolder. Undaunted, he thrashed his arms and legs wildly, unleashing a string of punches and kicks with dizzying speed.

"Penance Yang, stop! You've lost!" Zhao Zhijing shouted.

The boy paid him no heed. He continued to stamp his feet and swing his arms out of instinct, resolute and unflinching.

His martial brethren watching on the sidelines were amused at first, for they had never witnessed such a haphazard, slipshod mode of combat, but they soon grew alarmed by the reckless abandon the youngster was displaying and feared the two contestants would seriously hurt each other if left unchecked.

"Stop! Stop!"

"You're just sparring!"

"No need to take things so seriously."

Penance turned a deaf ear to their entreaties and pressed on with his assault. He was now the personification of the age-old saying: "When one man stakes his life to fight, ten thousand cannot hold him back."

The young monk ducked and dodged, trying to keep his frenzied opponent at bay. He might know more kung fu, but he was cowed by the raw aggression coming his way. He could neither compete with Penance's fighting spirit nor match the strength of Penance's pent-up emotions, for the boy was fuelled by grievances he had been nursing since his arrival. The novice soon gave up resisting and took to his heels, but Penance was relentless in his pursuit.

"Stinking Taoist! You're not getting away until you've had a taste of your own medicine." Penance's abuse insulted nearly everyone present, and a few of the monks made their displeasure known, grumbling that he ought to be disciplined.

"*Shifu! Shifu!*" the novice cried as he fled, hoping Zhao Zhijing would rein in his opponent, but Penance did not let up, taking no notice of the angry shouts ordering him to stand down.

A roar sounded from the crowd of spectators and out shot an overweight man. He grabbed Penance by the back of his collar, hoisted him up and – *pak pak pak* – cuffed the boy three times around the ear.

Penance was almost knocked unconscious, his cheeks turning a fiery red. When he could focus again, he recognised the fat monk immediately. Lu Qingdu. The man tasked with watching over him after he was snatched during Guo Jing's fight against the lone

Heavenly Northern Dipper formation when they first came to the Zhongnan Mountains. He had tricked the bulky man into untying his restraints, ambushed him with night soil, then left him tied up in a room in the path of the raging blaze that was devouring Chongyang Temple.

Penance had entered the fight with little hope of emerging unscathed, and now he knew his fate was sealed. He had made Lu Qingdu a figure of ridicule among his martial brothers and he was a mere child who knew no kung fu. Still, he tried to twist out of the monk's grasp, but his movements were hampered by the way he had been lifted up by the back of his robe.

Lu Qingdu snickered and – *pak pak pak* – smacked Penance thrice more. "You disobey your *shifu* and that makes you a renegade! And we are all permitted to give any traitor to our Sect a good beating!" The monk raised his hand again, his face twisted with malice.

"Qingdu, enough!" Cui Zhifang stepped in to calm his martial nephew, for he could tell he wanted to inflict real harm on the boy. He also suspected there was more going on here than met the eye, since Penance did not seem to know a single move of Quanzhen kung fu, and he had long known that Zhao Zhijing could be petty and small-minded.

"Martial Uncle, you have no idea how devious and slippery this lad can be." Lu Qingdu set Penance down with reluctance. "How do we uphold the rules of our Sect if we don't punish him severely?"

Cui Zhifang ignored the disgruntled junior and turned to Penance instead. The youngster was in a pitiful state: his face beaten black and blue, blood congealed under his nose and on his chin.

"Penance, why did you not use the kung fu your *shifu* has taught you? Why did you fight your brother in such a loutish way?" Cui Zhifang's voice was warm and friendly.

"*Shifu*? Ha!" Penance spat. "He has never taught me anything."

"You recited our mnemonics correctly."

"I'm not here to train for the Imperial Examination. What's the point of memorising such drivel?" Penance had decided the verses quoted by Zhao Zhijing must be unrelated to the martial arts, like the Confucian classics Lotus Huang had made him learn on Peach Blossom Island.

"Such insolence in the presence of an elder!" Frowning, the monk gave Penance's shoulder a firm shove.

One of the most capable martial artists of the third generation, Cui Zhifang was an expert in both internal and external techniques, though he lost out in terms of power to his elder martial brother Zhao Zhijing. He was feigning displeasure to find out if the boy was truly as unschooled in Quanzhen martial arts as he claimed.

The strike's strength and velocity were perfectly controlled to ensure that, at contact, it would trigger Penance's *neigong* force – if he had any – to engage automatically. The instant his palm connected, the Taoist could feel Penance's body turn a fraction in the direction of his push, and yet, at the same time, he could also sense power gathering in the boy and it dispersed a portion of the energy contained in his thrust.

How come he has such a store of internal strength? He's still a child and he's only been with us for half a year. And if he has already developed this level of *neigong*, he shouldn't be flailing so helplessly in a fight. Was it all an act?

Cui Zhifang could not have known that the inner kung fu displayed by Penance originated from the method Viper Ouyang had taught him, which the youngster had been practising over the past year. White Camel Mount internal strength was relatively easy to cultivate in the early stages, and Penance had already amassed sizeable reserves without realising what he had achieved, whereas the Quanzhen way was focused on building a firm and broad foundation. As such, students of White Camel Mount could muster much stronger internal strength in the first ten years of training, but disciples of the Quanzhen Sect would catch up and likely surpass them after another decade of hard work. And though the two *neigong* systems differed greatly, it was not possible for Cui Zhifang to distinguish the finer elements in such a brief moment of contact.

As the Taoist's hand smacked against his shoulder, Penance felt his breath catch in his chest. However hard he tried, he could not draw more air into his lungs. The strike made him reel and stumble back a few steps, but he somehow managed to maintain his balance. Bending low, he rammed his head into the monk's belly, believing the man was also out to chastise him. Right now, he was unafraid – he would fight the heavens and the earth if necessary, even Qiu Chuji himself, if he were standing before him.

Cui Zhifang gave Penance a gentle smile and stepped to the side to show that he was disinclined to engage. However, he was keen to gauge the true depths of the boy's kung fu, and said, "Qingdu, spar with your brother Yang. But show restraint, don't be too heavy-handed."

The instruction was exactly what Lu Qingdu had been hoping for. He stepped forward, his burly frame looming over Penance. His left hand shot out in a feint, luring the boy to dodge to the right and put himself in the path of the follow-up attack.

Pang! The monk's right palm hit Penance square on the sternum. The power of this Tiger Gate Hand would have left the youngster spurting blood from his mouth, if he had not been practising White Camel Mount *neigong*. Nonetheless, waves of pain seized his chest, turning his face as white as a sheet.

Unnerved to find Penance still standing, Lu Qingdu let fly with a right jab to his face. Penance threw his arms up out of instinct to shield himself. It was obvious to Cui Zhifang that the young man knew no standard moves for blocking and counter, something which a kung fu beginner should have learned in their first lessons.

While the right-handed punch flew in an arc, Lu Qingdu's left fist shot forth, plunging into the boy's gut with an audible thud. Penance doubled over in agony. The monk hacked down with the edge of his right palm, aiming at the exposed neck. He expected the ruthless strike to knock Penance out cold, but somehow the boy defied him.

Dizzy and limp, swaying from side to side, Penance summoned

every last drop of strength and willpower to keep himself from collapsing in a heap.

"Qingdu, stop!" Cui Zhifang needed no further confirmation that Penance was uninitiated in the art of combat.

The fleshy monk pulled back and hissed, "Do you submit, stinker?"

"I'll kill you one day, you crook!"

Lu Qingdu howled in anger and rapped Penance on the nose with a pair of rapid-fire punches.

The boy reeled. The blows had knocked all light from the sky and all colour from the earth. Just as Penance thought he was going to collapse in a faint, a jet of warmth surged from the Elixir Field in his lower abdomen. A third punch was now flying into his face. His mind was so dazed that he could barely raise his hands in his defence, but his body responded by itself. A croak issued from his throat and his legs bent from the knees. As he crouched low, his arms straightened, thrusting his palms out.

Into Lu Qingdu's belly.

The monk's bulky form was flung backwards and – *whump!* – he crashed down on his rump in a massive cloud of dust, some ten paces away.

Calls for Lu Qingdu to stop ceased that instant. Many of the senior monks, unsettled by the unfair match, had been voicing their objections, though Zhao Zhijing stayed silent throughout. But no-one had foreseen this reversal of fortune. The overweight man lay sprawled on the ground, stiff and unmoving.

"Oh no, he's dead!" the first Taoist to reach him cried.

"He's not breathing! His insides must be scrambled!" another added.

"Send for the Sect Grandmaster!" Once more, with no conscious effort, Penance had unleashed the might of Exploding Toad in a desperate moment. The first victim had been Erudite Wu on Peach Blossom Island. Now, he had managed to send a grown man flying. The advancement in his power was in part due to his intermittent practice over the past few months, but the intense hatred he felt towards Lu Qingdu had also contributed.

The cacophony of strained voices jolted Penance back to his senses. He dragged his battered, aching body from the confusion without anyone noticing.

Zhao Zhijing parted the throng to check on Lu Qingdu. He was horrified to see his junior's eyes rolled back, without any clear sign of life.

"Penance Yang!" he yelled. "What is this demoncraft?"

As the first disciple of Wang Chuyi, Zhao Zhijing had spent most of his life stationed at Chongyang Temple. So, despite being a capable fighter, his knowledge of other martial branches was limited, and he did not recognise the telltale signs of Viper Ouyang's signature repertoire.

"Penance Yang! Penance Yang!" Receiving no answer, Zhao Zhijing scanned the faces of the crowd. The youngster was nowhere to be seen.

The sneaky little thing must have slipped away! He can't have gone far in such a short time . . . The monk ordered all those present to split up and search for his student.

PENANCE TOOK off as fast as his battered body could carry him. With no notion of where he might hide, he headed into the densest vegetation at every turn to mask his progress, but he had not been fleeing long when he heard his name called from all sides.

"Penance Yang!"

"Come out!"

The monks' cries made his heart shudder. He bolted down an overgrown path and saw a shadow swerve abruptly up ahead.

He had been spotted. He spun around and flew off in a different direction.

"He's over here!" A voice sounded to one side of him.

Penance ducked low and burrowed headfirst into a thicket. The monk in pursuit was too large to squeeze in after him and had to circle round. By the time he had reached the other side, the youngster had long vanished.

The voices calling his name began to grow dim and distant, but Penance dared not ease his pace. He continued to charge through the brushwood, jinking between chest-high weeds and jagged rocks. Before long, he was so sore and sapped he had to sit down to catch his breath. All the while, a voice inside was screaming, *Fly! Fly!* But his legs seemed to weigh a thousand *jin*; he could not find the energy to stand up.

Sniggers sounded behind him. Penance snapped round. His heart almost leapt out of his mouth from sheer terror.

Zhao Zhijing. Glowering at him.

Shifu and disciple glared at each other. Neither made the slightest move.

With a yelp, Penance hopped to his feet and tore off. Zhao Zhijing pounced, his right hand reaching for the back of the boy's robe. Penance threw himself forward, narrowly avoiding the clawing fingers. He then picked up a rock and hurled it at his teacher.

Zhao Zhijing twisted away from the missile and widened his stride. The gap between hunter and the hunted was rapidly closing.

Penance glanced back over his shoulder, then fixed his eyes on the path ahead again, only to find his way forward cut off by a ravine. He could not tell what lay at the bottom, whether rocks or a stream, but he jumped without a second thought.

Skidding to a halt at the precipice, Zhao Zhijing caught a fleeting glimpse of Penance tumbling down a steep green slope before he disappeared into the undergrowth. From where he was standing, it was a sheer drop of about six or seven *zhang* to the nearest spot to offer a safe landing. Not a distance he could confidently jump.

The Taoist scanned the landscape and found a safer route to climb down. He then followed the trail of flattened grass into the woods, where he lost all trace of the boy. The further he ventured, the denser the forest grew, to the point that not a single ray of sunlight could find its way through the leafy canopy. He blundered on in the half-light for about ten *zhang* until it suddenly dawned on him that he was in the vicinity of Grandmaster Wang Chongyang's former residence, the Tomb of the Living Dead, which was strictly off limits to members of the Quanzhen Sect.

Zhao Zhijing knew he could not go any further, but he was loath to let Penance take advantage of this stricture and slip from his grasp.

"Penance Yang! Come out!" he yelled again and again.

The trees were still. He could not pick out any sound.

Boldly, he took another few steps. In the gloom, he came upon a rock carved with the warning:

NO TRESPASSING BEYOND THIS POINT

He paused, wondering whether he should continue, and decided against it.

"Penance Yang! Show yourself, you sneaky wretch! Or I'll beat you to death when I catch you!"

As his cry died away, Zhao Zhijing heard a buzzing sound rising amid the trees. Wisps of grey wafted between the leaves, zooming towards him at great speed.

White bees!

Zhao Zhijing twirled his wrists, whipping up a storm with his sleeves, channelling energy from his well of internal strength. He managed to disrupt the swarm, but the bees separated into two groups – one carried on bombarding him from the front, the other circled around to strike at his back.

The Taoist continued to flourish the long, flowing fabric of his sleeves to fend off the airborne attackers, but they simply broke into smaller units, diving at him from every conceivable angle.

Accepting that he could not beat them back, Zhao Zhijing focused on keeping them from stinging the exposed skin of his face as he fled from the forest, but the jade bees whirred persistently after him, undeterred by the powerful whisks of his sleeves. However abruptly he switched direction, they hummed around him, waiting for the moment when his frantic arms fell slack.

Eventually, a handful of bees broke through his defences and stung him on the cheek. An unbearable numbing itch spread across his body, reaching deep beneath the skin.

I'll die here today!

As the lament echoed through his inner ear, Zhao Zhijing stumbled, falling to the grass, and began to roll back and forth, screeching in agony. The bees cavorted around him, pricking any bare flesh they could find. Then, all of a sudden, they gathered themselves and returned to the woods.

CHAPTER FIVE

THE TOMB OF THE LIVING DEAD

I

STINGING PAIN. A DRONING BUZZ. PENANCE FORCED HIS EYELIDS apart. Bees everywhere, so many . . . white in colour . . . An incredible itch had taken hold of his body, creeping into the very marrow of his bones. He remembered jumping off the precipice and rolling down a steep slope into the undergrowth of a dense forest . . .

How long had he been out for?

A white mist clouded his vision, but before Penance could work out whether he was hallucinating, he fainted again.

Fragrant. Refreshing. Sweet. Liquid trickled down his throat and made its way into his stomach. Penance did not have the words to describe the soothing sensation it brought to his body. Still groggy, he opened his eyes a fraction and was met with an unsightly, pock-marked face, glaring down at him from two *chi* away. The shock nearly sent him under again. A hand reached for his jaw, its grip firm but not ungentle. Something cool, hard and smooth brushed his lower lip. He tasted the same fragrant, refreshing, sweet liquid on his tongue.

Soon, the pain and itching had subsided enough that he began to regain more of his senses. He was lying on a bed. The old woman must have tended to his injuries. He tried to curl up the corners of his lips in gratitude. The woman returned the smile, though hers was misshapen and hideous. Still, he could detect the note of tender kindness it conveyed, and it filled him with warmth.

Once Penance had swallowed the last of the sweet liquid and was feeling more in command of his body, he pushed himself up into a sitting position. "Please don't hand me over to my *shifu*."

"Who's your *shifu*, my dear child?"

Penance had not been spoken to so kindly for a long time. Something stirred in his breast and he broke down in sobs. The old woman held his hand, patted him lightly on the back and let him cry, her eyes full of motherly compassion.

A short while later, she asked, "Feeling better?"

The caring tone made Penance's tears flow anew.

She dabbed her handkerchief over his eyes. "Good child, don't cry. Don't cry. It'll stop hurting very soon."

Her words provoked another wave of sobs.

"Grandam Sun, why won't the child stop?" An airy female voice.

Penance turned in the direction of the new speaker. A slender hand, pure like white jade, parted the drape, and a maid of sixteen or so appeared.

Her white dress, though fashioned from humble materials, had a lightness to it that gave the impression she was shrouded in mist and fog. Other than her coal-black hair, colours seemed to have trouble latching onto her person. The rosy hue of blood could not tint her skin, and her complexion was as pale as her robe.

The instant Penance clapped eyes on this ethereal beauty he stopped sobbing and his face flushed crimson. He hung his head, mortified by his outburst of childish emotion. A moment later, he risked a glance from the corner of his eye and caught her watching him. He looked away immediately.

"I've tried . . ." Grandam Sun gave a helpless grin. "Perhaps he'll listen to you."

The young woman approached the bed, her gaze settling on the welts caused by the bee stings on his head. Then she ran her eyes over the bruises and bumps that disfigured his features, noting how badly he had been beaten, and placed her palm on his forehead to check his temperature. Her hand was strangely cold, and Penance shuddered uncontrollably at her touch.

"The jade bee honey will neutralise the sting in half a day." Her voice was mellifluous despite her dispassionate tone. "Why did you trespass into the forest?"

Penance raised his head and looked straight into her eyes. He had never seen anyone so graceful and otherworldly, and yet, there was a glacial aloofness about her. She was pristine like ice, and just as cold. There was no telling whether she was happy or angry, troubled or delighted, and he found it unsettling.

Is she made of crystal or snow? he wondered. Is she human? Maybe a ghost! Or perhaps a bodhisattva or a celestial?

Grandam Sun took from the boy's dazed expression that he was intimidated, and said with a smile, "Miss Long is the mistress of this place. You can speak freely to her."

The girl in white was the Dragon Maiden. She had lived in the Tomb of the Living Dead all her life and never ventured beyond its immediate vicinity. The internal *neigong* she practised required her to keep her emotions curbed, and as a result, she appeared a couple of years younger than her actual age – eighteen, going on nineteen.

Grandam Sun came to the Tomb as a serving woman, working under the Dragon Maiden's *shifu*, and now she was the young woman's only companion. Earlier in the day, she had been alerted by the buzzing of the bees that there were trespassers nearby and had headed into the woods to see who they were. There, she found Penance lying unconscious. She was aghast to note the signs of a rough beating beneath the welts left by the bee stings. The old woman could not bear to leave him unattended in his wretched state, and so, though outsiders were strictly barred from the Tomb and it also broke convention to admit men to the living quarters of women, she brought him back to treat his wounds.

Assured by the old woman, Penance climbed down from the bed and fell on his knees, touching his forehead on the ground twice. "Penance Yang thanks Grandam Sun and Auntie Long."

"Ah, Penance, there's no need to be so polite!" Beaming with delight, Grandam Sun helped the boy to his feet. It had been decades since she had interacted with anyone beyond the confines of the Tomb and she was taken by this well-mannered youngster.

Meanwhile, the Dragon Maiden acknowledged the obeisance with a curt nod and sat down on a stone seat near the bed.

"What brought you to the woods? Why were you beaten up? Give us the name of the villain who did this to you!" Grandam Sun rushed out of the room, leaving her questions hanging in the air, and returned with a plate of cakes and buns.

Penance ate a few pieces at Grandam Sun's urging and recounted his life story. He was gifted with words, and his passionate retelling won the old woman's sympathy. She sighed at his misfortune and seethed at the unfair treatment he had received, especially Lotus Huang's bias towards her petulant daughter, and Zhao Zhijing's petty spite. The Dragon Maiden listened impassively, save for when the name Blithe Li was mentioned, and her eyes met Grandam Sun's for a brief moment.

Once Penance had finished his tale, Grandam Sun clasped him to her bosom. "My poor child, my poor child . . ."

The Dragon Maiden rose unhurriedly to her feet. "His injuries are not serious. Grandam, please see him out."

Neither the old woman nor the boy had expected that response.

"I won't go back! I'd rather die!" Penance exclaimed.

"Miss, if we send him back, his *shifu* will surely beat him."

"You escort him. Tell his *shifu* not to."

"But we have no control over the Quanzhen Sect."

"Take a jar of jade bee honey and tell the old Taoist he must oblige." The Dragon Maiden spoke with a detached authority that demanded compliance.

Grandam Sun heaved a sigh. She knew how strong-willed her mistress could be – there was no hope of persuading her. She looked at the boy sadly, her conscience gnawing at her.

Penance put his hands together and bowed in respect. "Thank you, Grandam and Auntie, for looking after me. I'll take my leave."

"Where will you go?" the old woman asked.

Penance thought for a little while. "The land is vast under the skies." For all his bold words, he looked lost and forlorn. In truth, he did not know if there was a place for him in this world.

"Child, don't be upset," Grandam Sun said. "It's not that our mistress doesn't want you to stay, but we live by strict rules. Outsiders are not allowed to set foot inside the Tomb."

"Grandam, you don't have to explain – I understand. Please allow me to thank you and Auntie once more. I, Penance Yang, will never forget your kindness. We shall meet again, one day."

In Grandam Sun's eyes, the mismatch between his grown-up words and his boyish voice was almost too poignant to bear. She could see he was fighting to hold back the tears welling up in his eyes.

"Mistress, it is late. Let him stay until the morning?"

The Dragon Maiden shook her head. "Have you forgotten *Shifu*'s commandment?"

Sighing, Grandam Sun went up to Penance, who was steeling himself to leave. "Let me show you the way out. You won't find it by yourself." She took his hand, parted the drapes and led him out of the chamber.

After a few steps, Penance was plunged into impenetrable darkness. He held tight to the old woman's hand and scrabbled after her, following bend after bend down a winding route, wondering how she was able to navigate without any light to guide her.

The Tomb of the Living Dead, despite its name, was not originally intended to be a place for eternal rest. When Wang Chongyang rose up against the Jurchens, he had had it dug out as a subterranean store-house on a colossal scale, employing hundreds of labourers over the course of several years. A repository for weapons, food and fodder, and a base for patriots from the regions of Shaanxi and Shanxi, it was designed as a grand deception, since ancient burial complexes are common in this part of the realm. He also equipped the Tomb with countless deadly traps to guard against intruders, in case his enemies saw through the ruse. When the uprising failed, Wang Chongyang withdrew to his stronghold and shut himself away from the world. The Tomb contained many rooms and chambers, connected by a complex web of corridors. Anyone venturing inside would wind up hopelessly lost, even if its passageways were brilliantly lit. In pitch darkness, without a spark of light, trespassers did not stand a chance of finding their way.

2

"ZHEN ZHIBING, DISCIPLE OF THE QUANZHEN SECT, IS HERE to treat with Miss Long," a deep voice boomed from the far side of the forest just as Grandam Sun and Penance stepped out of the Tomb. The monk sent to parley was the second student of Qiu Chuji; he was held in high regard among his peers for his martial skills and his ability to manage complex Sect affairs.

"They've come for you." Grandam Sun could not hide her disquiet. "Let's not leave the forest just yet."

"Grandam, I take responsibility for what I've done," Penance said in a steady voice, though his body was trembling in fear. "I killed someone – by mistake. They'll claim my life as forfeit." He wriggled free of the old woman's grasp and marched resolutely ahead.

Grandam Sun hastened after the boy and took his hand again. "I'll go with you."

They emerged from the trees into the clearing beyond. Seven

monks spread out in a line; the injured Zhao Zhijing and Lu Qingdu were lying on stretchers, carried by two servants each. The Taoists were conversing quietly among themselves, but when they saw the youngster they stopped and took a few steps forward.

Penance let go of Grandam Sun's hand and strode towards the monks. "Kill me, flay me, do what you want! But you should not have disturbed the peace of this place."

No-one had expected him to speak with such confidence. The eldest disciple of Zhao Zhijing broke ranks and grabbed his youngest martial brother by the collar.

"Why so eager?" Penance sneered. "I'm not going to run!"

Angered by the boy's tone, the novice threw a punch at his face. He was furious that, thanks to the ingrate before him, the *shifu* he revered and honoured as a father figure was racked by excruciating discomfort. To make matters worse, the Quanzhen Sect had no effective treatment for jade bee stings.

Grandam Sun had intended to remain civil with the Quanzhen followers, but fury blazed in her heart to see Penance so roughly handled. She marched up to the young monk and flicked her sleeve, striking him on the wrist with the flowing fabric. Then she made a dash for the trees, pulling Penance along behind her.

The Taoists were stunned by the speed and precision of the feeble-looking old woman's movements.

"Unhand him!" one of the monks shouted, rushing after her with two of his brothers in tow.

Grandam Sun stopped and turned around. "What do you want?" She had already put a distance of at least a dozen *chi* between them.

Zhen Zhibing knew the relationship between the Tomb of the Living Dead and Chongyang Temple was deep-rooted and he did not want to risk causing offence. He hurried after his brethren, crying, "Stand down! Is this how we treat our seniors?" Then he bowed to the old woman. "Student Zhen Zhibing greets the Elder."

"Yes?"

A PAST UNEARTHED

"This child is a disciple of the Quanzhen Sect. I beg the Elder to return him to us."

"I refuse!" Grandam Sun cried with a frown. "Who knows how you'd torture him behind your walls! You've just struck him brutally before my eyes."

Zhen Zhibing strove to keep his temper in check. "The child is wayward and recalcitrant. He has flouted the rules of our Sect, defying, deceiving and disrespecting his *shifu* and other seniors. Veneration of one's teachers and forebears is what binds the *wulin* together. It is only natural that the Sect chasten him for his trespasses."

The monk's harsh words angered Grandam Sun further, turning her face puce and making her unsightly features ever more grotesque.

"Huh! That's just your side of the story. It was by your Quanzhen rules that the child sparred with that fat monk." She pointed at Lu Qingdu, who was being carried over to where Zhen Zhibing was standing. "Penance didn't want to enter the contest and you forced him. Every duel has a winner and a loser. Who is to blame if the lumbering oaf isn't up to the challenge?"

By now another dozen or so Taoist monks had arrived in the woods, gathering behind Zhen Zhibing and whispering among themselves about the identity of this audacious crone.

Zhen Zhibing knew that they could not fault Penance Yang for injuring Lu Qingdu, but he could not admit that to an outsider – he had a duty to preserve the Sect's reputation. "We shall, of course, lay the matter before our Sect Leader and he will make a just ruling. I call on the Elder to return the child to us."

"Just ruling?" Grandam Sun scoffed. "There is not one decent soul among you. Or else, why do we live so close and yet never cross paths?"

The Taoist found himself silently arguing back: It is you who keep to yourselves. We're not to blame! But he understood that it would do no good to instigate a battle of words and disturb their fragile coexistence. "I hope the Elder will grant us our request. If our

Sect has caused offence in the past, we shall return with our apologies at the command of our Leader."

Clinging to Grandam Sun's arm, Penance stood on his tiptoes and whispered into the old woman's ear, "Don't fall for his tricks."

Having lived in the Tomb of the Living Dead as a servant since her youth, it had not been Grandam Sun's destiny to bear children of her own, but fortune had placed a newborn babe in her hands eighteen years ago, and now she had come across this poor boy Penance Yang, who seemed genuinely fond of her, despite the short time they had spent together.

I won't let them take the child, no matter what, the old woman promised herself, determined to take him under her wing.

"No, you won't have your way this time," Grandam Sun declared. "He's not going back to your temple to be tortured!"

Stumped for a response, Zhen Zhibing decided to make a fresh appeal in a softer tone to reassure the old woman. "This lowly monk shares ties of martial kinship with the child's late father. I would not dream doing the orphan of my brother harm. There is nothing for the Elder to worry about."

Grandam Sun shook her head. "I've no time for this. Excuse us!" She turned her back on the monks and marched deeper into the trees.

Though Zhao Zhijing was tormented to distraction by the itchy and painful bee stings, he had heard enough to understand that words alone could not persuade the crone to relinquish the boy. Fuelled by exasperation, he leapt out of the stretcher, caught up with the woman and placed himself in her path.

"He's my disciple and I can chastise him however I like. There is no rule in the *wulin* that forbids a *shifu* to discipline his student."

Grandam Sun eyed the swollen, swinish face as she contemplated her reply. She could not deny that, as Penance's *shifu*, this cruel man did have legitimate authority over the boy, but she judged that the time for being reasonable with the Quanzhen monks had passed.

"Well, *I* forbid you," she said. "What can you do about that?"

"What's he to you?" Zhao Zhijing demanded. "You have no right to interfere in my business."

Grandam Sun allowed a brief silence then raised her voice to match the belligerent monk's tone. "He is not of your Quanzhen Sect. He has bowed to Miss Long and become her disciple. So, from now on, *she* decides on his well-being. Stop poking your noses where they don't belong!"

It was understood in the *wulin* that a disciple could not take another *shifu* without the expressed approval of the teacher they first bowed to when initiated into the martial arts, even if the new Master happened to be ten times more skilled. To do so would be considered a great betrayal, as the ties between mentor and protégé were regarded as equivalent to that of parent and child, and those guilty of such a breach of faith would be shunned by the martial world.

Grandam Sun's impulsive lie had left the Taoists speechless, but as she had never been part of the *wulin*, she had no way of knowing that she had invoked its greatest taboo. The monks gathered were mostly sympathetic towards Penance, for they suspected that Zhao Zhijing had been biased and unjust in his treatment of him, but they were outraged to hear that the boy had acted in defiance of the fundamental moral principle that guided their world – such flagrant treachery was unprecedented among their Sect.

The old woman's words sent a fresh burst of fury surging through Zhao Zhijing, followed by waves of pain and itchiness. It was so excruciating that for a moment the monk wished he were dead.

"Penance Yang, is it true?" he asked through gritted teeth.

The youngster was at that wide-eyed, undaunted age, where neither the height of the heavens nor the depths of the earth could intimidate him. He had not fully grasped the gravity of Grandam Sun's words, nor the menace in Zhao Zhijing's voice, but he was certain that the old woman was acting in his best interests, and even if she had claimed he had committed a thousand unforgiveable sins, he would have acknowledged them without a second thought. To bow to a new *shifu* was something that he had been dreaming of since his arrival at Chongyang Temple, and if Grandam Sun had told the monks that he had bowed to a smelly pig or a rabid dog as his martial Master, he would have admitted it readily. Why would he refuse the celestial Dragon Maiden?

"You stinking Taoist! You cur-face! You cow muzzle with goat whiskers! You've never taught me any kung fu. All you've ever given me is beatings. You think you're fit to be my *shifu*? Yes, I've bowed to Grandam Sun and Auntie Long. They're my *shifus* now."

Zhao Zhijing thought his chest would burst open from rage. He had never been so insulted in his life. Lunging blindly, he seized Penance's shoulder with both hands.

"What is the meaning of this?" Grandam Sun slammed her right forearm into Zhao Zhijing's wrist.

The impact forced them both back by two steps.

"You're not as feeble as you appear," Grandam Sun spat with disdain.

Despite his injuries, Zhao Zhijing was still a force to be reckoned with – he was one of the most capable fighters of the Quanzhen Sect's third generation of disciples, ranked alongside Qiu Chuji's proudest students, Harmony Yin and Zhen Zhibing.

Zhao Zhijing lunged again, this time at Grandam Sun. The woman ducked and twisted, avoiding his talons. Then, without warning, her foot flew up from the heavy folds of her floor-length skirt.

The Taoist leaned back the instant he sensed the gust of air whipped up by her kick, easing himself out of harm's way. But in the same moment an unbearable itch pulsed through every bee-stung welt on his body.

"*Arrrrrrgh* . . ." he screeched, cradling his head and doubling over in agony.

Grandam Sun gave him no respite, ramming the tip of her shoe into the bottom of his ribcage. The monk flew backwards, his cries cut short as the wind was knocked out of him.

Zhen Zhibing dashed forward, caught Zhao Zhijing and settled him with the servants manning the stretchers. He was shocked to see his martial equal undone with such ease – the old woman's initial kick had been launched with uncanny stealth, throwing him off balance and leaving him vulnerable to the decisive blow. It would be foolish to seek a duel with her one on one. Zhen Zhibing whistled. Six monks stepped forward, flanking him to form a Heavenly Northern Dipper formation and trapping Grandam Sun and Penance Yang in the middle.

"Pardon us." Zhen Zhibing's polite words signalled the first wave of attack, from the monks on the flanks of the formation, Heavenly Pivot and Shimmering Rays.

It took no more than a couple of exchanges for Grandam Sun to recognise the potency of the monks' coordinated assault, though she had not yet realised that she was already caught in the middle of their battle array. To make matters worse, she could only parry with one arm, as she was still holding Penance's hand. By the time a dozen moves had been traded, Grandam Sun was scraping through by the skin of her teeth. None of her blows could find its mark, and the monks were closing in. Another dozen desperate parries. An offensive sortie led by two Taoists threatened to overwhelm her outnumbered right palm, and in that very instant, a threat to her left flank emerged, with two more of their horde pressing close. She pulled Penance behind her and freed her other hand.

A shrill whistle from Zhen Zhibing was the signal for a third pair of monks to lunge, their fingers groping for Penance's robe.

The Taoists' efficiency was troubling Grandam Sun. They're more than I can deal with on my own, she admitted grudgingly, and she began to hum as she aimed two surreptitious kicks at the duo closing in on Penance. Her voice was so low at first that the monks thought little of it, but as the murmuring built up, layer upon layer, it got harder to ignore.

Zhen Zhibing had entered the fight cautious and alert, for he knew that the Master who had once lived in the Tomb of the Living Dead was his Grandmaster's martial equal – the heirs to her knowledge would surely pose a threat. When he first heard the old woman's low humming, he assumed it was a mind entrapment technique and focused his breathing and stilled his mind, and yet, he did not experience any ill effects as the drone grew more audible. It was then that he remembered what his *shifu* Qiu Chuji had told him about the night Chongyang Temple was attacked and the way the residents of the Tomb had repelled the rabble. In the near distance, a buzzing sound was rising in the air, merging with the woman's song, and it was getting louder and louder.

"Retreat!" he shouted.

The monks were baffled. Why did their martial senior look so perturbed? The fight was going in their favour and they were about to capture the old woman and the boy.

An angry grey blur surged between the leaves and branches, whizzing towards the Taoists. The sight of the bees reminded the monks of Zhao Zhijing's welts and how he had screamed and writhed in agony. Fear sent their spirits flying from their bodies and stung their legs into motion. They spun round and ran with all their might.

The sight of the fleeing monks brought a smile Grandam Sun's face, but her good humour faded when she saw two sparks of light approaching at speed through the gloom of the forest. An elderly Taoist, whose narrow face was framed by white hair and a silver beard, was waving a smoking torch in each hand to ward off the swarming bees. The blackened fumes sent the aerial attackers scrambling for clean air. They scattered in every direction, no longer a coordinated unit.

"How dare you chase away my bees? Who are you?" the old woman demanded.

The grey-haired Taoist smiled. "This impoverished monk, Hao Datong by name, hails the senior."

Grandam Sun nodded in recognition. One of Wang Chongyang's seven disciples, known by the title Infinite Peace. The younger monks had given her enough trouble – this old one would be even harder to shake off. And the pungent smoke, which smelt of insect-repelling herbs, was making her gag. Shorn of her apian allies, she had no choice but to retreat.

"You've harmed my mistress's bees. We shall seek recompense." She snatched up Penance and retreated deeper into the forest.

"Martial Uncle Hao, shall we pursue?" Zhen Zhibing asked.

Hao Datong shook his head. "Our Founder-Grandmaster decreed that we should never enter this forest. Let's return to the temple and plan our response."

3

GRANDAM SUN BROUGHT PENANCE BACK TO THE TOMB. THEIR encounter with the Taoists had further strengthened their fledgling bond, but the boy was still uneasy, as he suspected the Dragon Maiden would refuse to relent and take him in.

"Fret not, I won't let the matter rest until she permits you to stay." With that solemn promise, Grandam Sun settled Penance in a chamber and went to speak with her mistress.

Penance waited, but as time passed, he grew more and more restless. Just a couple of hours ago, Auntie Long had flatly declined to offer him shelter, even for just one night. What were the chances of her allowing him to remain with them for good? Grandam Sun was probably still trying to talk the young woman around, but even if she succeeded, did he want to live in a place where he was not genuinely wanted and welcomed? The answer was not long in coming. He stood up and walked resolutely out of the room.

The moment he stepped into the dark corridor, he heard hurried footsteps, followed by Grandam Sun's hushed voice: "Where are you going?"

"Grandam, I'm leaving. I'll come back to see you when I'm grown up."

"I'll see you off," the old woman said. "I'll take you to a place where no-one will mistreat you."

Penance had expected that he would have to leave, but the news still stung. "You don't have to. I'm nothing but trouble. I don't belong, no matter where I go. But, thank you, Grandam."

The old woman was angry at herself for failing to sway her mistress, and a slow-burning frustration was gnawing at her stomach. The sight of the crestfallen boy now stoked it higher.

"My dear child, others may not want you, but I like you very much. I'll stay by your side, wherever you go. Come!"

Penance was beside himself with joy. He took Grandam Sun's hand and followed her out of the Tomb.

The old woman reached into her robe to take stock of what she had on her person for the journey. She had made the decision to leave on the spur of the moment, with no chance to pack even a change of clothes. Her hand closed around a ceramic bottle – the honey she had taken with her the first time she left the Tomb with Penance. She had intended to give it to Zhao Zhijing, to heal his bee stings, but the encounter had turned violent before she could hand it over.

However repulsive she might find the Taoist, Grandam Sun had to concede that his offences did not warrant death, and it was not her place to refuse him treatment. With that in mind, she turned towards Chongyang Temple.

When Penance realised where they were headed, he asked with a quiver in his voice: "Grandam, why are we going there?"

"To give them the cure for your stinker of a *shifu*."

Flexing her toes, Grandam Sun sprang up and forward, tucking Penance under her arm. A few leaps later, they were standing at the foot of the temple's perimeter wall. She hopped up with Penance, landing on the tiles lining the summit, but before they could jump down, an urgent tocsin began to sound. Soon, a chorus of whistles filled the air, some closer than others, and the cacophony was completed by the shouts and roars of fighting men.

The Quanzhen Sect was one of the largest martial groups in the *wulin*, and its temple was closely guarded even under normal circumstances. Since their encounter with their neighbour from the Tomb of the Living Dead earlier in the day, they had been on high alert, posting additional sentries in every part of the monastery ready to sound the alarm at the first sign of intruders. Groups of Quanzhen disciples were also assigned to different parts of the complex as a mobile reserve, so there would be men at the ready to intercept trespassers and to cut them off from any reinforcements.

Grandam Sun screwed up her face at the militant reception. What an absurd show of force. *I haven't come here to fight!* Her already low opinion of the Quanzhen Sect sank even further. She looked down at the men gathered below and said gruffly, "Zhao Zhijing, come out! I want words with you."

A middle-aged Taoist – Zhang Zhiguang, the second disciple of Hao Datong – stepped forward. "What business has brought you to our temple, without invitation, in the middle of the night?"

"The cure for bee stings." She tossed the bottle of jade bee honey his way.

He caught the antidote, but it was clear he was doubtful about her intentions. "What is it made of?"

"You ask too many questions. Tell him to drink the whole bottle and that will tell you all you need to know."

"How do I know it's not poison?" the monk went on. "You subjected Elder Brother Zhao to such agonies. Why are you being merciful now?"

Grandam Sun could barely contain her rage. The querulous monk had not merely cast doubt on her good intentions, he had openly accused her of being a murderer. She jumped down from the wall with Penance, sprinted over and snatched the remedy from the Taoist's hand.

"Open your mouth!" she said to Penance.

The youngster obeyed without question. The woman uncorked the bottle and tipped it to his lips.

"See, it's not poison." She took the boy's hand again. "Let's go, Penance."

Zhang Zhiguang realised too late that the crone had come in good faith – his suspicions had deprived Zhao Zhijing of the remedy. Full of regret, he rushed forward and placed himself in the old woman's way, his arm thrown wide to stop her.

"Senior Elder, be not so fiery! I was jesting." The monk pulled a smile. "We have been neighbours for so many years – surely we're not strangers?" He gave a rather forced laugh. "I hope the Elder will grant us the antidote again."

"I have no more to give. You will have to figure out how to treat Zhao Zhijing yourself."

"There must be more than just one bottle," he said with a chuckle, his tone cloyingly overfamiliar. "I'll come with you."

Grandam Sun found the man's greasy lips and slippery tongue revolting. "I'll teach you how to respect your elders!" A backhand slap to the cheek. Fast, crisp, hard.

"This is Chongyang Temple," a Taoist on Grandam Sun's left shouted, thrusting out his palm. "Do you think you can come and go and act as you please?" A second monk advanced from another angle, poised to strike.

The prowess of the Heavenly Northern Dipper formation was fresh in the old woman's mind, and she was in no hurry to face it again, especially on the Quanzhen Sect's own territory. She grabbed Penance, jinked between the encroaching palms with a swerve of her hips and sprang into the air. They were about to land on the top of the wall when a monk appeared from the other side.

"Down!" he cried, hurling both palms into the old woman's face.

With no foothold to help her change direction mid-air, Grandam Sun thrust her right hand out to counter the double onslaught. She managed to beat the Taoist back, but her momentum was spent, sending her back down to the ground.

The instant she landed, seven monks surrounded her, forcing her back. They were all outstanding fighters of the third generation, handpicked for their ability to protect the temple.

Grandam Sun first thought was to charge past the men, for she was much fleeter of foot, but they linked arms and blocked all potential escape routes with their bodies. Her attempts only resulted in her being driven closer and closer to the wall.

A dozen blows were exchanged, with no sign of a breakout. Zhang Zhiguang could see that the old woman was flagging and sent word for torches to be brought forth. Lanterns and candles lit up the grand hall and courtyard, but their warm glow failed to add colour to Grandam Sun's deathlike pallor.

"Halt the assault!" Zhang Zhiguang called.

The seven monks who had been forming a human wall to contain the old woman leapt back as one, palms raised over their chests, taking up their respective positions in the Northern Dipper.

Grandam Sun was grateful for the chance to catch her breath, but she was under no illusions. There was now more space between herself and the Taoists, but she was still encircled, just like before.

"The Quanzhen Sect truly deserves its lofty reputation." Her voice dripped with sarcasm. "Sending dozens of young men in their prime against an old woman and a young boy. Most admirable indeed!"

Her words sent hot blood to Zhang Zhiguang's cheeks and he scrambled to justify their actions. "We are tasked with challenging intruders. Be it an old woman or young boy, it is our duty to ensure they do not walk in and out with impunity."

"Ha! So you want this old crone to crawl out on her knees?"

Zhang Zhiguang was reluctant to let her off lightly – his cheek was still smarting from the humiliating slap. "You are free to go if you do three things for us. First, give us the antidote for the bee stings. Second, leave the boy with us. He is a disciple of the Quanzhen Sect and he can only leave if our Sect Leader decrees it. Third, kowtow to the image of our Grandmaster Chongyang and beg his pardon on your uninvited entry."

Grandam Sun cackled wildly. "I've always said to my mistress that the Quanzhen Taoists are a bunch of good-for-nothings, and I was absolutely right. Come, come, come, gather around, I'll kowtow to you all!" She bent low in a graceful curtsy.

Zhang Zhiguang was stunned. He had never imagined the tough old crone would actually bow to him. By the time he had recovered from the initial shock, Grandam Sun was already straightening up. He blinked and caught a glint of something flying towards him.

"*Aiyooo!*" He tried to twist aside, but the clandestine projectile was faster.

A rounded object hit him by the outer corner of his left eye and smashed into pieces. Blood poured from the gash.

It was the empty vial of jade bee honey, thrown using a technique known only to the denizens of the Tomb of the Living Dead. The kung fu invented by the Master who had won the subterranean complex from Wang Chongyang had been tailored to suit the physique and deportment of her sex, and its subtle moves, powered by deft manipulations of inner strength, were as adaptable as they were varied. The path of Grandam Sun's projectile attack, Reverence Precedes Disdain, was impossible to predict, and when it was launched at such close quarters, the target was bound to be caught out.

The monks roared in anger at the sight of Zhang Zhiguang's bloodied face. Swords glittered in the courtyard. Grandam Sun looked around her with a sneer. She understood this would not be her night, but it was not in her nature to submit. Proud, resilient, unyielding – qualities that had defined her in her youth came even more to the fore in her twilight years, like the spicy sting of ginger that waxes with age.

She turned to Penance, who had been shielding behind her, and asked, "Child, are you afraid?"

The question made the boy think of Guo Jing. He would have no fear if his father's sworn brother were with them, but Grandam Sun could not tackle these Taoists by herself.

"Grandam, let them kill me." His voice was clear and calm. "This has nothing to do with you. Get out while you can."

The old woman's heart was bursting with fondness – for the

boy's iron will as much as his concern for her safety. "No! I'll stay and die with you!"

She followed her promise with a howl and a lunge. Thrusting her arms out, she wrapped her fingers around the wrists of the two monks closest to them and twisted. Their swords were now in her hands.

It was a Bare Hands Seize Blade technique unlike any the Quanzhen disciples had encountered. It looked as though she had grabbed the weapons with brute force, but in fact it was through a nimble manipulation of strength. Her attack came from an ingenious angle that the Taoists did not even think possible. They blinked and their steel was gone.

Grandam Sun handed a sword to Penance. "Child, does fighting these stinkers scare you?"

"No, but it's a pity no-one else is here to see it."

"What do you mean?"

"The Quanzhen Sect's fame reaches far and wide. Isn't it a shame that there's no-one to bear witness to their followers' heroic fight against a lone woman and an orphan boy?" He had grasped from Grandam Sun's exchange with Zhang Zhiguang that the monks' behaviour would not be considered honourable, and now he made sure he was enunciating clearly and that his voice sounded as young and childlike as possible.

Many of the Taoists present were mortified by his words – it was hardly valorous to lean upon their strength in numbers or take advantage of their fitter physical state.

"I'll inform our Sect Leader and seek his wisdom on the matter." It was a disciple of Tan Chuduan who spoke for them, his feeble voice betraying his anxiety. Events had escalated to a point that their actions would have a bearing on the Quanzhen Sect's reputation, and such a major decision ought to be made by the highest authority.

However, Ma Yu, the eldest disciple of Wang Chongyang and the most senior member of the Quanzhen Sect, was not there to make it – he had gone to seek enlightenment in a secluded cabin high in the mountains, a dozen *li* or so behind the temple, leaving his martial brother Hao Datong in charge.

"Let's take the evil crone first!" Zhang Zhiguang bellowed, overruling the suggestion. He could not let anyone go to Martial Uncle Ma. The benevolent monk would surely let the old woman go free, and he would have lost the use of his eye for nothing.

When the ceramic bottle hit Zhang Zhiguang's face, it had shattered into tiny pieces. The shards cut deep into his skin and blood pooled in his left eye, obscuring his vision. Since half of his face was stinging with pain, his head muddled by the embarrassment of having fallen for the crone's feint, he had jumped to the assumption that he had been blinded.

"Brothers, draw in!"

At Zhang Zhiguang's command, the Heavenly Northern Dipper formation tightened around the old woman. The seven monks felt certain that, any moment now, she would surrender and offer her hands to be bound.

When they were three steps away, Grandam Sun brought her sword into play, weaving a net of protection so intricate that they could come no closer.

Zhang Zhiguang shouted orders from the rear, screwing his left eye up in agony. Fearing that the bottle had been laced with poison, he hung back to avoid making any vigorous movements, lest he hastened the flow of blood and toxins through his body.

The monks were growing anxious. Nothing they had tried so far could break through the old woman's defences.

All of a sudden, Grandam Sun howled and threw down her sword. She launched herself at incredible speed through the glittering flashes of Taoists' steel and seized a teenage monk standing just beyond the formation.

"Let us pass!" she demanded.

At those words, Grandam Sun felt a tap on her wrist. A bolt of aching numbness shot down her arm and her fingers fell slack. It all happened so quickly that the hostage was snatched from her grasp before she had caught a glimpse of her assailant. The next thing she knew, a gust of air whipped up by a mighty strike was lashing into her face. Grandam Sun raised her palm in defence. *Pak!* Opposing hands smacked together and the old woman took a step back to steady herself.

Her assailant was also forced to shift his footing, but that did not prevent him from launching a second strike. Grandam Sun parried it in a similar way, the impact pushing her another step back. This time the man strode half a pace forward to deliver a third blow, and one more exchange saw Grandam Sun pressed right up against the wall.

"Give us the antidote and the boy."

He lowered his hands, giving her a chance to answer him, and the old woman finally had the breathing space to take a good look at who it was that had cornered her.

White beard, white brow. He had chased the jade bees away with his smoking torches earlier.

Hao Datong.

From the vital glow of his complexion and the strength that surged from his palms, Grandam Sun knew the monk's *neigong* far surpassed hers. Her prospects were grim if he chose to summon his full power.

"You'll have to kill me first if you want the child." Grandam Sun was uncompromising by nature. Even death could not force her to bow down and give in.

For his part, Hao Datong was keeping a tight rein on his inner energy. He did not wish to harm someone who shared a deep connection with his late *shifu* Wang Chongyang.

"We have been neighbours for decades. Let's not allow a child to shatter the peace we have maintained for so long."

"I came here in good faith with the cure for the bee sting. Ask your disciples if I am speaking the truth."

The moment Hao Datong turned to address the monk standing

behind him, Grandam Sun's foot flew up. The kick came with no forewarning: her body did not shift, her long skirt did not flutter.

By the time Hao Datong had detected the attack, it was already threatening his undefended lower belly. No time to step back or twist aside. He grunted – *Huh!* – channelling all the strength he could summon to his palm. The thrust that followed carried the full force of the most advanced Quanzhen *neigong*, accumulated through decades of training.

With her back against the wall, there was nothing Grandam Sun could do to lessen the impact. She was driven into the mass of pounded earth. The robust structure groaned and cracked under the pressure. Tiles and rubble rained down as blood spurted from the old woman's lips. Slowly, she slid to the ground.

Penance threw himself over her crumpled form. "Don't hurt her! It's me you want!"

Grandam Sun forced her eyes open and gave the boy a smile. "We'll stay together."

Penance wrapped his arms around the old woman and shielded her with his body. The position left the vulnerable points on his back open to attack, making it apparent to the Taoists that he would risk his life to keep her safe.

Hao Datong was full of remorse. It had not been his intention to hurt her, but he had been too forceful in his attempt to counter her kick. He went up to the prone woman, hoping to check on her condition and offer treatment, but the boy would not shift.

"Can you move aside, Penance, so I can see what is to be done?" he said warmly.

However, Penance would never again trust the word of anyone to do with the Quanzhen Sect. He hugged Grandam Sun tight and ignored Hao Datong. The monk asked several times and still received no answer. Growing impatient, he grabbed the youngster's arm to pull him away.

"Go on! Kill me!" Penance screamed. "I won't let you hurt my grandam."

4

"WHAT KIND OF A MAN BRAWLS WITH CHILDREN AND OLD women?" A frosty voice put a stop to Penance's howling.

Hao Datong turned around to find a young woman watching him. Her gaze, like her snow-white robe, was as cool as mountain ice.

"Who are you, Miss? What brings you here?" The Taoist regarded her warily.

The temple's warning bells had sounded when Grandam Sun was first sighted. For a dozen *li* around the monastery, sentries were posted at strategic points, and every single member of the Quanzhen Sect was on high alert. How could this young woman have slipped past so many pairs of eyes and ears unnoticed and arrived in the courtyard without the alarm being raised?

The young woman shot Hao Datong a black look and went to kneel beside Grandam Sun.

"Auntie Long! That evil monk . . . k-k-killed Grandam!" Penance sobbed.

Seeing the tears on the boy's face, the Dragon Maiden gave him a nod to acknowledge the protection he had been offering Grandam Sun.

"Everyone dies. It comes for us all," she said, her voice matter of fact.

The Dragon Maiden had been trailing Grandam Sun and Penance Yang since they had left the Tomb. She watched from the shadows as the monks surrounded them, but she stayed put in the belief that the Taoists would refrain from using deadly force. By the time she realised the situation was getting out of hand, it was too late to come to Grandam Sun's rescue.

Although the Dragon Maiden appeared impassive and unmoved, grief did flit through her heart at the sight of the old woman lying mortally wounded. After all, she was raised by Grandam Sun and knew that she had loved her as a mother would. But the *neigong* she practised required her to be dispassionate. Ever since she began her training as a child, she had kept her emotions in check, be it joy or wrath, sorrow or excitement. For eighteen years, her life had been a still pool of water, undisturbed by ripples.

For the first time since arriving on the scene, the Dragon Maiden cast her eyes over at the Taoists massed in the courtyard. The monks, by now, had gathered from Penance's address that they were faced with someone who had single-handedly expelled Prince Khudu and his ragtag followers from the mountains without even leaving the Tomb, a victory that had won her great fame in the *wulin*. They could not help but shudder when her eyes, clear as an autumn stream and cold as tundra ice, rested upon them. Hao Datong was the only one who could withstand her scrutiny, thanks to his deep well of inner strength and the peace that dwelt in his heart-mind.

The Dragon Maiden turned back to Grandam Sun and stooped to examine her injuries. "Where does it hurt?"

Wheezing painfully, the old woman croaked, 'Mistress, I beg you . . ."

"What is it?" A hint of a frown was forming on the Dragon Maiden's brow.

Grandam Sun tried to place her hand on Penance, but she lacked the strength to move or to speak.

Nevertheless, the Dragon Maiden had understood her meaning. "You want me to look after him."

Grandam Sun mustered the last of her fast-fading life force to gasp, "Look after him . . . keep him from hardship . . . For life . . ."

"For life?"

"I looked after you all those years . . . Nursed you . . . washed you . . . sung you to sleep . . . Do it for me?"

The Dragon Maiden bit down on her lip. "Yes . . ."

A pale smile illuminated the old woman's face. She looked at Penance and opened her mouth, but no words came.

Penance crouched down. "Grandam?"

"Closer . . ."

He lowered himself and put his ear to her mouth.

"She is all . . . alone . . ." the dying woman rasped. "Look after . . . her . . . for I—" Blood shot from her lips, spraying Penance in the face and staining the front of his robe.

Grandam Sun's eyes shut for the last time.

"Grandam! Grandam!" Penance clasped his arms around her lifeless body.

Hao Datong, rueing his actions, went up and bowed to Grandam Sun. "It was never my intention to hurt you, Grandam. This is a sin I am destined to carry. Go well."

The Dragon Maiden showed no visible reaction to the monk's obeisance, but as he remained motionless on the spot, a frown began to crease her brow. "Shouldn't you give your life in atonement?"

"What?" The Taoist could not believe his ears.

"You have taken a life, now you pay with yours. Put your sword to your throat, and I shall spare the monks in your temple."

A clamour broke out before Hao Datong had a chance to respond.

"Nonsense!"

"Kill himself to spare us?"

"Who do you think you are, little girl?"

"Begone!"

But a wave of the Quanzhen Immortal's hand silenced his martial juniors.

The Dragon Maiden paid them no heed. She removed a small silken bundle from inside her robe, unfolded it slowly to reveal a pair of white gloves and put them on. Then she turned to Hao Datong: "Old monk, you fear death and cling to life. Unsheathe your sword and we shall fight."

The conscience-stricken Taoist let out a dry laugh. He was keenly aware that, to honour the connection between his *shifu* Wang Chongyang and the young woman's martial forebear, he should do everything in his power to avoid aggravating the situation further.

Moreover, he could not see himself coming to blows with someone so much younger, who had earned her reputation through the manipulation of bees. Even if she had been trained in the subtlest kung fu techniques, he was certain that, given her tender years, she could not possibly pose a greater threat than the old woman.

"Take Penance Yang and be on your way," he said, his tone conciliatory. "It is to this impoverished monk's shame that Grandam Sun lies cold, but I have no wish to take another life."

The Dragon Maiden ignored his words and raised her left hand slightly. A white silk ribbon unfurled itself and swept towards Hao Datong's face. The strip of cloth sliced through the night without stirring the air or making any sound. As it came closer, the Taoist could make out, fastened to the very end of the fabric, a small golden orb, glittering in the flickering torchlight.

Through all his long years in the *wulin*, Hao Datong had never seen a weapon so peculiar. And though he was confident that he was the superior martial artist, he had enough combat experience to understand that, when faced with the unknown, one should err on the side of caution and shy away from direct confrontation. So, he swerved to the left, out of the likely course of the flying ribbon. But the strip of fabric defied the seasoned fighter's expectation and changed trajectory mid-flight, hurtling once more at his face.

The golden sphere at the end of the ribbon danced around Hao Datong's nose, striking with staggering speed and precision. Welcome Fragrance – *ding* – Tear Receptacle – *ding* – Water Trough – *ding*. The metal ball tinkled softly as it threatened each pressure point, and the strange sound burrowed deep into his being, making his heart shake and his souls sway.

Rattled, the Taoist bent from the knees and tipped backwards in an Iron Bridge, bringing his upper body parallel with the ground. The cloth ribbon shot past him, inches from his head. Fearing that the golden orb would come around in pursuit of him, he veered sideways by three *chi* while maintaining the reclining pose.

Clunk! The metal orb hit the courtyard paving stones and the Dragon Maiden retrieved the ribbon with a flick of her wrist.

Hao Datong straightened up, his cheeks pale and waxen from the knowledge that she had chosen to spare him. He had to admit that he had grossly underestimated her prowess and that she had caught him out with a sophisticated, first-rate technique.

The other monks were equally shaken. As Hao Datong's disciples or martial nephews, they had long admired their senior's kung fu and never imagined they would witness him scrambling about in such an undignified manner. Four of the most hot-headed among them raised their swords and lunged at the Dragon Maiden.

"You should have used your weapons from the start," she said, extending both arms with a flourish.

Two white silk ribbons slithered and glided, like a pair of water snakes, into the air. *Ding ding ding ding.* The golden orbs fell with quickfire precision at the Spirit Pathway acupoint on the monks' wrists. Four swords clattered to the ground.

The sight of his juniors being disarmed with such ease stirred Hao Datong's competitive spirits. He took a sword from one of his disciples. "Miss Long's kung fu is truly outstanding. Come, let this impoverished monk learn from you."

The Dragon Maiden nodded and swept the pair of white ribbons from left to right, the golden orbs chiming as they cut through the air.

The monks stepped back and formed a large circle around the two fighters, looking on intently. With each fresh exchange, the duel grew more intense. The young woman's white dress fluttered in the night, her snowy ribbons slicing through the darkness like a moonbeam. The aged monk's grey habit flitted like a shadow, his razor-keen sword a shaft of silver lightning.

Hao Datong's craft had been honed over dozens of winters and summers, and he was considered the third or fourth most accomplished swordsmen in the Quanzhen Sect. And yet, his blade could make no headway against the twirling, swirling bolts of silk. The ribbons curled and coiled at will, agile as divine serpents. The golden orbs jingled as they flew, setting teeth on edge and ears ringing.

The Taoist grew testy at his inability to force a breakthrough. Thus far, he had managed to keep his steel from getting entangled and dragged away by the ribbons, but he dreaded to think what a loss of face it would be if a Master of his stature required more than a hundred moves to best a teenage girl. He decided to change tack, adopting a more measured approach and drawing out his movements. Each thrust now took longer to realise, but more force was channelled through his blade, giving him the additional power to slice directly through the fabric.

It did not take long for the decision to pay off – moments later, his weapon nicked one of the golden orbs. *Clank!* The metal sphere bounced off the sharp steel and hurtled towards the Dragon Maiden's face, carried by fearsome *neigong* force. Emboldened by his success, the Taoist threw his weight behind his blade, aiming for his opponent's wrist. The thrust drew cheers from the Quanzhen followers. Hao Datong was confident that it would compel the young woman to let go of her cloth strip. If she tried to cling on, her flesh would be laid open to the bone.

And yet, the Dragon Maiden's response upended all expectations. She flipped her palm down and wrapped her gloved fingers around the midpoint of the blade.

The whetted steel snapped with a loud crack.

Hao Datong jumped back to gasps of shock. He stared stupefied at the useless hilt in his hand, his face a cadaverous grey.

"I concede." His weary voice almost broke. "Miss Long, you may go with the boy."

It seemed clear to him that the Dragon Maiden had mastered a supreme kung fu that fortified her against the keen edge of a blade, but, in fact, the feat had been performed by her gloves. Passed down from her *shifu*'s teacher, they were woven from the finest strands of white gold. Flexible but resilient, they could withstand the sharpest steel, allowing her to seize the monk's sword and shatter it using a deft application of inner strength without worrying about being cut.

"You killed Grandam Sun. Conceding is not enough," the Dragon Maiden stated coldly.

Hao Datong let out a resigned laugh. "I am indeed old and muddled." He pressed the broken blade to his neck.

Claaaang! What remained of the sword flew out of his hands.

The Taoist knew his elder martial brother Qiu Chuji must have returned. Who else could have hurled a copper coin with sufficient force to overcome his own *neigong*-fortified grip?

Hao Datong lifted his face towards the top of the wall, where the projectile had been launched from, and saw the towering figure of Qiu Chuji looking down. "Brother Qiu, I have been an insult to your teachings."

The monk eyed his despondent martial brother and burst out laughing. "If I were to slit my throat each time I faced defeat, I'd need eighteen heads and that still wouldn't be enough!" He drew his sword from its sheath and jumped down into the courtyard.

"Qiu Chuji of the Quanzhen Sect wishes to learn from our accomplished neighbour." He thrust the steel at the Dragon Maiden's arm.

The young woman made no attempt to dodge or parry. She simply grabbed hold of the blade with her left hand.

"Brother!" Hao Datong's warning came too late.

The instant the Dragon Maiden's fingers made contact, relaying her inner strength, she knew the monk's kung fu far surpassed his martial brother's – his power was coursing to the very tip of the sword. The two forces vied for dominance until the metal fractured with a *kacha!* The energy unleashed as it ruptured first deadened her arm then made itself felt as a dull ache in her chest. She knew that she could not hope to overpower this Taoist monk until she had mastered the whole of the Jade Maid Heart Scripture repertoire.

The Dragon Maiden cast down the broken sword, gathered up Grandam Sun's body with her left arm and lifted Penance Yang in her right, then flexed her feet and hopped over the wall, as though her burden weighed nothing and she was floating on the air.

Qiu Chuji and Hao Datong exchanged a look of surprise. They were confident the young woman was the lesser martial artist – certainly when compared with Qiu Chuji – though her kung fu was intricate and unusual. They had assumed her lightness *qinggong* would be on the same level, but what she had just demonstrated was proof of a virtuosity they had never before witnessed.

Hearing his martial brother's sigh, Qiu Chuji said, "Brother Hao, have you learned nothing in all your decades searching for the Way? Are you really unable to surmount one little setback? You know, we brothers ended up with a faceful of dust in Shanxi this time."

"What? Is anyone hurt?"

"It's a long story – I'll tell you when we reach Brother Ma's cabin."

IT WAS because of Blithe Li the Red Serpent Celestial that Qiu Chuji, Wang Chuyi and ten of their disciples had travelled to Shanxi. After harrying Lu Liding and his family in Jiaxing in the South, the Taoist nun had headed north-west to the heart of the Central Plains, where she came into conflict with and injured a number of martial heroes. Her vicious behaviour provoked the leading *wulin* figures in the area to send out summons throughout the land, rallying their martial brethren to join forces to capture her.

When the news reached the Quanzhen Sect, the monks agreed that, despite the evils she had committed, they would first try to reason with her and offer her a chance to mend her ways, in deference to the history between the founders of their two martial schools. Ma Yu sent his younger martial brother and sister, Liu Chuxuan and Sun Bu'er, north to track her down. Although they ran into her a few times, they could not bring her round to their way of thinking. The Red Serpent Celestial ended up maiming several more martial men in Shanxi, and that was when Qiu Chuji and Wang Chuyi were brought into the affair.

When Blithe Li had learned that the Quanzhen Sect was sending another two of the Immortals to pursue her, she devised a plan to goad them into single combat, knowing she would not last long against so many renowned fighters all at once. The first to accept the challenge was Sun Bu'er and she was caught out by the deadly Soul of Ice needles. After the duel, Blithe Li called on Qiu Chuji, offering the life-saving antidote. In accepting the remedy, the Quanzhen Sect were obliged to withdraw and could never again come after the Red Serpent Celestial, for it was against the martial code to wage war on those one owed a debt of gratitude. Wang Chuyi stayed in Shanxi and went on a pilgrimage to Taihang Mountain with their disciples, while Qiu Chuji returned directly to Chongyang Temple, arriving at the conclusion of Hao Datong's duel with the Dragon Maiden.

Qiu Chuji flew into a rage when he learned that the clash with the residents of the Tomb of the Living Dead had originated from Zhao Zhijing's unfair treatment of Penance Yang. He had hoped that the Quanzhen Sect would make an upstanding hero of the boy, offering redress for his failings in the education of the boy's father, Yang Kang. Now, all his plans were thwarted. He had lost custodianship of Penance to the Tomb of the Living Dead and he could not possibly take him back by force. Nevertheless, he promised himself that he would continue to keep an eye on the youngster, for he could not fail Guo Jing.

The Taoist was also thoroughly disappointed with Zhao Zhijing. He was the best fighter of the third generation, and Ma Yu had intended to nominate him for the post of the Foremost Disciple, which would give him a prominent leadership role in the Sect – but it was apparent his character and judgement were wanting. When he was tasked with defending the temple with the massed Heavenly Northern Dipper formations, he had allowed himself to become so single-mindedly focused on Guo Jing that he let their true enemies slip by. Now, with Penance, he had exposed the depths of his petty, violent nature. The Quanzhen Immortals decided to put Zhen Zhibing, a student of Qiu Chuji, forward for the premier position, and that made the jealous Zhao Zhijing resent Penance even more.

5

THE DRAGON MAIDEN SET PENANCE DOWN WHEN THEY WERE some distance from Chongyang Temple and shifted Grandam Sun's body to a more dignified position in her arms. She headed straight to the old woman's chamber when they entered the Tomb and placed her on the bed. She then lit a candle and sat down beside her in silence, cradling her chin in her hands. Penance buried his face in Grandam Sun's chest and sobbed.

The two of them stayed like this for a long time, then, out of the blue, the Dragon Maiden said, "She's dead. She can't hear you."

Her words shocked Penance. How could anyone be so unfeeling? But when he pondered her meaning, he could not deny her logic. It plunged him deeper into his grief and he cried even harder.

Silent and still, the Dragon Maiden watched the boy with unsympathetic eyes. Eventually, she said, "Come with me. We will bury her." She snuffed out the candle and carried Grandam Sun's body out of the room.

Wiping his face hastily with his sleeve, Penance scrabbled to his feet and hurried after the Dragon Maiden. He opened his eyes as wide as he could, but there was not so much as half a spark of light in the pitch-black corridor – he could not even make out her white dress. The only indication of her presence was the quiet scratching of her footsteps. He followed the noise, meandering east and twisting west, making sure he was never more than a step behind. When they at last stopped, he heard the grating groans of stone against stone and, a moment later, a flame burst into life.

He was standing at the entrance to a large chamber. The room was guarded by heavy double doors made of limestone. The Dragon Maiden had set Grandam Sun down on a long table and lit a pair of oil lamps. He stepped inside and shivered at the sight.

Five sarcophagi. Lined up, side by side.

"The Doyenne sleeps there and *Shifu* here." The Dragon Maiden gestured at the casket on the far right, then the one to its left, both of which were sealed.

Penance's eyes turned to the remaining three. The stone lids were half open, yet to be slotted into place. Are those occupied? What if they house the undead . . . ? His heart hammered in fear as his mind ran wild.

"Grandam Sun will sleep in this one."

He breathed out in relief to hear the rest of the coffins were empty. "What about those two?"

"For my martial sister Blithe Li – and for me."

Penance remembered the sadistic woman well. He would not have met Guo Jing and ended up here if Wu Santong had not taken shelter in the abandoned kiln he once called home and led that woman there.

"Will she . . . come back?"

"This is all as *Shifu* decreed, so she will return one day. We are missing yours though."

"I don't want one!"

"I gave Grandam Sun my word that I would look after you for life. You shall live where I live."

"I'll go where I want when you're dead!"

"I won't die before you. I said I would look after you for life."

"You're older than me!"

"I shall kill you before I expire."

"Grandam Sun told me to look after you for life too . . ."

"If we are both dead, then no-one has to look after anybody." The Dragon Maiden pushed open the lid of the sarcophagus in the middle and carried Grandam Sun's body over to it.

"Can I say goodbye?"

Penance's words made the Dragon Maiden pause. She could not understand why the boy was so attached to the old woman and she found his histrionics irksome – they had known each other for just one day. Furrowing her brow, she shot him a glare and laid Grandam Sun in her final resting place. Then she grabbed the stone lid and pulled. The heavy cover slotted into place with a loud crash.

"Let's go." She flicked her sleeve, extinguishing the lamps, and strode out of the chamber in complete darkness, without even a glance at the youngster, for she dreaded he would break down weeping again.

Penance scrambled after her, terrified that she would shut him in the room with the dead bodies.

THERE WAS no telling whether the sun had risen or set inside the Tomb, but they were both exhausted after wrangling with the Quanzhen Sect for a good part of the night. The Dragon Maiden took Penance to Grandam Sun's room. "You sleep here." She relit the candle on the table.

Finding himself standing by the bed where the old woman's cold body had lain not long ago, Penance was struck dumb with terror. He thought he had been toughened up by the years fending for himself after his mother's death, sleeping rough in the wild or in derelict temples, but right now, the prospect of closing his eyes in an underground burial complex with three occupied coffins was petrifying.

"Did you hear me?" the Dragon Maiden asked when she did not get a response.

". . . I'm scared."

"Of what?"

"I . . . I don't want to be here on my own."

Creases lined the Dragon Maiden's forehead. "Come to my room then." She put out the candle and led Penance back into the corridor.

Having grown up in the Tomb, the Dragon Maiden could move around and conduct basic tasks without the need for light.

Nevertheless, when they reached her chamber, she located a candle and lit it for the boy.

Penance had heard storytellers on street corners describing the boudoirs of beautiful ladies and his curiosity got the better of him, in spite of his physical fatigue and his unease among the dead. He was eager to see if the Dragon Maiden's room was as elegantly appointed as those in the stories. But when the candle flame came to life, the youngster was sorely disappointed. A spartan stone chamber, much like the sepulchre in which they had interred Grandam Sun. The only objects that could be described as furnishings were the folded white sheet and straw mat on a long strip of bluestone.

"You sleep there." The Dragon Maiden motioned at the bed.

"The floor is good enough."

"You must obey me if you want to stay. I will take your life without a second thought if you defy me."

"Alright, don't be so mean."

"How dare you talk back to me."

Penance stuck his tongue out. He could not understand why this elegant young woman was so determined to play the bully.

"What was the meaning of that?"

Ignoring her, Penance took off his shoes and climbed onto the bed. The instant he lay down, a biting frostiness leeched straight to his bones. He scrambled to get off.

"What is it now?" The Dragon Maiden's voice was cold, but the glint of a jest was unmistakable in her eyes.

Noting her amusement, Penance flashed a grin and spoke in a more familiar tone: "You've done this to make sport of me."

"Go to sleep. This is what the bed is like." She took a broom from a corner. "I'll thrash you ten times if you get out again."

Penance lay back on the straw mat with reluctance. Now he knew what to expect, the bed's freezing touch was less of a shock, but it still felt as if he were resting on a thick block of ice. In no time at all, the bone-chilling cold grew so unbearable that he started to shiver uncontrollably and his teeth clattered audibly. He thought he caught the Dragon Maiden watching him with a half-smile on her lips, relishing his suffering. Seething with indignation, he clenched his jaw and stiffened his joints to try to keep still.

Meanwhile, the Dragon Maiden took a piece of rope and fastened one end to a hook attached high on the wall, then secured the other to a robust iron nail at the same height on the far side, stretching it across the room. Then she sprang up, reclined on the suspended cord and waved her hand to put out the candle.

She can sleep on a rope? Penance was so awed by the feat he forgot all about his one-sided standoff. "Auntie, can you teach me this amazing skill tomorrow?"

"This little trick? I have many powerful techniques to show you, if you work hard."

Penance sensed the sincerity of her words beneath the nonchalant tone, and all the grudges and hard feelings he had been harbouring flew beyond the ninth heavens.

"You're so kind to me, Auntie!" Tears of gratitude trickled down his cheeks. "You know, I hated you earlier."

"I did throw you out."

"Not because of that. I thought you were like my previous *shifus*. They wouldn't teach me anything." His voice wobbled from his shivering.

"Are you cold?"

"Of course! What's the bed made of? Why is it so cold?"

"Do you like sleeping on it?"

"Er . . . no."

"Many martial Masters dream of spending a night on this bed."

"So . . . it's not a punishment?"

"I give you the best and you think I'm mistreating you?"

Realising his mistake, Penance pleaded in his sweetest voice: "Auntie, do tell me about this bed! What's so good about it?"

"Sleep and you will learn its benefits. Now, close your eyes and be quiet."

Penance had more questions, but he was intimidated by her terse

tone and astounded by the noise he had just heard. He was quite sure it was the rustle of fabric.

Did she just turn on her side? he wondered. But she's sleeping on a rope suspended several *chi* off the floor!

He stopped staring into the darkness and tried to doze off, but how could he find repose while being assaulted by grief on a frozen slab of rock?

"Auntie, I'm really cold," Penance said weakly after some time.

Gentle, even breathing was his only answer.

He called again in hushed tones. Still no response.

Keeping his breathing as quiet as possible, Penance slipped off the bed. He thought he had managed to avoid waking the Dragon Maiden, but the moment his feet touched the floor, he heard a faint tap. The next thing he knew, his left arm was being twisted behind his back, his face was pressed against the paving stones and the broomstick was falling on his buttocks.

He let out a yelp and gritted his teeth to brace himself for the humiliating chastisement, for he knew it would be futile to beg for mercy. The first five clouts were hard and painful, but by the sixth, he thought the broom was easing off. The final two strokes could be described as mild raps.

"You'll get another thrashing if you sneak out of bed again." With that, the Dragon Maiden tossed Penance back onto the straw mat. Then she put away the broom and hopped up onto the rope. She had expected him to wail and bawl and make a scene, but his stoicism took her by surprise. After a while, she asked, "Why did you not protest?"

"What's the point? You said you'd beat me if I got out of bed."

"You're cursing me in your head though."

"I am not. You're much better than the other *shifus* I've had.

"What do you mean?"

"You beat me, but you also care about me and don't want to hurt me too much. That's why the blows got lighter."

The Dragon Maiden's cheeks burned at having had her secret

called out. "Fie! Who cares about you? If you disobey me again, I'll beat you harder."

Noting her tone was much milder than her words, Penance replied glibly, "I don't mind." Then he added, sounding more earnest. "You do it for my own good, because you care. And you don't know how happy that makes me. Besides my late mother, my adopted father and Uncle Guo, you and Grandam Sun are the only people who have ever cared about me . . ."

"I don't care about you," the Dragon Maiden corrected him. "I only look after you because Grandam Sun told me to."

Hearing her cold response, Penance felt like he had been doused over the head with a bucket of icy water and it made the freezing bed even harder to bear.

"Why do you dislike me so?"

"I don't dislike you. This is who I am. I've spent my life in the Tomb, never liking or disliking anyone."

"Isn't it very boring? Have you never set foot in the world outside?"

"I have never left the Zhongnan Mountains. The world outside also has the sun, the moon, mountains and trees, has it not?"

"*Aiyo!* You've lived your life in vain! There are all kinds of wonderful things in the cities!" Penance proceeded to describe the sights and sounds he had come across in his years of roaming the countryside around Jiaxing on his own. A gifted storyteller, he embroidered his experiences into a patchwork of strange and fantastic encounters.

Having known only the Tomb of the Living Dead and its immediate surroundings for the eighteen years of her life, the Dragon Maiden believed every word of Penance's exaggerated account. When he was finished, she could not help but let out a sigh.

"Auntie, I'll show you the fun things out there."

"Nonsense. It is the Doyenne's decree that those who reside in the Tomb of the Living Dead should never step beyond the Zhongnan Mountains."

"What? So I can't leave either?"

"That's right. You can't."

But Penance was not disheartened. I managed to get away from Peach Blossom Island, in the middle of the sea! he reminded himself. No tomb can trap me for life!

"What about Blithe Li?" he asked. "She's your martial sister. She must have lived here. How did she leave?"

"She was cast out by *Shifu* for her defiance."

Ha! Now I know what to do when I want to leave, Penance said to himself. Though he was excited, he realised he must keep this idea a secret if he wanted it to work. He also noticed that, whenever he was speaking, he forgot about the cold, but the instant the last word left his lips, he was overcome by shivers again.

"Auntie, spare me! I don't want to sleep here."

"You didn't beg the Quanzhen monks. Why are you so weak now?"

"Because they're nasty to me. I won't give in to them, even in words. But those who are nice to me, I'd give them my life, so, I don't mind begging them for mercy." His cheeky response elicited a harrumph from the Dragon Maiden, but he could tell she was not actually displeased and seized the moment to play up his discomfort: "Auntie, I'm froooozen! I caaaaan't stand this anymore!"

"Hush now and I will tell you about the bed."

"Yes, please, I'll be quiet!"

"You are lying on a piece of primeval boreal nephrite. It is an excellent aid for developing advanced *neigong*."

"This rock?"

"It came from the bitterly frozen lands of the furthermost north, buried deep under the hardest ice. A close friend of the Doyenne devoted years of their life to excavating it. If you cultivate inner strength on this bed, the progress you'll make in twelve months will be equal to what another person can accumulate in a decade working on their own."

"That's amazing."

"The natural circulation of *qi* and blood is altered when we practise *neigong*, but when we sleep, everything returns to its original flow,

245

undoing nine tenths of our achievement. However, when you sleep on the boreal nephrite, you muster all the internal energy in the body to resist the cold, and over time, that becomes second nature, so as you doze, you are still utilising your inner power, consolidating and building on your training during the day."

"Sleeping in the snow has the same effect too?"

"No, the boreal nephrite is far colder."

"Now I see why I am all bundled up in quilted dark robes and you just wear a flowing white dress – because the chill of winter doesn't affect you!"

"I am not bothered by low temperatures and I care not what my clothes look like. The nephrite bed has another important function. It increases the rate of *neigong* attainment because it also lowers the risk of misfiring into the demonic way. Usually, half our focus is turned to resisting the heart-fire, but the boreal nephrite is the most *yin* and gelid material under the heavens, it can quench the heart-fire, so when we train sitting or lying on it, we can give our full attention to our practice."

"You're so good to me, Auntie. I don't know how I can repay your kindness. I'll live up to Grandam Sun's last request and look after you for life."

"How will you do that when you only know how to moan and whine?"

"I'll work hard! I'll catch up with Zhao Zhijing and the Quanzhen monks, and I won't fear the Wu brothers or Hibiscus Guo again."

"You live in the Tomb now. You must abide by the Doyenne's rules. Cultivate the heart, nurture the character, curb the urge to compete and compare."

"But the Quanzhen monks killed Grandam Sun! We're not going to let it pass, are we?"

"Death is inevitable. If Grandam Sun had not died at Hao Datong's hands, she would have met her end soon enough. What is the difference between living a few years longer or shorter? Talk not of revenge again."

The Dragon Maiden knew she should stop chatting to Penance, but she could not help being drawn into conversation. She had been brought up to disassociate from her emotions from a young age in order to practise Jade Maid Heart Scripture, and her *shifu* would chastise her if she laughed or cried. And Grandam Sun, although kindly and warm-hearted, had put on an icy distant front to avoid compromising her martial cultivation. In time, the young woman's personality and temperament became frosty cold. But Penance was the complete opposite of Grandam Sun in the way he acted and spoke – he burned with the fire of youth and she was captivated.

Hearing him squirm on the boreal nephrite, she said, "I will teach you how to withstand the cold," and began to recite a *neigong* mnemonic.

Penance followed her explanation and tapped into his inner strength. Within moments, the shivering abated somewhat. By the third circulation of *qi* throughout his body, a fire kindled in his core and he no longer minded the nephrite's frigid touch. It was now cooling and comfortable. His eyes grew heavy and he drifted off.

However, in less than an hour, the heat generated had dissipated and he was once more frozen stiff. He applied the same method and before long felt warm enough to doze. He woke up several times through the night to numbing cold, but he was surprisingly refreshed when he eventually rose, despite the interrupted rest. In just one sleep, he had not only improved his mastery of internal energy, he had also been initiated into the foundational kung fu devised by the Doyenne of the Tomb of the Living Dead.

6

THE NEXT DAY, AFTER THEY HAD BROKEN FAST AND PENANCE had washed the dishes, the Dragon Maiden said, "If you bow to me and call me *Shifu*, you must obey me for life. If you don't wish to do so, I will still give you kung fu lessons and you can leave the Tomb if you beat me one day. Think carefully before you answer."

"Of course, I will bow to you," Penance replied immediately. "I'll always listen to you whether you teach me or not."

"Why?"

"Because you treat me well – from your heart."

"Never let such words hang about your lips again," she said sternly. "If you are certain you wish to honour me as your *shifu*, we will perform the rites in the rear hall now."

Penance followed the Dragon Maiden to a stone chamber as spartan as all the other rooms in the Tomb he had seen so far. Other than a table and two candlesticks, all it contained were two paintings, affixed on opposite walls. On one side, a hanging scroll depicted a lady at her toilet. The woman sat before the dressing table, her back to the viewer. She was waited on by a girl of fourteen or fifteen carrying a basin of water. The lady's face was only visible in the mirror she was looking into. She was around twenty-five years of age, and her well-proportioned features, especially her eyes, conveyed a fierceness that demanded respect.

"This is our Doyenne. Kowtow to her." The Dragon Maiden motioned at the lady at the dressing table.

"She looks very young."

"She was when the portrait was painted. Then she grew old."

A pang of sorrow struck Penance. He could not take his eyes off the face in the mirror, and tears were threatening to fall.

The Dragon Maiden then gestured at the serving girl, oblivious to his emotional state. "This is my *shifu*. Kowtow to her too."

Penance tilted his head to one side and studied the image. This young woman, with the artless, open expression of a child, would one day become the Dragon Maiden's martial teacher. He knelt and – *thud, thud, thud* – knocked his forehead on the floor, his heart bursting with sincerity.

Once Penance was back on his feet, the Dragon Maiden pointed at the painting on the opposite wall. "Now spit at that Taoist monk."

The man was depicted from behind, so his face was not in view. Tall in stature, he was gesturing towards the top corner of the picture with his right index finger, and a sword hung from his belt.

"Who is he? Why do we have to spit at him?"

"He is Wang Chongyang, the founder of the Quanzhen Sect. It is the rule of our martial school that we spit at him after bowing to the Doyenne."

Tickled by this amusing requirement, Penance hawked with glee and aimed a huge gob of phlegm at the painted figure. He hacked again, sending more sputum flying, accompanied by a cry of "Stinker!"

"Enough." The Dragon Maiden stopped Penance when he tried to cough up mucus for a third time.

"The Doyenne hated Wang Chongyang, didn't she?"

"Yes."

"I hate him too! Why do we keep a painting of him? Why didn't the Doyenne tear it up?"

"I don't know why, but *Shifu* and Grandam Sun have both said that there is not a single good man under the heavens . . ." She cast a glance at Penance and her voice took on a hard edge. "I will show no mercy if you err."

"You'll forgive me."

The Dragon Maiden was stumped for a comeback. She had not expected the boy to counter her so boldly. "Now bow to your *shifu*!" she said, changing the subject.

"Yes, I will. But first, you must promise me one thing."

"What is it?" She eyed the youngster, her voice betraying no emotion. She remembered what Grandam Sun had said about the rituals when accepting disciples: it was common for *shifus* to ask their future protégés to make pledges, but the reverse was unheard of.

"You are my *shifu* in here," he said, placing his hand over his chest. "I will respect you, honour you, do anything you ask, but I won't call you *Shifu* – I will only call you Auntie."

"Why?" the Dragon Maiden asked after a pause.

"I was made to bow to that foul Quanzhen monk and call him by the title *shifu*. If I address you in the same way, the next time I curse him in my dreams, I'll be insulting you too."

A rogue smile stole upon the Dragon Maiden's lips. "As you wish."

"Disciple Penance Yang bows to Auntie Long." Penance went down on his knees and thumped his forehead on the floor loudly eight times to demonstrate his sincerity. "From now on, I pledge to always obey Auntie. I shall dedicate this life to looking after Auntie and keeping Auntie from danger. I also swear to slay anyone who means Auntie ill."

Being the far more capable martial artist, the Dragon Maiden had no need of Penance's protection, but she was moved by the solemnity with which the childish oath was delivered.

"There is little purpose to mastering the martial arts," she stated after a while, noticing how his eyes were glowing with excitement. "And I do not have the skill to best the Quanzhen Taoist Qiu Chuji or your Uncle Guo."

"I don't care how powerful they are. I'm happy because you are willing to teach me."

"It is simply a way to pass time."

"Auntie, what is the name of our kung fu branch?"

"We don't have one, because the Doyenne ceased all dealings with the *wulin* after moving into the Tomb. But it is said that people described Martial Sister Li as a disciple of the Ancient Tomb Sect. That can be our name."

"No!" Penance shook his head vehemently. "It's terrible!"

"What does it matter? They are mere words," the Dragon Maiden replied flatly, indifferent to his outburst. "Wait here."

"I'll come with you!" Penance did not wish to be left on his own in this place of death.

"You just promised to be obedient always."

"I'm scared."

The Dragon Maiden shot the boy a quizzical look, throwing back at him his bold manly promises to protect her.

Feeling self-conscious, he conceded. ". . . Come back quickly."

"I can't say how long it will take to catch them."

"Catch who?"

But the Dragon Maiden was already gone, leaving Penance to the echo of his own voice.

Auntie can't leave the mountains, so she must have gone after the Quanzhen monks, he reasoned, and he began to guess which one she would bring back, indulging in fantasies of what he would do to punish the Taoist cow muzzles. Then he remembered she had ventured out on her own. What if she ran into trouble?

Penance hurried out of the stone chamber, intent on finding the Dragon Maiden, but a dozen steps took him beyond the reach of the candlelight and he was engulfed by darkness. He placed his hand on the wall, turned around and carefully counted his paces.

"Twenty," he muttered under his breath, and yet, he was still surrounded by blackness. Panic seized his chest and he scampered faster. Each footfall took him further from his intended destination. He ran into walls and tripped over obstacles. He could see nothing, but he could feel the corridor splitting and forking into many passageways, none leading back to where he had started.

"Auntie! Auntie! Help!"

His cries bounced off the stonework. His distorted voice, muffled and indistinct, was his only answer.

He blundered on. Moisture was seeping into the thick cloth sole of his shoes. Mud splattered each time he lifted his foot. He had strayed off the paved walkways into some naturally formed region of the subterranean complex.

Auntie will find me eventually if I'm still in the built-up part of the Tomb, but here? Penance began to fret. Will she think I've run away? Will she be sad that I'm gone?

He dared not fumble any further. He groped around and found a piece of rock to perch on. Cradling his head, he wanted to cry, but his body would not make a sound.

So he sat there, waiting, for he knew not how long. Two hours?

Three? Suddenly, he thought he heard his name. He leapt up in joy and yelled at the top of his lungs, "Auntie! I'm here! I'm here!"

But the call of "Penance! Penance!" grew more faint with each repetition.

"Over here! Over here!" he bellowed with his whole being, but the only response was the hush of the earth, or the ghost of his voice.

After some time, Penance felt a cold touch on the tip of his ear, then a pinch and a pull and he was hauled from the rock onto his feet.

But instead of yelping in pain, he gushed, "Auntie! You're back! I didn't hear you coming at all!"

"What are you doing here?"

"I got lost."

The Dragon Maiden took his hand and guided him back to the main part of the Tomb. She navigated through the inky black environment as though they were above ground, her pace swift and sure, untroubled by the tunnels' labyrinthine twists and turns.

"How do you see your way?"

"I grew up in the dark. I have no need of light."

For once, Penance did not have a rejoinder. He trotted after the Dragon Maiden without a word, trying to grapple with the wild extremes of emotions he had just experienced, from the fear of being lost to the joy of being found.

When they re-entered the paved area of the Tomb, Penance said with relief, "I was really worried back there."

"Why? I would have found you eventually."

"No, not that. I thought you'd think I'd run away."

"Then I wouldn't have to keep my promise to Grandam Sun."

Penance tried to overlook the dispiriting answer and changed the subject. "Auntie, did you manage to . . . ?" he trailed off, unsure if he should ask outright.

"Yes. Follow me. We shall begin your training."

The youngster scuttered along, picturing how he would put the kung fu moves he was about to learn into practice against the Quanzhen monk she had captured.

What a fun way to learn! he rejoiced – his experience of martial lessons to date had been the tedium of memorising verses and mnemonics. Maybe Auntie has captured Zhao Zhijing. How thrilling will that be! I get to kick and punch that nasty man and he can't raise a hand to stop me.

The Dragon Maiden led Penance down a long, winding passage and pushed open a stone door. As she kindled the lamplight, the boy found himself shut in an incredibly cramped space with his teacher. There was barely room to twist around and face another direction. The ceiling was also much lower than in the other chambers he had visited. He reckoned the Dragon Maiden could touch it with her fingertips if she stretched her arm out.

"Where's the monk?" he asked.

"Hmm?"

"You said you'd captured someone for me to try out my kung fu on."

The Dragon Maiden shot him a look and picked up a sack tucked away in a corner. She undid the string tied around the opening, tipped the bag upside down and gave it a shake.

Three sparrows flew out.

"You went to catch these?"

Unruffled by Penance's astonishment, the Dragon Maiden issued the instructions for his first lesson – "Catch the sparrows without damaging their feathers or injuring them" – and leaned back to give him room.

"Yes, Auntie!"

Full of excitement, Penance jumped up and down, his arms reaching high. But the sparrows flitted away long before his grasping hands got anywhere near them. Soon, he was drenched in sweat and panting for air.

"Let me show you." She demonstrated numerous ways to spring high and dive low, as well as myriad techniques for the hands – swipe, grab, seize, pinch . . .

Penance committed every word and every move to memory, but he struggled to imitate them, let alone apply them with any efficacy.

The Dragon Maiden left him to practise on his own for the rest of the day. After supper, he lay on the boreal nephrite and channelled his inner strength. The next day, he noticed he was jumping a little bit higher and his hands seemed more dexterous, though he was still much slower than the sparrows and they continued to evade him with ease.

On the fifth day, Penance managed to wrap his fingers around one of the birds. Clasping the miserable creature between his palms, he ran to the Dragon Maiden's room, eager to show her he had at last succeeded.

"You are supposed to catch all three at the same time," she said flatly.

Although Penance had not received the praise he was hoping for, he was not disheartened and told himself it would not be hard to seize all three when he had managed to catch one. He went back to the cell, full of enthusiasm for his task, and yet, he failed to come near any of the birds. The bad spell continued the next day, and his lot did not improve even after another sleep. The Dragon Maiden came to check on his progress and saw how exhausted the sparrows were. She fed them grains of rice and set them free. Then she returned with another three so he could continue his training.

On the eighth day, the youngster finally triumphed.

Once the Dragon Maiden had verified his achievement, she said, "We are going to Chongyang Temple today."

Penance asked why as he hastened after his teacher, but no answer was forthcoming. He squeezed his eyes shut the instant they emerged above ground – it was the first time he had stood in the open air under the sun in days. Soon, he found they had arrived at the monastery's main gate. He stole a sideways glance at her and his heart grew ill at ease. He could discern no clue from her inscrutable face as to why they had come here.

Then he heard her call: "Zhao Zhijing, come out!"

CHAPTER SIX

THE JADE MAID
HEART SCRIPTURE

I

SCORES OF QUANZHEN DISCIPLES MARCHED FROM THE TEMPLE, their hands clasped over the hilts of their swords, ready for battle. The last to make an appearance was Zhao Zhijing. He shuffled out, supported by a teenage monk on each side.

The Dragon Maiden removed a ceramic vial from inside her robe and handed it to Penance. "Give this to Zhao Zhijing." She then addressed the monks gathered: "This honey neutralises the bee venom."

Penance was shocked to see his former *shifu*'s deterioration. It was plain that his tormenter lacked the strength to walk or stand by himself. His eyes had sunk deeper into their sockets, and his complexion was sallow and haggard.

Reluctantly, Penance trotted up to the sickly man and deposited the bottle unceremoniously on the ground. Clenching his jaw, he shot the Taoist a glare before turning around to go back to the Dragon Maiden's side.

The Quanzhen followers were dumbstruck. They thought the

Dragon Maiden had come to avenge Grandam Sun's death. That was why they had sallied out, armed for battle, as soon as they heard her challenge. They had alerted Ma Yu, Qiu Chuji and the other elders of her arrival. How could they have known that she had come to deliver the antidote?

"You think you can walk away after betraying us?" Lu Qingdu yelled as he darted out from the ranks.

That day at the trials, the overweight monk had been knocked unconscious by Exploding Toad kung fu and his breathing had stopped. But Penance had very little *neigong* power to speak of, so the blow's effects were short-lived. When Qiu Chuji had returned to Chongyang Temple later that night, he treated the injured man by massaging his vital points, and Lu Qingdu made a full recovery several days later. Now he was face to face with his attacker again, he was bent on vengeance.

"We will not raise our hands today, Penance."

The Dragon Maiden's reminder came as the youngster heard footsteps approaching behind him. The next instant he sensed the air parting at the back of his neck – a hand grabbing at his collar.

But Penance continued to walk in the same direction at the same pace, as though oblivious.

Just as Lu Qingdu's fingers grazed the fabric of his robe, Penance hunched and shot forward. At the same time, he reached behind and gave the Taoist's habit a tug. The bulky monk lurched and tumbled head over heels.

Of course, Lu Qingdu could not have guessed that, in just a matter of days, Penance had been initiated in the foundational techniques of the Ancient Tomb Sect's lightness *qinggong*, and that he had also begun to nurture his inner strength by sleeping on the boreal nephrite bed every night. That was why Penance could evade the attack and then retaliate by using the monk's own force against him.

Spluttering in rage, Lu Qingdu scrambled to his feet and prepared to launch himself at Penance again.

Just then, another Taoist flew out of the ranks, moving so fast that his feet barely touched the ground. He seized Lu Qingdu by the arm and dragged him back.

With half his body numbed by his brother monk's rough hold, Lu Qingdu opened his mouth to curse. Then he realised it was his martial uncle Zhen Zhibing who had pulled him back and he swallowed the insults.

When Lu Qingdu had calmed down somewhat, Zhen Zhibing relaxed his grip and bowed to the visitors. "I thank Miss Long for the antidote."

"Let's go home." The Dragon Maiden took Penance's hand and walked away without sparing the monks a glance.

AS SOON as they were back in the Tomb, the Dragon Maiden said sternly, "You should not have done that."

"Why not? That fat monk beat me half to death. And I listened to you. I didn't raise my hand at him."

She shook her head. "You shouldn't have done what you did — pulling him over. You should have made him slip and land on his backside, all by himself. That would have made a real fool of him."

"Teach me! Please!"

"I am you. And you are him. Now, try to catch me." She turned around and walked away.

With a chuckle, Penance made a grab for the Dragon Maiden, but the young woman seemed to have eyes in the back of her head. When he sped up, so did she. When he slowed down, she did too. Always maintaining a distance of three strides.

"Here I come!" Penance announced before diving after her. To his surprise, the Dragon Maiden did not try to evade him. However, just before his arms closed around her, she glided away at an angle and slipped from his grasp.

Twirling his arms around, Penance again tried to catch her, but the energy flow of this sudden action went against the forward momentum of the initial lunge. The powerful opposing forces rocked his footing and he tipped backwards and hit the cold stone floor.

"Auntie, what a clever manoeuvre!" Penance grabbed her extended hand and pulled himself up. The throbbing pain in his back did nothing to dampen his spirits. "How do you move so fast?"

"You can do the same too, if you spend another year catching sparrows."

"I can catch them already."

"You can?" she scoffed. "Do you think Ancient Tomb kung fu can be mastered so easily? Come along now."

The Dragon Maiden led Penance to a stone chamber twice the size of the cell in which he had first started practising with the sparrows. Six of the winged creatures were already flitting about inside. She then outlined a number of lightness *qinggong* techniques, and warned him that it would be much harder to capture the birds in the larger space. She expounded on ways to lift the body and spring into the air, as well as further grapple and lock methods to help him intercept them in flight.

Nine days later, Penance managed to trap all six sparrows in a single attempt. Whenever he succeeded in laying his hands on every one of his practice companions in the room, the Dragon Maiden moved him to a larger chamber with more of the chittering creatures. With each passing day, Penance grasped a little more of the Ancient Tomb Sect's martial foundations, and his *neigong* power also improved each night as he slept, thanks to the boreal nephrite. In three months' time, he emerged triumphant from the most spacious hall of the Tomb, having snared eighty-one sparrows in a single attempt.

"You have grasped the basic techniques underpinning the Supple Net. Now, we will test your skills outside." Seeing that Penance was visibly thrilled by the idea, the Dragon Maiden added, "Not a single sparrow, out of our eighty-one, can be allowed to escape."

IT WAS the third moon of the year and the tender green shoots of late spring adorned every branch. Penance stepped outside the Tomb and inhaled deeply, filling his lungs with the refreshing fragrance of grass and flowers.

The Dragon Maiden opened the sack she had brought along and out flew the eighty-one sparrows. They beat their wings, taking off in every direction.

A flourish of the hand here. A twirl of the arm there. She flitted around as swift as any bird, blocking the flock's access to the open sky and keeping them grouped together within a space of three *chi* before her.

Penance marvelled, mouth agape, at her lightsome movements. It was as if her arms were performing a complicated dance that multiplied her two palms, swishing and swirling, into a thousand.

The sparrows darted and dived here and there, but they could not break out of the invisible web woven by her hands.

Auntie is showing me some incredible palm kung fu! Penance began to observe more closely, following the myriad ways she reached out to block and drew back to strike. Her palms flew at great speed, but every thrust and gesture was crisp and clear-cut. Although he had yet to grasp the essence of the technique, he thought he could spot a pattern that allowed him to break her movements down into coherent groups and sequences.

When the Dragon Maiden's demonstration was finished, she stepped back and lowered her arms, clasping her hands behind her.

The pressure confining the sparrows vanished and they scattered skywards.

The Dragon Maiden leapt high and unfurled her long flowing sleeves, whipping up a gust that knocked the birds out of the air. "This kung fu to stop them taking flight is called Stretch and Flex in the Jade-Blue Sky."

The creatures squeaked and squawked and waggled about on the ground. It was some time before they were able to flutter their wings and fly beyond the treetops again.

Penance went up to the Dragon Maiden and held onto the hem of her sleeve, full of admiration. "I bet Uncle Guo can't do that!"

"Each martial branch has its own strengths." She brushed off the praise. "Once you have mastered the moves that make up the Supple Net, we will learn Stretch and Flex in the Jade-Blue Sky. They were both invented by our Doyenne. I expect you to work hard to master them."

Over the next fortnight, the Dragon Maiden taught Penance the technique's eighty-one moves and drilled him until he was familiar with each of them. Then she let him put his new-found knowledge into practice by blocking the ascent of a single sparrow.

Penance only managed two or three moves before the winged creature shot between his palms towards the blue yonder. The next few attempts yielded more or less the same result. He was largely too slow, and the odd occasion he was swift enough, his timing was off the mark.

However, the bird's bids for freedom were always short-lived. The Dragon Maiden, monitoring from the side, would claw it back with a casual stretch of her arm.

With the end of spring and the coming of summer, Penance's command of the Supple Net, honed over daily practice, had shown marked improvement. Quick of wit and nimble of limb, he was able to rein in more sparrows with each new session. By the middle of autumn, Penance was proficient in the kung fu, able to keep eighty-one birds from flying beyond the reach of his arm. However, from time to time, a few would slip away, as he had yet to attain mastery over the finer aspects of his powers and it would be years until he was as dexterous as his teacher.

"THE NEXT time you encounter the fat monk, you can send him flipping in a somersault," the Dragon Maiden said one day when they returned to the Tomb after their daily training.

"What about Zhao Zhijing?" Penance asked.

She looked at him in silence.

The implication was clear, but the youngster was not discouraged. "In a few years, I'll be stronger than him. Our kung fu is more powerful than the Quanzhen Sect's!"

"You and I are the only two in the world who believe that." The Dragon Maiden turned her eyes to the masonry vault. "I failed to best that old Taoist Qiu Chuji because I have yet to master the most sophisticated techniques of Ancient Tomb kung fu."

"What are they? Are they very hard? Can we start learning now?" Penance was eager to get even with the monks for the humiliation they had inflicted on him during his time at Chongyang Temple.

"Let me tell you the history of our martial sect. Remember you bowed to the Doyenne before you bowed to me? The Doyenne's family name was Lin, and her given name Chaoying. Many decades ago, she was one of the greatest martial artists in the *wulin*, together with Wang Chongyang. They began as equals, but, with his homeland threatened, Wang Chongyang devoted his energies into recruiting patriots to fight the Jurchen invasion. The Doyenne remained focused on her kung fu training and, in time, she outstripped him. But she was not interested in the everyday dealings of the martial world, nor had she any desire to show off her skills, so hardly anyone in the *jianghu* knew of her.

"When his uprising failed, Wang Chongyang shut himself away in the Tomb of the Living Dead and buried himself in kung fu learning. The Doyenne succumbed to a bout of low spirits around that period and suffered two major illnesses, so by the time Wang Chongyang emerged from the Tomb, she could no longer stand shoulder to shoulder with him when it came to matters martial. Somehow they entered into a wager and a duel. Wang Chongyang lost and vacated the Tomb, leaving it empty for the Doyenne. Come, let me show you what the two Masters left behind."

"I shall enjoy living here much more knowing this!"

"You don't like it here. You think it is boring."

"No! I don't care where I live. As long as I'm with you, I am happy!"

The Dragon Maiden turned her head from side to side with quiet amusement and led Penance to a part of the Tomb he had never visited before. As the candles flickered into life, he saw before him a sizeable chamber in a most curious shape. Around the entrance, it was very narrow, then it widened towards the far end. On one side of the doorway, the wall was curved in a half circle, and on the other side, it extended into a triangular shape.

"What a strange layout!" Penance blurted out.

"Wang Chongyang honed his martial learning in this room," the Dragon Maiden explained. "The narrow end is for practising palm kung fu. The wider end is used for the fists, the concave wall for the sword, and the pinched corner for training inner strength."

Penance paced around, trying to picture how the architectural features were meant to be utilised, but had insufficient knowledge to spark his imagination.

"The essence of Wang Chongyang's kung fu is up here."

He followed the Dragon Maiden's hand and tilted his head back to face the vaulted ceiling. Patterns, talismans and mnemonics were carved into the stonework. Some lines were bold and deep, others as faint as a scratch. He could make little sense of the markings nor discern any sequence or connection between them.

The Dragon Maiden guided him to the semi-circular wall, placed her hand on a tile at the base and nudged it several times. A large stone slab ground slowly out of place, revealing a portal. She picked up the candle and beckoned Penance to follow. The space was laid out in the opposite way from the previous chamber: wide at the doorway and narrow at the far end, and the half circle and the triangular space had also swapped sides. There were more symbols, drawings and writings on the ceiling.

"Up there are the secrets behind the Doyenne's kung fu," she said, gesturing at the carvings overhead. "Her physical prowess could not compare to Wang Chongyang's – it was through her wits that she won the Tomb. After she had moved in, she devoted herself to studying the marks Wang Chongyang left behind, inventing ways to overcome his martial techniques."

"Brilliant! Qiu Chuji and Hao Datong can't possibly outclass their *shifu*. Auntie, you can beat the stinking lot of them once you've learned the Doyenne's kung fu!"

"Perhaps, but, alas, I cannot train on my own."

"I'll help!"

The Dragon Maiden eyed Penance coldly. "You haven't got the skills." It was true, but her brutal delivery left his cheeks burning.

"The Doyenne named her repertoire Jade Maid Heart Scripture. The most advanced moves require you to work in tandem with a partner and the Doyenne's companion was my *shifu*. Although the Doyenne did eventually master her own martial creation, she passed away not long after, before my *shifu* had fully matched her achievements."

"I am your disciple. I can learn with you!" Penance was once more filled with hope.

"Perhaps . . ." Though the Dragon Maiden remained unconvinced, she was willing to give it a try. "Before we embark on the Jade Maid Heart Scripture, you must first become fluent in the techniques I can teach you, as well as Quanzhen kung fu. I was fourteen when *Shifu* died. At the time, she had only just begun to share her knowledge of the Quanzhen Sect's teachings. We will have to find a way ourselves."

THE CULTIVATION of *neigong* was integral to every advanced martial arts principle. Invariably, its purpose was to imbue kicks, punches, palm thrusts and blows of the sword with power beyond what could be contained in and summoned by the muscles. Instead of imparting a few bruises or causing someone to fall, a manoeuvre performed with inner strength could send an opponent's weapon flying, make them spew blood, or even extinguish their life. The outcome of a contest was often determined by the depths of the fighters' internal prowess, rather than their physical attributes and abilities.

However, the Ancient Tomb Sect's application of this inward energy was focused on boosting the speed of a strike rather than its intensity. As the store of power grew inside, one's body became lighter and one's footwork more deft. Your actions would become so swift that you could launch three or four offensives in the time it would take a Master of a similar level to summon a single response. Having said that, this single-minded pursuit of rapidity made it impossible to layer these assaults to multiply their power, which was the most sought-after function of *neigong* force in combat.

Nevertheless, this drawback had not been a concern for Lin Chaoying, as she did not practise martial arts to maim and kill. Her greatest wish was to best Wang Chongyang in a duel, to tap him lightly on the back, to nudge him gently on the nape of his neck, to catch him off guard, but never to cause him the slightest pain. She wanted to hear him chuckle and yield to her. Kung fu was her way of communicating her unspoken feelings and connecting with the man she longed for. As such, she strove to discover techniques that allowed the body to become quicker and lighter, and for ways to sneak up at angles undivinable without imparting wounding force.

Lin Chaoying devoted every waking hour and every waking thought to the task. She eventually emerged victorious, pioneering a strange new martial repertoire that was neither violent nor combative. She tested some of these inventions on Wang Chongyang and succeeded in ambushing the Master, who in time would become the Greatest Martial Master Under the Heavens at the Contest of Mount Hua.

It was these unpredictable palm strikes and sword techniques that Blithe Li adapted for the horsetail whisk, and with the aid of this unusual weapon, she terrorised the *jianghu*, prevailing over men far stronger and more formidable.

THE DRAGON Maiden continued to teach Penance the elemental kung fu of the Ancient Tomb Sect. When the youngster had become familiar with these new repertories, she brought him back to the stone chamber designed by Wang Chongyang. She let out three sparrows, allowing them to fly around freely. When one started to swoop, she shot forward and waved her hand, forcing it to hover just above the floor. She then turned her attention to the other two birds, bringing them under her influence. Soon, all three creatures were beating their wings in vain, confined to a small area in front of her.

"You already know the Supple Net," she said. "You can prevent eighty-one sparrows from flying out of your circle of control. Now, you're going to learn to round them up when they are flitting freely in the air.

"I will teach you how to use your palms to bring them down and stop them escaping. By the time you can keep eighty-one sparrows on the ground, you will have grasped the key to the Omnipresent Snare.

"This kung fu is very hard. We can't leap as high as a bird in flight and force them to descend, even with lightness kung fu. But we can train our eyes to be keen, our hands to be swift, and become more nimble than they are, launching our move just as they take wing.

"Sparrows weigh very little. A gentle flick of a finger or a light wave of the palm is enough to steer them in the direction we want. So, our main task is to train our internal strength to provide support for our *qinggong*. Our body responds as the impulse to act flashes through our mind. Our hands and our arms shoot out quick as lightning."

"What do we do when we're facing blows that carry more powerful inner strength than ours?" Penance asked. "We're agile, but our attacks have little force."

"I'll show you. Fight back with all your might."

The Dragon Maiden's right palm sailed towards Penance's face. He raised his right arm to push back, his counter swift and sure. *Pak!* Their hands met. She immediately twirled her wrist and gave him a cuff on the back of his head. At the same time, she raised her left arm and brushed her fingertips over the Celestial Well pressure point on the upper portion of his attacking arm. All strength drained from the limb and it hung drooping by his side.

"I see now! We don't compete on brute force. We best our opponents with speed and hit them before they realise an attack is coming!" Penance came to this conclusion after the Dragon Maiden had eased the numbing tingle in his arm by triggering the Four Rivers and Clear Cold Abyss acupoints around his elbow.

"Indeed, we train to become faster than our opponents and strike from the most unexpected angle, so even if they rack their brains for three days and three nights, they cannot work out how they have been beaten. When we are that agile, it matters little that our moves contain hardly any power."

"Amazing!" Penance rubbed his face and tugged his ears in excitement.

"Once you have learned the system of kung fu the Doyenne bestowed on us, this element of unpredictability will be at your disposal. As for how to outpace great martial Masters, that is something we must learn through practice. Not just you, I need training on that front too. We will eventually get there with the aid of the boreal nephrite." The Dragon Maiden went on to expound on strategies for darting high and diving low and came to this conclusion: "We can encircle anything with the Omnipresent Snare. Our foe can run to the heavens' edge and the sea's end, but they can't flee from the Snare's reach."

FROM THAT day on, the Dragon Maiden shared the Ancient Tomb martial heritage without reserve, teaching Penance *neigong* method and fist and palm kung fu, as well as the use of weapons secret and overt. These were skills invented by Lin Chaoying to suit her own sex's physique and habits, but the focus on dexterity was a better match for Penance's irreverent character than the might so sought after in a martial world dominated by men. In two years' time, he had learned everything the Ancient Tomb Sect had to offer, his grasp of their techniques augmented by the effects of the boreal nephrite bed. What remained now was to consolidate his power and fine-tune his control through sustained practice.

Now a handsome youth of sixteen, Penance had grown much taller and his voice had deepened. There was little trace left of the bruised and dishevelled child who had first arrived at the Tomb. He afforded the Dragon Maiden the utmost respect, honouring her as his senior and fulfilling her every request. He also took on the cooking and cleaning, so his teacher needed not be troubled by mundane housekeeping tasks.

In the Dragon Maiden's eyes, Penance was the same little boy she always had been. She thought she was still treating him with the icy and distant attitude she had adopted since the beginning, and speaking in the familiar stern tone as though there was little that tied them together, but, deep down, she had warmed to his company.

For his part, the young man had never been put off by her aloofness. He would sit quietly by her whenever she played the *qin* zither, listening closely to her restrained and unadorned performance.

AT LONG last, Penance had succeeded in using the Omnipresent Snare to corral the eighty-one sparrows shut up in Wang Chongyang's practice chamber into a tight flock before him.

"Well done. Now we can start training outside."

The Dragon Maiden was amused to see Penance's eyes light up at the chance to venture above ground. She gathered the sparrows in a sack and set them free when they reached a clearing. Once the birds began to flutter into the air, she led Penance in rounding them up using the Omnipresent Snare.

A few of the most defiant kept trying to break away. Penance jumped up and down, working with his teacher to drive them back to earth. From time to time, one or two slipped between their hands and shot beyond reach. There was nothing to be done but to let them fly to freedom, for there were scores of sparrows that needed to be contained.

After a while, the Dragon Maiden pulled back and let the sparrows take to the sky, pleased with Penance's performance. "We have so far been practising the first two levels of the Ancient Tomb kung fu. When we reach the third stage, many of the techniques will require us to join hands against our foes."

"We can thrash those Quanzhen cow muzzles together!"

"No, we won't do that. Grandam Sun may have died at their hands, but *Shifu* told me that the Quanzhen Sect does a lot of good helping those in adversity. We will hold Hao Datong alone accountable."

"We can take out ruffians together in the *jianghu*."

"What do they have to do with us? We live our lives in the Tomb – they can't do us any harm down there."

To hear the Dragon Maiden flatly refuse to consider the prospect of a life beyond these mountains was dispiriting for Penance, for he still hoped to leave the subterranean warren one day. But when he had given what she said more thought, he could sense that she had grown more welcoming of his companionship and his mood brightened.

"I will stay here with you for life." The promise tumbled from his lips. "You gave your word to Grandam Sun that you would never throw me out."

"Only if you behave," the Dragon Maiden clarified.

"Of course, I will always behave and listen to you, so you won't ever wish to part with me."

"You have a very high opinion of yourself," she noted. "I can adopt a little girl tomorrow and make her my disciple to keep me company."

"No!" Penance was stricken by an overwhelming sense of insecurity. "Auntie, please don't forsake me. If I misbehave, beat me – kill

269

me! I don't want to leave you even in death." Tears poured forth and he sank to the ground.

The Dragon Maiden was bewildered by his emotional display. The last time Penance had broken down like this was after Grandam Sun's death. She could not quite tell if he was truly hurt by her words or making a scene to win sympathy.

"Don't cry." Her tone was softer than usual. "I'm not throwing you out."

"You can't threaten me with it either!"

"You were so excited when I said we would train outside. I thought you were finding life inside the Tomb stifling."

"No! Not when I'm with you! I'm really happy! If you won't let me be with you, I'll run myself through with a sword."

"Obey and behave. Never again try to intimidate me with talk of taking your life." The Dragon Maiden's expression hardened. "If I want you gone, I care not whether you're living or dead."

Wounded by her forbidding tone and cold indifference, Penance curled up in a ball, his cheeks awash with tears.

"Get up, Penance! You're not a child anymore."

"I won't cry again!" He jumped back to his feet.

Presently, a pair of white butterflies fluttered by. Penance reached out and caught one in each hand. Much slower than sparrows, they were easy to capture.

"Don't hurt them."

Penance relaxed his fingers and watched the butterflies take to the air. "Stretch and Flex in the Jade-Blue Sky . . ." he said under his breath, wiping away the tears with his sleeve.

THAT EVENING after dinner, Penance tidied up as usual, collecting their used bowls and chopsticks, washing them up and leaving them on a wooden rack to dry. He then scrubbed the wok and set up the kitchen for breakfast in the morning. Afterwards, he got ready to retire for the night and lay down on the boreal nephrite to cultivate his *neigong* according to the Ancient Tomb method.

The same sleeping arrangement had been maintained over the years. Penance rested on the icy bluestone, as he had done on his first night in the Tomb, while the Dragon Maiden balanced on the suspended rope. She stayed in the room to monitor the circulation of his internal energy, as sometimes, in extreme heat or cold, it was known to flow the wrong way, and in case Penance came to a stumbling block and asked for help. The young man and woman treated each other with respect and rectitude, and neither thought much about the distinction between their sexes. It did not occur to them to keep separate chambers.

Penance had sent his inner strength around his body for one cycle when the Dragon Maiden entered the room. She had completed her toilet and was settling down for the night on her sleeping rope. Just as he was about to close his eyes, she turned on her side and he caught a glimpse of her bare feet. He had seen them many times, but somehow they held an inexplicable allure this night.

I won't be cast out so long as I obey and behave, he said to himself, thinking of the reassurance she had made earlier that day. I'd be content falling asleep every night to the sight of her luminescent little feet.

Penance's mind began to wander, but he reined it in and soon fell asleep. Some while later, a ball of heat gathered in his chest. It travelled slowly down his torso to his lower belly. A pair of white butterflies danced before his eyes, fluttering up and down and from side to side.

Entranced, Penance got to his feet and reached out in the Omnipresent Snare. His right palm hovered above the butterflies to prevent them from flitting upwards while he closed his left hand over one of them. Then he drew the fingers of his right hand around the other one. The butterflies were soft and ice cold to the touch. But they soon warmed up, quivering in his hands. He did not want to let go, though he kept his hold loose to avoid hurting them.

"Penance, what are you doing?" the Dragon Maiden barked.

The butterflies slipped from his grasp. He opened his eyes and realised he was standing under the suspended rope, his hands stretched out above him – where the Dragon Maiden's feet had been just a moment before.

"A-a-auntie . . . s-s-sorry!" he stammered as he staggered back onto the bed. "I was dreaming and I caught a pair of butterflies. I – I didn't realise they were . . . your feet. I – I . . . I didn't mean to . . ." He was so aghast at what he had done, he forgot to circulate his energy to resist the chill of the boreal nephrite. His body began to shudder and his teeth chattered in his head.

The Dragon Maiden tapped Penance on the sternum and sent a rush of warmth through his Chest Centre acupoint. He stopped shivering at once and feeling returned to his limbs.

Seeing that he had calmed down and started to fortify himself with *neigong*, she hopped back onto the rope and lay on her side. She drew her knees up to shield her feet under her skirt, keeping them out of sight.

The next night, when Penance saw the Dragon Maiden hanging her rope in the adjacent chamber, he pleaded, "Auntie, I'll tie my hands. If I cause offence again, cut me with your sword. The pain will wake me up."

"I let it pass last night because I could tell you did not do it on purpose. You have a good grasp of internal strength, but you need to be more cautious in your training to avoid misfiring."

Penance knew his mentor had made up her mind and returned to what was now to be his room. From then on, he kept his head clear whenever he was on the nephrite bed and did not encounter any more mishaps.

2

"YOU HAVE LEARNED ALL THE ANCIENT TOMB'S MARTIAL offerings," the Dragon Maiden said one day. "It is time to practise

Quanzhen Sect kung fu. This phase will not be easy. *Shifu* was no expert and my comprehension is superficial at best. We shall begin with their basic foundational moves. Do speak up if you find mistakes in my interpretation."

They returned to the irregular chamber designed by Wang Chongyang to study the carvings he had left on the vaulted ceiling.

Penance made good progress in the first few days. With a sound martial foundation and a sharp mind, he grasped the moves without requiring much by way of explanation from the Dragon Maiden. However, within a fortnight, he started to stagnate. The harder he worked, the more awkward he felt, to the point where his command over the techniques began to regress. When he raised the issue, it turned out the same thing had happened before.

"*Shifu* and I also failed to progress with Quanzhen martial arts. We had no-one to turn to with our questions and did not have access to their heart-approach. I offered to steal the secret from Chongyang Temple but *Shifu* was appalled by my suggestion. Eventually, we gave up, since learning another school's kung fu was not our priority. Still, it will not be difficult for us to surmount this. We can capture a Quanzhen monk and make him tell us what we need to know."

The Dragon Maiden's account reminded Penance of the verses Zhao Zhijing had forced him to learn by heart in the months he had spent at Chongyang Temple. One of them was called "The Great Way of Quanzhen". He recited the opening stanza:

"*Connect the Nine Openings to cultivate the Great Way.*
  The Nine Openings originate at the Tail Gate point:
  From the soles of the feet, the Gushing Springs surge,
  The Gushing Springs surge and rise to the knees,
  Passing the knees and unto the Tail Gate unhurried,
  Swirling ever faster atop the Earthy Pill.
  From the Golden Lock Gate down through the Magpie Bridge,
  From the Twelve Overlapping Towers to the Palace Chamber descends."

The Dragon Maiden pondered for a moment. "It sounds like their *neigong* formula."

Penance proceeded to chant the other Quanzhen mnemonics he knew. He had assumed they were nonsense since no-one had explained the meaning of the unusual names and phrases and he was never taught the methods for putting the words into action. Now, hearing the Dragon Maiden's analysis, he began to see their connection to internal kung fu training.

The Gushing Springs referred to the pressure points on the soles of the feet. The Tail Gate must be the base of the spine. The Earthy Pill was mostly likely the Hundred Converges on the crown of the head. It was confusing how one acupoint could have so many different names, but he could visualise the flow of energy now.

Armed with this knowledge, the two of them were able to try out the kung fu etched on the ceiling by Wang Chongyang.

MONTHS LATER, after a long day sparring with swords, the Dragon Maiden said, "I have always doubted the claim that the Quanzhen Sect is the orthodox martial school, but now I realise there is some truth to it. We hold the key to their training methods, and yet, we have a very long way to go before we are one with their techniques and are able to channel our energy with ease."

"Every mountain sits in the shadow of a loftier peak," Penance replied. "The Taoists may have sophisticated kung fu, but they aren't invincible. The Doyenne left us ways to outmanoeuvre them!"

The next day, the Dragon Maiden led Penance to the adjoining chamber constructed by Lin Chaoying and told him that they would be focusing on the Jade Maid Heart Scripture.

Referencing the drawings and patterns etched overhead, she explained the main concepts outlined and suggested ways of putting them into action. The core of the martial system had been passed on verbally from Lin Chaoying to her maidservant, then to the Dragon Maiden. It had never been written down.

The learning process was much smoother this time. The strategies for overcoming Quanzhen kung fu were rooted in the Ancient Tomb Sect's martial philosophy, so it took the two of them just a few months to attain a good grasp of the external combat techniques.

Now, when they sparred, one would employ Quanzhen swordcraft while the other fought with Jade Maid Sword. The Doyenne's martial invention allowed whoever mastered it to dismantle another's assault, thrust by thrust, until they could barely move. Jade Maid Sword was capable of forestalling and countering every conceivable variation of Quanzhen kung fu, keeping the opponent trapped within its influence, unable to fight back, unable to take flight.

Although a savage streak ran through each swing and slice of Jade Maid Sword, it was specified in the Scripture that the point of one's blade should be broken off and the keen edges made dull by hammering. As such, the repertoire exhibited all the qualities of the most intricate swordplay – except the ability to hurt one's foe.

This lack of an aggressive sting ran through all the Ancient Tomb kung fu, and this was the reason why Blithe Li had taken up the horsetail whisk. When performing complex swordplay with this unusual weapon, she gained an element of surprise and unpredictability, which counterbalanced the fact that her martial arts were non-lethal in nature, and allowed her to get the better of her adversaries, often in just a few moves.

Nevertheless, neither the Dragon Maiden nor Blithe Li were aware of the true motive behind the absence of a sharp edge to their swordcraft. The impetus for Lin Chaoying devising a new kung fu was to get the better of Wang Chongyang. She had never wished to cause the man she loved any physical harm, whereas the majority of martial repertoires had bloodshed and killing at their heart.

This blunted approach to sword fighting might seem tame at first, but at the least expected moment, it could throw up unforeseen variations of dizzying subtlety. Just when it looked as though one was about to throw down one's blade to admit defeat, an attack would lance out from an impossible angle, dazzling the eyes and confounding the limbs.

A duel with Wang Chongyang was a solemn affair for Lin Chaoying, but she sometimes introduced a touch of playfulness to their encounters. The two were martial equals and neither found it easy to overpower the other outright. But Wang Chongyang was mindful of his opponent's desire to win and his physical advantage over her as a man and would surreptitiously grant her an extra move over him. In those moments, the tenor of Lin Chaoying's attack would take a turn, sometimes skittish, sometimes brazen, as she discarded the poise and grace expected of a martial grandmaster, allowing her to catch Wang Chongyang unawares and seize control of the contest.

Her sword kung fu had limited power in a life-or-death struggle, but what made it hard to defeat was the endless variety of its flourishes and feints. By the time you realised you were ensnared, it was too late to extricate yourself.

ONCE THEY were familiar with the physical manoeuvres from the Jade Maid Heart Scripture, the Dragon Maiden decided they should embark on the internal elements of the martial system. After studying the images and words on the ceiling, she remained silent for a long time, deep in thought.

"Auntie, is it very hard?" Penance asked when he noticed her brow furrowing.

"*Shifu* said that it takes two to learn the *neigong* part. I thought we could do it together, but it is not possible."

"Why?"

"Because you are not a woman."

"Huh? Surely we can find a way."

"No . . ." The Dragon Maiden shook her head. "Look at the drawings."

Penance followed her gaze to a cluster of human figures etched into one corner of the ceiling. There were at least seventy or eighty of them, each holding a different pose. Thin lines radiated outwards from their unclothed bodies. He could not make out their significance and turned to the Dragon Maiden.

"*Shifu* once told me that our *qi* would bubble and roil at high temperatures when practising our inner energy," she began. "We are supposed to find a spacious, deserted place and leave our robes loose and unfastened so the heat generated can escape without hindrance, or else we could become grievously ill or even die."

"Why can't we do that?"

"It takes the two of us working together, when we reach the advanced stages, to guide each other's power within and to protect each other's energy flow. How could we possibly sit together in a state of undress?"

Penance had been so focused on his martial training, it had not crossed his mind that he was of a different sex. Now that the Dragon Maiden had pointed it out, he realised how improper his question had been.

The Dragon Maiden had also turned a blind eye to their physical distinctions. She might have lived for more than two decades, but she knew nothing about the world outside, having grown up in isolation in the Tomb. Her martial training had required her to repress her seven emotions and six desires, so, despite the fact that they were both in the fire of youth and spent nights and days in each other's company, neither had done anything that crossed the line of propriety – at least not in their waking hours. This need to disrobe to cultivate their *neigong* presented a problem for which there was no easy solution.

"Can't we sit side by side on the boreal nephrite?"

"Absolutely not! The chill would force the heat back into our bodies and we'd die within days!"

Penance thought for a moment before asking, "Can we train individually? If there's anything I can't understand, I can ask you another time."

"No." The Dragon Maiden shook her head slowly. "We have to tread with care every step of the way with this internal method. The energy flow can go the wrong way at any moment. If we do it alone without constant assistance, we could misfire into the demonic way. It takes two to surmount the dangers."

"Then what should we do?"

"Well, if we work harder on the external skills, it should be enough to beat the Quanzhen monks. We don't intend to fight them to the death anyway."

EVERY SO often, Penance would venture into the woods surrounding the Tomb after training to hunt for game. That afternoon, he caught a muntjac and then went in pursuit of a hare. The creature darted east one instant and swerved west the next. It was so agile and swift that the young man struggled to keep up, even with the aid of his *qinggong*.

Spurred on by the thrill of the chase, Penance decided not to maim it with weapons but to wear it out in a race. The hare bolted round a bend and vanished into a large shrub of red blossoms.

The luxuriant undergrowth stretched several *zhang* across the valley. Dense layers of leaves and flowers filled the air with a rich fragrance. By the time Penance had reached the other side, his prey was long gone. However, he was not particularly upset that the hare had escaped, for he had grown rather fond of the little creature.

Now, he had time to take in his surroundings. The thicket was like a folding screen decorated with red petals and verdant foliage. Above him, trees with luxuriant canopies provided natural shelter.

An idea struck Penance. He rushed back to the Tomb and led the Dragon Maiden to the secluded valley.

"Why do you bring me here? I am not interested in flowers."

"We can practise *neigong* here! You on one side of the thicket, and me on the other. We can't see each other through the dense layers of flowers, so it won't be a problem if we loosen our clothes. Isn't it perfect?"

The Dragon Maiden leapt up into the nearest tree. She looked to the east, to the south, to the west, to the north. No sign of human habitation. Just lush vegetation as far as the eye could see. The songs of birds and brooks came to her ears. Yes, they could cultivate internal strength here without the fear of being disturbed.

"We will begin this evening," she said.

They returned to their chosen spot after supper. The aroma in the air was more palpable in the still of the night.

The Dragon Maiden recited the opening *neigong* mnemonic from the Jade Maid Heart Scripture and explained its application. When Penance had no more questions, they took their places on either side of the thicket.

Penance removed his robes and put his arm through the branches to press his left palm against the Dragon Maiden's right. He could instantly feel her energy flow, and the connection allowed them to offer each other assistance whenever one of them encountered any hurdles in their training.

DURING THE day, they continued to work on the kung fu described in the Jade Maid Heart Scripture. They had now reached the seventh section, which involved moves that required them to fight in perfect synchrony. One focused on attack, the other on defence. The attacker could be secure in the knowledge that their partner would shield them, and this confidence doubled the power of their strikes. The defender, meanwhile, was able to steal in with the odd offensive strike, because the keen edge of their companion's onslaught would keep their foe from unleashing their full force.

When they tried out the moves, they pictured Hao Datong or another Quanzhen Immortal on the receiving end. Each time, the Taoist would lose spectacularly and beg for mercy on his knees.

Today, it was Qiu Chuji's turn to take an imaginary beating.

The Dragon Maiden realised she could not stop the corners of her mouth from curling upwards at the thought of the Taoist pleading for his life, though she knew it was against her training to indulge in joy or grief, and that she should always maintain a still heart. She quickly reined in her feelings, but Penance had already caught the rare blossoming of a smile on her face.

An urge the young man had never before experienced took over his body. He found her attempt to suppress her reaction indescribably alluring and he reached out without thinking. He wanted to press her body against his torso and plant his lips on hers. Just then, a voice sounded in his head, reminding him that she was his teacher, the person he most respected, and his arms fell back by his side.

Noticing his twitching, the Dragon Maiden asked, "What was that move?"

"Reverence Precedes Disdain," Penance answered quickly, praying that his forbidden thoughts had not been detected. "I feared Qiu Chuji would sneak a blow on you even though we had him on his knees. I'd give anything to keep you safe."

Penance was unaware that his remark captured the very essence of the seventh chapter of the Jade Maid Heart Scripture. Lin Chaoying created this kung fu system after she had won the Tomb from Wang Chongyang only for him to choose a celibate life as a Taoist monk over being with her. Alone in her subterranean lair, the great Master poured her lovelorn feelings into her martial inventions, dreaming up life-or-death situations in which her beloved would shield her with no regards for his own safety.

"IMAGINE I fall on the ground after being hit and our enemy launches another strike at me." The Dragon Maiden was instructing Penance in Luxuriant Loquat Tree, the nineteenth move of the seventh chapter of the Jade Maid Heart Scripture. "You leap over to shield me, placing your arms on either side of my body. Your legs too. Keep your core and spine straight so our bodies don't touch. Now I thrust my sword from between your thighs – into our attacker's lower belly.

"Our foe, seeing us tumble, will assume that we cannot defend ourselves. They will not see our retaliation coming. Your stance also conceals my weapon. They cannot possibly evade this move."

"Ingenious! But it's rather underhanded, isn't it?"

"Not at all. We are already down on the ground. That should have been the end of the fight. And yet, they pursue us and still want to hurt us. Because of that they run into our sword. This move only maims those with malicious intent."

In truth, Lin Chaoying was merely trying to console her lovesick self, fantasising that Wang Chongyang had loved her more than his own life and would sacrifice himself to offer her protection.

Penance and the Dragon Maiden practised the movements individually before combining them into a fluid whole. At the same time, they carried on with their *neigong* training and were soon seeing obvious improvement. Their attacks were now so swift and sudden that they could strike without giving any indication where the blow would come from or where it was aimed.

Subtle changes were also taking place in their dynamic. Penance had always sparred with the Dragon Maiden with utmost reverence. He maintained a respectful distance, not letting the edge of his palms graze even the hems of her robe. However, the moves he was learning now required him to fling his whole body over hers to intercept attacks with his flesh. He had to visualise her in mortal danger, threatened by a ruthless and brutal enemy, in order to realise the kung fu's potential. In time, the image of the Dragon Maiden in his head transformed from a superior fighter who had taught him everything he knew about the martial arts, to a hapless girl relying on him to deliver her from the hands of evil men. He even gained an air of dominance and maturity, as if he were now the elder of the two.

A similar shift also occurred in the Dragon Maiden. She began to see herself in the weaker position, physically and psychologically dependent on the younger man for protection. She was shedding the authority that came with being his teacher, becoming less distant and stern in her manner.

These new perspectives they had of themselves and of each other matched the original intent behind the creation of the Jade Maid Heart Scripture as well as the emotions underlining the moves. When they caught each other's eye in practice, they could see the connection in their hearts and their spirits – one protective, one dependent. They had now achieved such a level of synchronicity that they were truly fighting as one, in terms of emotions, internal energy and physical manoeuvres.

THE MOVE Be Your Armour required one person to wrap their arms around their partner, using their body as a shield to block any attack. In combat, the stance gave the one under protection a brief respite to smooth their elemental *qi*.

Penance tried out the sequence, embracing the Dragon Maiden without touching her.

At such close quarters, she noticed his eyes were burning bright with determination. She felt sure that for her sake he would brave, without a moment's hesitation, the keen edges of sabres and the sharp points of spears, as well as any number of punches and kicks.

Colour flushed her cheeks. She looked away and whispered, "No—" disturbed by a feeling she could not place.

Penance let go and leapt back.

Without either of them realising, ardour had been simmering beneath her remoteness and his reverence. The martial moves they had been practising required them to imagine each other on the brink of death while being physically engaged in close proximity. Over time, this stoked the natural passions and emotions they were born with. Even though they behaved with decorum at all times, the barriers established by the codes of social conduct were crumbling.

A few days later, they went over every martial move from the seventh section of the Scripture in the clearing outside the Tomb, including Luxuriant Loquat Tree. The Dragon Maiden took the recumbent position on the ground and Penance threw himself over her, channelling his strength to his spine to keep their bodies from making contact. Then his gaze met hers and he felt his whole being set ablaze. The shimmer in her eyes, the blush on her cheeks, the slight upturn at the corners of her mouth. Her striking features were more enchanting than ever. His self-restraint went up in flames. He clasped his arms around her and lowered his head to plant a kiss.

Something also ignited in the Dragon Maiden's heart. The weight of his body, the searing look in his eyes, the touch of his lips. Despite the two decades of training to stay calm, detached and controlled in any situation, her desires were stirred and amorous thoughts awakened. She shoved Penance away, cuffed him hard and ran into the Tomb.

Mortified and remorseful, he raced after her and let out a breath of relief when he found the entrance had been left open. He rushed inside, grabbed the broomstick and went straight to her chamber.

"Beat me. As hard as you want." Penance fell to his knees, offering the Dragon Maiden the instrument of punishment. "I was wrong."

She made no move to take the broom, but said firmly, in a quiet voice, "We won't practise that move again."

"As you say! But I vow to give my body and my life to protect you."

The Dragon Maiden made a soft noise in acknowledgement and the great weight that had been crushing Penance was lifted. He had been forgiven.

"I will always protect you and never do anything like that again," he pledged once more.

3

THE EPISODE DID NOT HINDER THEIR TRAINING. HOWEVER, both teacher and student maintained a cautious distance for fear of putting themselves in a situation where similar feelings might flare up again. Each night, they ventured out to practise, focusing on the *neigong* portion of the Jade Maid Heart Scripture, and during the day they rested in the Tomb.

Two months passed without incident. They had now reached the ninth chapter of the Scripture, which was wholly devoted to developing internal strength. They were beginning to understand how the methods described would help them strike more swiftly and increase the speed of their springs and jumps. They knew they had to train together to safeguard against misfiring into the demonic way, but they had yet to discover the true intent behind the Doyenne's invention – to bind the hearts and souls of the two learning in partnership, so they would act as one in the face of danger.

Lin Chaoying had hoped that one day she would practise the kung fu with Wang Chongyang, and that, through the intimate training, he would come to return her feelings towards him. Her bashful reticence and her pride prevented her from being the first to reveal her emotions. But she had never understood that this convoluted way of demonstrating her love would never bear fruit. If they had trained together, it would only have pushed them apart, because the ways they comprehended the world were often in opposition and it was the second nature of Masters with advanced *neigong* to be wary in their drill – they could never fully trust their peers.

Nevertheless, Lin Chaoying's creation eventually fulfilled its original purpose, for the Dragon Maiden shared her knowledge without holding back and Penance learned everything without doubt or hesitance.

THE INNER strength exercise in the ninth section of the Jade Maid Heart Scripture was split into nine stages. The odd numbered ones were called Yin Advance and they had to be completed in one sitting without pause or interruption to the circulation of energy. If a hare darted by and startled the practitioner, it could cause serious and lasting internal injuries. Whereas the even numbered levels were named Yang Retreat and one could stop and start as needed during training without any harm to the body.

The Dragon Maiden and Penance returned once more to the valley with the red flowers and took their places on either side of the thicket. She began to run through the seventh phase, while he practised the sixth.

The moon was reaching its zenith. In another hour or so, they would complete the training for their respective stages. Their bodies were emanating waves of heat, making the fragrance in the air more intense.

Somewhere not far off, grass was being crunched underfoot, breaking the quiet of the night.

The Dragon Maiden had reached a critical point and was oblivious to the noise, but Penance could hear the approaching footsteps very well.

Two men. Walking into the valley. Talking. Their voices sounded familiar. He pushed the *qi* gathered in the Elixir Field out of his body and made three deep inhalations to bring his training to a close.

The men were moving closer, speaking more loudly and in increasingly agitated tones, then they stopped, not far from where

Penance was sitting. He could now hear their exchange clearly and place their voices: his former *shifu* Zhao Zhijing and one-time martial uncle Zhen Zhibing.

"You can't hide anymore, Brother Zhen. I'll report you to Martial Uncle Qiu," Zhao Zhijing said. There was an edge to his voice.

"I know full well why you keep harassing me," Zhen Zhibing shot back. "You want to replace me as the Foremost Disciple of the third generation. You want to be the next Sect Leader."

"You've failed to abide by our monastic rules of purity and broken the Sect's commandments. How can you be the Foremost Disciple?"

"Which law have I transgressed?"

"The fourth! Thou shalt not succumb to lust."

From where Penance was sitting, he could make out the two men standing face to face, their features accentuated by the moonlight. Zhao Zhijing's accusation made Zhen Zhibing blanch and his hand shot to the hilt of his sword.

"I know your sense and spirits have taken leave of you since you set eyes on that Dragon Maiden from the Tomb of the Living Dead. I know you have had fantasies about embracing her, doing all manner of intimate forbidden things with her. The Quanzhen Sect prizes the cultivation of the heart and the nurturing of the character. You have trespassed by having these lascivious thoughts!"

A wild rage overcame Penance and his hatred for the Quanzhen monks bored into the marrow of his bones. How could they so besmirch the Dragon Maiden?

"Hogwash! How dare you presume to know what I'm thinking?"

"Well, I do know what Lu Qingdu and his three brothers saw in the woods outside the Tomb. I sent them to waylay that treacherous little bastard Penance Yang. They didn't see the boy, but they found someone else loitering. Multiple times. One Martial Uncle Zhen. Pacing back and forth, mumbling to himself. I bet you those words were 'Dragon Maiden'."

"This is pure slander!"

"Dare you deny your outings to the forest? It is the Sect Leader's express command that the area is out of bounds. My plan to capture Penance is well known among my disciples, whereas your furtive excursions . . . What do you think our martial elders will say when they find out?"

"Brother Zhao, it's clear you covert the title of Foremost Disciple and hope your scandalmongering can bring me down. If this becomes known, you do realise it will merely make you a laughing stock, don't you? Do you truly believe the honour will be yours if you manage to unseat me? Our brothers Li Zhichang, Wang Zhitan and Song Defang are all extremely smart and capable. They will be standing between you and the post."

"Scandalmongering? Who left a box of candied flat peaches and two jars of honeyed dates outside the Tomb on the Dragon Maiden's twentieth birthday? Who wrote the message 'Many happy returns of the day to Miss Long'?"

"You remember the date of her birth."

"How can any of us forget? Chongyang Temple was razed the day she turned eighteen. Don't try to deny your handiwork! The note was signed 'Presented by the humble monk Zhen Zhibing of Chongyang Temple'."

Zhao Zhijing pulled out the piece of paper found by Lu Qingdu – which was dyed an auspicious red – and flourished it before his martial brother.

"Shall we present this to our Sect Leader Martial Uncle Ma and your *shifu* Martial Uncle Qiu? Let them judge the calligraphy. Was it penned by you or forged by me?"

Sha! Zhen Zhibing unsheathed his sword and thrust its point at the provocative monk.

"Silence me with death?" Zhao Zhijing twisted away and tucked the note into his robe. "Let's see you try!"

Zhen Zhibing responded with three quick jabs with his sword, but his peer sidestepped them with ease. The ring of steel on steel halted his fourth attempt.

His blade flashing in the moonlight, Zhao Zhijing hurled slurs and insults as he parried, hoping to goad his fellow into a mistake. But Zhen Zhibing clenched his jaw and maintained his focus, channelling his frustration into ferocious waves of attack.

The two men were outstanding representatives of the Quanzhen Sect's third generation, considered by most to be martial equals. Zhen Zhibing was the second disciple Qiu Chuji took on, ranking just after Harmony Yin among Eternal Spring Immortal's students in terms of his kung fu. However, in recent years, Harmony had placed more emphasis on seeking the Way through the cultivation of internal elixir and the refinement of *qi*, leaving Zhao Zhijing, Wang Chuyi's first protégé, as Zhen Zhibing's only challenger for his position of honour.

A dozen thrusts and parries were exchanged in the blink of an eye. The monks flipped in the air. They rolled on the ground. One relentless in pursuit, the other fleet on his feet.

"I know every move you're making. You can't hurt me."

Zhao Zhijing's snide remark prompted a series of lunges from his martial brother, but Zhao maintained a robust defence, biding his time to retaliate. When the moment came, he let fly with his sword, sending forth three quick flashes of silver. Each successive strike forced Zhen Zhibing a step back.

At the sight of his opponent switching the blade to his left hand and drawing back his right palm, Zhao Zhijing spat out another taunt: "You haven't the skill to woo a woman, let alone do me harm!" Then he raised his forearm to fend off the blow aimed at his chest.

The tussle gained a new intensity. A whirlwind of thrusting swords and slicing palms.

Penance had been watching the fight with fascination. It was the first time he had seen Quanzhen swordplay in action since he started studying it with the Dragon Maiden. Every attack and retreat – each instinctive variation and fluid transition between moves – showed how insightful her interpretations had been. But though Penance was thrilled to have the chance to learn from this live demonstration, whenever the monks strayed towards the shrubbery that was concealing him and his teacher, his heart pounded wildly and his breath caught in his chest. He feared for the Dragon Maiden. She was oblivious to the outside world, having turned her awareness wholly inwards to cultivate her *neigong*. Any interruption could prove deadly, but there was little Penance could do but keep his eyes trained on the monks and pray that they kept their distance.

Zhen Zhibing let out an angry roar and launched a sequence of rapid-fire attacks, holding nothing back to guard against a counter. He would rather die than let his secret feelings be known.

Zhao Zhijing understood this, and the realisation unsettled him. Though he had never been fond of this disciple of Qiu Chuji's, he had no wish to slay or wound a martial brother. After all, fighting with total abandon was not in the spirit of Quanzhen kung fu. But as the fight wore on, it became clear that his scruples were putting him at a disadvantage.

Noting the signs of strain in his opponent's defence, Zhen Zhibing stepped up his offensive. Sword and palm sliced left and right at the same time, followed by a sly kick.

Three Interlocking Rings – a celebrated Quanzhen move.

Zhao Zhijing jumped up, springing more than a *zhang* from the ground to avoid the lethal combination, and hacked down with his steel from above.

Zhen Zhibing responded by hurling his blade at his opponent and thrusting both palms out with a *hah!*

Penance did not recognise these vicious moves, but they left a cold sweat on the nape of his neck. He was sure that his former *shifu* would be hit by the double palm strike, as it was nearly impossible to change direction when the body was falling downwards. He was expecting bones to snap and tendons to tear at the moment of impact . . .

And yet, somehow, Zhao Zhijing managed to twist into a backflip, making a graceful descent out of reach.

Penance leapt to his feet on instinct. He could not let the monk come anywhere near the spot where the Dragon Maiden was sitting. Riding his upward momentum, he thrust his left palm under his extended right arm in a move called Climb the Scaffold to Throw the Bouquet. His hand hammered into Zhao Zhijing's back, pushing the grown man two *zhang* away. However, Penance had put all his *neigong* power into the attack and left nothing to secure his landing. His legs buckled as he touched down, and he had to fight to keep his balance. A branch caught the fabric of his trousers without him noticing. He took a step to right himself, and in the process pulled free from the stray twig. It snapped back and struck the Dragon Maiden in the face.

The young woman did not know what had hit her. Sweat gushed from her every pore. The internal energy circulating rapidly around her body surged all at once into the Elixir Field and she blacked out.

Zhen Zhibing thought he was hallucinating. Had he really seen a young man jumping out of the undergrowth? And the woman he had been dreaming about night and day lurking among the flowers?

Zhao Zhijing rushed back to where the push had originated and saw the Dragon Maiden swooning in a half-naked man's arms, her clothes hastily draped over her body.

"How wondrous," he scoffed. "Here's your woman, doing all the things you dreamed of."

Penance was furious, but he was too concerned with the Dragon Maiden's well-being to pay his one-time *shifu* much attention. But, sensing the monks' prying eyes, he reached out with shaking hands and adjusted the robe to protect her modesty.

"Auntie, are you alright?" The skin on her forehead was ice cold to the touch.

The Dragon Maiden grunted weakly in reply.

Reassured that she had come to, Penance scooped her up. "I'll get you to the Tomb, then I'll come back to kill these two," he promised. He felt her body leaning pliantly into his embrace. It was alarming how little strength was left to her.

"Don't try to run! I'll be back for you!" Penance snarled at the Taoists.

It was hard to say if Zhen Zhibing had registered the words. He remained dumbstruck, rooted to the spot, but Zhao Zhijing let out a guffaw. "Brother Zhen, your sweetheart was doing the deed of shame with her lover. Shouldn't you turn your sword on him, instead of pointing it at me?"

No response still from Zhen Zhibing. But Penance had caught the vicious tone in his former *shifu*'s voice. He could not stand by and let him heap yet another insult on the Dragon Maiden. He set her down gently against a tree, snapped off a branch and jabbed it at the hostile monk. "Enough!"

For the first time, Zhao Zhijing got a proper look at the young man. Lean, muscular, stripped down to his waist – his moonlit features seemed familiar.

"Penance Yang!" The monk's voice cracked with anger. He was mortified that his turncoat of a student had sent him flying with a palm thrust.

"I don't care if you insult me. But you won't speak ill of Auntie!"

Zhao Zhijing snorted in derision. "It is said that the Ancient Tomb Sect is a martial branch for the fairer sex and their knowledge is passed down only to their own kind. We were led to believe their disciples were virgins purer than ice and cleaner than jade. In reality, it's a gang of filthy harlots, with lovers by the dozen. Monks, students, teachers, as long as they're male, the Ancient Tomb *maidens* will do the *deed* with them night and day, out in the open, with the earth as their bed and the sky as their blanket!"

The Dragon Maiden had turned her full focus to smoothing her energy flow, but fragments of the belligerent monk's tirade did find their way into her ears. Part of the *qi* circulation she had restored surged in the opposite direction, clashing, roiling. A crushing pressure mounted in her chest. A sure sign of internal injury.

"You lie—" A jet of blood shot from her lips.

Zhen Zhibing snapped out of his stupor and rushed over to check on the young woman.

Mistaking his intentions, Penance placed himself protectively before his mentor and prepared to strike. As Zhen Zhibing raised his hand instinctively to block the blow, Penance – recognising the move – flipped his palm around and caught his opponent by the wrist. He gave it a tug, pulling the Taoist towards him, then turned the forward momentum back on the man using an Ancient Tomb technique.

Penance was awed by the efficacy of his counter. He knew his reactions were quick, but his strength was still limited. He never imagined he could send a man with decades of martial experience reeling back by more than twenty steps. His success was due in part to the fact that Lin Chaoying had never used her kung fu on the Quanzhen monks, as by the time she had perfected it, she had shut herself up in the Tomb. The Taoists were blissfully unaware of the existence of a repertoire that, in the right hands, could thwart their every endeavour. Nor should it be forgotten that Zhen Zhibing's reflexes – mental and physical – were hampered by the shame of having his secret feelings exposed and by his concern for the Dragon Maiden's well-being. How else could he allow himself to be caught out by a boy with just a few years of training?

Flushed with success, Penance knelt by the Dragon Maiden's side. "Auntie, do not trouble yourself with them. I'll take you home."

"Kill them . . . can't let them . . . slander me . . ." she muttered between painful gasps.

Penance did not need to be asked twice. He lunged for the nearest Taoist, spearing the branch he had snapped off earlier at his former *shifu*'s chest. Zhao Zhijing twirled his sword with a sneer and hacked down at the feeble makeshift weapon. The tip of the branch quivered and curled away from the blade, flicking an acupoint on the wrist below the monk's sword hand and numbing the joint. Then it cut horizontally towards his left cheek.

Zhao Zhijing was forced to choose between clinging onto his steel and dodging the strike aimed at his face. The monk decided to put his faith in his combat experience and ducked, letting Penance take his sword from his hand. He was confident that he could snatch it back with his next move.

The Taoist thought he had been clever, luring his one-time student in by feigning weakness. How could he know that the kung fu Penance was using against him had been designed to counteract every possible permutation of Quanzhen martial arts? Or that the youth was so well drilled that his responses were reflexive?

Straight away, Penance recognised the sequence Zhao Zhijing was about to launch and swung the stolen sword down at the monk's hand.

Zhao Zhijing jerked his arm back from the blade's whetted edge, only to find its sharpened tip pointing at his heart.

"Down!"

As Penance's roar filled his ears, Zhao Zhijing felt a foot hooking around his ankle. The next thing he knew, he was on the ground, with the sword's point plunging towards his exposed lower belly.

"He is your *shifu!*" Zhen Zhibing yelled as he lunged, desperate to parry the lethal blow.

Feeling the air parting behind him, Penance stabbed backwards. *Dooong!* Steel clashed as the two blades locked.

Zhen Zhibing was impressed by Penance's quick and precise response, then shocked to find his arm straightening against his will and his weapon being drawn away from him. He summoned a rush of internal strength to resist. Naturally, he prevailed and even managed to pull Penance's sword towards him, making the most of his far greater store of *neigong* power.

The monk thought he had the situation under control, but in fact he was reacting in the exact way Penance had hoped. All of a sudden, Zhen Zhibing found he was unable to drag Penance's blade any further and it fell from the young man's grasp. The hilt bounced off the ground and the sharp point came flying his way, with Penance's hands thrusting into his chest at the same time.

Zhen Zhibing flung his sword at the airborne blade, knocking it off course, and pulled his arms across his chest, folding his elbows at a severe angle. It was difficult to channel much energy in this awkward position. His forearms took the brunt of the palm thrusts, but stabs of pain still reached his torso. He scuttled three steps back to dissipate some of the power of the blows, thankful that Penance's internal energy was not strong enough to fracture his bones.

The entire exchange unfolded in the brief time it took Zhao Zhijing to get back on his feet. The warring martial brothers now set aside their differences and joined forces against the young turncoat. But, to their shock and shame, they soon found themselves so hard-pressed that it was as if their limbs were tangling up. They pulled back to stand shoulder to shoulder, maintaining a defensive posture until they had figured out a pattern to the boy's kung fu.

At first, with Penance now armed with both swords, the young man's blistering attacks held sway over the contest, but in time, the monks grew more sure-footed in their watchful stance. And Penance was beginning to realise that he could not repeat the success he enjoyed when fighting sword to sword. Lin Chaoying had invented the Jade Maid Heart Scripture with the sole aim of outsmarting Wang Chongyang in an equal contest, each equipped with the same weapons. She would never have lowered herself to pitching steel against flesh, so her swordplay had no answer against Quanzhen fist or palm strikes. This was the reason why Zhao Zhijing and Zhen Zhibing were able to hold their ground barehanded, though their superior martial training and their willingness to work together to avoid defeat also played a part.

Penance swung the swords up and down and side to side, hacking and slicing, and yet, he could not find a crack in the monks' defences. To make matters worse, the two blades were getting heavy and burdensome under the hail of Taoist palm strikes.

As Zhen Zhibing swatted away yet another slash of the sword, the absurdity of the situation struck him. Two martial seniors brawling with a teenage boy, while the woman of his dreams lay slumped against a tree, grievously injured.

"Penance Yang, stop this nonsense!" he called. "Help Miss Long back to the Tomb."

"Auntie told me to kill you."

Zhen Zhibing replied with a thumping palm thrust, knocking the sword in Penance's left hand askew.

"Enough!" the monk cried, jumping back three steps. "You can't kill us, Penance. It's impossible." He held his left palm skywards. "To reassure you both, I, Zhen Zhibing, solemnly vow not to breathe a word about what has come to pass today. If I reveal the smallest detail, I shall slit my throat . . . If I break this promise, I shall die a horrible death and be cast down to the Eighteenth Hell, and in my next life, I shall be reborn as a pig or a dog, and always reincarnated as a beast!"

"A dog would suit you," Penance shot back, though Zhen Zhibing's solemn tone had convinced him that his words came from the heart. He turned and strode two steps forward, as if he were walking away, before swinging one of his swords to the rear.

The sly, underhand attack – Mulan Shoots Backwards – threatened to spill Zhao Zhijing's guts. Though the monk had remained alert, as any martial man would in the situation, he had not imagined his erstwhile disciple had the skill to launch a strike like that undetected. But now the prick of steel on his lower belly was proving otherwise. He tucked in his abdomen by gathering *qi* in the Elixir Field and struck the flat of the blade with his right foot, sending the weapon flying into the air.

Unruffled, Penance swiftly jabbed his finger at his former *shifu*'s leg, triggering the pressure point in the crook of the knee. Zhao Zhijing buckled and fell in a genuflecting position.

Penance caught the sword as it fell and touched its tip to the monk's throat, keeping him in his humiliating stance. "I honoured you as my *shifu* and kowtowed eight times to you, but you were never my teacher. Return those bows to me. Now!"

Zhao Zhijing nearly passed out at the outrageous demand. His face was puce – almost black – with rage.

Seeing that the Taoist would not budge, Penance pressed the sword point harder into his skin.

"Go on, kill me!" Zhao Zhijing shouted in defiance.

"Penance, no," the Dragon Maiden said weakly. "Don't hurt him. Make him swear . . . and let him go."

Penance relaxed his grip somewhat. "Promise you will never speak of what you saw today!"

"I won't talk . . ." Zhao Zhijing's tone was conciliatory, but he could not resist adding a retort. "But why must I swear?"

"Swear on your life!" the young man demanded.

"Fine! What has come to pass today is known only to the four of us. If I share it with a fifth person, let me be despised by all in the *wulin*, thrown out of the Sect, my reputation ruined, and suffer a horrible death."

Unschooled in worldly matters, neither the Dragon Maiden nor Penance had noticed the catch in Zhao Zhijing's oath. But Zhen Zhibing had heard it loud and clear. He wanted to warn Penance, but how could he without alerting his martial brother? While he deliberated, the youth disappeared into the night with his teacher in his arms.

4

PENANCE HEADED STRAIGHT FOR HIS ROOM WHEN HE STEPPED inside the Tomb, and set the Dragon Maiden down on the boreal nephrite.

"Not here . . . too cold," she whispered, her voice quivering at the freezing touch of the stone.

The young man berated himself for his thoughtlessness. Of course, it was impossible for his teacher to handle the icy slab right now. He carried her gingerly to the next chamber, with its standard stone bed. When he was helping her to lie down, a guttural grunt rocked her body and a spray of blood shot from her lips. The warm crimson liquid clung to his bare chest. She wheezed and gasped and spewed forth another jet of blood.

Shocked by the severity of her injuries, Penance began to weep.

"Why the tears?" The Dragon Maiden managed a smile. "It'll stop when I have no more blood to cough up."

"Don't die, Auntie, please!"

"You're scared, aren't you? Don't worry. I shall kill you before I expire." Noticing his distress, she added, "If I don't, who will look after you when I am gone? How am I to face Grandam Sun in the netherworld?" Blood trickled from the corners of her mouth as she spoke, yet her demeanour was calm and composed, as though nothing was amiss.

Penance remembered she had said something to the same effect when he first arrived at the Tomb and he grew more flustered. Not knowing what to say, he ran out and fetched a large bowl of jade bee honey and fed it to her.

The sweet liquid seemed to have remarkable healing properties. The Dragon Maiden stopped coughing blood and fell in a deep slumber. The tightness in Penance's chest at last began to ease and his body succumbed to the night's exertions. He curled up on the floor and dozed off leaning against the bed.

Suddenly, Penance felt the chill of metal pressed against his neck. He had lived in the Tomb long enough to see in the subterranean darkness without the need for candles. He parted his eyelids to find the Dragon Maiden sitting up, her sword in her hand.

"Auntie!"

"I am not going to get better, Penance. I shall take your life now and we will find Grandam Sun together."

"Auntie!"

"Afraid? It will be quick. Just one strike." Her eyes flashed with resolve. She was ready.

Penance had never imagined he would raise his hand against his mentor, but the desire to stay alive burned bright. He rolled sideways and threw a foot out at the blade.

The injury had not slowed the Dragon Maiden's reactions. She turned away from the kick, but her sword's aim stayed true. He tried another move, then another, but everything he knew he had learned from her, and she could predict his every response. The steel trailed him like a shadow, never more than three inches from his throat.

She's determined to kill me!

The palpable threat drenched Penance in cold sweat. It also compelled him to act. He held up his palms side by side and thrust them forward. He was hoping the Dragon Maiden would withdraw since she had no *neigong* power left for a head-on confrontation, but her sword did not waver. She merely veered a fraction, shifting out of the blow's direct course.

Penance hesitated. If he struck down now, he could knock the weapon out of her grasp, but how could he lay a finger on his teacher? He angled his arms upwards and let his hands glide past her shoulder.

"This is futile, Penance."

The Dragon Maiden reached a little further with her sword hand and flexed her wrist. The blade quivered – a feint left and a flick right – in an attack known as Parting Flowers, Flicking Willows. The sharp point now rested on the thinly stretched skin over Penance's windpipe. She turned to meet his gaze, ready to end it all, but the instant she caught the pleading look in his eyes, all energy drained from her being. The blade clattered to the ground.

Penance bolted the moment he was free from the threat of steel, but he turned round for one last look before he stepped through the doorway.

The Dragon Maiden had slumped to the floor, the sword lying forgotten by her side. Her eyes were squeezed shut. Two rivulets of blood flowed from the corners of her mouth. Her skin had lost the usual white jade luminosity – it was now a lacklustre grey.

I can't leave Auntie to die! If she wants to kill me, so be it.

His mind made up, Penance sat down and shifted the Dragon Maiden into a more comfortable position leaning against his chest.

He saw the bowl of jade bee honey from earlier and remembered its efficacy. He parted her lips and poured some of the sweet liquid into her mouth.

The Dragon Maiden recovered a little when she tasted the honey. After swallowing a few mouthfuls, she became aware of the warmth emanating from his embrace. Joy spread from her heart and colour returned to her cheeks like the bloom of spring.

"Why . . . did you stay?"

"I can't bear the thought of leaving you! You can kill me, or I'll take my life when you die. I'll follow you to the netherworld, so you won't be alone."

The sincerity and depth of feeling in his words filled the Dragon Maiden with a profound sense of peace. Her breathing became less ragged and her eyes grew heavy. Penance scooped her up and placed her gently on the bed. He pulled a thin blanket over her and lit the candle on the nearby stone side table. It was a relief to see a hint of colour returning to her face and the corners of her lips curling up. She no longer looked like she was at death's door.

A short while later, the Dragon Maiden turned to Penance and parted her eyelids a little. "*Shifu* once said ginseng, notoginseng, safflower and dong quai could be used to cure internal injuries . . ."

"I'll find them now."

She closed her eyes and murmured, "Be careful . . ."

PENANCE HURRIED out of the Tomb and stepped into dazzling sunlight. Birdsong and the scent of flowers riding on the breeze flooded his senses. The world above ground was far removed from the gloom and misery down below, but he was in no mood to appreciate the change of scenery. He raced down the mountain using his fastest lightness *qinggong*, pausing briefly at a creek to wash the blood from his skin, and reached the foothills around midday, just as his empty stomach was beginning to protest. He spotted corn growing on a slope to the west and decided to stop for a quick snack before finding his way to the nearest marketplace for the medicinal herbs required.

The crop had yet to fully ripen, but from his time drifting on his own after his mother's death, Penance knew they were edible. He picked five ears and roasted them on a fire built with dead leaves and stalks found in the field. He wolfed down three cobs and wrapped the rest up for the Dragon Maiden. Then he heard footsteps approaching. Assuming it was the farmer who owned the field, he squatted down to scatter the ashes and conceal the uneaten corn. He would prefer to avoid a squabble and be on his way as soon as possible.

But when he looked up, his eyes lighted on a Taoist nun in an apricot-yellow habit heading in his direction. The young woman carried two swords on her back. The blood-red silk tassels attached to the hilts were swinging as she walked. Judging by her outfit and her light gait, she was clearly trained in the martial arts – probably a disciple of Sun Bu'er the Sage of Tranquillity from Chongyang Temple. He bent down again to finish cleaning up.

The Taoist hailed Penance and asked, "Which is the path to ascend?"

How can a Quanzhen disciple not know her way around the Zhongnan Mountains? Penance suspected something nefarious was afoot and kept his head lowered. "Follow the main road uphill."

The nun cast her eyes over the young man. He was stripped to the waist, crouching on his heels, busy picking at dead leaves. His trousers were worn and stained dark with paint or remnants of food.

"I'm speaking to you. Stand up and turn to me!"

The young woman was keenly aware of her physical allure and was not used to being ignored. Men usually gawked and stared at her, and yet this farmhand had taken one look and returned to gathering broken twigs. His indifference was vexing.

Penance pretended not to have heard her. He hated anyone associated with the Quanzhen Sect and he did not wish to tarry here.

"Did you hear me?"

He grunted an acknowledgement.

The Taoist let out a girlish titter and said in a voice coy and sweet, "Oh, do turn around and look at me."

Perplexed by her odd tone, Penance did as she asked and found her regarding him with a sidelong gaze. He could not detect any malicious intent lurking in her fair skin, rosy cheeks and gleaming eyes, and busied himself with moving stalks and branches around in the hope that she would lose interest and leave him alone.

"Do you know the way to the tomb up in the mountains?"

Penance froze for a brief moment, then shouted, "No!"

The young woman dismissed his agitation as superstitious fear of the dead, but it also confirmed that he knew what she was talking about. She kept her eyes trained on him, wondering how she could coax him into revealing the location of the Tomb of the Living Dead, since he had already shown he was too young and uncouth to recognise her beauty. She produced two *sycee* ingots of silver from inside her robe and struck them together.

"These will be yours if you do as I say."

Although Penance wanted to go on his way and be rid of her, he was curious as to why she was seeking directions to the Tomb, and the truth was he could use her money. No silver was kept in the underground complex and he had planned to take the herbs needed by stealth or by force when he got to the market. He decided to feign ignorance to lure the young woman into divulging her purpose. He fixed his eyes on the ingots and asked in oafish manner, "What are they?"

The Taoist flashed a radiant smile. "This is silver. You can buy new clothes, a big fat hen and polished white rice with it."

Penance scrunched up his face in disbelief – "You're lying!" – as he wondered how he might snatch the silver from her hands.

"I'm not." She beamed in good humour. "Tell me your name."

"They call me Clod. What's yours?"

"Well, you can call me Celestial. I need an axe. You have one at home? Bring it here."

Penance shook his head fervently.

"I'll give you this for your trouble." She tossed an ingot at him.

Penance reached out clumsily. The metal nugget hit him on the shoulder then bounced off his foot.

"You hurt me!" He yelped and hopped and grabbed the silver, all the while edging downhill with each ungainly movement.

The Taoist nun watched the boy's over-the-top response with amusement and let him run off. Then she unwound her belt and whipped the long strip of fabric towards his back.

Sensing the rush of air, Penance looked over his shoulder and was shocked to see an Ancient Tomb martial move in action.

She's not a Quanzhen nun! Is she here for Auntie? Despite the unsettling discovery, Penance kept up his act of a coarse rustic with no kung fu knowledge. He let the sash curl around his ankle and toppled forward heavily. When she began to retrieve the belt, he relaxed his body and allowed her to reel him in, while loudly protesting his treatment.

The Taoist looked at the grubby captive at her feet. He's not bad looking for a country lad, she thought. Unsheathing one of her swords, she pointed it at his heart.

"Do you want to live or die?" she asked with a friendly smile.

Penance recognised the technique immediately. Blossom Blooms under the Brush. Another Ancient Tomb kung fu. He was now certain that she was a student of Blithe Li, which meant she could not have come in peace, since her *shifu* had left the Tomb on acrimonious terms. He decided to continue to play the yokel to keep her guard down, so he screwed up his face in fright and shouted, "I want to live! I'll do what you say!"

"If you defy me, boy, I'll cut you down."

"As you say!"

"Bring me an axe. Now."

The Taoist flicked her wrist and the long cloth belt wound around her waist by itself. She did so to flaunt her martial mastery, but the dazed look on the lad's face showed no appreciation at all.

In truth, Penance was awed by her meticulous control. He recognised that his original plan to escape, get the herbs and rush back to the Tomb would not work. The Dragon Maiden was injured and all alone . . . what if this nun found her way to the Tomb? Who knew what infernal plan she was harbouring? He could not possibly let her out of his sight. All he could do now was go along with her and find out what she was up to. And so, he bumbled towards the closest cottage, stamping his feet heavily and unsteadily.

His lumbering steps irritated the Taoist and she cried after him, "Don't tell anyone about me! And come back quickly!"

Penance grunted in reply. He opened the door and peeped around inside. Empty. The habitants were probably working in the fields. He took the hatchet hanging on the wall, grabbed a tattered old shirt draped over a stand, pulled it over his head and waddled back.

"Why do you look so glum? Smile!"

Penance forced a grin and croaked out a laugh. He had not realised that, although he had been successful in acting the part of a bumpkin, his worries about the Dragon Maiden were clouding his expression.

"Take me up the mountains."

"No, Ma says I'm to stay here."

"Really?" The nun pinched the boy's ear and twisted. At the same time, she raised her sword in menace.

"I'll go! I'll go!" He squealed like a pig at the slaughter.

The young woman seized Penance's sleeve and pulled him along using lightness kung fu. He stumbled after her, planting his feet awkwardly, struggling to keep pace. After a while, he flumped down on a rock, panting hard, and refused to take another step.

When she urged him to get up, he shot back, "You run like a hare! How can I keep up?" and continued to mop the sweat from his brow.

The Taoist's patience was wearing thin. She looked up at the sky. The sun was already slanting westwards. She grabbed his arm and sprinted uphill. Penance kicked his legs in all directions as he scrambled after her, trampling on her toes every so often.

"You!" The nun hissed in frustration after one particularly hard stamp, but she checked her temper when she registered how laboriously the lad was wheezing and how exhausted he looked. She put her arm around his waist and half lifted him before darting ahead in her fastest *qinggong*. In a matter of moments, they had ascended several *li*.

Penance could feel her warmth through his back, and they were in such close proximity that he could also pick up her unique scent. As he grew more accustomed to the position, he allowed himself to lean fully into her shapely figure and let her carry him up the mountains.

The Taoist soon felt the load on her arm growing heavier. She looked down and saw the enjoyment on the swain's face and the upturned corners of his mouth. She immediately let go and cast him to the ground.

"*Aiyooo!* That hurt!" Penance rubbed his backside and refused to take another step.

AS PENANCE had guessed, the Taoist nun was a disciple of Blithe Li the Red Serpent Celestial. She was the teenager sent to take the lives of Lu Liding and his family, only to be chased away by Madam Wu.

Ripple Hong sat down on a rock and started to smooth the locks of hair that had been blown loose by the wind.

Penance watched her, his head inclined to one side. She is rather pretty, he thought, but of course, no-one can compare with Auntie.

"What are you looking at?" She shot him a glare, but the sight of him spluttering for a reply made her chuckle. "Do you think I'm pretty?"

Without waiting for a response, she took out a small ivory comb and rearranged her hair. When she was done, she took his arm and continued their ascent.

Soon, the outline of Chongyang Temple appeared in the distance at the end of the road, but here Ripple Hong turned west – in the general direction of the Tomb of the Living Dead.

So she really is here for Auntie, Penance said to himself. He started trying to think of ways to stall their progress.

Some time later, Ripple Hong took a map from inside her robe to orient herself.

"We shouldn't go any further," Penance said under his breath, trying to make himself sound scared. "There are ghosts."

"How do you know?"

"There's a big tomb in the wood yonder and evil spirits live inside. No-one goes near it."

Ripple Hong was thrilled to learn that she was nearing her destination. She had first heard about the Jade Maid Heart Scripture when she was in Shanxi helping her *shifu* take on the heroes of the *wulin*. Blithe Li had told her that, if they studied the martial system, they would have no need to fear the Quanzhen cow muzzles and she would not have to resort to trickery to best them – but its secrets were buried in the Tomb of the Living Dead in the Zhongnan Mountains. Ripple Hong asked her teacher why she had not returned to the Tomb to learn this kung fu. Blithe Li mumbled something about how she had handed over the subterranean structure to her younger martial sister and they were not on speaking terms. In time, she let slip that her martial sister was much younger and rather mediocre in her learning – to turn up at the Tomb would be to risk appearing a bully, given her seniority.

Since first learning of the Scripture, Ripple Hong had often urged her *shifu* to take back the martial inheritance that was rightfully hers, but Blithe Li would simply smile and say nothing. The proud fighter would never divulge the truth of the matter: her attempts to break in had left her injured, fleeing in desperation. And yet, not a single day went by that the Red Serpent Celestial did not think about circumventing its defence mechanisms.

Frustrated by her *shifu*'s indifference, Ripple Hong began to ask questions about the Tomb to get an idea of its location and layout, marking all she could discover on a map, waiting for the right moment to go in search of the Scripture.

Before long, Blithe Li sent her to Chang'an to dispatch an enemy. The man had limited kung fu and she dispatched him without difficulty. Now she had the chance to extend her trip and make a quick detour to the Zhongnan Mountains, which lay not far south of the city.

PENANCE WAS made to cut a path through the thorny undergrowth. He swung the hatchet clumsily to keep up his pretence, grumbling loudly about the futility of it all. He had been at it for more than an hour and they had barely progressed one *li*.

The gloomy forest floor was now pitch-black with the coming of night. Anxiety was threatening to overwhelm Penance. He was still stuck with the student of Blithe Li, and he could not let her out of his sight in case she found her way to the Tomb and accosted the Dragon Maiden while she was injured and unprotected. Who knew what malicious purpose had brought her there in the first place?

He had not forgotten his original mission, but it was too late to head back down the mountains to find a shop that sold the medicinal herbs needed. Even if he could locate such a place, he would have to slip away from the Taoist first. On top of everything, all he really wanted was to see his teacher as soon as possible.

Penance forced himself to take stock of his options. After spending the afternoon with the nun, he was confident he could get the better of her, especially since he was familiar with their surroundings and she was not. He continued chopping branches in his haphazard way and surreptitiously took aim at a rock.

Sparks flew.

"Oh no, I've broken the axe!" he cried, pointing at the dented cutting edge. "Papa will beat me! I – I'm going home!"

"No! You can't!" Ripple Hong grabbed him by the shoulders. She had to enter the Tomb tonight.

"Are you scared of ghosts?"

"I'll cut them in half with my sword."

"If you promise to chase the nasty things away, I'll take you to the big tomb."

"You know the way? Take me there now!"

Penance babbled on about ghosts and spirits to maintain his guise, urging the nun to swear over and over that she would protect him. He took her hand and led her onto a concealed trail.

By the time they emerged from the woods, the night was far advanced. In the darkness, without a hint of the moon or the stars overhead, Penance was keenly aware of the warm hand in his grasp. He could not help but compare it with the Dragon Maiden's.

Why are Auntie's palms so cold to the touch? he wondered as he tensed and relaxed his fingers unconsciously to gauge the temperature of the soft and smooth skin.

If a man of the *wulin* were so brazen, Ripple Hong would have given him a taste of her sword, and yet, she did not find this country lad repulsive. Perhaps it was because she needed him to take her to the Tomb of the Living Dead, or it might be the disarming combination of his dim wits and his handsome features. She could not deny it was pleasing that he at last seemed to have recognised her charms.

5

PENANCE'S HEART THROBBED WILDLY WHEN HE SAW THAT THE Tomb's entrance was wide open, realising he had neglected to shut it in the rush to set off in the morning. He stepped inside, praying nothing untoward had befallen the Dragon Maiden while he had been away.

Ripple Hong found the boy's assured strides curious, but in the absolute absence of light, just keeping pace demanded her full focus. Her *shifu* had said one wrong step along the meandering passage was all it took to become hopelessly lost underground, and yet, the lad raced ahead without any hesitation, stopping once in a while to push open a door or shift a rock. She began to doubt her *shifu*'s warnings. *Did she exaggerate to put me off coming here?*

But before she could decide on an answer, the farm boy halted. He nudged open a stone door and paused at the threshold.

After a moment's silence, she heard him whisper, "We've arrived," as if he were worried about disturbing whatever lay within.

Although this part of the Tomb was no darker than any other, Ripple Hong felt the oppressive blackness more keenly now that they had stopped moving. She fumbled in her robe for tinder and flint, and only ventured forward once she had sparked a small flame into life.

A woman clad in a white robe was lying on her side, her back turned towards the doorway. Ripple Hong assumed she was the Dragon Maiden and was surprised that she had not stirred. Was she deep in slumber? Or so confident in her skills that she could afford to ignore intruders?

The Taoist nun lit the candle on the table and raised one of her swords to guard her approach. "Student Ripple Hong bows to her martial elder."

Penance's heart had been in his throat since they had entered the chamber. A part of him longed to rush up and fold the Dragon Maiden into his arms, but he also dreaded to find out why she was lying so still. He waited for her to respond to the greeting. When he heard a weak, breathy *hmm*, the heavy rock that had been crushing his chest dropped away and he was so relieved that he burst into tears.

"Hush . . ." The Dragon Maiden turned around slowly.

Ripple Hong, who had never set eyes on a more beautiful face, suddenly felt rather ashamed of her own looks.

"Is my martial sister here?" the Dragon Maiden asked weakly.

"*Shifu* sent me to convey her good wishes."

"Leave now . . . You and your *shifu* . . . are not allowed here . . ." But her warning was rendered ineffectual by her waxen pallor, blood-spattered dress and ragged breathing.

Recognising that the Dragon Maiden was mortally hurt, Ripple Hong relaxed her watchful stance. This was a chance sent by the heavens to make her the heir to the Tomb of the Living Dead!

"*Shifu* tasked me with retrieving the Jade Maid Heart Scripture." She stated her purpose outright, for she feared the Dragon Maiden might die at any moment and it would be very difficult to find the martial tract in this dark subterranean labyrinth. "Hand it over and I will help you with your injury."

"Where is my martial sister? I wish to . . . speak to her."

Sniggering, Ripple Hong withdrew two long silver needles from inside her robe. "I believe you recognise these. Give me the Scripture."

Penance knew them all too well. The deadly poisonous Soul of Ice. He had suffered terribly from just touching them. He would do anything to get them away from the Dragon Maiden.

"Ghost!" he screamed, throwing his arms around Ripple Hong and hugging her from behind. In the process, he flicked the True Shoulder pressure point by her shoulder blade and Capital Gate on the side of her waist. He then jabbed the Great Bone point on her collarbone firmly several times, in case she had a way to unblock her meridian flow.

It had never occurred to Ripple Hong that the cloddish farm boy could be trained in the martial arts, let alone in such advanced techniques. An aching numbness spread rapidly through her body and she slumped to the floor before she could even spit a curse at him.

"Auntie, should I give her a taste of her own needles?" Penance stooped, picked one up with the hem of his shirt and grinned at the Taoist nun.

His words sent Ripple Hong's spirits flying and her souls scattering in fright. She would have begged for mercy if she could part her lips, but all she could do was look at him with beseeching eyes.

"Shut the Tomb, Penance," the Dragon Maiden ordered.

A coquettish female voice answered from the corridor. "I'm here already, my little martial sister."

Standing in the doorway was an attractive woman dressed in a Taoist habit. Her eyes were in the much-admired apricot shape and her skin glowed with the blush of peach blossom. A barely perceptible smile played on her lips. Blithe Li the Red Serpent Celestial.

She had long suspected that her disciple had designs on the Jade Maid Heart Scripture. Since she had first mentioned the Tomb of the Living Dead after her tussle with the Quanzhen monks in Shanxi several years before, their conversation had turned from time to time to its location and layout. So, when one of her enemies was sighted in Chang'an, she sent Ripple Hong there alone, to see if she would take action. Of course, Blithe Li was trailing behind in the shadows. So swift and fleet-footed was she that no-one detected her presence until she chose to make herself known.

The Dragon Maiden sat up – "Sister!" – and succumbed to a coughing fit.

"Where's Grandam Sun?"

"She's dead."

Visibly pleased by the news, Blithe Li then pointed at Penance. "Who's this? Why is he here? The Doyenne decreed that no man should ever step inside the Tomb."

Penance moved to stand protectively in front of the Dragon Maiden, who had been seized by another bout of coughing.

Blithe Li let fly with her horsetail whisk. A flurry of deadly strikes, once, twice, thrice. Three Birds Fly into the Wood – a formidable Ancient Tomb move. Most fighters on the receiving end would be left with snapped tendons and fractured bones, but Penance was privy to the secrets behind it and veered away with relative ease.

"Sister, who is he?" Blithe Li reined in her weapon with alarm. The boy had dodged her attack using a technique from her own kung fu heritage.

"Bow to your martial elder, Penance." The Dragon Maiden's voice was muffled by her attempts to hold down another lungful of blood.

Penance spat at the command.

"Come closer," the Dragon Maiden heaved with difficulty. "Listen to me."

He bent down reluctantly and brought his ear to her lips.

"There's a stone lever down by my feet," she whispered. "Tug it hard to the left and jump up on the bed at once."

Nodding, Penance pretended to straighten the bedclothes so he could locate the trigger. Once his fingers had closed around it he adjusted his stance and said in a voice bright and loud: "Student Penance Yang bows to his martial elder." Then he pulled the lever and hopped onto the bed.

The stone bed began its rumbling descent. At the same time, a rock slid over the open doorway, closing off the room.

Blithe Li had always known that the Tomb was full of mechanical traps, but she was kept in the dark regarding their triggers and locations because her *shifu* liked the Dragon Maiden better. She had not expected her bedridden martial sister and her young male disciple to offer any kind of resistance and had been wondering how she could force them to hand over the Scripture rather than paying attention to their interaction.

The noise of the trapdoor pulled the woman's focus back to the here and now. She shot her hand out, but before she could secure her grip, Penance's palm knocked it askew.

Paa-aang! A stone slab slotted into the cavity the bed had left behind.

The Dragon Maiden and Penance were now sealed in the chamber beneath. It took a moment for Penance's eyes to adjust to the gloom. He could make out a table and went up to it. He felt around its surface, found a candle stump and lit it with the tinderbox he carried on his person.

The Dragon Maiden pushed herself to a sitting position and let out a sigh. "I have lost too much blood to channel my internal strength to heal myself. And even without this injury, the two of us couldn't beat—"

Penance bit into his wrist and pressed the bleeding wound against her lips, cutting her short. Warm blood flowed into her mouth and chased away the iciness in her body. She knew it was not right to indulge in such things and struggled against it with what remaining strength she had, but his arm was wrapped tight around her waist, keeping her from making the slightest movement.

The wound soon congealed and Penance tore it raw again. Then he sank his teeth in his other wrist. He pulled away from her when his head began to spin and he started seeing double. He felt as if his life force had been drained from his body. He could barely sit up straight.

The Dragon Maiden watched Penance in silence. After a while, she heaved out a sigh, closed her eyes and started channelling her energy around her body. Penance, meanwhile, searched the room for fresh wax lights to replace the dimming, flickering stump. Then he joined his teacher in circulating his inner strength to ease the fatigue caused by the blood loss.

The Dragon Maiden opened her eyes several hours later. She could sense that her internal flow had been partially restored and she no longer felt she was at death's door.

"Auntie, you're better!" Penance gushed when he saw that a hint of colour had returned to her cheeks. Now her complexion had the quality of a piece of immaculate white jade dabbed with a touch of rouge. In truth, ingesting blood had done little to replace all she had lost, but its nutritious value had revived her somewhat.

Nodding with a smile, she said, "Let's go back," then got out of bed, went up to a wall, found a hidden lever and wrenched it this way and that. A doorway opened up in the stonework.

Penance followed the Dragon Maiden into the corridor. Despite the darkness, he could tell that he had never been in this passageway before, but he soon found himself back in familiar territory, arriving at his own room.

The Dragon Maiden lit a candle, found a knapsack and started to pack Penance's clothes, followed by her white gold gloves and two jars of jade bee honey.

"What are you doing?" he asked, baffled. "Are we leaving?"

"You are."

"What about you?"

"I swore an oath to *Shifu* that I would stay in the Tomb for life. Unless . . ." She shook her head. "I am staying."

"I'm not going without you."

"Martial Sister Li is here for the Jade Maid Heart Scripture. She won't let us be until it is in her hands. Her grasp of the martial arts far exceeds mine and I am weakened by this injury. Our stores of food will last twenty days at most. With the honey, perhaps a month. What will we do after that?"

"We may not win a fight, but we have to try."

"If you were familiar with her temperament and her skills, you'd know we stand no chance. She will torture and humiliate us, then kill us in the most painful manner—"

"I can't leave—"

The Dragon Maiden ignored Penance's interjection and continued to outline her plan. "I will challenge her and lead her deep underground. You grab the chance to run. Once you're outside, shift the rock to the left of the entryway and pull the lever. Two tenthousand-*jin* boulders will fall and seal the Tomb."

"You know another way out, right?"

"There is no other exit. The Tomb was built by Wang Chongyang as an arsenal and granary for his rebel army . . ." The Dragon Maiden spoke slowly and paused every so often to catch her breath. "He installed many devices to safeguard his supplies. The Dragon Severing Rocks outside the Tomb form the final line of defence.

"Once they fall into place, they block the Tomb's only entrance. It is final and irrevocable and this reflects the strength of Wang Chongyang's resolve. He would rather lure the Jin into the Tomb and die with them than bend his knee." She gulped a few mouthfuls of air and concluded her speech. "Wang Chongyang shared every detail of the Tomb's defences with the Doyenne when she won it from him in their duel."

"I'll stay with you, Auntie." Penance proclaimed through tears. "Dead or alive!"

"You've said the world outside is fun. Go and enjoy it. You can beat the Quanzhen Taoists easily with your kung fu now. You're also very clever. You tricked Ripple Hong. You don't need me to look after you."

"I can never be happy without you." Penance threw his arms around his teacher.

The embrace was stirring physical reactions that the Dragon Maiden could not place or recognise. Hot blood surged through her as tears pricked her eyes.

Unsettled by what was happening to her body, she thought of her *shifu*'s bidding from her deathbed:

> *"Your kung fu training requires you to cut off your seven feelings and stamp out your six desires. If you give your heart away or if you shed tears for another – especially for a man – you will do damage to your martial skills and put yourself in mortal danger. Beware, beware!"*

She pushed him away. "You must obey."

Silenced by her frosty demeanour, Penance let the Dragon Maiden strap the knapsack to his back and accepted the sword she pressed into his hand.

Then she gave her final orders: "Run when I tell you to. Trigger the Dragon Severing Rocks once you are out. You only have a narrow window to seal the Tomb. You will do as I say, won't you?"

"Yes," he promised with a sob.

"If you don't follow my instructions, I will resent you for eternity."

The Dragon Maiden took Penance's hand and led him down the unlit corridor. He noticed her palm was hot one moment and cold the next, rather than consistently icy to the touch, as he was used to, but his hammering heart and sizzling mind were too preoccupied by the confrontation ahead to find any meaning in this.

After a while, the Dragon Maiden stopped and said in a whisper, "They are on the other side of this wall. I will hold my martial sister back. You take the side door in the north-west corner of the room. Use the Jade Bee Needles if her student gives chase."

These needles laced with bee venom were as fine as a hair. Wrought from fine steel, they were gilded with layers of gold – the heavy metal gave them the weight they needed to fly a significant distance. They were unknown in the *wulin* because Lin Chaoying had hardly used them. She considered it dishonourable to use weapons that could not be detected, and later in life, her martial virtuosity was such that she had no need for clandestine means of attack. Although Blithe Li knew of the needles' existence, she was not made privy to the details of their production because she refused to pledge to stay in the Tomb of the Living Dead for life.

The Dragon Maiden allowed a moment for her and Penance to prepare themselves before triggering the mechanism in the stone-work. A large slab of rock shifted to one side, groaning. She made a flourish with her arms and sent her twin weapons – a pair of silk rib-bons – through the opening. One flew towards Blithe Li, the other made straight for Ripple Hong.

Blithe Li brandished her horsetail whisk, whipping its long hairs at the ribbon hurtling her way. The Dragon Maiden's sudden appearance did not catch her off guard – though it did interrupt her chastisement of her student. Her swift parry carried such power that it turned the strip of fabric back the way it came.

Twirling both arms, the Dragon Maiden altered the trajectory of the ribbon flying back at her and redirected the other from Ripple Hong to Blithe Li. The silken strands swished and swirled in a series of nimble, high-speed strikes.

Shifu never showed me this kung fu! Blithe Li noted with bitterness, reminding herself of the need to hold back. She wanted to see what other skills her *shifu* had kept from her. And she must not forget why she had come to the Tomb – to seize the Jade Maid Heart Scripture. She needed her martial sister alive to show her where it was hidden. Given the size of the underground complex, she would never find it by herself.

Meanwhile, Ripple Hong had unsheathed her second sword and was now lunging after Penance. She had always prided herself on being astute and capable, so it was especially maddening and humiliating that she had failed to see through the boy's tricks. She thrust one sword forward and swung the other athwart, raining down a torrent of savage strikes.

Penance raised his blade to block, but his eyes were blurred by tears and his mind was in a whirl. All he could think of was his impending separation from the Dragon Maiden. At any other time, he would have relished the contest, jeering and taunting his opponent between blows, but, as it was, he was reacting mechanically, making no attempt to retaliate.

Ripple Hong grew angrier with herself with each passing moment. From the boy's limp response, she judged that his kung fu was average at best, and yet, he had managed to immobilise her through her acupoints earlier because she had underestimated him.

More than a dozen moves had been exchanged between the two martial sisters in this short space of time. Sensing an opening, Blithe Li swished the horsetail whisk and wound its hairs around the nearest ribbon.

"Watch carefully now!" Blithe Li said gleefully, letting her inner strength flow through her weapon. The horsehairs cut through the fabric and a length of ribbon fluttered to the ground.

In a fight with steel, breaking the opponent's blade requires superb skill and precision. But both Blithe Li and the Dragon Maiden's weapons were soft and pliable, and it was ten times harder to imbue hair and silk with enough firm, incisive internal energy to sever a similarly supple material.

The Dragon Maiden showed no reaction to the curtailing of her weapon or her martial sister's self-satisfied smile. With a flick of the wrist, she brought what was left of the ribbon back to life. It licked out and curled around the whisk's long hairs, and in the same moment, its counterpart shot out and coiled itself around the handle. She then drew in both ribbons, making them pull in opposite directions. *Pak!* The horsetail whisk snapped in two.

Blithe Li tossed her broken weapon away and snatched for the silk ribbons with her bare hands. It was difficult for her to accept that, even in her injured state, her younger martial sister could execute moves with such swiftness and sophisticated control.

The Dragon Maiden was forced to withdraw in the face of this new wave of aggression, and in fewer than twenty moves, she had retreated so much that her back was pressed against the east wall of the chamber. She twisted one arm behind her and called "Penance!" while pushing at a tile.

The rumble of stone grinding against stone filled the room and a small opening appeared in the north-western corner.

Blithe Li spun round to stop Penance, but the Dragon Maiden dropped the ribbons and sent forth a flurry of the deadliest palm strikes with both hands, forcing her martial sister to shift her focus back to her.

"Penance! Go!"

"Yes, Auntie." Penance looked into the Dragon Maiden's eyes, understanding that he had to carry out her command, and brandished his sword with a vigour missing from his lacklustre parries so far. *Sha sha sha!* The razor edge of his blade cut through the air, forcing Ripple Hong to leap back, and he seized the chance to dash towards the open door.

In the meantime, the Dragon Maiden was using the knowledge from the Jade Maid Heart Scripture to keep Blithe Li rooted to the spot. But when she saw Penance turning his back on her and heading through the opening, her eyes began to prick and burn – this would be the last she saw of him. The strength of her emotions, which had already overwhelmed her not long ago when they had first escaped, terrified her, diverting her attention from the fight for a brief moment.

Penance cast one last glance around the chamber as he bent low to pass through the doorway. He saw the Dragon Maiden falter and Blithe Li seizing her wrist at the Gathering Convergence point, then swiping her foot at her ankle. The Dragon Maiden swayed and toppled. Blithe Li raised her hand to deal another blow.

"Noooooo!" he yelled. A rush of blood surged from his chest. He charged back into the room and locked his arms around the Taoist nun's waist, using his weight to frustrate her attack.

A raw, instinctive reaction drawn out of desperation rather than formal martial training.

Blithe Li writhed against Penance's grip, but she could not break free. She was infuriated with herself for being so careless, over-confident in her skills and single-minded in her assault on the Dragon Maiden. As she struggled, she began to feel the heat emanating from his body and the contours of his figure – firm and muscular. The sensations passed through her clothes, searing her insides, scorching her spirits. It sent her heart racing, her mind in a whirl. In all her years roaming the *jianghu*, she had never had such close contact with a member of the opposite sex, even during her courtship with Lu Zhanyuan. She might be notorious for her wanton brutality and scorn for convention, but she had always held her chastity to be her most precious treasure.

In fact, Penance had thrown his arms around Blithe Li like this some years ago, when she had tried to kill Lu Wushuang and Cheng Ying, who had been taking shelter in the abandoned kiln he had been camping in. But, at the time, he was still a child, and now he was on the cusp of manhood.

Blithe Li grew more alarmed as she fought and twisted against Penance's hold. Somehow her efforts to free herself were draining her strength, weakening her core and causing her cheeks to burn.

Shocked to see her *shifu* so firmly shackled, Ripple Hong lunged with both swords flashing, one striking at Penance's back and the other held high in defence.

From the floor, the Dragon Maiden saw the young Taoist's attack and seized Blithe Li's wrist, squeezing her pulse to limit her mobility.

She then rolled to the left, pulling both Penance and Blithe Li along after her, out of the blade's path.

"Go! Now!" The Dragon Maiden climbed to her feet, her fingers still gripping her martial sister's wrist.

"You run, Auntie. I've got her. She can't go after you." Penance locked his arms more tightly around the Taoist nun.

A dozen thoughts were racing through Blithe Li's mind. She was well aware that she was a hair's breadth from death right now and she ought to disentangle herself promptly, but a part of her was so intoxicated by the embrace that it was urging her to stop resisting.

The Dragon Maiden was certain her martial sister could slip away from Penance in a trice, if she so wished. How come he still had a hold on her? Could he have locked her acupoints? But she did not have time to dwell on the matter. One of Ripple Hong's swords was stealing up on Penance again.

Still clutching Blithe Li's wrist, the Dragon Maiden reached out her free hand and tapped the foible of the blade Ripple Hong held in defence. It veered into the attacking sword in a shower of sparks. The impact numbed the young woman's fingers and both weapons clattered to the floor.

The noise jolted Blithe Li from her reverie. The appraising look in the Dragon Maiden's eyes left her mortified.

"How dare you!" she spat. She summoned strength to her arms and cast Penance off. Then she wrenched her wrist out of the Dragon Maiden's grasp and retaliated with a palm thrust.

Distracted by her concern for Penance, the Dragon Maiden only noticed the attack when it was almost upon her. There was no time to launch a counter to dissipate its power, so she raised her arm to block the blow head on. The heavy strike shook her to the core, and a dull ache throbbed in her chest.

Penance got back to his feet and rushed over to check on his teacher, but she pushed him away. "You promised to heed my words."

"Yes, but I also swore to look after you till my last breath! I want to live with you and die with you."

The Dragon Maiden could feel emotions churning in her heart again, but Blithe Li was bearing down on her with her palm readied for another strike. She was too injured and drained to engage directly, so she ducked and swerved out of the way. She then grabbed Penance's arm and pushed him through the side door before darting through it herself.

However, Blithe Li was following close behind them like a shadow. She shot her hand out to grab the Dragon Maiden, but in that moment, her fleeing martial sister spun around and flicked her wrist. A dozen Jade Bee Needles took flight.

A faint scent, sweet like honey, wafted through the air. Blithe Li bent backwards and pushed with her feet to launch herself across the room in a hasty retreat. She slammed into Ripple Hong, who was rushing in pursuit of Penance and the Dragon Maiden, and the two tumbled in a heap.

The needles hit the opposite wall in a series of quiet tinkles. The grinding reverberation of stone against stone sounded in the chamber. The side door was sealed once more.

CHAPTER SEVEN

CHONGYANG'S LAST ENGRAVINGS

I

THE DRAGON MAIDEN AND PENANCE RAN ALONG THE UNLIT corridors until they reached the entrance to the Tomb. The night was no longer as dark and oppressive as before. A handful of stars were twinkling in the sky.

Penance sucked in a few mouthfuls of fresh air then said, "I'll release the Dragon Severing Rocks."

The Dragon Maiden watched him bustle around, searching for the trigger, and shook her head lightly. "Let me go inside first."

"Why?"

"*Shifu* told me to guard the Tomb and never let it fall into another's hands."

"But they'll die in there."

"Yes, but I'll also be shut out forever. I am not you. I will not go against *Shifu*'s bidding."

Sensing her gaze, Penance held her arm and promised, "I will do as you say, Auntie."

The Dragon Maiden bit down on her lip and closed her eyes. She feared she would give in to the stirrings in her heart if she tried to say another word. Freeing herself, she strode across the threshold then stopped.

With her back to Penance and the outside world, she gave her order: "Let the rocks fall." She stared down the dark passageway, terrified her resolve would melt away if she looked back now.

Penance took a deep breath. The scent of flowers, grass and trees filled his lungs. He looked up to the heavens.

This is the last time I will set eyes on the starry sky . . .

He went to the left side of the Tomb entrance and found a round piece of stone concealed behind a large boulder. Following the Dragon Maiden's instructions, he shifted the rock then pulled the trigger. The stone came loose and sand gushed out of the hole it left behind. The enormous Dragon Severing Rocks were being lowered over the entryway. It had taken several hundred men to haul them into place with specially made cables, and once they were released, no-one would ever step out of the Tomb again. Not Blithe Li. Not Ripple Hong. Not the Dragon Maiden. The sheer weight of the rocks would defeat the most sophisticated martial learning.

Tears trickled down the Dragon Maiden's cheeks when she heard the rocks' rumbling descent, and she turned to take one last look at Penance. She watched the dark shadow engulf his silhouette. His face then his torso.

When the rocks were a mere two *chi* from the ground, he dived in a Jade Maid Throws the Shuttle.

The Dragon Severing Rocks crashed down with a thunderous roar.

"You can never kick me out now." Penance's voice echoed in the pitch-black passageway. "I'll be with you even in death!"

The Dragon Maiden folded him in her arms. Overcome by fear then joy, she felt lightheaded and gasped for air. Penance returned her embrace and put his hands on her back, patting it lightly to smooth her breathing.

After some time, she murmured into his chest, "We will be together even in death," then took his hand and headed into the dark heart of the Tomb.

BLITHE LI and Ripple Hong had been groping around, blind and anxious, knocking on walls and pushing tiles to find a trigger that would let them out of the Tomb. Though they had been in the light-less tunnels long enough to make out vague shapes, it was still a huge relief when they heard the approach of footsteps after the earth-shattering rumble and knew they were not alone.

Blithe Li squeezed past the Dragon Maiden and Penance, trapping them between herself and her disciple.

"Would you come with me?" the Dragon Maiden said to her martial sister, undaunted.

Blithe Li hesitated. It was unlikely that she and Ripple Hong would be able to find their way out of this underground maze on their own, whereas the Dragon Maiden knew the place inside out . . . including the traps.

What if this is a ploy to lead me into one, though? I'd be at her mercy.

Receiving no response, the Dragon Maiden added, "I would like to take you to *Shifu*'s final resting place—"

"Don't try to trick me by mentioning *Shifu*," Blithe Li cut her short.

The Dragon Maiden started off down the corridor again, walking hand in hand with Penance and leaving her back undefended. She was taking no precautions to protect herself.

Something about the Dragon Maiden's poise and presence compelled Blithe Li to follow her. She beckoned Ripple Hong to come along, planting each step with care, her senses on high alert.

They soon arrived at the spirit chamber with the five sarcophagi. Blithe Li had never set foot in this part of the Tomb before.

Memories of her *shifu*, raising her, teaching her, came to the surface, tinged with grief and gratitude, but they were soon washed away by bitterness and anger at the woman's undisguised favouritism towards her martial sister. She stood upright in irreverent defiance, refusing to perform the expected obeisance at the memorial.

"Why did you bring me here?" Blithe Li demanded. "*Shifu* cut all ties with me long ago."

"These two coffins are empty." The Dragon Maiden gestured at the caskets that were not completely closed. "Choose one. I'll take the other."

Incensed, Blithe Li let fly with a palm thrust, but the Dragon Maiden stood still, showing no intention to fend off or evade the hefty blow falling on her chest.

When her hand was mere inches away, the Taoist reminded herself – I need her alive for the Scripture! – and pulled back.

"The Dragon Severing Rocks have been lowered," the Dragon Maiden resumed, once Blithe Li had calmed down somewhat.

All colour drained from Blithe Li's face. She remembered the time when *Shifu* was going to lower the rocks to keep their enemies out, but at the last moment they managed to repel the invaders with Soul of Ice and Jade Bee Needles.

"You know another way out, don't you?" she asked in a shaky voice. She refused to believe that her younger martial sister had shut herself up for good.

"The Dragon Severing Rocks seal the Tomb forever. You know that."

"No!" Blithe Li grabbed the Dragon Maiden by the collar.

Unfazed, the Dragon Maiden reached inside her robe and pulled out a well-thumbed bound volume. "Here's the Jade Maid Heart Scripture!" She tossed it into one of the unoccupied stone coffins.

The book was in fact a Taoist classic called *Kinship of the Three*, studied by all who sought the enlightenment of the Way. The Dragon Maiden had been reading it to pass the time when Penance left to find medicinal herbs to treat her injury.

"The Scripture is yours," she continued. "You can advance your kung fu, but you will not leave this place alive or meet new foes again. If you want to kill us, go ahead."

The martial tract Blithe Li had dreamt about night and day was at last within her grasp. She was ready to bend down and reach into the sarcophagus when she realised she would be leaving her back exposed and unprotected.

I'd better dispatch the two of them now . . .

She swung her hand at her martial sister's face.

Penance planted himself before the Dragon Maiden. "You'll have to kill me first!"

Blithe Li lowered her palm and let it hover menacingly over his torso. "You'll protect her with your life?"

"Yes!" Penance had never been more certain of anything.

The Taoist shot her left hand out at an angle and snatched the sword in Penance's grasp. "I will only kill one of you." She twirled the blade around and touched its point to his throat. "Which of you will die today? You or her?"

Penance gave his teacher a radiant smile and looked into Blithe Li's eyes.

"Kill me."

He was truly fearless in the face of death and no threat could sway his heart.

Sighing, Blithe Li said to her martial sister, "You are free from your vow. You can leave this Tomb and these mountains."

WOUNDED BY her unrequited feelings for Wang Chongyang, Lin Chaoying, the Doyenne of the Ancient Tomb Sect, decreed that her true heiress must swear to spend her life in the Tomb of the Living Dead and never to leave the Zhongnan Mountains. The only circumstance in which the martial descendant would be released from this pledge was if she met a man who would willingly give his life for her, without the foreknowledge that his act of self-sacrifice would free her from a lifetime in the subterranean complex.

Lin Chaoying believed all men under the heavens to be fickle and that there was not one living who would readily die for the woman he loved, since even the upright and heroic Wang Chongyang had failed on that front. How could she expect any better from the rest of his sex? But if such a man did exist, her successor would have a reliable companion when she ventured into the world.

Blithe Li should have inherited all the Ancient Tomb kung fu, as she was taken on as a disciple before the Dragon Maiden, however, she refused to swear the oath. As a result, the custodianship of the Tomb and its martial legacy was passed to her younger martial sister.

PENANCE'S DEVOTION fanned the flames of envy and rage in Blithe Li. She furrowed her brow as suppressed memories of the faithless cheat Lu Zhanyuan began to resurface.

"You are very lucky, little sister." Her voice dripped with rancour. She had never enjoyed love herself. Why should her martial sister be favoured with what she had never had? She let her inner strength course through her arm.

Sensing her murderous intent, the Dragon Maiden flourished her left hand, and a dozen Jade Bee Needles took flight. Blithe Li sprang up and the secret weapons flew under her feet.

The Dragon Maiden seized the opportunity and pulled Penance out of the room. She stopped once they were in the passageway outside and called out to her martial sister.

"Whether I am free from my vow or not, we four are destined to die in this tomb. I do not wish to see you again. So, let us each meet our fate on our own terms."

With these words, she tapped the trigger by the doorway and shut the spirit chamber.

2

THE BRIEF ENCOUNTER HAD SO EXHAUSTED THE DRAGON Maiden that she was now straining to lift her feet, let alone walk. Penance put his arm around her back and half carried her to the room she had rested in during the day. Once he had helped her onto the bed, he lit a candle, poured a cup of jade bee honey, held it to her lips and made sure she drank it all. Then he guzzled down a portion of the sweet liquid too.

"Why are you prepared to die for me?" the Dragon Maiden said after a while.

"I have no other family but you in this world. I can't bear to be parted from you."

Silence hung in the air.

"If I had known about this . . ." she muttered at length. "We didn't have to come back . . . but if we had not . . . I would have never found out . . . and I would not be released from my vow."

"Shall we look for a way out?"

"The Tomb's layout is too complex. We will never—" The Dragon Maiden heard Penance suck in a deep breath and asked, "You're regretting your choice, aren't you?"

"No." His answer was firm and resolute. "In here, I've got you. Out there, no-one cares about me."

Before today, she would have put a stop to such blatant articulations of feelings, but now they warmed her.

"Then why do you—?"

"I can't help but think, what a wonderful time we would have . . . if we could leave . . . There are so many exciting things under the skies."

The Dragon Maiden was a newborn babe when she was taken into the Tomb of the Living Dead. Her *shifu* and Grandam Sun had never told her about the outside world. She could not imagine what life above ground and beyond the Zhongnan Mountains would be like, her heart as calm as a pool of undisturbed water. The first she had heard about the thrills of towns and marketplaces was when Penance described his own adventures.

Now that he mentioned the outside world again, thoughts and feelings she had never known before swelled like a rising tide, hot blood surged and dashed against her bosom like crashing waves. She channelled her *qi* to try to smooth this strange sensation, but tranquillity eluded her. She had never before experienced this unsettling state and it frightened her. For the first time, the idea that the injury might have done irreparable damage to her martial capabilities crossed her mind.

The stillness of the heart so crucial to her kung fu training came from an outright suppression of the seven feelings and six desires, which in itself went against the natural course of things as governed by the heavens. The feelings and desires were not eradicated, but merely choked and muted. But how could any human being fail to be stirred when they realised someone was ready to die for them to keep them safe?

Passion gushed forth over the breached dam, thoughts and fancies raced headlong through her mind.

Unable to quell the storm within, the Dragon Maiden got out of bed and started pacing, but it only made her more agitated and her stride grew brisker. She could feel heat emanating from her cheeks and nervous energy contorting her features. She slumped back down on the bed and turned to Penance. He was looking at her with affection and concern in his eyes.

Why should we be bound by the ties of teacher and disciple or aunt and nephew when we are both going to die in a matter of days? she asked herself. If he puts his arms around me now, I won't push him away. I will let him hold me.

Penance noticed the Dragon Maiden heaving her bosom in ragged breaths and thought the injury was bothering her again.

"Auntie, how do you feel?"

"Come here." She took his hand as soon as he drew near and touched his palm against her cheek. "Do you like me?"

Disturbed by her feverish skin and the unusual bright glint in her eyes, Penance overlooked her whispered question.

"Is your chest hurting a lot?"

"No, I feel good, especially here." She put her hand to her heart and gave him a reassuring smile. "I am not long for this world. So, Penance, tell me, do you like me, truly?"

"Of course! I have no other family but you."

"If someone else treats you as I do, will you respond to her in the same way?"

"I am nice to anyone who's nice to me." As soon as the words left his mouth, Penance felt a tremor pass through the hand that was clasped over his, its warm touch turning ice cold in an instant. The blush on the Dragon Maiden's cheeks faded before his eyes. Alarmed, he cast his mind back to her words.

There are women in the tens of thousands – if they're all nice to me, will I like them all? He put the question to himself. Say the Taoist nun Ripple Hong. It was nice to be spoken to with affection and to have her arms around me . . . but how can I compare her with Auntie?

"I may be nice to others, Auntie, but with you, it's different," Penance declared. "When I set off the Dragon Severing Rocks, I realised I'd never see you again and it felt worse than dying. I'd rather starve to death here with you. I don't mind being killed by Blithe Li as long as I am with you. If I can't be by your side, then let death come. If another woman treats me as well as you, I'd think her a nice person, a good friend, but I wouldn't die for her – no, never!"

"Why? Just because I am good to you?"

"I like being able to see you. I like being next to you. It doesn't matter how you treat me. Whether you're nice to me or not. You can beat me every day. You can tell me off. You can scar me anew with your sword. I will still adore you with all my heart. The Lord of the

Heavens can make me your dog, your cat, and you can whip me and kick me at your whim. I will still stay by your side and follow you wherever you go. Auntie, in this life, this incarnation, you are the only person I will ever like."

The Dragon Maiden and Penance had spent every waking and sleeping hour in each other's company over the past few years. Though they talked only of the martial arts, tender feelings had been developing unnoticed, taking root deep in their hearts. Now, as they tottered on the brink of death, they at last recognised the smouldering ardour within.

To separate from, or to let go of, the other was inconceivable.

"I feel the same too." Smiling, the Dragon Maiden held Penance's hand tighter and let out a happy sigh. "I am so pleased." And yet, a moment later, her grasp slackened and she muttered, "Penance, I've been awful."

"No! You're wonderful!" he protested, missing the warmth of her hand pressing into his.

She shook her head. "I was nasty to you. I threw you out. Luckily, Grandam Sun stood by you. If I hadn't turned you away, she wouldn't have died!" Tears began to trickle from her eyes.

The Dragon Maiden had not shed a tear since she had started her martial training when she was five years of age. This explosion of emotions left her shaken. She was racked by sobs, and her bones and joints creaked audibly, as if her *neigong* power were pouring from her body.

"Auntie!" Penance cried in fright. "How are you feeling? What's going—"

The stone doors to the room opened with a groan and in strode the two Taoist nuns. Blithe Li had accepted that she was shut in the Tomb with no hope of getting out, and she found, with this shift in her frame of mind, the defence mechanisms that had compelled her to tread warily were no longer so intimidating. Drawing on her memories of living in the Tomb, she strode boldly ahead and forced her way through several chambers without triggering any of the traps, back to the one where she had first found the Dragon Maiden earlier. She was thrilled by her luck, but in fact her smooth passage was due to the design of the Tomb. The bulky rocks and heavy boulders that safeguarded the underground complex from the anticipated Jurchen intruders had to be launched manually, and the Dragon Maiden had not been in a state fit to operate them – and nor had she the inclination to do so.

The instant Penance heard the doors opening, he shifted his stance to shield the Dragon Maiden with his body.

"Move!" Blithe Li bellowed, but the young man would not budge. She could sense distrust emanating from him: he was expecting her to attack at any moment. Irked by his watchfulness, she shot him a piercing look, then let out a sigh. "There are few men like you under the heavens."

"What do you mean?" the Dragon Maiden asked as she raised herself off the bed.

"Sister, you've been down here all your life, you don't know how foul and wicked the human heart is," Blithe Li said wearily. "You won't find another as devoted and steadfast as he beneath this sky."

Pleased to hear Penance spoken of so highly, the Dragon Maiden muttered to herself, "To die in his company has made my life worthwhile . . ."

"Who is he to you? Are you two married?"

"He is my disciple—"

"Show me your arm!" Blithe Li interjected in disbelief. She grabbed the Dragon Maiden's hand, flipped her palm upwards and pulled up her sleeve.

On the inside of her forearm, a crimson dot stood out on her snow-white skin.

The Taoist nun was amazed to find the proof of chastity tattooed by their *shifu* still on her martial sister's arm.

They've been living in great intimacy, and yet they've never overstepped the bounds of decency.

Blithe Li regarded the Dragon Maiden with a newfound respect.

331

She rolled up her sleeve and revealed her own Chastity Cinnabar. However, she was keenly aware of the fundamental differences between these two dabs of bright red pigment. It was not by choice that she had maintained her maidenhood, whereas the Dragon Maiden had chosen to hold on to her virtue while living alongside a man who would willingly die for her.

Blithe Li heaved a sigh and lowered her arm. She took a moment to gather herself, then said in an appeasing tone: "Sister, I have come to apologise."

The Dragon Maiden was taken aback. The Blithe Li she had known was too proud to ever bow to another. What was she trying to gain from this?

"You have your ways of doing things and I have mine," she said coolly. "There is nothing to apologise for."

"Do hear me out, Sister. You know the ancient saying, don't you? 'A priceless treasure is easy to find, a true-hearted man is hard to locate.' I have lived through bitter hardships and I can see this young lad is very good to you. With him by your side, you will not want for anything in life."

The Dragon Maiden smiled at the kind words. "I am very happy. I know he will always be good to me."

Thinking of her own misfortunes, the Taoist nun continued, "You have no idea how many false-hearted men there are out there. Most of us struggle to meet half a faithful soul.

"I once had a beloved. He said many honeyed words to me. He claimed he'd die a thousand deaths for me without regret. And then, we had to part for two months. In that time, he met a pretty young girl.

"When we saw each other again, he took no notice of me, as if we were strangers. I asked him why and he said, 'Miss Li, we are compeers of the *jianghu*, sharing a belief in justice and righteousness. I am grateful for the kindly way you have treated me. In future, if there are matters by which I can repay this favour, I shall of course do my part.' Then he had the audacity to add: 'On the twenty-fourth of the next month, I shall wed Miss He of Dali. It would be our honour if you would grace us with your presence at the banquet.'"

Blithe Li imitated Lu Zhanyuan's impersonal tone as she repeated his parting words. It was clear that she was still reliving the moment of her heartbreak years later. She took a deep breath before concluding her tale.

"I retched up blood in my outrage and blacked out. He brought me around, settled me in a room at an inn to recuperate and left for good."

"What happened next? You didn't just let him go, did you?"

"What could I do? Force him back with a sabre to his neck? Let myself be fooled by flowery words and false feelings for a little longer? That would merely leave an unsavoury taste in the mouth. A thousand horses cannot drag back a man whose heart has fled elsewhere.

"Men. They lust after the new and toss out the old. Every single one of them. Their attachments shift with their eyes. Even a heavenly creature with allure beyond measure cannot be sure that her man will always be constant and true.

"Sister, I no longer envy you for your knowledge of the Jade Maid Heart Scripture. I envy you for having such a wonderful disciple. He is prepared to die for you. I have prayed night and day for the good fortune to meet such a one as him. Let him be thick. Let him be plain. But I will give him my whole heart. And you've met yours! You're so blessed."

"I am the truly blessed one, Elder Li," Penance said earnestly, his attitude softening.

"Fortune smiles on the both of you." Blithe Li let her words hang in the air, then sighed dramatically. "Such a shame you're trapped here. This place of death where the rays of the sun can never reach you. And at your tender age too. You'll never feast your eyes on the myriad wonders of the outside world. You will live to rue this."

"Never, never, never, never!" Penance shouted at the top of his voice. He turned to the Dragon Maiden. "Strike me with your sword if I display the slightest sign of regret. I will not flinch."

The Dragon Maiden regarded him with tenderness in her eyes. "I believe you, Penance. I believe you."

Penance reached out and took her hands in his. As their palms touched, their hearts were joined. Despite the low light, they could read a hundred promises and a thousand declarations of love in each other's eyes. They would be true to each other, this life, this incarnation. Never would they see the day when their hearts changed. Never would they betray each other. They knew. For certain.

Watching the lovers, Blithe Li snorted quietly then said, "You are young, Sister, you don't know how wretched the human heart can be. Let me share with you how you may protect yourself. *Shifu* could not teach you this because she never left the Tomb."

"Thank you, Sister."

"If your man seems different one day – if he doesn't appear as warm, if it feels like he's grown distant, polite – then he has changed his heart. This shift is subtle. It is often impossible to tell when it started. Be vigilant at all times. Look for the smallest clues. They can be as fine as spider silk. And never let him get away with it."

"We live here in the Tomb – what is there to be heedful of? I thank you, Sister, for telling me about your experiences, but I don't need to protect myself. Penance will never change his heart, not in a thousand, ten thousand years."

Her conviction made Blithe Li's heart ache. "In that case, wonderful . . . You two should leave these mountains and enjoy life, flying off, wing to wing, into the glorious world beyond. There is nothing more joyous than that."

The Dragon Maiden looked up, but her eyes were not focused on anything in particular. "Too late now," she muttered.

"What do you mean?"

"The Dragon Severing Rocks are in place. There's no way out of the Tomb, even if *Shifu* comes back to life."

Rage and frustration seized Blithe Li. She had tired out her tongue and her lips, speaking humbly in meek tones, hoping to fire up the Dragon Maiden's lust for life. She had hoped her martial sister would search her knowledge of the Tomb's layout to find a path to the light. But it had all been in vain. She had relived her worst memory, the moment of her betrayal, and it was all for nothing. She was still trapped – alive but buried in this tomb. She wanted blood to slake her fury. Flipping her wrist, she sliced her palm down at the Dragon Maiden's head.

Penance crouched down instinctively, croaking, and thrust both hands at Blithe Li. He had not practised the Exploding Toad kung fu that had made Viper Ouyang's name since that fateful day in Chongyang Temple, but as the first powerful martial technique he had learned, it was ingrained into his being. He unthinkingly turned to it whenever he was in dire peril.

A ferocious wave of *neigong* power crashed towards Blithe Li. She aborted her attack and twisted her arm around to push back, but the blow was more formidable than she had expected. *Pang!* It threw her off her feet and she slammed into the wall.

Penance's store of internal strength had grown significantly over the past few years. Even though Exploding Toad kung fu channelled a different kind of energy, the Ancient Tomb Sect's training had improved his control and speed when summoning and unleashing it, and he was able to generate more power than ever before.

Paralysing pain shot down Blithe Li's spine. Furious with herself for the humiliation she had suffered, she began to rub her hands together. Presently, a nauseating stench filled the room.

The Dragon Maiden recognised that her martial sister was preparing to launch her deadliest skill, Red Serpent Palm. Not a kung fu she could counter head on, even with Penance's help. She shot her hand out and – *smack!* – slapped Blithe Li on her left cheek while she was still drawing back her palm to strike.

"This is what the Jade Maid Heart Scripture can do!" she cried as she cuffed Blithe Li on the other side of her face. Then she grabbed Penance's arm and sprinted out of the room.

The slaps did not overly hurt, but they landed with a crisp crack.

Stunned by the swiftness of the attack, Blithe Li could only watch as the doors slammed shut.

She has shown me mercy, the Taoist thought as she gingerly touched where she had been hit. I would be dead if she had used any inner strength.

Blithe Li was able to pick out some familiar elements in the Dragon Maiden's movements, but she could not fathom the essence that allowed the slap to be executed with such rapidity and unpredictability. She was loath to admit it, but she was unnerved at being caught so utterly unawares. Little did she know that the Scripture's techniques, though speedy and mercurial, delivered hardly any sting, as they were not designed to injure the person on the receiving end.

3

THE INSTANT THE DOORS GROUND SHUT, PENANCE SAID WITH glee, "Blithe Li can't match the Scripture—" but he was cut short by the trembling hand on his arm. "Auntie, are you . . . what's going on?"

"I – I . . . c-c-cold . . ."

In launching the slaps, the Dragon Maiden had drawn power from the depths of her *neigong* foundation, which had been damaged by the interruption to her training the night before. She was now in a worse state than when she had first sustained the injury; she no longer had the strength to suppress the iciness in her core that had been accumulated over years of martial cultivation on the boreal nephrite. She felt as if she had been plunged into an ancient glacier thousands of feet thick. The freezing cold bore into the marrow of her bones. She could not stop her teeth clattering.

"What can I do?" Penance hugged her tightly, hoping his body heat would warm her up, but the chilling touch of her skin grew more and more intense. Soon, he was also struggling.

The Dragon Maiden could sense her internal energy trickling away in drips and drops. "Carry me . . . to the coffin . . . I won't recover from this."

A twinge in his heart robbed Penance of his voice. But he recalled that they were inside the Tomb and their days were numbered anyway. Did it matter if the inevitable was brought forward? No. As long as they were together.

PENANCE SET the Dragon Maiden down gently against one of the sarcophagi and lit a candle. In the flickering flame, she looked even more fragile and frail next to the bulky stone casket.

"Put me inside this one."

Penance pushed the lid further back and lifted her into the coffin with care.

The Dragon Maiden was surprised by how calm Penance seemed, but before she had time to ponder his uncharacteristic cool-headedness, he had lowered himself into the sarcophagus, lying down next to her, their bodies were pressed close together.

"What are you doing?" she asked, but she had to admit that she found the proximity both strange and delightful.

"I'm staying with you," he answered. "Those two can sleep in the other coffin."

The Dragon Maiden turned to look at Penance and caught him watching her. His gaze brought a sense of tranquillity to her heart and the frigid sensation in her bones seemed less biting. As she leaned into him, the weight of his arm on her waist felt more prominent. It was pulling her closer to his body. The intimacy made her bashful, but his embrace thawed the iciness and kindled a fire within. She averted her eyes to calm her spirits and that was when she noticed writing on the underside of the coffin lid.

Large characters, set down with robust, rigorous brushstrokes in black ink, were visible in the gloom. Even though she was viewing

them from an oblique angle, the characters were clear enough to be discerned.

> *TRY TO BEST QUANZHEN WITH*
> *JADE MAID HEART SCRIPTURE*
> *BUT CHONGYANG IN HIS LIFETIME*
> *HAS NE'ER LOST TO ANOTHER*

"What does this mean?" she said quietly to herself.

Penance followed her sight and scanned the calligraphy. "Is that Wang Chongyang's hand?"

"Very likely. Is he saying that he's the stronger fighter?"

"The cow muzzle was bluffing."

The Dragon Maiden noticed a string of smaller characters under the large ones, but they were too far away to make out.

"Penance, can you step out?"

"No!"

"There's writing at the other end. I want to see what it says, then you can come back."

Reassured, Penance climbed out of the stone coffin and brought over the candle.

The Dragon Maiden took the wax light and lay down the other way. The smaller characters were now directly above her, but they were upside down. She studied the passage, reading it twice under her breath. For a brief moment, all her strength left her, making her hand wobble. The candleholder tipped over, but Penance snatched it up and helped her out.

"Are you alright?" He was alarmed by her countenance. "What does it say?"

It took the Dragon Maiden a while to gather her wits. She inhaled deeply before exhaling slowly. "After the Doyenne's death, Wang Chongyang came to the Tomb to pay his last respects. He saw the Jade Maid Heart Scripture carved into the ceiling. Though the Doyenne believed her invention could outmanoeuvre every Quanzhen

339

martial move, he left this message to say that it was no match for truly advanced martial techniques and that the way to beat it was set down in the chamber beneath this one . . . but I know nothing of such a room."

"We'll find a way, won't we?"

The Dragon Maiden was bone weary, but she nodded and gave Penance an indulgent smile, then cast her eyes around, wondering where the access to this secret chamber might be found. Her sight lighted on the coffin they had lain in: Did Wang Chongyang set this casket up?

"See if you can lift the base."

Penance hopped into the sarcophagus and ran his hands along the stonework. In time, he discovered a hollowed-out spot at the bottom that would admit all five fingers. Firming up his grip, he heaved upwards. Nothing moved.

"Try turning it to the left, then pull."

To his amazement, the slab of stone came loose with a grinding noise.

"It worked!" he exclaimed, getting ready to jump down into the opening.

"Wait! Let the air clear first."

Penance rejoined the Dragon Maiden in the chamber, but moments later, he started to fidget and sniff noisily. "Can we go in now?"

"Be patient." She straightened up slowly, picked up the candle-holder and climbed back into the coffin. Its base opened onto a narrow staircase. She headed down the steps, followed a short corridor around a bend and came to an empty chamber. She tilted her head back – the ceiling was etched full of words and symbols.

On the far right were four characters written in a very large hand:

THE NINE YIN MANUAL

The Dragon Maiden had never heard of this tract, but she could see that it offered some very sophisticated martial skills underpinned by complex theories that she could not quite comprehend.

"Even the most powerful kung fu has little use for us now . . ."

Subdued by her wistful tone, Penance was beginning to calm down from the first flush of excitement at entering the chamber. But when he looked away from the overhead carvings, he caught a cluster of curved lines engraved in a corner – they seemed to have little to do with the martial arts.

"What is that?" he asked, pointing.

The Dragon Maiden turned to look. When her eyes lighted on the etchings, she began to stiffen up. She stared at them for a long time, without moving or even seeming to breathe.

Penance tugged her sleeve and called out with a tremor in his voice, "Auntie . . ."

She made a sound with her throat to show that she had heard him, then buried her face in his chest and broke down in sobs.

"Are you hurting?" He helped her sit down against a wall before joining her on the floor.

"No . . ." She took a moment to collect herself, then whispered, "We can leave . . ."

"Really?" Penance's whole person was heaving with anticipation.

Nodding, she explained: "This is a map of the Tomb and it shows a secret exit."

"That's fantastic! Why are you crying?"

Tears glinting in her eyes, she gave him a radiant smile. "I've never feared death, because I was destined to stay in this tomb for life. It made no difference dying sooner or later. But – but over the last day, I haven't stopped thinking how good you are to me. I want to be with you. I want us to be happy together. I want to go out there and see the world for myself. Oh Penance, I am scared and I am excited."

"We will go out together." He clasped her hands in his. "I'll pick flowers and put them in your hair. I'll catch crickets and give you the most invincible general!"

The Dragon Maiden listened intently to Penance's animated descriptions. Even though they were games from his childhood, they were entirely new to her as she had never had a playmate growing up. Soon, she succumbed to drowsiness, her head resting on his shoulder.

Feeling her weight on him, Penance watched her sleep in the flickering candlelight. Her eyelids drooped softly, her breathing gentle and even, she was deep in slumber. He felt truly relaxed for the first time in days and he too entered the land of dreams.

4

PENANCE DID NOT KNOW HOW LONG HE HAD BEEN DOZING when he thought he felt something poking into the back of his waist. A stab of soreness hit his Central Pivot acupoint and he woke with a start. He tried to jump up and defend himself, but someone had seized him by the nape of the neck with a Grappling technique, locking his movements. From the corner of his eye, he could make out Blithe Li and her disciple Ripple Hong standing to one side, smiling in satisfaction. He could also sense the weight of the Dragon Maiden slumped against him and it appeared her pressure points were bound too.

In all the excitement of their discovery, they had forgotten to replace the stone slab and conceal the entrance to this secret chamber, giving Blithe Li a chance to find and waylay them.

"So, this is where you young 'uns have been enjoying yourselves. What a secluded spot!" the Taoist said with a sneer. "Now, Sister, I think you can figure out a way to leave this place if you put your mind to it."

Blithe Li had gone to the Tomb entrance to see the Dragon Severing Rocks with her own eyes, but she was still not ready to submit to her fate, even though she knew the Dragon Maiden was most likely telling the truth about their situation.

"I wouldn't tell you even if I knew."

The response was not what Blithe Li had been expecting. The slightly confrontational tone suggested the Dragon Maiden really was hiding something.

"If you guide us out of here, my dearest sister," Blithe Li said in her sweetest voice, "I promise I will never bother you again."

"You found your way in – you can find your way out."

Vexed by the Dragon Maiden's defiance, Blithe Li jabbed at the Heaven's Vent acupoint between the collarbones and the Fifth Pivot point on the front of her hip, using the Ancient Tomb Sect's locking technique. Then she did the same to Penance.

The Taoist was no stranger to her martial sister's stubbornness. She recalled their *shifu* yielding to the girl's uncompromising nature when she was a just a few years old. But Blithe Li's will to live was strong. She was prepared to employ any means necessary to find a way to escape the Tomb.

The pressure points she had triggered were both at the intersection of meridians – the rivers along which one's internal energy flowed – and, once activated, they sent out waves of unbearable numbing itchiness to every part of the body. Blithe Li was certain they could not withstand the discomfort for long. They would soon be forced to reveal the hidden exit.

The Dragon Maiden closed her eyes and said nothing. Penance clenched his jaw against the irritation and shot back, "Do you think we'd still be here if we knew the way out?"

"Don't deny it. She's already let it slip," Blithe Li said, beaming, before turning to the Dragon Maiden. "You know a secret passage and you'll leave once you've rested up. Am I right, Sister?"

"You'll carry on killing if you get out."

The nun was not ruffled by the retort. She sat down with her arms around her knees, a cryptic smile playing on her lips.

The silence and the itching were too much for Penance to bear. "The Doyenne didn't pass on her martial skills for you to hurt your own kin. Don't you feel bad doing this to your martial sister?" Then he whispered into the Dragon Maiden's ear, "As long as she doesn't know what we've learned, she won't kill us."

The Dragon Maiden could see the map in her peripheral vision and now she reminded herself to keep her eyes averted, so as not to lead Blithe Li to their discovery.

GRIEF OVERWHELMED Wang Chongyang when he learned of Lin Chaoying's passing. He had always known about her love for him and valued her devotion, even though he could not return her feelings. That they were now separated by the great divide between the living and the dead made his heart ache. He stole into the Tomb, avoiding her maidservant, and found the chamber where she was interred.

At the sight of his old friend's stone coffin, Wang Chongyang broke down in tears and sobbed in silence. He wandered through the subterranean network he had planned and constructed, coming across the portrait Lin Chaoying had painted of him – the one in which he stood with his back to the beholder – and discovering the room where she had inscribed her final martial invention, the Jade Maid Heart Scripture. He was fascinated by the kung fu repertoire, but when he realised it picked apart the Quanzhen combat strategy blow by blow, he staggered out into the open, ashen faced.

After that, Wang Chongyang ventured deep into the Zhongnan Mountains and built himself a thatched hut where he remained for three years. During his stay there, he made some inroads into countering the moves described in the Scripture, but he failed to devise a comprehensive system akin to Lin Chaoying's – one that embodied both internal and external fighting methods. He gave up, disheartened, but also in awe of his late friend's wit and imagination.

A dozen or so years later, Wang Chongyang won the custodianship of the Nine Yin Manual and the title of the Greatest Martial Master Under the Heavens at the Contest of Mount Hua. He had fought for this fabled compendium of the most powerful kung fu to stop the trail of blood left by *wulin* heroes in their scramble to lay their hands on the text. Although he had made it known that he and his martial descendants would never study the techniques within, he did read the Manual out of curiosity.

He spent a fortnight contemplating the skills set down in it and conceived of a way to overpower the Scripture. He stole into the Tomb, went to the hidden room beneath the spirit chamber, and carved the Manual's key ideas on the ceiling to demonstrate how they could be used to dismantle the Scripture, move by move. He then left a message in the empty coffin that housed the secret trapdoor, so the successor of Lin Chaoying who chose it as their final resting place would learn in their last moments that the founder of the Quanzhen Sect had never lost to anyone in his lifetime and that he had ways to beat the Jade Maid Heart Scripture. He assumed only someone on the point of death would lie in the coffin and that this would be a secret they took to the netherworld.

It was Wang Chongyang's competitive spirits that made him so determined to have the last word and claim the final victory in his lifelong duel with Lin Chaoying. This pride, this need to be paramount, to always come out on top, had also been the root of their estrangement.

They should have been a match made by the heavens and supported by the earth. Two martial geniuses of comparable standing. No rival or suitor had come between them. No feud within their families – blood or martial – had threatened to tear them apart. What stifled their affections was their pride. Each refusing to admit that they could be less than the other.

Deep down, Wang Chongyang recognised Lin Chaoying was the more talented martial artist, but he struggled to accept coming second to a woman. Instead, he devoted himself to repelling the Jurchen invaders, telling himself that he had no time for affairs of the heart, suppressing his feelings for her at every turn. Even when Lin Chaoying pulled him out of his wallowing after his failed uprising, he chose to renounce all worldly ties and become a Taoist monk, leaving her to sequester herself for the rest of her years, embittered and despondent.

His stubborn refusal to bow persisted even after Lin Chaoying's departure from this world, first in his determination to invent a response to the Jade Maid Heart Scripture, then – more than a decade later – in his need to make the power of the Nine Yin Manual known to her successor. It was only once he had carved the Manual's secrets into the ceiling of the hidden chamber, that he at last accepted his inferiority – it was the wisdom of another, not his own, that had trumped Lin Chaoying's martial creation. When he returned to Chongyang Temple, he urged his disciples to always be humble and open-minded, and to face their shortcomings with courage.

In truth, neither Wang Chongyang nor Lin Chaoying could explain how they had ended up drifting further and further apart. Perhaps, they would say it was not to be, not realising that it was their own doing. Their pride had led to this destiny of separation.

It was also concern for his own image that had stopped Wang Chongyang from telling Lin Chaoying about the secret exit when he explained the defence mechanisms he had designed for the Tomb. The map had been engraved in that chamber since the underground complex was first built, but he feared she would deride him for designing an escape route, and kept from her the existence of both the room and the exit. Wang Chongyang's goal was to repel the invaders of his country, and he had made plans to extricate his army if it found itself locked in an extended stand-off with the Jurchens – they could abandon their base and continue the struggle after trapping their Jin pursuers inside. But the Dragon Maiden had no way of knowing any of this. To her mind, once the Dragon Severing Rocks were triggered, they would be cut off from the world of the living.

THE DRAGON Maiden was staring vacantly ahead, keeping her gaze away from the escape map, when four characters caught her eye.

On unlocking pressure points

She skimmed the passage and her heart skipped a beat. She could feel excitement rushing to her extremities. If she had not trained all her life to conceal her emotions, she would have cheered out loud.

The section gave instructions on how to unblock one's acupoints. The technique was not intended for the situation she was in now, as a martial artist familiar with the Nine Yin Manual's teachings was unlikely to be caught out in that way. It was included in case one's energy misfired during practice and caused a blockage, as the *neigong* techniques in the Manual were so sophisticated that no outside force could restore the circulation.

To unlock the acupressure points, one must first master Breath Sealing and Soul Switching. The first method involved halting the movement of *qi* through the body by restricting respiration. Stopping the energy flow within would clear obstructions along the meridians and at specific pressure points.

However, breathing was a fundamental process of the body, and it was very difficult to hold off for long. By mastering Spirit Separation – one of the basic skills of Soul Switching kung fu, which allowed the mind to roam beyond the body's physical confines and the heart to disengage from the corporeal – one could do so for an extended period without being asphyxiated.

In short, through a separation of the body and the spirit, one's breath was sealed, which in turn unlocked the pressure points. The two methods came together as an interconnected whole.

Though the Dragon Maiden was thrilled by the discovery, a cautionary voice sounded in her head:

Even if you regain your movement, you don't have the kung fu to subdue your martial sister, so it's still futile.

347

It prompted the young woman to revisit the writings on the ceiling. She scanned them as surreptitiously and as quickly as she could, hoping Blithe Li would not notice. However, there was nothing she could make use of immediately, it would all take months to master.

As she pondered her options, she realised that Penance had been waging a war of words with Blithe Li and Ripple Hong, and the Taoists were so infuriated that neither had been paying her any attention.

The mindless argument gave the Dragon Maiden an idea. She quickly memorised the method for unlocking pressure points and turned to Penance, whispering her plan into his ear.

Penance carried on squabbling while he listened, in an attempt to keep the women distracted. Now, as he put their escape plan into action, he shouted even louder, delivering a barrage of insults and nonsensical gibberish.

"*Aiiiiyooooooooo!*" he exclaimed, elongating his cry before leaving a dramatic pause. "Martial Elder Li, you are cruel and evil and mean!" He let the words hang in the air. "What you've done . . . you've wronged our Doyenne – and her grandmamma too!" Another short pause. "*Eeeeeiiii* . . . You're still in your prime, Martial Elder Li, and very pretty too . . . though not as lovely as my teacher . . ." He trailed off and waited a moment before resuming. "But you've got such a black, black heart! Aren't you worried that the poison will seep out – and ruin your good looks?" He broke off again and let the silence linger. "That would be such a shame . . . How come you're not worried about wronging our Doyenne's great grandmamma?"

While he was blathering away, Penance was trying out the technique the Dragon Maiden had described, letting his souls and his spirits roam beyond his corporeal being. During each pause, he held in his breath to loosen the bind on his pressure points. And the Dragon Maiden had seized the chance to do the same.

At first, Blithe Li was annoyed by Penance's nonsense, but soon, an amused smile crept onto her face – it flattered her self-esteem to be called Martial Elder and to receive compliments on her looks, even though she knew they did not come from the heart. But after a while, she noticed a change in the aura of her two captives and barked, "What are you doing?"

The Dragon Maiden jumped up and struck Blithe Li on the shoulder with an intricate backhand strike from the Jade Maid Heart Scripture. "Do you want to leave the Tomb, Sister?"

Blithe Li reeled back in shock. *How did she manage to regain her movement? She's been toying with me ever since I stepped foot in here!* The realisation filled the Taoist nun with rage, but she forced herself to rein in her temper. The priority was to get out of the Tomb, then she could take revenge to soothe her injured pride. Once she had calmed down, it also occurred to her that every move launched by the Dragon Maiden so far had lacked strength. She refused to believe it was due solely to her benevolence. The thought reassured her, and she put on an ingratiating smile: "I apologise, my dear sister. I have been most unreasonable. Please do show us the way out."

"We can only take one of you," Penance answered for the Dragon Maiden, in an attempt to sow division between Blithe Li and her disciple. "So, who will it be? You or her?"

"I wasn't talking to you!" Blithe Li hissed at the youth.

"Yes, we can only take one." The Dragon Maiden repeated Penance's claim, though she did not know why he had made it – she was sure he had his reasons.

Penance flashed the Dragon Maiden a smile and turned back to Blithe Li. "Martial Elder, you should let Sister Hong come with us. She is not as pretty as you, but you are older – you have lived long enough."

Reminding herself that her freedom depended on their goodwill, Blithe Li clenched her jaw and fumed in silence.

"That's settled then!" Penance said. "Auntie leads the way. I follow her. The last in line stays in the Tomb forever!"

The Dragon Maiden took Penance's hand and strolled out of the stone chamber. Blithe Li and Ripple Hong scrambled after them, pushing and shoving at the doorway, vying for the next spot. They both believed the Dragon Maiden would seal the room the instant the third person emerged into the corridor.

"What do you think you're doing?" Blithe Li pressed her palm on her disciple's shoulder.

Ripple Hong froze at the menacing tone and threatening touch and let her *shifu* pass. She knew the woman would have no qualms about striking her dead if she tried to take another step.

Blithe Li walked on the heels of Penance, keeping the distance between them to a single stride. She could make out little in the dark, but from the sloping floor, she knew they were burrowing steadily deeper underground. The earth had grown moist and soft underfoot, a sign that they were leaving the main structure of the Tomb behind. They twisted and turned in shifting shades of black, their path fanning out into myriad branches. The descent steepened and in time it became a sheer drop. Their kung fu was the only thing keeping the four of them from slipping into the dark unknown.

How much further to go? Blithe Li wondered. At this rate, we'll reach the foot of mountain soon.

They had been walking for another hour when the passage began to level out. The air felt more humid and soon they heard trickling water. The next thing they knew, they were wading through a pool that got rapidly deeper. One moment they were ankle deep; a few steps later, the water was swirling around their knees, then their hips, and up to their chests.

With the sloshing of water masking her voice, the Dragon Maiden whispered to Penance, "Remember the Breath Sealing method?"

"Yes," he answered softly.

"Take care not to inhale any water."

"You too, Auntie."

When Wang Chongyang was planning his underground storehouse, he chose a site close to a stream and diverted its flow to provide fresh water for those stationed within. It was the path of this river that the Dragon Maiden had been following.

It originated high up in the Zhongnan Mountains, and after

passing through the Tomb, it was filtered through the rocks into an underground lake before emerging in the foothills as part of a larger watercourse.

The four of them were now shuffling forwards with water up to their necks.

"Sister, do you know how to swim?" Blithe Li asked with a tremble in her voice.

"No."

The woman took comfort in the fact that they were equally ill-equipped to deal with the terrain. She lifted her foot to take another step, but when she lowered it, she could find no firm ground and toppled forwards. Water rushed into her nose and mouth. She threw herself backwards, only to see the outline of the Dragon Maiden and Penance Yang marching resolutely ahead, even as they became entirely submerged.

Determined not to be left behind, Blithe Li steeled herself to face the water again. She would blaze her way through a forest of sabres and a sea of swords to reach life and light at the other end. Just then, Ripple Hong grabbed her robe from behind, forcing her to stop dead. Blithe Li threw a merciless backhand slap, but the strike was dulled by the water and she failed to shake off her disciple. The brief tussle diverted her attention from anchoring her feet and she was dragged down by the silent undertow – with Ripple Hong clinging tight to her habit.

Blithe Li floundered about, splashing, kicking, her kung fu rendered utterly useless by the water. Swept along by the current, limbs flailing, her body was no longer hers to control. Then her fingertips grazed something solid. She seized it with all her might.

Blithe Li held tight to Penance's arm. Even as water rushed relentlessly into her nostrils and mouth. Even as she was on the verge of blacking out. She would not let go of the hope clenched between her fingers.

Penance had been trudging forward hand in hand with the Dragon Maiden along the bottom of the underground lake. The instant he sensed Blithe Li's fingers close around him, he twisted his arm in a series of grappling moves, but he failed to loosen her grasp or pull away. He dared not put in more force or thrash about, in case he swallowed water, so he reluctantly towed her along after him.

The underwater march proceeded for quite some time. Both the Dragon Maiden and Penance felt starved of air even with the Breath Sealing technique. They tried thrusting with their feet to push up above the surface to breathe, but not knowing how to swim, they gulped water with each attempt. It was sheer good fortune that the lake was getting shallower and the undercurrent was weakening.

At last, a glimmer of light.

The Dragon Maiden and Penance emerged into the open, gasping for air. They set the unconscious Blithe Li and Ripple Hong down at the mouth of the cave and collapsed in exhaustion. When they had smoothed their breathing somewhat, they circulated their *qi* to force out the water they had swallowed.

Even though Blithe Li had passed out, her fingers were still locked around Penance's arm. Now that he had recovered his strength a little, he prised open her grip, finger by finger. Free at last, he carried the two comatose women over to a large, flat rock nearby, settling them in a position that allowed the water in their bellies to trickle from their lips. The Dragon Maiden came up and tapped the pressure points on their shoulders.

"Auntie, this place is beautiful," Penance said, looking around him.

The Dragon Maiden nodded with a smile.

Flowers in full bloom amid the luscious greenery. Everywhere they turned, it was full of light, full of life. A stark contrast to the darkness and desperation of the Tomb.

A groan disrupted this idyllic scene. Blithe Li opened her eyes to the sun's radiance. Her body was numb and limp, but her heart felt more sprightly than it had for a long time. She trembled at her memories, trapped in the gloom of the Tomb, then submerged and washed away by the underswell. She was grateful to see the open sky again.

The Dragon Maiden noticed that both Blithe Li and Ripple Hong had come to and said, "Martial Sister, please be on your way."

The Taoist nuns exchanged a silent look. They could feel that their control of their arms had been taken away by the locks on their acupoints. Given all they had just experienced, they departed without another word.

5

THAT NIGHT, THE DRAGON MAIDEN AND PENANCE SLEPT ON the soft grass under the shelter of a tree in this secluded valley of the Zhongnan Mountains. In the morning, Penance suggested that they should go to the nearest town, but the thought terrified the Dragon Maiden, who had never experienced the hubbub of ordinary life. "I need to get better first, and we have yet to master the Jade Maid Heart Scripture."

"Arrgh!" Penance smacked himself on the head. "How could I forget about your injury?"

They decided to settle for a time by the riverbank. The isolated location was ideal for completing their training in the Scripture. The lush vegetation provided the privacy they needed, so they would have no fear of being disrupted. They built two simple shacks near a large pine tree to keep out the wind and the rain, and draped the roofs with vines of wisteria. Partial to fragrant flowers, Penance planted shrubs of rose and jasmine outside his hut, whereas the Dragon Maiden, who preferred nature at its simplest – the refreshing scent of pine and fresh grass – left the wild weeds to thrive.

During the first fortnight, Penance helped the Dragon Maiden heal her injury, channelling his *qi* through his palm to guide the flow of her internal strength. Once she had recovered, they resumed their work on the Jade Maid Heart Scripture, sleeping during the day and training at night. The Dragon Maiden mastered the remaining sections in a few moons' time, and Penance reached the same level a month or so later. After that, they focused on refining the kung fu and internal strength techniques they had learned, until they could draw on them in combat without a moment's hesitation. It was then that Penance once more suggested leaving the mountains.

The Dragon Maiden was content with her lot and doubted if life beyond the valley could measure up to what they had now. However, she was aware that Penance had always longed for the red dust yonder and that he could not be tied down to a small patch of uncultivated land for the rest of his days. Nevertheless, she made up another reason to stay: "Penance, I know our kung fu has improved, but compared to your Uncle and Auntie Guo, where do we stand?"

"I'm far behind, obviously, but you have strengths they don't."

"What about their daughter and the Wu brothers? They will have been learning kung fu all this time. They may be a match for us."

"If they try anything, I'll make them regret it!" Penance jumped up in anger.

"Empty words. You don't know if you can beat them."

"Help me, then."

"I can't best your Auntie Guo."

Penance lowered his head and weighed up his options. "I won't quarrel with them – out of respect for Uncle Guo," he said eventually.

The Dragon Maiden was impressed by his mature response. It seemed the years living in the Tomb and learning Ancient Tomb kung fu had quenched his fiery nature somewhat.

It was true that Penance was less hot-headed than when he had first arrived in the Zhongnan Mountains, but that was mostly due to his age and to a better understanding of human relationships. He could now look back without prejudice and see that Guo Jing had treated him with genuine care, so he was willing to concede any dispute out of gratitude. After all, there had never been any real feud between him and Hibiscus Guo, or with the Wu brothers. It was a childish fight over a cricket and he could not care less about it now.

"I am glad you've outgrown the urge to brawl. But you have said before, out in the *wulin*, others may still pester you after you have given ground. We should master the martial skills set down by Wang Chongyang, so we're not left helpless in those situations."

Penance sensed the Dragon Maiden was hesitant about leaving this tranquil spot and he was happy to indulge her. "Yes, let's start learning the Nine Yin Manual tomorrow."

After this conversation, they stayed in the valley for another year. Every so often, they returned to the Tomb via the underground river, to the chamber where Wang Chongyang had engraved portions of the Nine Yin Manual. They would remain there for several days to memorise a section of the text until they could recite it flawlessly before returning to their huts. Their internal and external kung fu saw considerable advancement over these months. However, Wang Chongyang had only set down passages from the Manual that were relevant to outmanoeuvring techniques from the Jade Maid Heart Scripture, and he had not been able to decipher the Manual's key tenets, which were set down in a Sanskrit-inspired code. Needless to say, the Dragon Maiden and Penance's grasp of this supreme martial text could not compare to that of Guo Jing and Lotus Huang.

AFTER A fruitful day of training, Penance walked back to their camp with a spring in his step, but the Dragon Maiden was unusually quiet and subdued. He told joke after joke to cheer her up, but she stayed silent and made no response at all. At first, Penance was unsure what was behind her low spirits, but then it struck him that they had just learned everything they could from Wang Chongyang's writings in the hidden chamber.

Is she worried because she's run out of excuses to stay?

As the thought crossed his mind, he said, "Auntie, we can live here forever, if that's what you want."

"That would be nice—" The Dragon Maiden checked herself. She knew Penance would remain there to keep her company, but he would never be truly happy.

"We will talk tomorrow." She ended the discussion curtly and went inside her hut.

Penance sat on the grass and waited for the Dragon Maiden to re-emerge, but she did not make an appearance even at dinner time. Still, he waited, until the moon peeked out from behind the mountains. Then he retired to bed.

That night, a shrieking gale tore into Penance's dream. He sat up and cocked his ear in the direction of the disturbance. The air was whistling with gusts of the kind whipped up by punches and palm strikes. He jumped out of bed and crept hurriedly through the darkness to the Dragon Maiden's hut.

"Auntie? You hear that?" he whispered through the gap between the two rustic door panels fashioned from branches lashed together.

No reply.

Penance called again, softly. He did not wish to alert the fighters to his presence.

Still nothing. But surely it was impossible to sleep through the racket. He nudged the doors open. The hut was deserted. He ran towards the noise with a trembling heart. He was too far away to make out the duellists' silhouettes, but from the stirring in the air, he knew that one of them was the Dragon Maiden and that she was facing a fearsome martial artist. He sprinted faster. Soon, he saw his teacher, illuminated by the moon, battling a tall, stout man.

Standing rooted like a mountain, the man thrust his palms, slowly, one after the other, weaving a net of internal strength. The Dragon Maiden flitted left and right, always on the move. Though she had been successful in avoiding a direct clash thus far, it was unlikely she could withstand the weighty pressure exerted by the man's onslaught for long.

"Auntie! I'm here!" Penance flexed his foot and, after two great leaps, landed by the Dragon Maiden's side. He turned his eyes on her attacker and was stunned to see a familiar face under a huge bristly beard, stiff like a hedgehog's spines. His adopted father Viper Ouyang!

"Stop!" he cried. "We're friends!"

Friends? The Dragon Maiden was quite certain that she did not know this hairy lunatic, but the quick dip into her memory distracted her momentarily, making her movements a touch slower than before.

Taking full advantage, Viper sent his right palm scything up from under his left elbow in a savage diagonal slice. A powerful gust of air rushed into the Dragon Maiden's face.

Penance saw the Dragon Maiden raising her left hand to parry and threw himself forward. He knew his adopted father's reserves of *neigong* power were far superior and even fleeting contact could result in grave internal injuries. He extended all five fingers and brushed them over the man's elbow in a move called Strum Five Strings. He had yet to fully master this technique from the Nine Yin Manual, but as his aim was precise, the glancing touch was enough to numb Viper Ouyang's arm and dissipate the attacking force within.

Taking her chance, the Dragon Maiden lunged to retaliate, but Penance seized her wrist and used it as leverage to squeeze himself in between the two fighters.

"Please stop! We are friends!"

Viper Ouyang did not recognise the young man standing before him, but he was alarmed by his advanced kung fu. The tap on his elbow had rendered him defenceless, and the woman could have done serious damage with a mere nudge.

"Who are you?"

"It's me, Papa! Your son!" Penance was not hopeful that the older man would remember him, given how addled he had seemed in the short time they had spent together.

Confounded, Viper pulled Penance closer and turned his face to better catch the moonlight. The child had grown tall and his kung fu was now outstanding, but he soon picked out the familiar features of the adopted son he had been looking for all these years. He wrapped his arms tightly around Penance and sobbed with joy.

"Son, I've searched far and wide for you!"

Penance returned the embrace, tears streaming down his cheeks.

The Dragon Maiden sat down on the grass, relieved but suddenly pensive. Having grown up with emotionally reserved older women, she had always imagined that the fire of passion burning in Penance was the exception rather than the norm. Now, as she witnessed Viper Ouyang being overwhelmed by his feelings, she dreaded leaving the mountains and entering the world beyond even more.

THE LAST time Viper Ouyang had seen Penance Yang was in the Iron Spear Temple in Jiaxing, some five or six years before, when he fought Ke Zhen'e, the eldest and only remaining member of the Seven Freaks of the South. At the time he was suffering internal injuries sustained during an earlier confrontation with Guo Jing and he had barely managed to repel his opponent, enduring several blows from the Freak's weighty metal staff. Penance helped him take shelter under a large bronze bell, where he stayed for seven days and seven nights, channelling his *neigong* power around his body to heal the damage inside. After that, he took a room in a nearby inn and remained there for another twenty days until he had recovered from the muscular injuries caused by Ke's weapon.

Once Viper Ouyang was well enough, he began to look for Penance. But it had been more than a month since their parting. How could he hope to find any trace of the boy's whereabouts in this vast land? In his foggy mind, he recalled that Guo Jing and Lotus Huang had taken the lad under their wing, so it was likely that he would have gone to Peach Blossom Island. He set off eastwards for the coast, chartered a boat and set sail. He made the boat master dock under the cover of darkness, as he knew he could not overpower the Guo couple. His fellow Martial Great, Apothecary Huang, might be on the island too. Were he twice as skilled, he would not stand a chance if the three of them banded together. He kept himself hidden in a cave on a remote hillside during the day and would only venture out timidly at night. Even in his muddled state, he had memories of the island's deadly traps and treacherous paths.

Viper kept up his nocturnal sorties on Peach Blossom Island for more than a year without being discovered. One evening, he overheard the Wu brothers saying that Guo Jing had taken Penance to the Quanzhen Sect to continue his education. He stole a boat that night, sailed back to the mainland and headed north for Chongyang Temple.

By the time he reached the Zhongnan Mountains, Penance had fallen out with the Taoist monks and taken shelter in the Tomb of the Living Dead. The humiliating episode was a taboo in the Quanzhen Sect, so no mention was made of his stay there. Still, Viper was intent on finding the boy and searched every peak of the Zhongnan Mountains, as well as the surrounding towns, cities and countryside, covering several hundred *li* to no avail.

That night, he had come upon the valley for the first time and seen a young woman, dressed head to toe in white. She was sitting on the ground, her knees hugged close to her chest, gazing wistfully at the moon.

"Young lady! Have you seen my child? Where is he?"

The Dragon Maiden cast the stranger a sidelong glance and turned away, ignoring him.

Viper Ouyang strode up and grabbed her by the arm. "Where is my child?"

The Dragon Maiden was stunned by the older man's fierce, swift and incisive movements. He might look and sound unhinged but his kung fu far surpassed that of the strongest Quanzhen fighter she had faced. Forcing herself to calm down, she twirled her arm in a Miniature Grapple and Lock move to break free.

It was Viper's turn to be surprised. He could not believe the girl had extricated herself with such ease. His other hand shot forth, out of instinct, and suddenly they were caught up in a deadly tussle — for no cause whatsoever and without either knowing who the other was.

VIPER OUYANG had been in a half-crazed state since the second Contest of Mount Hua almost two decades before. The past was a blur he struggled to put into words, and he listened to Penance's account of the years since their encounter in Jiaxing with indifference. Only one detail managed to cut through the haze in his mind: his adopted son had received training in the martial arts from the girl in white.

"The lassie's kung fu is nothing compared to mine. Why would you learn from her? I'll teach you!"

With a thin smile on her lips, the Dragon Maiden moved further away to give the father and son some space.

"Papa, she's very good to me," Penance tried to explain.

"She's good? So I'm bad?" Viper snapped.

"No! You're good! You're the only two people in this world who've been good to me," Penance cried out in a placating tone. Although he could barely piece together what his adopted father had been up to in the past few years, it was clear he had gone to great lengths to find him.

Viper clasped Penance's hand with a chuckle, and after a while, he said, "Your kung fu is passable. But it's a shame you don't know the two most wondrous martial systems of this world."

"What are they?"

"You don't know?" Viper scrunched up his face. "Your *shifu* taught you nothing?"

Will he ever recover his wits? Penance wondered, disturbed by his father's mood swings.

"Papa will show you!" The Martial Great burst out in gleeful laughter. "The first is Exploding Toad, the other is the Nine Yin Manual." He began to recite the mnemonics that underpinned his own signature kung fu.

"You've taught me this before. Don't you remember?"

Viper scratched his head. "Show me what you can do."

Penance happily obliged, though he had not practised the technique since he had moved into the Tomb. Drawing on his understanding of Ancient Tomb *neigong*, he gave a flamboyant and florid rendition.

"Very pretty!" The old man chuckled. "But useless! Not right! This is how you do it." He waved his arms and kicked his feet as frenzied explanations poured forth from his lips. One moment he was rambling on about Exploding Toad, the next he turned to the inverted Nine Yin Manual. He rattled off whatever came to mind, caring little how much of it Penance could comprehend.

Aware that his adopted father's words contained great martial wisdom, Penance gave him his full attention, but it was impossible to grasp even a few morsels of knowledge, so confused was his delivery.

"*Aiyooo!*" Viper's eyes lighted on the Dragon Maiden. "No, no, no, we can't let your little *shifu* listen in on my secrets." He walked up to her. "Oi, lassie, I'm teaching my child. You mustn't eavesdrop."

"I'm not interested and I'm not listening."

Viper cocked his head to consider her answer. "Good, then go away."

The Dragon Maiden leaned back against a tree. "I come and go as I please."

Viper's beard and eyebrows bristled in rage at this insolent reply. He raised his hand to strike the Dragon Maiden in the face, but he paused when he heard Penance's voice.

"Pa, don't be rude to my teacher."

"Alright, alright, we'll go far, far away. But you mustn't sneak up on us."

The Dragon Maiden turned her head aside, deciding to ignore the crazed man. Presently, she felt a prod in the back and a numbing sensation spread from the point of contact. She realised with horror that she had been ambushed. She wanted to retaliate but she had lost control of her upper body. Then she felt another jab, this time to her waist.

"Don't fret, girl. I'll free you when I'm done teaching my son." Viper left her under the tree and marched over to Penance. "Let's go over there," he urged. "Out of your little *shifu*'s earshot." Penance was too busy trying to make sense of his adopted father's jumbled martial wisdom to register any of what had just happened. He let Viper take his hand and lead him away, as he knew he could not convince him that the Dragon Maiden had no interest in his martial secrets and would never listen in.

Hearing their fading footsteps, the Dragon Maiden laughed at herself. What was the point of being skilled in the martial arts if she lacked the combat experience to detect a surprise attack? Last time, it was Blithe Li; now, this bearded madman. But it was not in her nature to dwell on such things. Restoring her movements was foremost on her mind, as the weight of her body had already dragged her from a sitting position to lying prone on the ground.

She began to unlock her pressure points using the method from the Nine Yin Manual. Not long after she had sealed her breath, the numbing tingle intensified around the acupoints that had been tapped. Confused, she tried again, then again, but there was no hint of the binds loosening – and the discomfort was getting harder to ignore.

The Dragon Maiden did not dare make another attempt. If she kept blundering on, she might end up strengthening the restraints. Since fretting was not in her nature either, she gazed at the stars for a time then closed her eyes to rest.

A light touch on the eyelids woke her. She did not know how long she had been dozing, but when she opened her eyes, she could not see a thing. Alarmed, she blinked hard. Darkness remained, stubborn and impenetrable. She had never had her vision taken away. The years living in the Tomb meant that she could see in even the scantest light.

She felt the touch of a hand. Her upper body was scooped up off the ground. Hands slid down her back. Arms wound around her body. Loose and timid at first, but soon they grew bold and tightened in an embrace.

Petrified, she tried to scream, but she could not part her lips or move her tongue.

A fleeting touch on her cheek. Warm breath . . . Soft lips brushing her face . . . Smooth skin. Not Viper Ouyang . . .

Her heart hammered.

Terror began to recede. Something else had gripped her, taking its place. A name formed on her locked lips: Penance.

The arms were no longer content with wrapping themselves around her. The hands started to roam. Over her torso. Pulling loose the ties holding her robes. Peeling off layers of clothes. Tugging at propriety.

She had no choice but to lie there and let the hands do what they wanted; her movements were still locked by the pressure points. She was bewildered by what was happening, bashful about how she was feeling. She could tell the owner of the hands was craving intimacy, and she desired the same – to become one, to be intoxicated body and heart, to sway and swirl from the very depths of her souls and spirits.

6

VIPER OUYANG HAD NOT EXPECTED PENANCE TO GRASP MUCH of his teachings, but he was thrilled by how receptive his son proved to be, committing his every word to memory, and this encouraged him to offer more of his knowledge. The Martial Great talked and talked until the sun rose to light up the sky. At last, he had passed on the key ideas behind his two proudest martial achievements.

Penance took some time to consider all he had heard. "The kung fu from the Nine Yin Manual I've learned is very different from yours . . ."

"How can that be?"

"When you describe Transforming Muscles, Forging Bones, the third step reverses the flow of *qi* and blood and forces them through the Celestial Pillar point. But Auntie said we should focus the mind on the Elixir Field to open the Camphorwood Gate—"

"No, no, that's wrong!" Viper said with a vehement wag of his head. "Hmm, wait . . ." He tried it the way Penance had just out-lined. His internal strength flowed with ease, and he had never felt so effortless when putting the Nine Yin Manual's techniques into practice. Of course, he still did not know that his version had been altered by Guo Jing.

"What just happened?" The Martial Great blinked in confusion. "Am I wrong? Or is she? Can this be true? I . . . who am I?" He gazed ahead, his eyes vacant, his face blank, as if his spirits had abandoned his body.

Penance hailed his adopted father several times, but the man was lost to the tempest in his mind, deaf to all sounds. Then Penance remembered that the last time he had seen the martial artist afflicted in this way was when Lotus Huang shouted a string of family names to muddle his thoughts. He had realised then that his father did not know his own name, and he was planning to share the one he had overheard the Guo couple use, the next time they met, but things had spun out of control in the temple in Jiaxing.

"Papa, you are Viper Ouyang. Does that sound familiar?"

A flash of lightning sliced through the fog in Viper's head and floods of memories surged to the fore. He sprang high into the air with a cackle.

"Yes! Yes! Viper Ouyang!" Laughter overcame the older man once more. "Viper Ouyang!" He broke off a branch from a nearby tree and brandished it in a move from his Serpent Staff repertoire, thrash-ing the air noisily. "Viper Ouyang is unrivalled! Viper Ouyang is the Greatest Martial Master Under the Heavens! Viper Ouyang's kung fu is supreme! Viper Ouyang fears no-one!"

Still shouting and guffawing, the Martial Great took off like a gust of wind, leaving his adopted son behind.

PENANCE WAS about set off after Viper Ouyang when he heard a twig snap not far away.

Auntie?

He doubted it was her, but he had never come across another soul in the valley until now.

A moment later, he caught a streak of indigo blue hurtling through the undergrowth.

The colour of a Quanzhen Taoist robe.

"Who's there? Stop!" Penance gave chase using lightness *qinggong*, convinced that the furtive stranger was up to no good.

Hearing the shout, the shadowy figure quickened his pace, but Penance was faster. Rallying his internal strength, he shot ahead like a dart and caught up with the fleeing man.

"What are you doing here?" Penance wrenched the monk around by his shoulder and found he was looking at a familiar face.

Zhen Zhibing.

Panic was etched across his features. His mouth hung open without a sound. His hair and clothes were in disarray. His cheeks white one instant and crimson the next.

Penance was surprised by how flustered the Taoist seemed. As he recalled, Zhen Zhibing had always been calm and dignified, and he had seemed sincere when he pledged never to speak of the night he had seen the Dragon Maiden in the meadow of red flowers. For that, Penance had held him to be one of the more palatable members of the Quanzhen Sect.

Relaxing his grip, Penance spoke in a less aggressive tone: "Be on your way."

Zhen Zhibing took his leave without a word, though he did cast a few worried glances back as he blundered out of the valley.

PENANCE DECIDED to return to his hut. On the way, he wondered what had caused the monk to look so anxious, until he noticed two bare feet poking out of a flowering shrub, absolutely still, as though the person they belonged to was sound asleep.

"Auntie! Auntie!"

No response.

He parted the vegetation and found the Dragon Maiden lying on the ground, a scrap of blue cloth draped over her eyes. The sight made him uneasy. He lifted the fabric. The eyes that looked back at him . . . he could not describe her gaze. There was a peculiar glint he had never seen in all their time together. A blush rose to her cheeks and she looked away bashfully.

"Auntie, who put this over your eyes?"

Hearing his question, the Dragon Maiden shot him an accusing look.

Penance realised she had not moved since he had found her, and that her stance exuded a lethargy that came when someone's movements were frozen by way of their pressure points. He took her hands and pulled her up to lean against him. Her pliant body contained no strength.

Auntie could have freed herself easily from standard acupoint-locking kung fu, he reasoned. Papa must have used the reverse method he was telling me about.

Penance put what Viper Ouyang had taught him into practice and released her. And yet, she continued to drape herself over him. Her body was soft, supple and docile, as if her bones had melted away.

Mystified, Penance put his hands on her shoulders to help her sit up. "Papa isn't right in the head and he acts funny. Please don't be angry with him."

But the Dragon Maiden buried her face in his chest and whispered, "You're the funny one."

"Auntie . . ." Penance was unsure how to respond. He had never known her to speak in such a girlish tone or act in such a clingy manner.

"Why do you still call me that?" The Dragon Maiden straightened up somewhat to look him in the eye.

"What else if not Auntie? Should I call you *Shifu*?" Penance was more confused than ever.

"After what you've done . . ." She gave him an enigmatic smile. "How can I still be your *shifu*?"

"What . . . what did I do?"

"Look." The Dragon Maiden rolled up her sleeve. Her forearm was as delicate as a tender snowy lotus root, her skin unblemished like the purest white jade. The cinnabar mark of chastity had disappeared.

"Auntie . . ." Penance scratched his ear, bewildered.

"Don't call me that," she snapped, but her demeanour quickly softened at his panicked expression. "The knowledge of the Ancient Tomb Sect was passed on from maiden to maiden. Here –" she pointed to the inside of her forearm – "my *shifu* drew the Chastity Cinnabar, but . . . after last night . . . after what you . . . did—"

"What do you mean?" Penance cut in, too impatient to hear out her halting explanation.

The Dragon Maiden flushed bright red. How could she put that private act between them into words? After a while, she broke the silence in an almost inaudible whisper: "I was scared of leaving this valley, but now I will follow wherever you go."

"Oh, Auntie!" Penance cried with joy.

"Why do you still call me that?" Her voice was sharp, but she calmed herself a little before asking, "Didn't you mean it?" She waited for an answer. When none came, she added, in a tremoring voice: "Who am I to you?"

"You are my teacher," Penance replied with earnest conviction. "You have shown me compassion and shared your knowledge. I took an oath to honour and respect you and to do your bidding as long as I live."

"You don't see me as your wife."

The blunt statement stunned Penance. He had never imagined their bond developing in this way and he did not know how to respond.

"N-n-no . . . I – I don't . . ." he stammered eventually. "I am not . . . good enough for you . . . You're my *shifu*, my mentor, my Auntie."

The Dragon Maiden did not know what to think. She had been petrified when she was roused from her slumber by those invasive hands. She had no knowledge of intimacy and her pressure points had been locked – she had no way to resist what was being done to her. But when she deduced that it could only be Penance, since no-one other than Viper Ouyang had ventured into their secluded valley in the time they had lived there, all her fear and repulsion had vanished. She began to welcome and relish the caresses. She believed it meant Penance had resolved to take her as the love of his life. She was no longer just Auntie or *Shifu*. She also admitted to herself that she had felt the same way about him for some time. She started to imagine the vows and pledges they would make to each other, witnessed by the mountains and the seas, tying them forever as man and wife. She looked forward to the loving tenderness he would show her with the arrival of dawn. She wondered what name he would address her by. Would he use the endearing term "Sister"? Would he simply call her gruffly as "Wife"? How should she greet him? The same as before? Perhaps "my lord"?

Those sweet questions were still swirling in her head when he cruelly and repeatedly hailed her as "Auntie". He remained cool and unconcerned when she hinted that she had given him her most precious treasure, something that was more important than life itself. His refusal to acknowledge their passionate moment in the cold light of day had shattered her visions for the future. Her martial sister's voice sounded in her head:

> "*If your man seems different one day – if he doesn't appear as warm, if it feels like he's grown distant, polite – then he has changed his heart. This shift is subtle. It is often impossible to tell when it has started. Be vigilant at all times. Look for the smallest clues. They can be as fine as spider silk.*"

Blithe Li was right! He has already changed his heart. He does not want me to be his wife. He has said it with a certainty that could cut through iron. Her body shuddered as a surge of rage flooded her veins and – *wah!* – blood shot from her lips.

"Auntie! Auntie!" Penance was at such a loss that he knew not where to put his hands or feet.

Glaring at the fickle youth, the Dragon Maiden raised her palm. She wanted to hack down at the crown of his head, to dispatch him from this world once and for all, but her arm would not comply. The fury burning in her eyes was smothered by a pall of self-blame. When that dissipated, only the ashes of rueful sorrow remained.

"I know now." She heaved out a long sigh and added in a hushed tone, "You want to be free. You want to be on your own, unfettered . . . It will be as you wish. You will not see me again . . . To stop my heart from breaking." With a flick of her long flowing sleeves, she ran from the valley.

"Auntie! Where are you going? Don't leave me!"

"Stop. Don't follow me." She slowed down but kept her back to him as tears welled up in her eyes. "If I see you again, I – I may not . . . be able to check myself . . . I don't want to take your l— I want you to live."

"Are you . . . upset that I learned kung fu from Papa?"

"It's – you . . . you've changed . . . your heart." The Dragon Maiden flew off using her fastest *qinggong*.

Penance was utterly bewildered. He could not begin to understand the cause of their bizarre exchange. His body had frozen up, rooting him to the spot. His eyes followed her white dress, fluttering among the greenery, gliding further and further away, until it disappeared from the valley.

Stricken with grief at his loss, he slumped to the ground, his body racked by sobs. He could not fathom what he had done to offend the Dragon Maiden. He had no notion what had caused the change in her countenance, from fawning and affectionate to bitter and distant in no time at all.

Why did she forbid me to call her Auntie? Why did she say she wanted to be my wife? Why did she accuse me of changing my heart? What did Papa do to upset her? These questions tormented Penance, whipping up suffocating waves of anxiety that crashed in his skull.

He looked vacantly into the sequestered valley – with nothing to disturb its peace but the occasional snatch of birdsong – and roared at the top of his lungs: "Auntie! Auntie!"

The only answer he received was the echo of his broken tearful voice.

CHAPTER EIGHT

THE GIRL IN WHITE

I

PENANCE HAD NOT SPENT A SINGLE DAY AWAY FROM THE Dragon Maiden since he first came to live in the Tomb. Their bond was closer than that which commonly existed between *shifu* and disciple. In some respects, she was both a mother and a big sister to him. To be abandoned so resolutely, so abruptly and for no apparent reason was gut-wrenching. He even considered ramming his head against a rock to be done with it all, but in the very depths of his being, there was a flicker of hope that would not be snuffed out.

Auntie has left so suddenly . . . perhaps, she'll return without warning too, he told himself. She'll realise I have nothing to do with Papa's wrongdoing and come back to me.

That night, however, was destined to be sleepless. The whispering wind, chirring insects, nocturnal birds beating their wings . . . Penance jumped from the bed at the slightest sound and rushed outside.

"Auntie! Auntie!"

But, each time, he dragged himself back to the hut with heavy steps and a heavier heart. He decided to stay up and scaled the nearest peak to keep a look out until the sky grew bright.

Penance gazed at the clouds pooling in the valleys and the fog shrouding the peaks. It felt as if he were the only person left in the vast expanse between the heavens and the earth. He howled and thumped his chest.

I'll look for Auntie, he decided. She can strike me, shout at me, but I'll never let her part from me. If she wants to kill me, then so be it!

Buoyed by his resolve, Penance wrapped his clothes and some of the Dragon Maiden's robes in a piece of fabric, then tied the bundle onto his back and marched downhill.

PENANCE STOPPED at every village, asking the locals if they had seen a beautiful young woman dressed head to toe in white. They all shook their heads. He had now been walking for most of the day, and had questioned more than a dozen people. His patience was wearing thin, and his tone was brusque. The country folk, affronted by his manner, suspected he was up to no good. One demanded he explain how he was related to the maiden he was asking after.

"That's none of your business," Penance retorted. "Just tell me if you've seen her."

Before more sharp words could be exchanged, an elderly man stepped forward and tugged Penance by the sleeve to get his attention.

"I saw the girl heading that way last night," he said, pointing out a path to the east. Penance put his hands together in a gesture of thanks and hurried off in the direction indicated as the man continued to speak: "I thought it was Guanyin the Observer of Sound descending from the heavens. I didn't realise she was your sweetheart . . ."

Penance did not catch the rest of the old man's arch words or the jeers that pursued him out of the village. He had no idea the sighting had been fabricated to pay him back for his rudeness.

Soon, he came upon a fork in the road. Knowing the Dragon Maiden preferred peace and quiet, he chose the narrow rocky track that looked less travelled, but after a few bends it widened and joined the main road. He could even make out the distant outlines of pitched roofs clustered together in the approaching gloom. He decided to head for the town. As he walked, his stomach started to grumble, reminding him that he had not had a drop to drink or a morsel to eat since the night before. He quickened his pace and took a table in the first tavern he came across.

"Bring me some food."

The waiter brought him a simple dish with a bowl of rice. Penance gobbled down a few mouthfuls, then he felt a tightness in his chest and a lump in his throat that made swallowing difficult.

I should keep looking, he said to himself. If I don't find her tonight, I may never see her again.

He set down the bowl and beckoned the waiter over. "I'd like to ask you something."

"What can I do for you, Sir?" The man approached with a smile, his eyes lighting on the untouched dishes. "Is the meal not to your taste? I can ask the kitchen to prepare something else. What would you like?"

"No, no, this is fine," Penance said, waving the matter away. "Have you seen a beautiful young woman passing through this town? She is dressed all in white."

"Is she in mourning?"

"Have you seen her?" Penance snapped, frustrated that no-one would give him a straight answer.

"Well, I did see a girl, and her robe was white . . ."

"Which way did she go?"

"She passed by this morning, so she has half a day's start." The waiter then lowered his voice. "Young man, she isn't someone you'd want to . . . Trust me, it's best not to look for her."

"Why?"

"Are you aware that she knows kung fu?"

"Of course!" Penance's voice quavered in excitement. At last! He had found the Dragon Maiden.

"Then why are you looking for her? She's very dangerous."

"What do you mean?"

"Tell me, who is she to you?"

Penance realised that if he did not offer up some kind of explanation, he would get no more information out of the waiter.

"She is my . . . big sister. I need to find her."

The waiter's expression turned thoughtful and he shook his head. "Never mind . . ."

"Tell me what you know!" Penance seized him by the collar.

The man's tongue lolled out his mouth and he spluttered incomprehensibly.

"What are you muttering about?"

"Sir, let me go . . . I can't breathe . . ." He coughed out the words. "It's difficult to talk like this . . . I can if I have to, but . . ."

Penance let go, frowning at this dramatic performance.

The man hacked and wheezed for some time before he found his voice. "Sir, I mean, you two don't look alike. That wen— that gir— errr, your big sister, well, she looks younger than you. I'd say she's your *little* sister, if anything. But you are rather similar in some ways. Fiery, hot tempered . . . and you both speak with your fists!"

"She . . . she fought someone?"

"Oh, yes! She didn't just fight. She hurt two Taoists. Look." He pointed at the deep marks hacked and scored into the table. "It was terrifying. Your sister's a real Master. One swing of the sabre and she took an ear from each of them."

"Which Taoists?" Penance smiled at the thought of the Dragon Maiden handing out a thrashing to a pair of Quanzhen monks.

The waiter opened his mouth to answer but stopped dead. His eyes lingered for a moment at the tavern's entrance then flitted away as his cheeks turned pale and he scurried from the table.

Penance could only assume some intimidating figures had arrived. He pressed his bowl against his lower lip before looking over the rim towards the doorway while shovelling rice into his mouth. Two Taoists, around twenty-six or twenty-seven years of age, both wearing bandages that stretched over their cheeks. They sat down at the table next to Penance's, and shouted for food and drink.

The waiter soon came simpering with their order. He caught Penance's eye, winked and lifted his chin towards the newcomers.

Penance pretended not to have seen the signal and carried on stuffing his face. His mood had brightened now he had fresh news of the Dragon Maiden, and his appetite had returned. He wolfed down a second helping of rice, smacking his lips loudly to blend in with the other diners. In the simple, rough-spun clothes the Dragon Maiden had made for him, he did look like an ordinary rustic youth, dusty and grimy after a long day's journeying down country lanes.

THE TWO Taoists spoke in low voices as they ate. "Brother Pi, are you sure Master Han and Master Chen will be here tonight?"

"They are heroes of the Beggar Clan and they trust Martial Uncle Shen with their lives." Brother Pi cleared his throat. "They will come at his invitation."

Penance stole a hurried look at the adjacent table from the corner of his eye. The monk who had spoken first had bushy eyebrows, while Brother Pi had a wide mouth. They were so focused on their meal and each other that they had not even glanced in Penance's direction and they were unaware that he was listening in.

I can't let them see me, Penance thought, shifting in his seat to make it harder for the Taoists to see his face. I don't recognise them, but there are cow muzzles by the hundred at Chongyang Temple and they probably all know what the boy who defected from their sect looks like.

"What if they're too far away and can't make it in time?" asked the monk with the prominent eyebrows.

"Don't worry so much, Big Brother Ji," Pi rasped. "She's just a girl, how formidable can she be—"

"Drink!" Ji knocked his cup on his martial brother's, unwilling to continue this line of conversation. He drained his wine and shouted for the tavern's best room to be prepared for their stay.

Penance had heard enough to work out that the monks had enlisted the beggars' help in dealing with the Dragon Maiden, and they were meeting them later that night. All he had to do to find her was follow them!

Once the men had gone to their room, Penance asked the waiter for the chamber next to theirs.

"Sir, you must take care," the waiter whispered as he lit the candle in the guest room. "Your sister cut off their ears. They're plotting revenge."

"What? Never! My sister is the nicest person."

"She may be nice to you, but not to others," the man replied. "She was dining here . . . Tell me the truth, is she really your big sister? I'm not convinced . . . Anyway, the monks were sitting at the next table and glanced at her legs. Your sister flew into a rage. They exchanged heated words then she attacked them with her sword—"

Penance shushed the waiter with a gesture, shooed him from the room and snuffed out the candle. He had heard one of the monks through the wall saying he was ready to retire for the night.

Those lecherous Taoists must have offended Auntie with their stares, he reasoned, sitting on the *kang* bed-stove in the dark. I've always known there's not a decent soul to be found in the Quanzhen Sect. They probably recognised her from the fight at Chongyang Temple . . .

Penance then turned his mind to the martial techniques Viper Ouyang had shared with him during their brief reunion, for he needed something to occupy his thoughts while he kept an ear out for developments next door. He could recall less than a third of the disorganised jumble his adopted father regurgitated, and the complex training methods of Nine Yin and Exploding Toad kung fu were not easy to make sense of even in the right order. He ran through what he had grasped, but refrained from dwelling on any of it for too long, lest he missed any action from his neighbours.

The tavern quietened down as the hour grew late. Not long after midnight, two indistinct taps in the courtyard broke the silence. It sounded to Penance as though someone had jumped over the perimeter wall. A window opened with a creak and he heard a whispered question through the wall: "Is it Master Han and Master Chen?"

"Yes," came the hushed reply.

"Please come in."

The doors to the Taoists' room parted with a muffled creak.

"Your humble monk Ji Qingxu." Penance recognised the voice of the Taoist with bristly eyebrows. "This is my younger martial brother Pi Qingxuan. We are honoured to meet Hero Han and Hero Chen."

The given name of a Quanzhen disciple reflected their place in the martial school's lineage. When Wang Chongyang founded the Sect, four of his seven protégés took on the character *chu* in their names, and the Immortals' students, the third generation, were granted the character *zhi*. The fourth generation, which Penance was once part of, adopted the character *qing*, and their successors would assume the character *jing* in their names.

So they're of the fourth generation, the young man said to himself. Which old cow muzzle is their *shifu*? Hao Datong or Liu Chuxuan?

Then a high-pitched voice interrupted his thoughts: "We came as fast we could the moment we received your Martial Uncle Shen's message. How is the little minx's kung fu?"

"Brother Pi and I have come to blows with her and, to our shame, we were no match for her."

"Who trained her?" the same voice asked.

"Martial Uncle Shen's first thought was that she hails from the Ancient Tomb Sect," Ji Qingxu replied. "But when he asked her, the lass's only response was to curse Blithe Li the Red Serpent Celestial—"

"In that case, it seems unlikely. Where is your rendezvous? How many champions will she bring?"

"Tomorrow noon, Jackal Valley. Forty *li* south-west of this town. We don't know who she will enlist to aid her, but I know we have nothing to fear with the heroes of the Beggar Clan on our side."

"Brother Han and I will be there. So long."

The two monks walked the beggars to the doors, then Ji Qingxu said under his breath, "Chongyang Temple isn't far from here. Please keep this contest a secret. If word reaches our Grandmasters, we will be in great trouble."

Beggar Han, who had not spoken a word so far, gave a dry chuckle. "Your Uncle Shen has already reminded us. Why else would you need us when you have so many Masters close at hand?"

"Rest assured, we will not breathe a word," Beggar Chen promised in his squeaky voice. "There would be trouble enough if your other martial uncles found out, let alone the Six Immortals."

The four of them spoke in hushed tones at the doorway for a little longer before crossing the courtyard. Out of courtesy, the Taoists vaulted over the perimeter wall after the beggars and accompanied them back to their lodgings.

2

THE INSTANT THE TAOIST MONKS LEFT THE TAVERN, PENANCE sneaked into their room via an unlatched window. An oil lamp was burning on the table and there were two cloth bundles lying on the *kang* bed-stove. Penance picked up the smaller one. It was surprisingly heavy. He unwrapped it to reveal twenty *taels* of silver.

Perfect! I've got the money to pay for my room now, he told himself as he stuffed the ingots into his shirt.

Then he unwrapped the other bundle, which was about four *chi* in length, and found two swords. He unsheathed them, snapped the blades and slipped the broken pieces back into the scabbards, before packing them up as he had found them.

Let's see how they serve you tomorrow! Penance detested the

two monks for both their run-in with the Dragon Maiden and their chicken-hearted ways, turning to outsiders for help while hiding the encounter from their martial elders.

Just before he left the room, Penance decided to bestow one last parting gift on the monks. He untied the string holding up his trousers and emptied his bladder onto their bedding. Catching scrabbling noises from beyond the tavern wall, he made himself decent and climbed out through the window. He was in no particular hurry, as he had already observed that the monks' lightness kung fu was middling at best and they could not clear the wall in one leap. They would have to hop up to the summit before jumping down, and that would give him enough time to get back to his own room.

Penance tiptoed through the darkness, closed the doors softly behind him, then pressed his ear against the partition separating the two chambers. Soon he heard the Taoists entering, then the rustle of fabric. As they removed their outer robes to get ready for bed, they talked in hushed tones about the contest the next day and how they were confident of victory.

Suddenly, a loud croaky voice rang out. "Why are the bedclothes wet?" Penance remembered the monk was called Pi Qingxuan. "And they stink too! Big Brother Ji, what did you do?"

"Nothing!" Ji Qingxu yelled back. "Was it a cat?"

"Cats don't piss that much."

"Are you sure?" Ji Qingxu moved their belongings off the soiled linen. "Wait, where's our silver?" He thundered about the room, lifting and shifting everything in sight to look for the money.

Penance listened with glee.

"Innkeep! Innkeep!" Pi Qingxuan shouted. "Thieves in the house! Our silver's gone!"

The disturbance brought a drowsy tavern attendant to their room. Pi Qingxuan seized the man by the front of his robe and bellowed in his face, denouncing the establishment as a nest of bandits. The man screeched and shrieked, proclaiming his innocence, waking every single person in the courtyard.

Drawn by the racket, the tavern's cashier, chefs, waiters and some of the overnight guests gathered outside the monks' chamber. Penance concealed himself amid the nosy onlookers. He recognised the man grabbed by Pi Qingxuan as the prying waiter who had served him earlier, and from their brief interaction, he had a sense that he enjoyed picking quarrels and waging wars of words.

Barely pausing for breath, the waiter hurled slanders and slurs at the monks amid sprays of spittle. Mortified, the Taoists stood helpless and mute, clearly eager to shut the man up with their fists. But to use violence against one untrained in the martial arts was a serious breach of the rules of the Quanzhen Sect, especially when the man had claimed he had nothing to do with the theft. The monks had not forgotten that they were in a town at the foot of the Zhongnan Mountains and that what happened here would inevitably reach the ears of Chongyang Temple. They swallowed their retorts and shut the doors, leaving the waiter to shout at no-one in particular.

Early the next morning, the waiter was still muttering darkly about the Taoists. Penance beckoned him over with a grin and ordered a bowl of noodles for breakfast, then asked, "What happened last night?"

"Those whoreson thieves!" the waiter hissed. "They came here to dine and take a room for free. We would have let the matter pass as a courtesy to Chongyang Temple, but they called us bandits! We're here to do honest business. We can't afford to have our reputation smeared. The Taoist vagabonds sneaked away at the crack of dawn, but I'll go to the temple with my complaint. I remember their ratty faces well!"

Penance could barely contain his laughter. As he filled his stomach, he fanned the flames of the waiter's indignation. He then settled the bill and asked for directions to Jackal Valley.

THE SUN'S rays had yet to lose their early morning slant when Penance arrived at his destination. With a few hours to go until the midday rendezvous, he decided to find somewhere to hide and watch the Dragon Maiden trounce the villains. Wouldn't it be amusing to disguise himself as a peasant boy so she would not recognise him at first glance, and play the same trick on her as he had with Ripple Hong? He headed for the nearest farmstead to find what he needed for his deception. On the way, he passed a raging bull butting its horns into its enclosure, making the wooden structure squeak and groan.

An idea struck the young man: I'll dress as a cowherd. Auntie will never recognise me!

He tiptoed close to the farmhouse and jumped in through an open window. Two small children were playing with clay on the floor. Dumbstruck by shock and fear, they watched without making a sound as the stranger changed into their father's clothes and straw sandals.

Penance rubbed some earth onto his face and made for the bullpen. He put on the conical hat hanging on the side of the enclosure, then grabbed the short bamboo flute next to it and tucked it into the straw rope tied around his waist. Pleased with his disguise, he let the beast out. It charged straight for him, bellowing angrily.

The muscular creature, weighing at least seven hundred *jin*, was a magnificent specimen with a luscious coat and proud horns. Penance waited until it was moments from goring him, then placed his palm on its head and vaulted onto its back.

In a twinkling, the bull had taken Penance to the main road. The irate beast bucked and leapt and spun, trying to throw off its rider, but he sat perfectly poised.

"Behave, or it'll hurt," Penance warned with a laugh and hacked the edge of his palm on the animal's withers. The blow contained one-fifth of his internal power, and it was enough to make the bull bleat in pain. Still the feisty creature would not yield, plunging and jumping in an attempt to cast off the unwelcome stranger.

A dozen chops of the palm later, the bull relented. Now, when the animal was prodded on the left side of its neck, it would turn right, and steer left when poked on the right. Amused, Penance slapped it on the rump and on it trotted, then a jab on the forehead sent it backwards.

Another smack on the bull's behind and off it shot at great speed like a stampeding horse. It took Penance through a dense forest and stopped in a dell hemmed in by vertiginous hills on all sides.

It matched exactly with the tavern waiter's description of Jackal Valley.

Penance hopped off and led the bull by the rope attached to its nose to a grassy incline. He sat down, stretched out on his back and closed his eyes. To anyone passing, he was a cowherd taking his mid-morning nap. However, as the sun moved higher in the sky, he began to fret. What if the Dragon Maiden doesn't turn up?

Except for the occasional snort of the bull, all was quiet under the midday sun. Then a handclap broke the silence. An answer came from the opposite direction.

Penance remained lying on the turf, but shifted his position sur-reptitiously to get a better view. He propped his mud-caked ankle over his knee and shielded most of his face with his hat, leaving one eye uncovered.

A short while later, three Taoists came into Penance's line of sight. He recognised Ji Qingxu and Pi Qingxuan from the tavern. The monk walking with them also looked familiar. Short and com-pact in build, this more senior figure appeared to be in his forties.

He must be their Martial Uncle Shen, Penance thought. I've prob-ably seen him in Chongyang Temple.

At the same time, two men were sweeping across the meadow towards the Taoists. Both were dressed in rags, and one was stocky and heavyset, while the other had a shock of white hair and a face full of wrinkles. They were Han and Chen from the Beggar Clan.

The five men greeted each other in silence by touching their palms over their fists, then spread out in a line, facing west. The thudding of hooves could now be heard echoing between the craggy hills. The men exchanged glances and turned their eyes on the path leading into the valley.

A splash of black and white appeared amid the greenery. A white-clad young woman on a black donkey was charging towards the five men.

Who is she? Penance's heart froze. Is she with those men? Where's Auntie?

The young woman tightened the reins to her mount and stopped several *zhang* from the Taoists and the beggars. Contempt written across her features, she swept her cold eyes over them, not deigning to speak first.

"Little lass," Ji Qingxu called. "We did not expect you to come yourself. Where are your champions?"

The young woman sneered and – *sha!* – drew a curved sabre from her belt. The thin and narrow blade, shaped like a crescent moon, dazzled with its silver glint.

"When will they arrive?" Ji Qingxu pursued. "We have not come here to stand around."

"This is my champion!" The young woman brandished her weapon. Its keen edge hummed as it sliced through the air.

The men had not imagined their opponent would be so foolhardy as to turn up alone to a contest with reputed fighters of the *wulin*. Penance, meanwhile, was bitterly disappointed that the girl in white he had been told about was not the Dragon Maiden. A rush of *qi* pushed upwards from his chest, against his regular flow of energy. He could no longer suppress his emotions and broke down in wails and sobs.

The martial artists noticed Penance for the first time, but they assumed he was a mere cowherd and ignored his outburst.

Ji Qingxu spoke again, gesturing at the vagrants. "Here we have Hero Han and Hero Chen from the Beggar Clan." Then he pointed at the middle-aged Taoist. "And you have met our martial uncle Shen Zhifan."

The young woman said nothing, but eyed each of them with her icy condescending stare.

"We won't fight you today, since you come alone," Shen Zhifan said. "You have ten days to enlist four champions. Then we will meet here again at the same time."

"I said, I have already got my champions. I need no help thrashing wineskins and rice-sacks of your ilk."

"Conceited little girl!" Shen Zhifan restrained himself from offering further insults in case her audacity was a front and she had helpers waiting in ambush. "Were you trained by the Ancient Tomb Sect?"

"Why do you care, cow muzzle? Are you too craven to accept my challenge?"

"Let me ask you one more time, Miss." Again, the monk forced himself to check his temper. He could not afford to get on the wrong side of someone associated with the Red Serpent Celestial. "Why did you injure my Quanzhen fellows? If we have done you wrong, we shall beg forgiveness from your *shifu*, but if you won't state the reason, then you cannot accuse us of being discourteous."

The young woman sniggered. "Your two cow muzzles over there were indeed discourteous. That's why I cut off their ears."

Her frank admission made Shen Zhifan wonder if they should keep pursuing her, but Beggar Chen had no such qualms – his fiery temper had yet to be cooled by age.

"Little lass, dismount when you address an elder!" As he spoke, the vagrant lurched forward and grabbed for the young woman. There was no time for her to veer away and her sword hand was caught in his grip.

And yet, she managed to twist her arm around and the cold glint of steel flashed once.

Beggar Chen let go and scrambled back, but two of his fingertips had been sliced open to the bone despite his swift reaction. Enraged, he unsheathed his sabre. "Face your death, strumpet!"

The other men also reached for their weapons. Beggar Han brandished a pair of maces linked by a chain and the senior Taoist charged with his sword. However, when Ji Qingxu and Pi Qingxuan grabbed the hilt of their swords to draw them from their scabbards, their weapons felt . . . lighter. They gasped at the broken blades.

The monks' dumbfounded expressions made the young woman giggle. Her voice jolted Penance from his wallowing and the fruits of his handiwork brought a smile to his face. Intrigued, he watched her closely to see what she would do next.

Still mounted, the young woman leaned forward and – *swish!* – slashed her sabre down at Pi Qingxuan. As the monk ducked, she flicked her wrist ever so slightly. The blade changed direction mid-air and sliced across his cheek, drawing blood.

Penance knew the mercurial move well. It was typical of Ancient Tomb kung fu.

Shen Zhifan and the two beggars closed in around the young woman, provoked by her brutality and shocked by her unpredictable attack. Ji Qingxu seized the chance to pull his martial brother back. The monks clung to their sword stumps, reluctant to part with the useless hilts.

Whistling, the young woman tugged at the reins and the donkey shot past her assailants. The beggars ran after the animal, threatening it with their weapons, while Shen Zhifan thrust the point of his sword at the young woman's vital points.

Penance could tell that the monk was launching some of the most ferocious Quanzhen sword strokes with the intent to maim, but his control lagged far behind that of his martial brothers Zhen Zhibing and Zhao Zhijing.

A third-rate fighter! Penance thought, turning his attention to the young woman. He now understood why the tavern waiter had refused to believe this pretty girl with an oval face was his older sister, because she looked at least a year or two younger than him. She appeared suntanned compared with the Dragon Maiden, whose snow-white complexion stemmed from a lifetime of living underground. He watched her fluid and lightsome movements, noting she mainly thrust and sliced with her blade as though it were a double-edged, sharp-pointed sword, rather than hacking and hewing as one usually would with a single-edged curved sabre.

Are you a disciple of Blithe Li? Penance wondered as the young woman sent the men leaping and tumbling with her Ancient Tomb kung fu. But he soon lost interest in the brawl. He disliked both sides and he could not care less about the outcome. He folded his arms behind his head and gazed up at the sky instead.

Meanwhile, the five men were yet to make any headway against the young woman, who held the high ground, seated on her donkey.

Tiring of his broken sword, Ji Qingxu called, "Brother Pi, come with me!" and sprinted to the nearest copse. He picked a willowy young tree and cut it down with his sword stump, then shaved off the branches to fashion a pike. Pi Qingxuan followed suit and they rushed back to the fight with their new weapons, thrusting their sharp points at the donkey's flanks.

"Have you no shame?" The young woman parried the improvised spears, but her response left her front and back vulnerable. Beggar Han swung a mace into her face while Shen Zhifan thrust his sword into her back. She ducked, leaning to one side, while swinging her sabre backwards. The mace shot past her cheek and her weapon met the Taoist's steel with a resounding clang.

The next moment, the donkey brayed and reared up, having been jabbed by Ji Qingxu. Beggar Chen grasped the opportunity to roll towards the animal and strike its hind legs with the blunt edge of his blade using Earthbound Sabre kung fu. The creature buckled, kneeling on its front legs. Shen Zhifan and Beggar Han aimed their weapons at the young woman once more.

She grabbed Pi Qingxuan's pike and vaulted up from the saddle, avoiding their pincer assault. As she descended, she used her weight to snap the makeshift weapon. The instant she touched down, she twirled her sabre and sliced it horizontally to block Beggar Chen's blade.

Penance's interest was piqued when he heard the thud of her feet on the ground. The landing was heavier than he had expected. Was she injured? He looked her up and down and observed that her left leg was slightly shorter, which put a strain on her leaps and jumps. Now he understood why she had refused to dismount. He felt compelled by his natural sense of justice to take her side. It was not honourable for five grown men to band together against a teenage girl with a limp. Yet, at the same time, he could not help begrudging her for dashing his hopes of finding the Dragon Maiden, and resenting her connection with Blithe Li. Were it not for that malicious woman, he would still be living in peace and isolation in the Tomb of the Living Dead with Auntie. He turned the other way, unwilling to spare another thought for any of the brawlers. However, the clink and clank of weapons stirred his curiosity before long and he was tempted to steal a glance.

The fight had turned on its head. The young woman was now swerving and dodging, wielding her sabre in defence instead of attack. As Penance looked on, she ducked away from Beggar Han's hurtling mace. The iron ball shot past her cheek, but Shen Zhifan was slicing his sword down at the same moment. There was a sharp metal tinkle and black tresses tumbled over her face. The silver loop fastening her hair had been cut in half.

The young woman furrowed her brow and puckered her lips. The frost of displeasure hardened her features.

Penance was struck by the change in her countenance: *Auntie sports the same expression when she's upset with me.* This firmed up his resolve to come to the young woman's aid. He grabbed a handful of stones and waited for an opening.

Finding space for a backhanded swing, the young woman hacked her sabre at the senior Taoist monk in retaliation, but within a handful of moves, she was on the defensive again, scrambling left and right.

"Who is the Red Serpent Celestial to you?" Shen Zhifan demanded. "Tell us the truth, or we shan't be civil any longer."

She answered by sketching a horizontal arc with her sabre. Its vicious curved point was now threatening the back of the monk's head as she drew it back in a hooking motion.

"Watch out!"

So swift and stealthy was the strike that, by the time Beggar

Chen's warning reached Shen Zhifan's ears, it was too late to veer out of the way. Ji Qingxu came to his martial uncle's rescue, blocking the blade's edge with his pike.

The five men now set about the young woman with less inhibition. At first, Shen Zhifan had been worried about bringing trouble to the Quanzhen Sect by hurting a disciple of Blithe Li. Then he recalled that his martial elders had crossed swords with the Red Serpent Celestial some years ago in Shanxi, so he was unlikely to incur their wrath. He quickly convinced himself that, since the young woman was fighting alone, he should seize the chance to rid the martial world of one of Blithe Li's underlings, and unleashed a series of lethal assaults, aiming his sword at her vital points.

The situation was turning nasty for the young woman. Penance knew he had to act without delay. He directed the bull towards the fighters, then hopped onto its back and slid around to hug its belly, hooking his feet around its body. Thus positioned, he dug his heels into its rump. It bolted straight into the battle, sending the martial artists fleeing in every direction.

Concealed under the bull's girth, Penance flicked the stones he had gathered earlier into the men's backs in quick succession, hitting either the Gate of the Soul or Spirit Hall acupoints. Their arms flopped to their sides, numb and sore, and their weapons clattered to the ground in a chorus of clangs and thuds and yelps.

Penance steered the bull back onto the grassy slope and yelled, "Look out! It's on the rampage!"

Shen Zhifan paid the cowherd no heed. He was too preoccupied by the young woman's secret defender. Only a supreme martial Master could have disarmed all five of them without being detected or revealing themselves. The Taoist knew the smartest course of action was to retreat while he still had control of his legs.

"Brother Chen, Brother Han, let's go!" he cried as he sprinted out of Jackal Valley. The beggars followed his lead, but Pi Qingxuan was so addled by the invisible attack that he ran without looking, bumbling straight into the young woman.

"Over here!" Ji Qingxu called, catching his martial brother's mistake.

Pi Qingxuan whipped around, but the young woman had taken a step in his direction and was now swinging her sabre down. Unarmed, he twisted his body to veer out of the way. However, her strike was deceptive. It appeared to be falling on his left side, and yet its true target was his right. It looked to be flying up high, but it was in fact swinging low. The blade flashed, its edge was slicing down at the Taoist's face. Pi Qingxuan lifted his hand to shield himself out of instinct and the sabre cut clean through three of his fingers. So intent was he on escaping, he did not even register the pain.

Beggar Han had been running for a while when he realised the young woman was not giving chase. She's lame, he recalled. Of course, she can't keep up with us! He glanced back and his eyes lingered momentarily on her shorter left leg.

She felt his gaze and flew into a rage. "You think you can outrun me?" Twirling her sabre several times, she hurled it at the beggar. *Whoosh!* A glittering silver beam cut through the air and impaled the man's shoulder, making him stagger and almost fall. But he steadied himself and made off at an even swifter pace, the weapon still lodged in his body.

3

THE YOUNG WOMAN WATCHED THE MEN DISAPPEAR BEHIND A cluster of trees with a snicker and picked up the sabre Beggar Chen had dropped. She was rather upset to have lost her Silver Curved Blade, which had accompanied her for so long, but the pressing issue at hand was to find out who had come to her aid. Weapon in hand, she checked the thickets around the valley. All was silent and still. She did not chance so much as a shadow resembling the human form. She headed back into the open and saw the cowherd lying on the ground, his face crumpled in misery, wailing at the heavens and earth.

THE GIRL IN WHITE

"What's the matter?" she asked.

"The bull got scratched when he charged at you. My master will beat me."

She cast her eye over the animal. Not a mark on its glossy coat. But it did come barging in at a most opportune moment, she thought, reaching inside her robe for an ingot of three *taels*.

"Here you go." She threw the silver on the ground.

The boy shook his head glumly and did not spare it a glance.

"Money for your trouble," she added, assuming his lack of gratitude was because he was too foolish and uncouth to understand the value of her gesture.

Then she heard him mumble, "Not enough."

She tossed another ingot down. This time, the cowherd took a peep. Still, he shook his head. She raised her eyebrows and her face darkened. "I'm not giving you more!"

Her countenance brought to mind the Dragon Maiden. A rush of hot blood surged from Penance's chest and his eyes pricked. An idea took shape in his head: It may be some time before I find Auntie. If I stay close to her, at least I have a reminder of Auntie's mannerisms.

He wrapped his arms around her legs. "You can't go!"

"Unhand me!" She twisted and kicked to no avail.

Her mounting irritation delighted Penance. "I can't go home. You have to help me!"

"Let go!" She raised her sabre. "Or I'll chop you into pieces."

"Go on!" Penance squeezed his arms tighter and pretended to cry. "They'll beat me to death at home."

"What do you want?"

"I don't know. I'll go where you go!"

The young woman had had enough. The blade flashed down. She had no desire to kill him, but she was not averse to giving the lad a taste of her steel to be rid of him.

Penance clung on. He never imagined she would hurt him, but the sharp edge was now mere inches from his head. He rolled away, shrieking, "Murder! Murder!"

She strode after him and hacked down again.

Squirming on the ground, Penance kicked his muddy feet in a frenzy as he hollered, "I'm slain!"

Somehow, the young woman had failed to land one single blow on the boy, and yet she had come close to being struck several times by his wild movements.

"Get up!" she ordered when she noticed the intense way he was staring at her.

"You won't kill me?"

"No."

Penance climbed slowly to his feet, panting and huffing. He summoned his *qi* surreptitiously to seal his blood flow. His face turned ashen-white in an instant.

The young woman was delighted to see him so cowed by the threat of her blade, as if his souls had taken leave of his body in fright. "This is what happens if you displease me." She gestured with the sabre at Pi Qingxuan's severed fingers. "I trimmed that mad dog's claws."

Scrunching up his features in mock horror, Penance recoiled from the bloody stubs. The young woman tucked her weapon into her belt and looked around for her black donkey, but the animal had long taken flight. She had no choice but to continue her journey on foot.

"Wait! Take me with you!" Penance stowed the silver ingots in his shirt and hurried after the young woman, pulling the bull along with him.

WHEN SHE had put some distance between herself and Jackal Valley, the young woman decided to rest her legs, but just as she was about to set off again, she saw the cowherd approaching with the bull in tow.

"Take me along!" he called out.

Furrowing her brow, she sprinted away using lightness *qinggong* for several *li* without pause. She slowed down when she thought she had left him far behind, but then a faint cry of "Don't leave me behind!" reached her ears.

Rage swelled in the young woman's breast and she charged with her sabre held high. The youth screamed and ran the other way, cradling his head.

Believing she had chased him off, she turned around and continued on her way. Before long, she heard the guttural lowing of a bull. And there was the teenage cowherd, trailing thirty or forty paces behind her. She halted and waited for him to catch up, but he too stopped and kept his distance. When she moved again, he followed suit, but when she raced towards him brandishing her weapon, he fled.

The sun began to dip below the horizon. All afternoon, the two of them had journeyed along in this stop-start manner. Every so often, the young woman would turn back and lunge at the cowherd, but he always managed to roll, crawl or tumble in the most undignified manner away from her sabre – avoiding its keen edge by a hair's breadth. And her attempts to knock him out or whack him on the legs to stop him from shadowing her had not succeeded.

In time, the young woman grew impressed by the lad's stamina and persistence. However, she assumed he was fit and hardy from hiking up hills and mountains with his bull and it was simply luck that had saved him from her blade. She had never once considered that he might be more than a common swain. In any case, the running back and forth was taking its toll on her weaker leg and the young woman decided to call a truce.

"You can come with me – if you do as I say."

"Really?"

"Let me ride on your bull. I'm tired."

Penance dragged the animal over to her. As he drew close, he caught a glint in her eyes and concluded that she must have hatched a plot against him. Bracing himself for what was to come, he climbed clumsily onto the bull.

With a tap of her right foot, the young woman sailed into the air and landed gracefully in front of him.

Not a bad substitute for the donkey, she thought as she dug her heels hard into the bull's ribs. The pain made it shoot forward. In that same moment, she elbowed her fellow rider in the chest.

"*Aiyoooo!*" Penance exclaimed as he rolled off the animal's back.

At last, the nuisance was gone! Smirking at her success, the young woman kicked the bull again to drive it on. However, to her surprise, the boy's yelps and cries did not fade as she sped away. They persisted, right behind her. She looked around.

He was clinging onto the bull's tail with both hands. The animal was hurtling at such a pace that his feet were barely touching the ground. Dust flew into his face and tears and snot ran down into his mouth, but he was holding on tight.

The young woman raised her sabre, ready to swing it down at his hands, when the bull ground to a sudden halt and the din of conversation rang in her ears. They had careered into a bustling market and the animal could make no headway in the cluttered surroundings.

Penance sprawled on the ground and squealed, "*Ooooowww*, my chest! That nasty trick of yours will be the death of me!"

There had always been a streak of frivolity in Penance's character and he had relished making sport of others since he was a child. However, out of respect for the Dragon Maiden he had kept it strictly in check over the past years. Now, that side of him was coming to the fore, because whenever he provoked the young woman, it distracted him momentarily from his inability to locate the Dragon Maiden. He was also finding solace in her angry looks, as whenever she shot one his way, he could almost convince himself that he was in the company of his teacher again.

By now, a crowd had gathered around Penance, bombarding him with questions about what had happened and gossiping among themselves.

The young woman melted into the throng, hoping to make her

getaway, but within a few steps, she felt two arms winding around her right leg – her good leg.

"Don't leave me!" Penance cried.

"What's going on between you two?" one of the onlookers asked.

The memory of the Dragon Maiden asking if he wanted her to be his wife flashed through Penance's mind and he said, "She's my lady wife. She beat me up because she doesn't want me anymore."

Her brow creasing in displeasure, the young woman launched her foot at Penance, who was still writhing on the ground. The instant he saw her kick coming, he shoved the man standing closest to him into its path and the blow landed on the man's belly.

The man howled and threw a punch at the young woman in retaliation, but she was not intimidated, even though his fist was the size of a vinegar vat. She reached out and gave his elbow a firm push, sending the burly man, who weighed at least two hundred *jin*, shrieking and squawking into the air. He crashed into the swarm of busybodies watching from the sidelines and the marketplace erupted into screams and confusion.

The young woman tried once more to free herself, but Penance's arms were locked tight. Several men from the nosy horde had extricated themselves from the tangle of limbs and were closing in with menace.

"Unhand me – and you can come along," she whispered.

"You won't hit me again?"

"No."

Penance released his hold and got to his feet. Together, they darted through the angry rabble and fled from the clamour.

"Did you hear them?" Penance asked with a grin when they had made it out of the market with the bull. "They say no wife should strike her man."

"Shut up! I'll cut your head off if you call me that again," she said, hefting her sabre to emphasise her point.

Penance put his hands around his neck and ran several paces ahead. "As you say, good Miss!"

"Who'd want to marry a filthy smelly bumpkin like you!"

With a silly giggle, Penance trotted back to walk beside her.

In the deepening gloom, wisps of cooking smoke were coiling into the sky from the marketplace, but after the earlier squabble, they had no choice but to make their way into the wilderness on an empty stomach.

"Go back to the town and buy ten *mantou* buns," the young woman said after a while.

"No!"

"Why?"

"You'll run away."

"I won't."

But Penance did not believe her and kept shaking his head. Frustrated, the young woman threw a punch. He sidestepped her clumsily and took cover behind the bull. She gave chase using lightness *qinggong*, but the screaming stumbling boy managed to swerve away every single time, circling the beast as if they were playing hide and seek.

With each stride she took, the young woman grew more baffled and infuriated. She knew her limp slowed her down, but why were her efforts to bring the dirty stinky swain under control proving so ineffectual? It was a heavy blow to her confidence in her wit and her martial capability, but it was yet to cross her mind that it was indeed impossible for an ordinary cowherd to evade her again and again.

She decided to stop pursuing him for the time being and set off south along the main road. She had come to the conclusion that she would have to resort to extreme measures to shake him off, but she could not think of a way to dispatch him without revealing her deadly intent, so she let him follow her at a distance with his bull.

She was trudging along, turning ideas over her head, when she saw a temple that looked deserted. Perhaps they could stop there for the night since it was already getting dark, and she could finish him off in his asleep. She pushed open the doors and a cloud of dust rushed into her face. The place had been abandoned for so long that even the statues of the deities were crumbling away. She cut some tall grass and twigs to sweep the altar table, which, fortunately, was still fairly sturdy. Once she had made it as clean as she could, she lay down and closed her eyes, waiting for him to follow her into the temple. And yet, she could not hear his footsteps at all.

"Hey, boy, where are you?"

No reply.

Free of his pestering presence, at last! However, the young woman did not feel the elation she had been expecting, only a heightened sense of solitude. She found herself wishing for his company as she drifted off.

Some time later, she was woken by the smell of freshly cooked meat. She headed outside and found the cowherd sitting by a fire, tearing into a large joint. Chunks of meat were being roasted over the flames on a spit fashioned from branches, filling the air with a mouth-watering aroma.

Hearing her approach, Penance turned to her with a smile. "Want some?" He tossed a piece of meat over.

The young woman picked off a small mouthful and tasted it. There was no seasoning, but the meat was flavoursome. Muntjac, perhaps? She joined him by the fire and pulled off another strip, eating gracefully despite the inhospitable surroundings.

Penance ate with a voracious appetite, slurping the juices and crunching the bones noisily, sending scraps and spittle flying.

The young woman was put off by his revolting manners, but her empty stomach could not be ignored. She shifted around until he was out of her line of sight before finishing her meal. Then she was handed another joint.

"Hey, clod, tell me your name," she asked as she tore at the piece of meat.

"How did you know?"

"Clod's your name? Really?" She laughed. "Where are your parents?"

"They're gone. What's yours?"
"Why should I tell you?"

THE YOUNG woman's name was Lu Wushuang. In fact, she had met Penance when she was nine years old and he was around thirteen, outside the abandoned kiln where he had been sleeping rough at the time, on the day her life turned upside down.

It was the morning after she had broken her leg. The night before, she had been with her cousin Cheng Ying and their new friends, the Wu brothers, who were travelling with their mother and had sought temporary accommodation at her home. She had tried to leap to the top of the perimeter wall to pick flowers, but she missed and plunged to the ground, fracturing her left leg. The boy's mother was resetting the bone when she was interrupted by Ripple Hong, sent by her *shifu* Blithe Li to bring carnage to the Lu household, and as a result, the realignment was imperfect. By the time Lu Wushuang could move around again, she found her injured leg was slightly shorter and she was walking with a limp. Since then, she had been very sensitive about her gait and her physicality.

Although Lu Wushuang was taken to safety after Ripple Hong's attack, she was tracked down and captured by Blithe Li hours later. She had planned to send the girl to join her dead parents, but her resolve wavered at the sight of the handkerchief around her neck. It was the love token she had given Lu Zhanyuan – Lu Wushuang's uncle – and it brought back the tender feelings she once had for him, which lingered even when he cast her away for another. Eventually, the Taoist nun took the girl back to her hideout, Crimson Cloud Manor.

Lu Wushuang had always been good at reading people and quick to adapt. She swiftly understood her fate rested on Blithe Li's whims for she had no hope of stealing away from the woman's watchful eyes. She would endure the threats and insults and ingratiate herself with her captor. She would pretend to have lost her memory thanks to the fall and conceal her knowledge of the blood feud with her family, hiding her vengeful heart behind appeasing acts. Whenever she sensed that Blithe Li was brooding over her late uncle, she exaggerated her limp and made herself look more wretched by leaving her hair unbrushed and her face unwashed. She observed over time that the Taoist nun was not necessarily cruel and evil by nature. Her heart would soften somewhat if her captive appeared in a pitiful state, and at those times, Lu Wushuang would only have to put up with a brief scolding and a mild beating.

Lu Wushuang tried to make herself useful and waited on Blithe Li when she gave Ripple Hong martial lessons, handing them swords, towels, cups of tea or plates of food before they even thought to ask. She committed as many of the moves as she could to memory and tried them out in stolen moments when she was left to her own devices. She had also made a deliberate effort to get on the right side of Ripple Hong, so she might put in a sympathetic word or two for her when Blithe Li was in a good mood.

In time, a curious rapport was formed between captor and captive. Blithe Li was no longer compelled by the bloodlust that had inspired the killing spree at Lu Manor and had even accepted Lu Wushuang as her student and a resident of Crimson Cloud Manor. Nevertheless, the Taoist was guarded about sharing her knowledge and would only grant the girl a morsel here and there, strictly limited to second-rate martial techniques. In the end, Ripple Hong took pity on her little martial sister and offered her furtive guidance whenever she could. Lu Wushuang worked hard, consolidating the foundational training she had received under her father, and her martial capability saw substantial improvement over the years. Although she was still a long way from becoming a kung fu Master, she was no longer a mere novice.

When Blithe Li sent Ripple Hong to Chang'an on an errand, she departed herself soon after, leaving Lu Wushuang on her own. The young woman waited for their return as she had been told, but neither had made an appearance days after the appointed time. Lu Wushuang saw her chance to escape and head back to the South to find out what had happened to her parents. She remembered they were grievously wounded by Blithe Li, and she knew they were unlikely to have survived their injuries, but until she saw their cold bodies with her own eyes, a flicker of hope would always live within her. Before fleeing the manor, she stole Blithe Li's most treasured possession, *The Secrets of Five Poisons*, a hand-copied volume with detailed descriptions on how to make various toxins and their antidotes.

AS LU Wushuang was picking through the second piece of meat, she sensed the boy's eyes roaming more blatantly over her and promised herself that she would strike back later, drawing her sabre across his throat as he slept. Her family's cruel fate and the humiliation she had endured since just to stay alive had poisoned her heart. She had grown ruthless and uncaring while living with Blithe Li and bearing witness to the Taoist's callous ways. She finished her food, retired inside the temple and dozed off again. When she stirred some time later, she tiptoed outside with her sabre and saw the youth curled up on his side by the cold ashes of the fire, deep in slumber. She raised the blade and hacked down. *Claaang!* Pain radiated from her hand between her thumb and forefinger and her weapon flew into the air.

Lu Wushuang scrambled back in shock. Was he using some kind of body toughening kung fu? What she had struck was as hard as iron or granite. She retreated further before glancing back. He was lying in exactly the same position.

"Hey!" No answer. She peered at his huddled form. Something felt odd. She crept closer. Though she recognised his shirt, what lay beneath it did not quite resemble the outline of the human body. She gave him a prod with her foot. Rock hard. She tore off the garment. It *was* a piece of granite.

"Oi! Where are you?"

She looked around and listened intently with her head cocked. There was snoring coming from inside the temple. She rushed back and found the cowherd fast asleep on the altar table she had vacated mere moments ago. He was lying with his back to the doors, grunts rumbling in his throat. She lunged and thrust the point of her sabre into his back. This time, she could feel steel piercing through flesh, but it did not interrupt the noise he was making.

"It tickles," he mumbled. "Stop . . ."

Blood drained from Lu Wushuang's cheeks. What kind of creature was he? She plucked her sabre out with shaking hands. She wanted to flee, but her legs were stiff with fear; she could not take a single step.

"Itchy . . ." He reached under his shirt to scratch his back. "Trying to steal my muntjac, mousey?" A slab of meat fell to the floor with a wet slap.

Is this what I stabbed? So, he is human after all . . . Lu Wushuang breathed out in relief. I'll finish you off this time!

Tightening her jaw, she hacked her weapon down.

Penance let out a snore and rolled onto his front. Thwack! The blade's edge sank deep into the wood. Presently, he twisted onto his back and writhed around like he was having a nightmare, crying "Aaaah! Don't bite me, you nasty thing!" and kicking his feet into the air.

The next thing Lu Wushuang knew, the boy was digging his left heel into the crook of her elbow, precisely at Pool at the Bend, and his right foot made contact with the spot where her neck joined her shoulder, the Shoulder Well acupoint. Her movements were locked instantly, but she could still move her lips. "Take your stinky feet away!"

He answered with a confused, sleepy snort.

At a loss, she spat at his face. He shifted as though turning in his sleep and avoided the sputum. His movement brought his right big toe to the Great Bone point just above her shoulder blade. A numbing ache spread through her body. Now she had lost control of her facial muscles.

The stench of his feet attacked her nose, but frozen to the spot, she had no choice but to endure the humiliation. She swore she would cut him into a dozen pieces with her sabre when she could move freely again.

A short while later, Penance rolled onto his side and drew his legs up to his stomach, pleased to have caught a glimpse through half-closed eyes of her exasperated expression, which so reminded him of the Dragon Maiden.

4

THE MOON began to dip in the west and its beams reached in through the temple's half-opened doorway. Lu Wushuang could now see that Penance was not asleep – his squinting eyes were catching the light. He was watching her with a dazed smile on his face.

Did he bind my pressure points on purpose? Has he been playing the fool all along? Questions whirled in her mind as a cold sweat began to dampen her undershirt. She was considering the likelihood of this filthy cowherd being trained in sophisticated kung fu, when she noticed his gaze had shifted to the floor and looked in the same direction.

Three elongated shadows, armed.

Panic started to mount in Lu Wushuang. Her pressure points were still locked.

"Come out, wench!" one of the men shouted.

"We're here to claim two ears and three fingers." A second voice.

"Turn around and face us!" And a third. The shadows shifted as the three men spread out in a semi-circle before the temple entrance.

Penance stretched and yawned, sitting up slowly as if he had just woken up. "What's that noise?" He gave the young woman a nudge in the back. "Why are you standing so still?"

Potent internal strength rushed through Lu Wushuang's body to the three locked acupoints, restoring her movements. She snatched up the sabre embedded in the altar table and marched outside to face the three men. Without a word, she thrust the blade at the one on her left with a flick of the wrist.

The man twisted around and swished his weapon – an iron riding crop. The slender metal bar landed precisely on the tip of the sabre. The blade flew out of Lu Wushuang's hand and clattered to the ground.

Now the man in the middle – dressed in a Taoist habit – jabbed his sword forward. Lu Wushuang retreated from the thrust and flung her left hand out at an angle.

Penance made himself cosy, resting on his side. That monk can say goodbye to his steel, he thought, sensing the gist of what she was planning.

As he predicted, Lu Wushuang flipped her palm and took hold of the man's blade using an Ancient Tomb move. She then sliced it down at his shoulder.

Hollering in pain, he withdrew from the fight, tearing a strip from his robe to bandage his wound.

The man with the iron crop threw himself at Lu Wushuang, while the third fighter, who was shorter and smaller in build, harassed her with his spear from a safe distance, thanks to the length of his weapon. Within a dozen moves, they had her in a tight spot, but they took pride in their superior martial standing and chose not to take advantage of her weakness when she faltered.

Once the injured monk had bound up his wound, he re-entered the fray, swinging his fists. Lu Wushuang flashed the stolen sword in response, slicing into his back with his own weapon, but, at the same moment, the spear was thrusting into her from behind and the sharp tip of the iron crop was striking at her collarbone.

There's nowhere she can turn to avoid these blows! Taking matters into his own hands, Penance slipped down from the altar table, grabbed two small pieces of broken floor tile and hurled them at her attackers. One struck the spearhead, diverting its path. The other hit the crop-wielder's right wrist, halting the metal rod's progress, but the man reacted quickly and shot his left palm forward, swift as lightning.

Thump! Lu Wushuang was struck square in the chest.

Penance did not have the combat experience to foresee this blow. The depth of the man's kung fu had taken him by surprise. He rushed to Lu Wushuang's aid, seizing him by the back of his collar and flinging him several *zhang* away. The other two rushed to help their companion to his feet and together they fled the scene, unwilling to face such a skilled new entrant to the fight.

Lu Wushuang had collapsed to the floor, unconscious. Her face had the waxy lifeless colour of gold leaf, and her breathing was shallow and weak. Penance placed his hand on her back to help her sit up and heard the muffled cracks of broken bones grinding against each other. The pain brought her around and a groan escaped her lips.

"Are you in a lot of pain?" he asked.

"Of course, stupid!" Lu Wushuang hissed through clenched teeth. "Take me inside."

He scooped her up, but the movement caused her fractured ribs to grate again, and the pain was so intense she thought she would die from the agony.

"You're hurting me!"

Penance said nothing, focusing on keeping his steps steady to avoid jostling her any further.

"Where did those men go?" Lu Wushuang asked when the pain had eased a little.

"Gone. They thought you were dead."

"Why're you smiling?" Though relieved, she was riled by the grin with which the news was delivered. "You enjoy seeing me suffer, don't you?"

Her chiding words reminded Penance of the morning the Dragon Maiden had disappeared, when she had spoken to him in a similarly accusing tone. Then he recalled the other times she had scolded him, always out of concern for his well-being. These thoughts warmed his heart, for the years spent in the Tomb of the Living Dead had been, without a doubt, the happiest of his life. He was aware that his Auntie and this young woman were not really alike – one was aloof, distant and sparing with her words, while the other was fiery, hot-headed and clearly relished lambasting him. However, he had already felt less alone and abandoned having spent the day in Lu Wushuang's company, which was why he had borne her sharp tongue and her attempts on his life with good humour.

Penance set Lu Wushuang down lightly on the altar table, but the slight change in posture caused the splintered bones to scrape against each other again. The pain made her yelp and heave, putting further stress on the fractures. Beads of sweat formed along her hairline and her jaw locked tight as she tried to resist making any more sharp movements.

"Do you want me to reset the bones?"

"You know how?"

"I fixed my mangy mutt when the big yellow dog next door snapped her leg. Oh, and Uncle Wang's sow – her ribs were crushed."

Lu Wushuang squeezed her eyes shut and cursed the boy in her head. She was loath to suffer the comparison with farm animals in silence, but her every breath was sending shards of pain through her torso. If she attempted to speak, it would be worse.

"The mutt was running around in a few days," he continued. "Like she'd never broken any bones!"

Perhaps he really does know what he's doing. The young woman weighed up her options. I'll die from the pain if I don't get this tended to soon. But he'll have to place his hands on me . . . and I'll be . . . sullied . . . Whether he succeeds or not, he must die! No man can live after touching my body.

"Fine!" she said eventually.

Naturally, Penance seized the chance to tease her. "Uncle Wang's daughter begged me and called me 'Dear Big Brother' a hundred times before I—"

"You—" A surge of acute pain cut her short. "*Aiiiyooooo!*"

"Your choice." Penance stood up and headed out of the temple. "I'm going home."

Racked by unbearable agony, Lu Wushuang swallowed her pride. "What do I have to do?"

"I'd have helped you just now, if you had agreed to call me 'Dear Big Brother' a hundred times. But I've changed my mind. You've said too many nasty things to me . . . So, you'll have to call me 'Dear Big Brother' a thousand times."

Lu Wushuang swore to herself that she would have her revenge when she got better, and spat out in a voice distorted by groans, "Dear big brother . . . dear big brother . . . dear big brother . . ."

"I'll make a note of the nine hundred and ninety-seven times you owe me," Penance said, reaching out to untie her clothes.

"What are you doing?" she shrieked, recoiling involuntarily.

Penance took a step back, startled, and tried to make light of the situation. "Pigs and dogs don't wear clothes."

Lu Wushuang could not deny his logic but the thought of being undressed by a member of the opposite sex horrified her.

Eventually she whispered, "Go on . . ."

But before Penance could get to work, a female voice came through the open doorway. "She can't have gone far. Find her!"

Blood drained from Lu Wushuang's face, and for a moment, she forgot about the pain in her chest. She clapped her hand over the boy's mouth.

Blithe Li is here? Penance was equally shocked.

"The sabre in the beggar's shoulder – " he recognised the voice as Ripple Hong's – "looked like little sister's Silver Curved Blade. Pity we didn't manage to pull it out."

AFTER THE ordeal in the Tomb of the Living Dead, Blithe Li and her disciple Ripple Hong had returned to a deserted Crimson Cloud Manor. Lu Wushuang's escape did not bother either of them all that much, until Blithe Li discovered that her copy of *The Secrets of Five Poisons* was missing.

The Taoist nun terrorised the *jianghu* not just with her martial arts, but also with her knowledge of poison. Fast-acting toxins were integral to her most feared skills, Red Serpent Palm and Soul of Ice, and the book contained the secrets behind these two venoms, among others – how they were made and what was required for the antidote. If the details became widely known, the Red Serpent Celestial would be left toothless and impotent.

Blithe Li had learned the deadly recipes by heart many years before, so she never carried the book on her person. She had kept it hidden in the manor in a place known only to herself, but she had underestimated how watchful Lu Wushuang could be.

White with rage, Blithe Li set off with Ripple Hong, vowing to capture her treacherous student. They journeyed for days without stopping, but Lu Wushuang had been on the run for some time and she had been careful, keeping to narrow, little-used paths that were off the beaten track. The two Taoists travelled from their base in the North to the South and back again on several routes without finding a trace of the runaway.

Earlier that evening, when Blithe Li and Ripple Hong were approaching Tong Pass, they got wind of a Beggar Clan assembly for its members in the region and decided to see if they could find news of Lu Wushuang. The vagrant network reached every town and village under the heavens, and their followers were known to keep their eyes and ears open – one of them must have come across Lu Wushuang over the past weeks and months.

As they were on their way to the meeting site, they overtook a crowd of seventeen or eighteen Beggar Clan members surrounding a wounded man who was being carried on another's back. Over his ragged clothes, the man wore five sacks – denoting that he was a

Disciple of Five Pouches – and there was a curved sabre lodged near his shoulder. Blithe Li recognised the weapon as Lu Wushuang's straight away. Thrilled, she pulled Ripple Hong aside and eavesdropped on the beggars' conversation, gathering from their indignant remarks that the injury was caused by a girl with a limp.

The man's wound still looks fresh – Blithe Li observed – so Lu Wushuang can't have gone far. She paid close attention to the exchange, listening for clues to her disciple's whereabouts.

The two Taoist nuns eventually came across an abandoned temple. The ashes of a recent bonfire and the faint scent of blood told Blithe Li that they must be on the right track. She struck her tinderbox and located traces of fresh blood in the flickering light of her match. She tugged Ripple Hong's sleeve and gestured at the temple. With a nod, the younger Taoist tiptoed up to the half-open double doors and entered with her sword held before her.

LU WUSHUANG knew her fate was sealed the moment she heard the familiar voices. She lay still on the altar table and waited for the inevitable. The doors creaked and a blur of pale blue-green slipped through.

Ripple Hong went straight up to her martial sister, raised her sword and pointed it at the girl's heart. She thrust aside all thoughts of their camaraderie. The only thing she could do for her now was spare her from a slow, excruciating death at their *shifu's* hands.

Just as the tip of her sword made contact with the girl's robe, Ripple Hong felt a tap on her shoulder and her arms fell slack by her sides.

"What's the rush?" Blithe Li questioned her disciple archly, then turned to her renegade student. "Will you not bow to your *shifu*?"

Lu Wushuang knew that the Taoist's calm concealed a burning rage. Whether she pleaded for mercy or spat back curses, the same fate awaited her – torture and death.

"You killed my parents." She glared at Blithe Li defiantly, shedding the placating facade she had assumed for so long.

Blithe Li regarded the young woman with a faint smile and her eyes betrayed no emotion.

Lu Wushuang had seen this expression before. It surfaced whenever the Taoist was about to unleash her brutal side. And yet, she felt curiously calm, the constant fear of being caught had left her. She even started to wonder where the cowherd had gone. The thought of him brought a touch of warmth and comfort.

The pounding of hooves shattered the loaded silence and torchlight threw stark shadows on the walls. A bull was charging straight at the altar table. A flaming branch was lashed to one horn and a sharp sabre to the other. Blithe Li and Ripple Hong hopped out of the beast's way and watched with bewilderment as it careered around the worship hall before storming out again in the blink of an eye.

Who dressed the bull's horns? As Blithe Li searched for an answer, she twisted round and let out a gasp. The altar table was empty. Lu Wushuang had vanished. The Taoist immediately sent Ripple Hong to search the temple grounds while she ran after the bull. The blazing torch was a luminous beacon in the darkness. She could see it hurtling through the woods, but no-one was riding on its back.

Blithe Li took a moment to think through what had happened and decided that the bull must have been driven into the temple as a distraction to make it possible for Lu Wushuang's accomplice to sneak in and steal her away. Still, she decided to check the animal for clues first. She caught up with the beast and leapt onto its back. Finding nothing to indicate where Lu Wushuang might have gone, she jumped down, giving the animal a sharp kick in the rump to send it on its way. She then whistled, signalling Ripple Hong to come down from the temple roof where she had been keeping watch and to start searching to the east, while she herself went south to look for the runaway.

5

WHEN PENANCE HAD FIRST HEARD BLITHE LI'S VOICE, HE slipped out the back of the temple and listened in through an open window on one side. The instant the Taoist parted her lips, he sensed the hunger for blood in her tone and rushed off to find the bull, dressing its horns with Lu Wushuang's discarded sabre and a burning branch before clinging to its belly and urging it into the temple. He made the animal charge close to the altar table, pulled Lu Wushuang into his arms and escaped from under Blithe Li's nose, shielded by the beast's great girth. They took shelter among some tall weeds before Blithe Li realised her captive was gone.

The pain had been so intense that Lu Wushuang was left with only a fleeting impression of her rescue. A groan rose from her throat as she began to emerge from her stupor. Penance clapped his hands over her mouth and shushed her with a look.

The crunch of footsteps.

"Where did she go?" Ripple Hong muttered to herself, mere paces from their hiding place. "I blinked and she disappeared."

"Let's move on. There's nowhere for her to hide round here." Blithe Li's voice drifted in from somewhere a little further off.

Footfall sounded again, heading away from them.

Suffocating and in agony, Lu Wushuang struggled to stifle cries of anguish, but both Penance's hands were clamped over the lower part of her face. She squirmed instinctively against his hold, but it only brought his arm snaking around her, clasping her tight, and his weight pressing close, restraining her movements. Then she felt his breath and the touch of his lips on her ear.

"They're still here," he whispered.

A moment later, they heard Blithe Li say from just a few steps away, "She really has fled."

Lu Wushuang realised she would have died a second time on this one night were it not for the cowherd. Blithe Li's exchange with her disciple was a ploy to trick her into lowering her guard and revealing herself, while the Taoist silently circled back using lightness *qing-gong*.

When Penance was certain that the two nuns were truly gone, he removed his hand from Lu Wushuang's face and gave her a smile. "We're safe."

"Take your arm away."

Gingerly, Penance freed her from his embrace. "I'll reset the bones, then we'll leave while it's still dark. It's not safe to move in daylight."

Seeing her nod, he tapped her pressure points to numb her body in case she cried out from the pain and brought the two women racing back.

"Don't make a sound. No matter what."

Penance unfastened her outer robe to reveal a pale white under-shirt. He untied this garment with hesitant fingers and unveiled an apricot yellow undervest. He dared not allow his gaze to linger on this most private item of clothing and looked away, and when he did so he noticed that Lu Wushuang's eyes were squeezed shut and her brow scrunched up. There was no trace of the bold young woman he had got to know during the day. Penance thought he caught a fragrance emanating from her unblemished skin and his heart began to pound.

Sensing his fingers falter, Lu Wushuang parted her eyelids a fraction and urged him on in a feeble voice. "Do it." Then she screwed her eyes shut again and turned her head to one side.

With trembling hands, Penance pulled up this last garment. The sight of her breasts, tender and white like milk curd, made him pause.

If Auntie needed her bones reset, would I look at her body? he asked himself. Without his realising it, his reverence for the Dragon Maiden had become coloured by the yearning between man and woman.

Lu Wushuang braced herself for the pain, but the chilly night breeze on her exposed skin was all she could feel. She opened her eyes a sliver and caught Penance staring.

"What . . . what are you looking at . . . ?"

Snapped out of his musing, Penance placed his hands on her chest and steeled himself to find the fractures. But the sensation of her skin on his fingertips struck him like a thunderclap, as if he had plunged his hands into a coal fire. He jerked back.

"Shut your eyes! If you look again, I . . . I . . ." Tears glistened on the young woman's face.

"D-don't cry. I – I won't look." Penance closed his eyes and located the broken bones by touch. Two of her ribs were fractured. He re-aligned them with care, then quickly pulled down the under-vest. Taking a moment to calm his mind, he stood up, opened his eyes and hurried over to the nearest tree. He snapped off four branches, peeled a few strips of bark and rushed back, all the while looking anywhere but at the girl. He bound the branches over her torso with the bark to hold the broken ribs in place, then fastened her under-shirt and outer robe and released the binds on her pressure points.

When Lu Wushuang felt she had been fully clothed, she opened her eyes and saw in the moonlight that the young man's face had flushed bright red. He seemed to be more awkward and embarrassed than she was, stealing glances at her to gauge her mood. The instant their eyes met, he looked away.

Her chest still hurt, but the pain was now bearable. She was genuinely impressed by his skill. Naturally, she had figured out by now that he was no unwashed swain or country simpleton, but she was too proud to change the churlish way she had been treating him.

"Hey, you!" she said curtly. "What's your plan?"

"What do you want to do?"

"Run, of course, you idiot. I'm not waiting here for death to catch up with me."

"Where will you go?"

"South. To Jiangnan."

"I can't go that far. I've got to find Auntie."

"Fine!" Lu Wushuang's face darkened. "Go! Leave me here to die."

If she had pleaded with warm words and soft tones, Penance would have outright refused, but her angry glare instantly brought the Dragon Maiden to mind and he could not bring himself to abandon her.

Perhaps Auntie headed south too? He looked for ways to convince himself. A good heart is rewarded by blessings. If I see this girl south safely, perhaps the heavens will take pity and let me run into Auntie?

Rationally, Penance knew it was nigh on impossible that he would chance upon the Dragon Maiden, but he bent down with a sigh and scooped Lu Wushuang up.

"What are you doing?"

"Taking you to the South."

"Fool! It's thousands of *li* from here." But she relaxed into his arms with a chuckle.

The bull was long gone, so Penance had to journey on foot. He picked the least-trodden trail to avoid crossing paths with Blithe Li and Ripple Hong. His legs moved fast, but he held his upper body still and steady.

Lu Wushuang watched in awe as the trees flashed past her at great speed. She could have been riding a galloping horse with the smoothest gait – she was not in the least bit jostled or jolted.

His lightness kung fu is on a par with Blithe Li's, she observed. He's carrying me, and yet, he's faster than I've ever been. How did he acquire such impressive skills at such a young age?

The faint light of dawn began to glow in the east. For the first time, Lu Wushuang took a good look at the cowherd. Though his face was caked in grime, it could not obscure his handsome features or his lively bright eyes. A stirring in her heart took her mind off the pain in her chest and she soon fell asleep in his arms.

The sun had now risen fully. Feeling a little tired, Penance stopped, placed Lu Wushuang gingerly against a tree and sat down beside her.

She opened her eyes and gave him a smile. "I'm hungry, are you?"

"We'll keep moving till we find a tavern." His arms were sore from carrying her half the night, so he lifted her to sit on his shoulders and set off at a slower pace.

Lu Wushuang's legs swung gently in time with his steps, tapping against his chest. "Hey, tell me your real name. I can't keep calling you Clod or Stupid."

"I don't have one."

"Fine! Who's your *shifu*?"

Penance had been enjoying playing the fool, but he would never jest about the Dragon Maiden.

"Auntie," he uttered the word with reverence.

So, he's from a martial family, she noted before asking, "Why did you save me?"

Penance was not even sure of the answer himself. He thought for a moment, then said, "Auntie told me to."

"Who's your auntie?"

"Auntie is Auntie. I do what she says."

Lu Wushuang sighed, deciding that he was indeed a blockhead after all. The tender feelings developed over the past few hours hardened into distaste once more.

Later that morning, they arrived at a small market town and ate a quick meal at a modest inn. Lu Wushuang gave Penance some silver and sent him to buy a donkey. She climbed onto its back, but the tetchy animal bucked against her weight and rubbed its flank against the closest wall in an attempt to dislodge her. The impact rattled the reset bones and stabbing pain radiated from her ribs, snatching all strength from her person.

Too weak to hold on with her hands or secure her position with her knees, she toppled from her mount. Though she managed to land on her good leg, thanks to her martial training, another agonising wave of pain spread out from her chest.

"Why didn't you help me?" Lu Wushuang took out her frustration on the cowherd, but his only response was a silly giggle.

"Give me a hand," she ordered.

Obediently, Penance helped her back onto the donkey, but the animal brayed and jerked again.

"Take the lead-rope!"

"No, it'll kick me."

Lu Wushuang eyed the young man, once again doubting that he was dull in the head. She had a feeling he was letting this struggle happen, so she would be forced to ask him to ride with her. It infuriated her, but the pain was so intense, she had no choice but to swallow her pride.

"Come up."

Penance mounted the donkey with a grin. Placing one hand on her waist, he took the whip from her grasp and squeezed his legs hard. The animal yielded to the pressure on its flanks and trotted forward submissively.

"Where shall we go?" he asked.

Lu Wushuang's first thought was to head east for Tong Pass before journeying through the plains of Zhongzhou. However, this involved taking the most well-travelled route through the Qin Mountains, which divided the land into North and South, and there was a high chance of running into Blithe Li or the Beggar Clan. She decided it would be best to take smaller trails and pointed south-east.

"That way."

This longer meandering route would first take them to the fort town of Dragon Steed, then through Bamboo Forest Pass and Red-bud Seed Pass, after which they could head straight for Jiangnan in the South.

Tak, tak, tak . . . The donkey's hooves beat the ground rhythmically as it ambled out of the town. A child ran out and stopped them.

"Miss Lu, this is for you." He threw a bunch of rapeseed flowers at Lu Wushuang and sprinted off.

She caught the golden blossoms and saw there was a note slipped in among the stems. The sheet was rough and tainted with a yellow dye, but the calligraphy was elegant.

Your shifu *will be here very soon. Hide!*

Lu Wushuang's mind was reeling: Who is this child? How does he know my name or who my *shifu* is?

"You know him, don't you?" She looked round at Penance. "He was sent by your auntie, wasn't he?"

"No . . ." Penance had seen the message over her shoulder and his thoughts were also racing. The child was a local peasant boy, and whoever had sent the note seemed to mean well. The advice was undoubtedly sound. He might have a foundation in two of the most potent martial repertoires ever devised, the Jade Maid Heart Scripture and the Nine Yin Manual, but he had just begun to scratch the surface of both and he had little chance against Blithe Li if it came to a fight. He scanned the surroundings. Blue sky, white sun – nowhere to hide in this open countryside.

What should they do?

Blaring *suona* flutes and clanging cymbals wrenched Penance out of his thoughts. The tune was crude, but the joy it conveyed was unmistakeable. A bright red flower-palanquin had appeared on the trail, escorted by dozens of men. A groom had just picked up his betrothed and they were on the way to their wedding ceremony.

Penance leaned into Lu Wushuang. "How would you like to play the bride for a day?"

TO BE CONTINUED . . .

CHARACTERS

As they appear in this, the first volume of
Return of the Condor Heroes

THE LU FAMILY

A well-to-do family from the city of Jiaxing. The head of the house-hold **Lu Zhanyuan** 陆展元 made a name in the martial world together with his wife **He Yuanjun** 何沅君. His younger brother **Lu Liding** 陆立鼎 is also trained in kung fu, but he and his wife **Mistress Lu** live an ordinary life with their daughter **Lu Wushuang** 陆无双 and their niece **Cheng Ying** 程英.

Madam Wu is a traveller who comes to stay one night at Lu Manor with her sons **Earnest Wu** 武敦儒 (Wu Dunru) and **Erudite Wu** 武修文 (Wu Xiuwen). Her husband **Wu Santong** 武三通 was Captain of the Imperial Guard of the Kingdom of Dali during the reign of Duan Zhixing the King Gongji, also known as the King of the South, one of the Five Greats.

THE FIVE GREATS

These sophisticated martial artists became known as the Greats after taking part in the original Contest of Mount Hua, which was held to determine the Greatest Martial Master Under the Heavens.

Wang Chongyang 王重阳 the Double Sun Immortal, also known as Central Divinity, was the founder of the Quanzhen Sect and the winner of the original Contest, which granted him the custodianship of the sought-after martial compendium, the Nine Yin Manual. A real historical figure, he lived between 1113 and 1170.

The Heretic of the East, **Apothecary Huang** 黄药师 (Huang Yaoshi), makes his home on Peach Blossom Island in the Eastern Sea. An all-round scholar with exceptional knowledge of the *I'Ching*, he cultivates a reputation as a loner and a radical who holds traditions and conventions in contempt.

Hailing from White Camel Mount in the Western Regions, **Viper Ouyang** 欧阳锋 (Ouyang Feng), the Venom of the West, is a master of poisons and venomous creatures. His martial inventions, most notably the Exploding Toad, are inspired by the deadly companions he keeps.

Once the monarch of the Kingdom of Dali, **Duan Zhixing** 段智兴, the King of the South, abdicated from his throne and became a Buddhist monk under the name Sole Light. His unique pressure-point locking kung fu, Yang in Ascendance, is an attacking system that also has great healing powers. A real figure in history, he lived between 1149 and 1200.

The Beggar of the North, **Count Seven Hong** 洪七公 (Hong Qi Gong), was once the leader of a vast network of vagrants, the Beggar Clan, and is respected across the *jianghu* for his sense of justice and righteousness. He loves good food as much as he loves kung fu, and his most admired martial repertoire is the Eighteen Dragon-Subduing Palms.

PEACH BLOSSOM ISLAND

The Peach Blossom Island has shed its savage reputation since **Lotus Huang** 黄蓉 (Huang Rong), daughter of Apothecary Huang, moved back with her husband **Guo Jing** 郭靖. They are the only two formal disciples accepted by Count Seven Hong, and Lotus has also taken on the duty of the Beggar Chief from the Martial Great. They have a daughter, **Hibiscus Guo** 郭芙 (Guo Fu).

Ke Zhen'e 柯镇恶, the Flying Bat, the eldest of the Seven Freaks of the South and the man who first initiated Guo Jing into the world of kung fu, lives with the couple on the island.

Penance Yang 杨过 (Yang Guo), the orphaned son of Guo Jing's sworn brother Yang Kang and Mercy Mu, joins the Guo family on the island after a chance encounter on the mainland.

THE MONGOLIANS

Khudu is believed to be a Mongol Prince related to Genghis Khan, and together with his martial senior, **Darbai**, he has made a name for himself in the *wulin* with kung fu hailing from the Vajra Buddhist lineage.

THE QUANZHEN SECT

Chongyang Temple and the Zhongnan Mountains, south of Chang'an (modern-day Xi'an), are important sites to this real-life branch of Taoism founded by Wang Chongyang, whose name means "Way of Complete Perfection".

The Seven Immortals, students of Wang Chongyang, are all real figures from history:

Scarlet Sun **Ma Yu** 马钰, the most senior among them and the leader of the Sect

Eternal Truth **Tan Chuduan** 谭处端

Eternal Life **Liu Chuxuan** 刘处玄

Eternal Spring **Qiu Chuji** 丘处机

Jade Sun **Wang Chuyi** 王处一

Infinite Peace **Hao Datong** 郝大通

Sage of Tranquillity **Sun Bu'er** 孙不二

A number of followers of the Seven Immortals are featured in this volume, the majority of them fictive characters invented by the author.

Student of Qiu Chuji: **Zhen Zhibing** 甄志丙

Students of Wang Chuyi: **Zhao Zhijing** 赵志敬, **Cui Zhifang** 崔志方

Other members of the Quanzhen Sect: **Zhang Zhiguang** 张志光, **Shen Zhifan** 申志凡, **Lu Qingdu** 鹿清笃, **Pi Qingxuan** 皮清玄, **Ji Qingxu** 姬清虚

THE ANCIENT TOMB SECT

Founded by the reclusive Master **Lin Chaoying** 林朝英 (sometimes known as "the Doyenne") and her unnamed maidservant, who both vowed never to leave their base, the Tomb of the Living Dead in the Zhongnan Mountains, this group only becomes known and acquires its name when one of its martial descendants **Blithe Li** 李莫愁 (Li Mochou), the Red Serpent Celestial, ventures into the *wulin* with her disciple **Ripple Hong** 洪凌波 (Hong Lingbo). The Tomb, together with Lin Chaoying's full martial inheritance, is passed onto Blithe Li's younger martial sister, who is believed to be of the family name Long, and is known to the outside world by the title, the **Dragon Maiden** 小龙女, taken from the meaning of her family name. She lives in the underground complex with **Grandam Sun**, who was the serving woman of the Dragon Maiden's *shifu*, Lin Chaoying's unnamed maidservant.

THE BEGGAR CLAN

A fictional group that has appeared in countless works of martial-arts literature, the Beggar Clan has followers all over China, the majority of them being actual beggars, though some martial men of fixed abode also join up because they share the same upright morals and sense of justice. Led by Chief Lotus Huang, the clansmen are ruled over by their Elders, each of whom has responsibilities for a different geographical region. The Clan's clear hierarchy is illustrated by the number of pouches a member is granted, with the Elders given nine such rough-spun sacks to symbolise their senior status. Two representatives, **Beggar Chen** and **Beggar Han**, appear in this volume.

NOTES ON THE TEXT

PAGE NUMBERS DENOTE THE FIRST TIME THESE CONCEPTS OR
names are mentioned in the book.

ON TRANSLATING CHARACTER NAMES

The names Jin Yong chose for his fictional characters are often tied
to their fate or personality traits, and it is this body of information
imbued in the written form – the meanings rather than the pronunciation – that stays with Chinese readers, making these heavily loaded
names an integral part of the reading experience. For certain characters in the story, this semantic connection is vital to their perception
in readers' minds, and in those cases, we have tried to reflect that in
their English names, so readers of the translations can share similar
associations to those enjoyed by readers of the Chinese originals –
an interpretation that is rooted in the Chinese culture of naming and
understanding a person's name.

P.1 OUYANG XIU

Poet, historian and statesman, Ouyang Xiu (1007–72) exerts a lasting
influence on Chinese culture. He led the compilation of two major
histories, one on the Tang dynasty (618–907) and one on the Five
Dynasties period (907–60). His prose and poetry departed from the

strict, ornate conventions popular at the time, pioneering a new simpler style, cementing his reputation as a literary master. His works are still studied in Chinese schools to this day.

P. 1   TUNE OF "BUTTERFLIES ADORE FLOWERS"

In Chinese literature, there is a genre of verse known as *ci* 词, or lyric poetry. These poems are written to fit a specific tune or melody, like song lyrics, and they follow strict rules that define not only the length of each line and the rhyme scheme, but also the tone pitch of each character within the line. These tunes are now mostly lost, with only their titles known to us, though it is occasionally possible to reconstruct some semblance of the underlying harmony through the sonic qualities of the words. "Butterflies Adore Flowers" is one such tune title, and many poets have set lyrics to variations of this melody over the centuries.

P. 2   HORSETAIL WHISK

Made by tying hair from a horse's tail to a longish handle, the horsetail whisk was originally designed to flick away insects without hurting them and to wipe away dust. It is an object of ritual and ceremonial significance in Taoism and Buddhism due to a symbolic interpretation of its function and serves as a reminder of one's spiritual calling. It was held to be a weapon of compassion since it has no whetted edge. The whisk can also be made with hair from other animals or plant fibres.

P. 34   JIANG ZIYA

A statesman and tactician from the 11th century B.C., Jiang Ziya only came to be appreciated by the rulers of the time in the eighth decade of his life. He helped King Wen of Zhou to overthrow the despot King Zhou of Shang, marking the end of the Shang dynasty (c. 17th to 11th century B.C.) and the founding of the Zhou dynasty (c. 11th to 3rd century B.C.). He was granted numerous names and titles during his lifetime and after his death to honour his contribution, including that of Grand Duke. His wisdom continues to influence

Chinese culture to this day and his story has been reimagined many times in fiction and on screen.

P. 76 *HUNDRED FAMILY SURNAMES*

Believed to be compiled in the early Northern Song (960–1127), *Hundred Family Surnames* originally contained more than four hundred surnames and was later expanded to more than five hundred. The family names are arranged in easily memorable rhyming lines of four characters, and the text has been used as one of the introductory works for children when learning to recognise Chinese characters.

P. 83 IRON SPEAR WANG / GENERAL WANG YANZHANG

A famous general of the Later Liang state (907–23), Wang Yanzhang (863–923) was known for his prowess on the field and his loyalty to his country. He was captured by Later Tang (923–37) forces and subsequently beheaded when he refused to defect.

Later Liang was one of the states of the turbulent Five Dynasties and Ten Kingdoms period (907–79) that preceded the founding of the Song dynasty (960–1279) during which our story is set.

P. 98 COURTESY NAME

In times past, educated Chinese men assumed a courtesy name *zi* 字 when they came of age at twenty. This would be the one used in polite company, as opposed to the name given to them by their parents at birth, known as *ming* 名.

P. 117 SOULS AND SPIRITS

In Taoist belief, there are three *hun* 魂 and seven *po* 魄 within the body that make one a living, thinking, feeling human being. The *hun* is believed to be the "immortal" portion that will be reincarnated after death, and the *po* is linked to feelings and emotions that will dissipate when one expires. Traditionally, certain illnesses – particularly those that are psychological in nature – are attributed to the loss of one or more of these intangible elements. This concept of human essence enters the everyday Chinese vocabulary as *hunpo* 魂魄, and here it is translated as souls and spirits to reflect the multiplicity encoded in the phrase.

P. 120 GENERAL FAN KUAI

A general and statesman from the 3rd century B.C., Fan Kuai was known for his loyalty and physical prowess, as evidenced when he saved the life of the Han dynasty (202 B.C.–220) founder Liu Bang.

P. 163 ZIFANG / ZHANG LIANG

A strategist and statesman from the 3rd century B.C., Zhang Liang used his wits to help Liu Bang establish the Han dynasty (202 B.C.–220). His legacy was a general acceptance that wisdom was as important as military might on the battlefield and his exploits won admiration from commentators and literati from subsequent ages.

P. 177 SEVEN-STRINGED *QIN*

The seven-stringed *qin* is held to embody and express the ideal qualities of a refined, learned person in Chinese literati culture. It has an oblong, fretless wooden body and the strings are traditionally made of silk. Its music, made by plucking the strings, tends to be low and subdued in timbre and gentle in pace, so it is typically played on its own, though it is sometimes accompanied by quiet singing or with the end-blown *xiao* flute, whose tone is also soft and subtle. The instrument is usually called the *guqin* today.

P. 328 SEVEN FEELINGS AND SIX DESIRES

According to the *Book of Rites*, the seven feelings are joy, rage, sorrow, fear, liking, loathing and craving. The six desires are defined in *Master Lü's Spring and Autumn Annals* as those relating to the human wish for life and against death, as well as those stemming from the senses of hearing, sight, taste and smell. These feelings and desires may vary somewhat in other areas of Chinese culture, such as in traditional medicine or Buddhist writings.

P. 332 CHASTITY CINNABAR

An ancient mythical medicinal mixture that was tattooed on the skin and would supposedly fade away should a woman lose her maidenhood. The earliest extant written record of this practice can be dated back to the Qin and Han periods (221 B.C.–220), but its efficacy was already being called into question in medical books that survive from the 7th century. However, the technique captured the imagination of storytellers and entered into the folk culture.

P. 372 GUANYIN THE OBSERVER OF SOUND

The Chinese representation of the bodhisattva of compassion, Avalokiteshvara, and the name is a translation of the deity's Sanskrit title. Guanyin is worshipped by Buddhists and Taoists in China and is sometimes referred to as the Goddess of Mercy in English.

P. 376 *KANG* BED-STOVE

Found in central and northern China to this day, the *kang* bed-stove is an important interior feature that warms homes during freezing winters. A brick or fired-clay platform, often taking up a third of the room, its hollow interior is connected to the dwelling's cooking fire. The latter's hot exhaust heats up the earthen mass of the *kang*. A well-built bed-stove can retain heat for a long time without requiring much fuel or attention. Its warm surface is the site of social life and household activities during the day and provides ample space for restful sleep at night.

P. 400 FIVE POISONS

The Five Poisons usually refer to five kinds of venomous creatures: centipedes, vipers, scorpions, geckos and toads.

P. 407 TONG PASS / ZHONGZHOU

With the Yellow River to its north and the Qin Mountains to its south, Tong Pass is one of the most important military strongholds in the history of China. Its unique geographic position allowed it to defend Chang'an (modern-day Xi'an, once capital to numerous dynasties) from attacks coming from the north and the east. If armies coming from the west could seize it, they could ride with little topographical hindrance across the plains of Zhongzhou (modern-day Henan province), heading for key cities like Luoyang and Kaifeng to the east and Beijing to the north-east, or south-east towards the wealthy Jiangnan region for cities such as Hangzhou and Suzhou. However, so long as the soldiers garrisoned there did not sally out to engage the enemy, it was nigh on impregnable, and legend has it that two men behind its walls could hold back a company of a hundred.

P. 415   DRAGON STEED FORT / BAMBOO FOREST PASS / REDBUD SEED PASS

Dragon Steed Fort and Bamboo Forest Pass are strategic mountain passes and strongholds in modern-day Shangluo, to the south-east of the Zhongnan Mountains. Redbud Seed Pass is another key position that was prized by both military tacticians and merchants, as it connects northern and southern China by road and water. It lies further south-east at the meeting point of three provinces – Shaanxi, Hubei and Henan – in modern-day Nanyang.

P. 416   *SUONA*

The name of this double-reed woodwind musical instrument points to its origins in Arabia, where it is known as the *zurna*, while its European variation is referred to as the shawm. The shrill, penetrating sonic quality makes the *suona* ideal for religious processions and military functions, and it is heard in folk and traditional music from various Chinese regions to this day.